MOONSTRUCK

MOONSTRUCK

Edward M. Lerner

BAEN

MOONSTRUCK

This is a work of fiction. All the characters and events portrayed in this book are fictional, and any resemblance to real people or incidents is purely coincidental.

A Baen Books Original

Baen Publishing Enterprises
P.O. Box 1403
Riverdale, NY 10471

ISBN: 0-7434-9885-2

Cover art by Doug Chaffee

Production by Windhaven Press, Auburn, NH (www.windhaven.com)
Printed in the United States of America

To friends and colleagues too numerous
to mention in and around NASA.
And to the Hard SF authors who
steered me in that direction.

MOONSTRUCK

PROLOGUE

"T MINUS FIVE minutes, and holding."

It wasn't even ten in the morning, but the day was already hot. Kyle Gustafson squirted another dollop of sunscreen into his palm, then rubbed his hands together. Smearing it over his face and neck, he grimaced: he reeked of coconut oil. He made a mental note to avoid all open flames until he showered.

Kyle had a Scottish-American mother and a Swedish-American father, a combination that Dad called industrial-strength WASP. He didn't belong below the forty-fifth parallel, let alone outside beneath Cape Canaveral's summer, subtropical sun—but he never missed an opportunity to witness a launch. His job helped: who better than the presidential science advisor to escort visiting foreign dignitaries to Kennedy Space Center?

"You could wear a hat, my friend."

I look really stupid in hats, Kyle thought. Turning toward his Russian counterpart, he suppressed that answer as impolitic. Instead, he changed the subject. "Sorry for the delay, Sergei. The hold is built into the schedule to allow time for responding to minor glitches."

"T minus five minutes, and holding."

His guest said nothing. Sergei Denisovich Arbatov was tall, wiry, and tanned. He'd been born and raised in the Crimea, the Black Sea peninsula once popularly called the Russian Riviera.

That nickname had gone out of vogue when the USSR self-destructed, and an independent Ukraine had made it clear that ethnic Russians were no longer welcome. In 1992, Sergei had moved his family to Moscow, where he'd moved up rapidly in the new, democratic government. It wasn't clear to Kyle how Sergei avoided the Muscovite's traditional pallor—unless it was by finagling trips to Florida.

"T minus five minutes, and counting."

The single-word change in the announcement made Kyle's pulse race. Across the plain from their vantage point at the VIP launch viewing area, *Atlantis* shimmered through the rising waves of heated air.

The shuttle on Launch Pad 39B stood 184 feet tall, the dartlike body of the orbiter dwarfed by the solid rocket boosters and external fuel tank to which it was attached. All but the tank were white; the expendable metal tank, once also painted white, was now left its natural rust color to reduce takeoff weight by 750 pounds.

"T minus four minutes, thirty seconds, and counting."

Kyle continued his standard briefing. "The gross weight of the shuttle at launch is about 4.5 million pounds, Sergei. Impressive, don't you think?"

"Apollo/Saturn V weighed a half again more." The gray-haired Russian smiled sadly. "We never made it to the moon, and you Americans have forgotten how. I don't know who disappoints me more."

Kyle had been thirteen the night of the first moon landing. Afterward, he'd lain awake all night, scheming how he, too, would sometime, somehow, make a giant leap for mankind. The idealist in him still shared Arbatov's regrets. Many days, only that boy's dream sustained Kyle through Washington's game-playing and inanity. Someday, he told himself, he *would* make it happen.

Someday seemed never to get closer.

"T minus four minutes, and counting."

Nervously, Kyle ran his fingers through hair once flame-red. Age had banked the fire with ashes, for a net effect beginning to approach salmon. Too late, he remembered the sunscreen that coated his hands. "We'll go back, Sergei," he answered softly, speaking really to himself. "Men will walk again on the moon. Will visit other worlds, too." He shook off the sudden gloom. "First, though, we've got a satellite to launch."

"T minus three minutes, ten seconds, and counting." Loudspeakers all around them blared the announcement.

The Earth's atmosphere is effectively opaque to gamma radiation. In 1991, to begin a whole new era in astronomy, *Atlantis* had delivered the Gamma Ray Observatory to low Earth orbit. After years of spectacular success, the GRO had had one too many gyroscopes fail. NASA had deorbited it in 2000, in a spectacular but controlled Pacific Ocean crash.

Now another *Atlantis* crew was ready to deploy GRO's replacement. Major Les Griffiths, the mission commander, had proposed that the mission badges on the crew's flight suits read, "Your full-spectrum delivery service." The suggestion was rejected as too flippant. A mere three missions into the post-*Columbia* resumption of shuttle flights, American nerves remained raw.

"*Da*." Arbatov turned to the distant shuttle. He sounded skeptical. "Then let us watch."

The remaining minutes passed with glacial slowness. Finally, a brilliant spark flashed beneath *Atlantis*. Golden flames lashed at 300,000 gallons of water in the giant heat/sound-suppression trench beside the launch pad, hiding the shuttle in a sudden cloud of steam. Kyle's heart, as always, skipped a beat, anxious for the top of the shuttle to emerge from the fog. A wall of sound more felt than heard washed over them. Faster than he could ever believe possible, no matter how often he saw it, the shuttle shot skyward on a column of fire and smoke. Chase planes in pursuit, it angled eastward and headed out over the ocean. The sound receded to a rumble as he shaded his eyes to watch.

"Kyle!"

The American reluctantly returned his attention to his guest. Arbatov still stared at the disappearing spacecraft, one of the mission-frequency portable radios that Kyle's position had allowed him to commandeer pressed tightly to his ear. Kyle's own radio, turned off, hung from his wrist.

"*Nyet, nyet, nyet!*" shouted the Russian.

The presidential advisor snapped on his own radio. "Roger that," said the pilot. "Abort order acknowledged." The hypercalm, hypercrisp words made Kyle's blood run cold.

A speck atop a distant flame, the shuttle continued its climb. The far-off flame suddenly dimmed; the three main engines had been extinguished. *What the hell was happening?* "Shutdown sequence complete. Pressure in the ET"—external tank—"still rising. Jettisoning tank and SRBs." Unseen explosive bolts severed the manned orbiter from the external tank; freed from the massive orbiter, the tank and its still-attached, nonextinguishable, solid-fuel rocket boosters quickly shot clear. The manned orbiter coasted after them, for the moment, on momentum.

Clutching their radios, Kyle and his guest leaned together for reassurance. "Pressure still increasing."

Light glinted mockingly off the sun-tracking Astronaut Memorial, the granite monolith engraved with the names of astronauts killed in the line of duty. It seemed all too likely that the list was about to grow by five more names.

"Pressure nearing critical." He recognized the voice from Mission Control. "Report status."

What pressure? In the ET? Was it about to blow? Two Sea-Air Rescue choppers thundered overhead as he did a quick calculation. *The ET must still contain at least 250,000 gallons of liquid hydrogen!*

"Beginning OMS burn."

The distant speck regrew a flame—had the orbital-maneuvering-system engines ever been fired before inside the atmosphere?—and began banking toward the coast. Unaided by SRBs, its main engines unusable without the ET, the orbiter seemed to lumber. Seemed mortally wounded. "Suggest my escorts make tracks."

"Pressure at critical. Crit plus ten. Crit plus twenty. Twenty-three. Twenty-four."

An enormous fireball blossomed above the escaping orbiter. From miles away, Kyle saw the craft stagger as the shock wave struck. "Tell Beth that I love her." The distant flame pinwheeled as *Atlantis* began to tumble. Moments later, the roar and the shock wave of the blast reached the Cape, whipping Kyle and Sergei with a sudden gale of sand and grit. The distant spark extinguished as safety circuits shut down the tumbling craft's rocket engines.

The orbiter began its long plunge to the sea, with both chase planes diving futilely after it.

Like its mythical namesake, the orbiter *Atlantis* slipped beneath the silent and uncaring waves to meet its fate.

GIFT HORSE

CHAPTER 1

WITHOUT WARNING, the Toyota pickup swerved in front of Kyle. He tapped his brakes lightly—this near the I-66 exit to the Beltway, such maneuvers were hardly unexpected—and gave a pro forma honk. The yahoo in the pickup responded with the traditional one-fingered salute. The truck's rear bumper bore the message: Have comments about my driving? Email: biteme@whogivesashit.org.

Such is the state of discourse in the nation's capital.

Sighing, Kyle turned up his radio for the semihourly news summary. There was no preview of this morning's hearing. That was fine with him: he'd never learned to speak in sound bites. If the session made tomorrow's *Washington Post*, his testimony might rate a full paragraph of synopsis.

The good news was today's topic wasn't the *Atlantis*.

Reliving the disaster in his dreams was hard enough; the science advisor's presence had also become de rigueur for every anti-NASA representative or senator who wanted to use the disaster to justify ending the manned space program. *Challenger, Columbia,* and now *Atlantis* ... after three shuttle catastrophes, they spoke for much of the country. By comparison, today's session about technology for improved enforcement of the Clean Air Act would be positively benign.

As traffic crept forward, he tried to use the time to further prepare for the senatorial grilling. He knew the types of questions his boss would have posed to ready him: What would he volunteer in his opening statement? What information needed to be metered out in digestible chunks? Whose home district had a contractor who'd want to bid on the program? Who was likely to leave the session early for other hearings? All the wrong questions, of course, when Kyle wanted to talk about remote-sensing technology and computing loads. There was too little science in the job of presidential science advisor.

In any event, he had to swing by his basement cranny in the OEOB for last-minute instructions. He turned off his radio, which was in any event unable to compete with the bass booming from the sport-ute in the next lane.

The Old Executive Office Building was as far as Kyle got that day—or the next one. About the time he'd traded witticisms with the driver of the Toyota pickup, the emissaries of the Galactic Commonwealth had announced their imminent arrival on Earth by interrupting the TV broadcast of *A.M. America.*

The White House situation room held the humidity and stench of too many occupants. Men and women alike had lost their jackets; abandoned neckties were strewn about like oversized, Technicolor Christmas tinsel. Notepad computers vied for desk space with pizza boxes, burger wrappers, and soda cans.

In clusters of two and three, the crisis team muttered in urgent consultation. A few junior staffers sat exiled in the corners, glued to the TV monitors. Everything was being taped, but everyone wanted to see the aliens' broadcasts live. Watching a new message, even if it differed not a whit from the last twenty, provided momentary diversion from the many uncertainties.

Neither Kyle's PalmPilot nor the remaining pizza had wisdom to offer. He looked up at the entry of Britt Arledge, White House chief of staff and Kyle's boss and mentor. The President's senior aide could have been a poster child for patricians: tall and trim, with chiseled features, icy blue eyes, a furrowed brow, and a full head of silver hair. Within the politico's exterior sat a brilliant, if wholly unscientific, mind. Arledge's forte was recognizing other people's strengths, and building the right team for tackling any problem.

Kyle wondered whether his boss's legendary insight extended to the Galactics.

"So what have we got?"

He parted a path for them through the crowded room to the whiteboard where he'd already summarized the data. The list was short. "Not much, but what we do have is amazing.

"The moon now has its own satellite, and it's two-plus miles across. Not one observatory saw it approaching. Once the broadcasts started and people looked for it, though, there it was."

Arledge had raised an eyebrow at the object's size. The NASA-led international space station, two orders of magnitude smaller, was still only half built. "But they can see it now."

Kyle nodded. "It's big enough even for decently equipped amateur astronomers to spot." Far better views would be available once STSI, the Space Telescope Science Institute in Baltimore, finished computer enhancement of various images. Too bad the supersensitive instruments on the Hubble Space Telescope would be struck blind if it looked so close to the moon. "To no one's great surprise, it doesn't look like anything we've ever seen. Or ever built. The way that it simply *appeared* suggests teleportation or subspace tunneling or some other mode of travel whose underlying physics we can't begin to understand."

"What else?"

"You've seen the broadcasts, obviously." At Britt's shrug, Kyle continued. "That's a pretty alien-looking alien. Also, White Sands, Wallops, Jodrell Bank, and Arecibo *all* confirm direct receipt from the moon of the signal that keeps preempting network broadcasts. Overriding network satellite feed, to be precise.

"So far, that's it. I suspect we'll know a lot more soon."

"Commercial," called one of the exiles.

At the burst of typing that announced redirection of the signal, everyone turned forward to the projection screen. A famous pitchman vanished from the display almost so quickly as to be subliminal (it was enough to make Kyle think of Jell-O), to be replaced with the increasingly familiar visage of the Galactic spokesman. No one could read the expression on the alien's face, not that anyone knew that the aliens provided such visual cues, but Kyle found himself liking the creature. What wonderful wit and whimsy to present their announcements only during the commercial breaks.

"Greetings to the people of Earth," began his(?) message. "I am H'ffl. As the ambassador of the Galactic Commonwealth to your planet, the beautiful world of which we were made aware by your many radio transmissions, I am pleased to announce the arrival of our embassy expedition. We come in peace and fellowship."

Kyle studied the alien's image as familiar words repeated. The creature was vaguely centaurian in appearance: six-limbed, with four legs and two arms; one-headed; bilaterally symmetric.

Any resemblance to humans or horses stopped there. His skin was lizardlike: faintly greenish, hairless, and scaled. The legs ended in three-sectioned hooves; the arms in three-fingered claws better suited to fighting than to making or manipulating tools. A wholly unhorselike tail—long, muscular, and bifurcated, with both halves prehensile—appeared to provide counterbalance to the elongated torso. The head had four pairs of eyes, with a vertical pair set every ninety degrees for 360-degree stereoscopic vision. A motionless mouth and three vertically colinear nostrils appeared directly in the torso. The best guess was that H'ffl both spoke and heard through tympanic membranes atop the head.

"Our starship has assumed orbit around your moon. Two days from today, at noon Eastern Standard Time, a landing craft will arrive at Reagan National Airport in Washington, DC."

The control-tower radar at Reagan National tracked the spacecraft from well off the Atlantic coast to touchdown. The blip was enormous: the "landing craft" was larger than an Air Force C-5 cargo carrier. (That heavy-lift air transport had been dubbed the "Galaxy" ... *How ironic*, Kyle thought.) Fighters scrambled from Andrews AFB reported a lifting-body configuration: a flattened lower surface in lieu of wings. The turbulence behind the spacecraft, visible to weather radars, suggested powered descent.

The spacecraft swooped into sight, following the twists of the Potomac River as agilely as a radio-controlled model plane. The Air Force officer to Kyle's right scowled. "What's the matter, Colonel? You'd rather they fly over the city?"

"I'd rather that their ship wasn't so maneuverable."

Comparing capabilities? Kyle recalled the enormity of the mother ship in lunar orbit, and stifled a laugh.

Civil air traffic had been diverted to Dulles International; the Galactic vessel shot arrowlike to the center of the deserted field, settling onto the X of two intersecting runways. A mighty cheer arose from the throng that nothing short of martial law *might* have kept away. The shouts faded into an awkward hush as thousands realized that nothing was happening.

Kyle hurried to the tower elevator, descending to join the coterie of welcoming dignitaries. They were already boarding the limos that would drive them to the Galactics' vessel. He wound up in the last car, between a deputy undersecretary of state and an aide to the national security advisor. The woman from Foggy Bottom studied papers from her briefcase.

Stepping from the car, Kyle obtained some new data: the concrete beneath the landing legs of the spacecraft was broken. That thing was *heavy*. The shout of greeting must have drowned out the report of the runway cracking.

The welcoming party formed two concentric arcs facing the spacecraft, heavy hitters up front, aides and adjutants in back. Kyle took a spot in the second tier, vaguely pleased with his position: his craning at the ship was less obtrusive this way.

Away from the crowd, only the creaks and groans of the ship cooling down from the heat of reentry broke the silence. The sun beat down unmercifully. Kyle tried to memorize details of the ship—shape and proportion, aerodynamic control surfaces, view ports, thrusters and main engines, antennae—even though photographers around the airport and in helicopters overhead were busily capturing everything with telephoto lenses. Sensors hastily installed in the limos were measuring and recording any radiation from the ship.

His overriding impression was one of age, that this ship had been around for a while. Why? After a moment's thought, he focused his attention on the skin of the ship. Under the cloudless noon sky, not a bit of surface glinted. He wasn't close enough to be sure, but the shadowed underbelly of the ship seemed finely pitted. How many years of solar wind had it withstood? How many collisions with the tenuous matter of the interstellar void? Beside him, the diplomats were absorbed in their own unanswered, perhaps unanswerable, questions.

And then, at long last, with soundless ease, a wide ramp began its descent from the underside of the alien ship.

CHAPTER 2

THE RAMP STRUCK the concrete runway with a solid *thunk*. The walkway faced about 20 degrees away from the crowd, a shallow enough angle that no one moved. Necks twisted and craned slightly towards the shadowed opening. An inner door—an airlock port?—remained closed.

Kyle snuck a peek at the meter in his pocket. The counter showed an increase in radiation levels since the ramp had descended, but not enough to worry about. Still, he chided himself for losing the argument that the welcoming party wear dosimeters. That battle lost, he'd done the best he could: the meter in his coat would beep if his cumulative exposure exceeded a preset threshold.

Inference one, he thought, eyeing once more the cracked runway. Radiation plus massive weight, enough weight for a *major* amount of shielding, denote nuclear power. Then a sharp intake of breath from the diplomat beside him returned Kyle's attention to the ramp. As he watched, the airlock door cycled silently open.

Four aliens cantered down the incline, their scales iridescent in the sunlight. The ramp boomed under thudding hooves, with a tone that reminded Kyle of ceramic. The creatures halted on the runway at the base of the ramp. For clothing, each wore only a many-pocketed belt from which hung a larger sack like a Scottish sporran. Only slight variations in skin tone, all shades of light green, differentiated them. Each had about twelve inches on Kyle, himself a six-footer.

The aliens didn't turn toward the human dignitaries. If rude by human standards, the position nonetheless made sense: a face-to-face stance would have given a good view to only one pair of eyes. *They're not human,* Kyle reminded himself. For them to act like us would be strange.

One of the aliens walked slowly toward the waiting humans. Pads on the bottom of his hooves rasped against concrete. Extending both arms, hands open, palms upward, the alien stopped directly in front of Harold Shively Robeson.

"Thank you for meeting me, Mr. President," said the creature, the bass voice rumbling eerily from the top of his head. "I am Ambassador H'ffl. I bring you greetings from the Galactic Commonwealth."

The President reached out and clasped one of the alien's hands. "On behalf of the people of America and planet Earth, welcome."

So many mysteries; so little time.

Kyle stood in the White House basement command post of the science-analysis team. There was no place on Earth he'd rather be, except possibly upstairs in the Oval Office where the President and sundry diplomats met with the F'thk themselves. Should he be *here,* helping to make sense of what data they already had, or *there* trying to gather more? The obvious answer was yes.

"How's it going?"

He'd been staring at a wall covered with Post-it notes. Each paper square bore, in scribbled form, one comment about the aliens. As he turned to the doorway where Britt Arledge had appeared, one of the drafted wizards from DOE did yet another reshuffle of the stickies. Two more squares, green ones, denoting inferences, appeared between the rearranged yellow factoids. One of the relocated squares, its adhesive dissipated by too many moves, fluttered to the floor. A secretary scurried over to rewrite its content on a new sheet.

Kyle gestured over toward his red-eyed boss, wondering who looked more exhausted. "We're learning."

Britt nodded; it was all the encouragement Kyle needed. "For starters, our guests have a fusion reactor aboard their landing craft. That technology alone would be invaluable."

"Is that so?" The response was nearly monotonic; Arledge seemed singularly unimpressed. "The F'thk didn't mention that."

"Gotta be." Kyle warmed to his subject. The meter he'd taken to National hadn't differentiated between types of radiation, but the gear he'd had stowed aboard the limos was far more sophisticated. The drivers, following his instructions, had parked the cars in positions well spaced around the spaceship. "There's definite neutron flux at the back of the ship and magnetic fringing like from a tokamak quadrupole."

"Uh-huh."

"Magnetic-bottle technology to contain the plasma, and lots of shielding to protect the crew. Tons and *tons* of shielding, Britt. You saw what their ship did to the runway."

"Okay."

"On our own, we *may* have practical fusion in fifty years." Thinking, suddenly, of the distant mother ship, two-plus miles across, he nervously ran both hands through his hair. "Momma must have one *big* fusion reactor aboard."

"Oh, I doubt it," said Britt, a cat-who-ate-the-canary grin lighting his tired face. "My friend H'ffl says it uses matter-to-energy conversion. He wondered if we have antimatter."

Antimatter! No wonder Arledge was so unimpressed by his own news. "Fleetingly, for research, and then only a few subatomic particles at a time. Nothing you could power a spaceship with." Or a lightbulb, for that matter. A flurry of new Post-it notes suggestive of more progress distracted him. "What was that?"

"I asked, is antimatter dangerous? H'ffl says it's standard practice to park antimatter-powered vessels in the gravity well of an uninhabited moon when near an inhabited planet. Something about protecting against the remote likelihood of a mishap. Does it make sense for them to keep the mother ship out by the moon?"

"Yes, it's dangerous, and I don't know ... Equal amounts of matter and antimatter *do* convert totally to energy, at efficiencies far greater than fission or fusion. Orbit just a thousand miles above Earth, though, and there's no atmosphere whatever. No friction. Even without engines, a ship would circle forever. If, for some reason, it blew up, there'd be beaucoup radiation, but nothing—I should do some calculations to confirm this—nothing the atmosphere wouldn't effectively block.

"So, no, I don't see any reason to stay a quarter-million miles away. Then, what do *I* know? It's not like Earth has technology remotely like theirs."

The chief of staff persisted. "Is the mother ship a danger where it is? What if it crashed on the moon?"

"A really big crater, as if one more would matter. The point is that won't happen. The moon has no atmosphere. Any orbit higher than the tallest lunar mountain should last forever." Kyle had fudged a bit for effect: given enough time, he suspected, gravitational perturbations from lunar mascons or other planets, or tidal effects of the Earth, or solar wind would have disastrous effects on an orbit *that* low. None of which applied, in less than geological time, to the altitude at which the F'thk ship actually orbited the moon. One glance through a telescope had convinced him that the mother ship wasn't ever meant to land.

"The President will be relieved."

When had the Post-it notes stretched around to a second wall? "What else can I tell you?"

"Nothing, really—I was mostly making conversation. I actually came by to invite you to dinner." He waved off Kyle's protest. "A state dinner, upstairs, tonight at eight. Perhaps Ambassador H'ffl or one of his companions can enlighten you on F'thk orbital preferences."

Something was odd about the ballroom, thought Kyle, something other than the green aliens making chitchat with Washington's elite. What was it? He settled, at last, on the absence of hors d'oeuvres. The F'thk would not eat in public: they said that trace elements in their food were toxic to terrestrial life. White House protocol officers had then decreed that the humans wouldn't eat either.

Some dinner! He wished someone had mentioned this decision before he'd arrived. He'd gone home to change into a tux; any nuke 'n puke meal from his freezer, if not up to White House banquet standards, still would've beaten fasting.

He sipped his wine; the F'thk with whom he and a gaggle of civil servants were talking held tightly to a glass of water. The microcassette recorder in Kyle's pocket was hopefully catching the entire conversation. If not, well, he'd handed out others.

"You've been very quiet, Dr. Gustafson. I'd expected more curiosity from a man in your position."

Kyle needed a moment to realize that the comment had come

from the alien. Earth's radio and TV broadcasts had served not only as beacons but also as language tutorials—lessons the F'thk had learned extremely well. "Lack of curiosity is not the problem, K'ddl." Despite his best efforts, a hint of vowel crept into the name. "Quite the opposite. I have so many questions that I don't know where to begin."

"Oh, God," whispered a State Department staffer behind him. "He's going to babble in nanobytes per quark volt."

Kyle ignored the crack, his mind still wrestling with the afternoon's conversation about the mother ship. "I'm puzzled about one thing. Why keep the F'thk mother ship in lunar orbit? It seems excessively cautious."

Swelling violins from the chamber orchestra—Mozart, Kyle thought—drowned out the alien's response. He shrugged reflexively, realizing even as he did it how foolish it was to expect the alien to understand the gesture.

Except K'ddl did. "I said, it's not F'thk. The mother ship is Aie'eel-built. They fly it, as well." The alien made a periodic rasping noise which, Kyle decided, must be a form of laughter. "You thought it coincidental that the Commonwealth's representatives were so humanlike? You would consider the Aie'eel so many headless, methane-breathing frogs. The Zxk'tl and the #$%^&"—Kyle couldn't even begin to organize that last sound burst into English letters—"and other crew species aboard the mother ship would seem less human still.

"We F'thk were chosen as the emissary species because we so closely resemble you. We are accustomed to similar gravity, temperature, sunlight, and atmosphere." He hoisted his still-filled glass and took a drink. "We are even both water-based."

That was when too much wine on an empty stomach betrayed Kyle. The room spun. His ears rang. Visions of . . . things . . . too inhuman even to lend themselves to description assailed him. All thought of orbits and exotic energy sources fled. He missed entirely the last comment K'ddl made before turning his attention to another White House guest.

The tape recorder in Kyle's pocket, however, was made of sterner stuff. K'ddl had added, "I do not wish to offend, but no F'thk would ever invent such dark nights or such a paltry number of moons."

＊　　　＊　　　＊

Two sandwiches and four cups of coffee later, Kyle felt almost himself again. He ignored the disapproving sniffs of the White House chef. It was unclear, in any event, whether the criticism dealt with Kyle's plebeian taste for peanut butter or his part in that afternoon's delivery to the kitchen of so much bulky equipment. So many instrument-covered counters . . . perhaps it was just as well that dinner for three hundred had been canceled.

A Secret Service agent turned waiter for the evening came through the double doors, a single half-empty glass on his tray. "One of the aliens set this down. K'ddl I think, but I can't really tell 'em apart yet. Sorry it wasn't any fuller."

Kyle nodded his thanks. "Doesn't matter. It's more than we need." He tore the sterile wrapper from an eyedropper, then extracted a few milliliters from the alien's glass. The sample went into an automated mass spectrometer.

The analyzer beeped as it completed its tests. The color display lit up, chemical names and their concentrations scrolling down the screen. Water. Very dilute carbonic acid: carbon dioxide in solution, basic fizz. Traces of calcium and magnesium salts. Kyle compared the list to a sample taken before the aliens had arrived. As best he could tell, the glass contained pure Perrier.

"Kyle?"

He turned to the casually dressed engineer, a friend from the nearby Naval Research Labs, who'd spent the evening in the kitchen. "Yeah, Larry?"

"The *air* samples are different." To an eyebrow raised in interrogation, Larry added, "Check the plots yourself."

Kyle rolled out two strip charts, one annotated "6:05 P.M." and the other "9:00 P.M." Spikes of unrecognized complex hydrocarbons appeared on only the later sheet. If what passed for alien saliva held no trace of metabolic toxins, apparently their exhalations did. Still, the nine-o'clock spike seemed somehow familiar.

Ah.

"Can I bum a cigarette, Lar, and a match?" He lit up clumsily, almost choking as he inhaled. Waving away the suddenly solicitous engineer, he took a more cautious drag. He directed part of this lungful into a test tube, which he quickly stoppered.

Larry, catching on quickly, ran the latest sample through the mass spectrometer. The resulting strip chart, marked "10:11 P.M.," soon lay beside the others.

The evening's addition to the White House air was simply tobacco smoke. Whatever toxins the aliens ate didn't appear in their breath, either.

Kyle poured a fresh cup of coffee, only in part to wash the unaccustomed and unwelcome smoke residues from his mouth. He also hoped for a caffeine jolt to settle jangled nerves. First, the conundrum about the aliens' inconvenient orbit around the moon; now, undetectable toxins.

He wondered when, or if, his study of the aliens would begin to make sense.

CHAPTER 3

H'ffl Is Father of My Baby

—*National Investigator*

UFO Sightings Precede F'thk "Arrival"

—*Star Inquirer*

Satyr-like F'thk Are Devil's Spawn
—yesterday's most popular dialogue on the
Modern Revelations News Group, *AmericaNet*

F'thk Evaluate Earth for Commonwealth Membership
—*Washington Post*

BETWEEN TWO PARALLEL lines of the Marine honor guard, a ramp descended from the Galactics' ship. What looked like a Hovercraft floated down the incline, any noise that it may have been making drowned out by the crowd. Four F'thk and a large cylindrical object filled the house-sized vehicle's open rear deck. The one-way glass of the front compartment gave no clues as to the species of the driver. From the shortness of the cab, it seemed unlikely that the driver was another F'thk. Then again, maybe there was no driver.

At a stately ten miles per hour, the craft slid across the runway toward the George Washington Parkway. Four Secret Service cars pulled out in front of it; limos and more Secret Service fell in behind to complete the motorcade.

At that speed, it'd be a while before the aliens arrived here at the Mall. Kyle moved the inset TV window to the back of the palmtop computer's display before turning to his companion.

Darlene Lyons was quietly attractive, with twinkling brown eyes, a daintily upturned nose, and full lips slightly parted in a smile. In faded jeans and an even more faded Metallica T-shirt, her black hair flowing to the small of her back, she looked not at all like the business-suited and bunned diplomat with whom he'd shared a limo to the airport on Landing Day. Then again, it wasn't as if he routinely wore cutoffs, a sleeveless sweatshirt, and an Orioles cap to the OEOB. Alas.

"I'm glad you joined me."

"I'm glad you asked. You were right, too. I'll learn a lot more watching people during the ceremony than seeing it live myself." She raked both hands, fingers splayed, through her lustrous hair. "Though I wouldn't have minded selling my ticket for the grandstands."

Laughing, Kyle tapped a query into the comp. As they watched, the bid on eBay for a bleacher seat popped up another three hundred dollars, to over fifteen grand. "I don't think the Secret Service would've gone for either of us scalping a seat on the presidential reviewing stand. Beside, this way I'll have something to tell my folks the next time they try to impress me with having been at Woodstock."

Another reason went unstated. For the soon-to-be-appointed head of the soon-to-be-announced Presidential Commission on Galactic Studies, today was probably his last chance to get an unfiltered assessment of the public's mood.

As far as the eye or network helicopters *thp-thp-thp*-ing overhead could see, the Mall was packed. There would be other ceremonies like today's, of course, celebrations all around the world—Tiananmen Square tomorrow, Red Square the next day, Jardin de Tuileries the day after that—but today was different. Today was the first. Kyle and Darlene wanted to be in it, not just watching it. Judging from the crowd, much of the Eastern Seaboard had felt the same way.

He offered an elbow. "Shall we mingle?"

Giving only a snort in response, whether to the anachronistic gesture or the impracticality of walking side by side through the crowd, he couldn't tell, she plunged ahead. He hastened after. Only by heading *away* from the National Gallery of Art, in front of which the Fellowship Station was to be placed, were they able to make slow progress.

" . . . Growing up as a . . . " " . . . Incalculable opportunity . . . " " . . . Soulless monsters . . . " " . . . Food around here?" "Devils . . . " " . . . To the stars?" Bits of conversation rose and fell randomly from the milling, murmuring crowd.

Devils and monsters? "Wait a sec." Kyle pivoted slowly, listening in vain for more of one conversation. "Did you hear someone mention monsters?" She shook her head.

He dug the computer out of his pocket. A few finger taps retrieved the sampling of today's headlines that had been radio-downlinked from the White House's intranet. He grunted as the tabloid headlines rolled into view. He'd come here to learn, and he had: however inventive these nutty headlines were, there really were people who believed them. A double tap on the AmericaNet entry made him blink in surprise: 547 postings just yesterday to the Modern Revelations news group. A quick scribble with the stylus across the touch screen, "f'thk OR alien OR galactic" matched only 403 of these entries; "monster OR creature OR devil OR demon OR satan" yielded 516 entries. Wondering if he'd missed any synonyms, Kyle wrote himself a softcopy note to check out this news group.

A roar arose from across the Mall. The crowd pivoted toward the National Gallery, aligning itself to the north like so many iron filings. People all around them retrieved their radios, portable TVs, and pocket comps. As one, they turned the volume settings to max.

Once more, the aliens had arrived.

The Hovercraft coasted gracefully to a halt at the presidential reviewing stand. A ramp slid from the deck area. A F'thk (Kyle couldn't decide from the small screen if it was one that he'd met) guided the cylindrical Fellowship Station down the slope. No longer partially obscured by the side of the Hovercraft, the cylinder could now be seen to have a flared base, a skirt for containing its own air cushion, perhaps. To yet one more cheer, the cylinder settled to rest on the grassy surface of the Mall.

As the President completed his words of welcome and introduction, Darlene poked Kyle with a sharp finger. "Coming to
Washington first. Odd, don't you think?"

His home VCR was taping everything anyway. "So? They'll see
other capitals, meet other heads of state at other ceremonies,
starting with Chairman Chang tomorrow in Beijing."

"They've picked favorites, or seemed to, by coming to Washington, first. Why not New York and the UN?"

"Maybe they didn't know about it."

"Yeah, right. They speak perfect English—and French, Spanish, German, and Russian. People I respect say their Mandarin,
Japanese, and Hindi are just as good. They made themselves folk
heroes by interrupting only commercials. You really think they
never heard of the United Nations?"

"You don't buy that?"

"Hardly."

"Does everyone at Foggy Bottom feel this way?"

Her look of disgust was eloquent.

So . . . someone who didn't take the aliens at face value. Someone
whose thinking was, at the same time, orthogonal to his own.
Kyle made a snap decision. "Congratulations."

"For what?"

For being selected a member of the Presidential Commission
on Galactic Studies. Trying to look enigmatic, he turned back
to his computer screen, on which Ambassador H'ffl had just
appeared.

"Ask me tomorrow."

After speaking of fellowship and galactic unity for fifteen minutes, Ambassador H'ffl extended an arm toward the just-dedicated
Fellowship Station. In one smooth motion, a talon sliced through
the ribbon and depressed the single control button. The crowd
didn't go silent, that was too much to expect from what the
media now estimated at 720,000 people, but there was a decided
abatement of the din. An inset door in the station slid aside. H'ffl
removed something that sparkled in the sunlight and handed it
to President Robeson.

"On behalf of the Commonwealth, I offer you this orb, symbol of galactic unity. May the peoples of Earth soon qualify for
membership."

Renewed shouting drowned out much of the President's response. As Kyle and Darlene watched, H'ffl and his associates presented one orb after another to the assembled dignitaries. A phalanx of Secret Service agents, Park Service police, and DC cops held back the crowd while the VIPs filed back to their limos. Honking as it went, the motorcade receded.

Darlene and Kyle were among the lucky ones: they reached the Fellowship Station and received their orbs in only a bit over five hours. Each was an ever-changing crystalline sphere, resting in a metallic bowl atop a ceramic pedestal. It seemed a nice enough souvenir, if hardly worth the hoopla.

The next morning, an exhausted Kyle found an orb waiting on his desk. The note left beneath the galactic memento read: *When I told H'ffl about your new duties, he insisted that you get one of these. Britt.*

CHAPTER 4

Economic Impact of Galactic Technology Uncertain
—*The Wall Street Journal*

Thousands Pray for Deliverance from Space Devils
—yesterday's most popular dialogue on the
Modern Revelations News Group, *AmericaNet*

Gustafson Commission Opens Hearings Today
—*New York Times*

AIDES SCURRIED AROUND the enormous conference table, double-checking the placement of name tags, distributing glasses and pitchers of ice water, straightening network taps and power cords for laptop PCs, and setting out pencils and pads of paper. The secretaries were silent; the considerable noise within the room all came from the milling crowd on the opposite side of the closed double doors. From, that was, the press and the commission members...

The chairman of the Presidential Commission on Galactic Studies scowled at the totally anachronistic pads of paper, and at the inclusion of so many committee members apt to use them. He'd turned out to have less authority than expected—far less, for example, than the President's chief of staff. Kyle could name as many *staffers* as he wished; the *commissioners* were to be chosen more for their political correctness ("A diversity of viewpoints," Britt had gently rephrased Kyle's complaint) than for any insight they were likely to have.

The list of private-sector members on which he and Britt had finally converged was simultaneously top-heavy with CEOs from New New Economy companies and light on technologists: more campaign contributors than researchers. Kyle could at least hope that these executives would tap their organizations' expertise, and he'd had some success in holding out for execs whose firms did relevant R&D. As to the Wall Street and Hollywood types, he could only hope that the deliberations would put them to sleep. Would it be unseemly to ask his token clergyperson to pray for that?

The next largest group of members was drawn from mid-tier executives of key federal agencies and departments: EPA, Energy, NASA, Homeland Security, DoD, Commerce—and State. He smiled, recalling a rare victory: Darlene Lyons was one of "his" diplomats.

The smallest set of slots was for practicing scientists and engineers. With only ten member spots to work with, he'd scoured academia and the federal labs for twenty-first-century Renaissance people. *Damn!* He needed biologists, physicists, and engineers of every type; astronomers; psychologists and sociologists; organic and inorganic chemists; economists . . . the list seemed endless, and ten seats didn't begin to cover it. After considerable anguish, he'd filled the few experts' positions. Time would tell what happened when seven Nobel laureates focused on one problem.

The hubbub outside was rising to a crescendo; he caught the eye of Myra Flynn, his admin assistant. She did a final scan of the facilities, then nodded: the room was ready. He nodded back, dispatching her to open the doors.

Let the Galactic games begin.

Squinting under the onslaught of massed videocam lights, Kyle studied the faces arrayed around the table. Despite his earlier misgivings, he had to admit it: the hearing room was packed with achievers and overachievers, great Americans all. For this mission, it was impossible to be too competent.

It was time to stimulate their thinking. He took a sip of water while he tried yet again to vanquish his stage fright.

"Fellow commissioners." The words came out as a croak. Another sip. "You have all been invited, and have graciously accepted the call, to serve your country at a time when great issues must be addressed. Great issues, indeed." He tapped the keyboard built into the lectern. An image popped up on the projection screen beside him, and onto the display of every PC whose owner had logged on to the committee-room network. The still picture was a close-up of the Galactics' highly impressive landing craft. "This is the tip of the iceberg."

Click. A second picture appeared, a telescopic close-up of the two-mile-wide mother ship. H'ffl said it was named *S'kz'wtz Lrrk'l*, which he'd translated as "*Galactic Peace.*" "*This* is the iceberg. The civilization capable of building this vessel represents opportunities, and risks, which, I am convinced, we cannot yet even begin to fathom. It is our responsibility to explore those opportunities, to investigate those risks, and to chart a prudent course between them."

Click. An aerial photo appeared of the Washington Mall, with any trace of grass obscured by the myriads of people patiently awaiting the arrival of the Fellowship Station. "The people of America..." Click: a montage of aerial shots of major capital cities around the globe, each showing a sea of citizens greeting the Galactics. "... And of the world now look to their leaders in hope."

Click. For the first time, sound issued from the projection system: xenophobic rantings. After a few seconds tightly focused on the contorted face of the charismatic speaker, the camera panned back to reveal a few dozen rapt faces, then hundreds, then thousands. Kyle muted the harangue. "Or they look in fear. Fear of the unfamiliar. Fear of the unknown."

Click. A back-lit close-up of an orb, the instantly famous symbol of galactic unity, the crystal slowly, subtly, hypnotically changing colors and texture. The larger-than-life image emphasized the variations occurring throughout the sphere's crystalline depths: a thing of beauty beyond words. Kyle noticed, for the first time, that several commissioners had brought their own orbs to the session. "Our task, and it is a most challenging one, is to advise the President on whether, and how, to respond to an offer from the Galactics, should one be forthcoming.

"Let us all be up to that challenge."

Chords crashed. Arpeggios rippled their way up and down the keyboard. Speakers all around Kyle poured out music so pure that his fingers imagined the stiff bounce of each key; his shoulders and arms tensed in sympathy with the pianist's.

As the Saint-Saëns second piano concerto enveloped him in its lengthy crescendo, he peered into a Galactic orb. Colors shimmering and swirling throughout its depths drew him ever inward. A lava lamp for the twenty-first century, whispered some quirky corner of his mind.

He'd never seen the orb transform so rapidly. Colors flowed one into another. Textures waxed and waned, one blending imperceptibly into the next. Patterns formed and faded before a merely human intellect could capture their meaning.

The final chords, and some epiphany, seemed to hang in the air, tantalizingly just beyond his reach. As the music stopped, so, too, did the changes within the orb. Sighing, he picked it up from the coffee table. Not for a lack of trying, all that he, or anyone, had learned was that the galactic unity icon responded to light and sound. Like snowflakes, no two orbs were ever quite the same, nor had any orb ever been seen to repeat itself. Fellowship stations kept manufacturing them on demand, requiring only occasional redeliveries of raw material from the F'thk.

From its cabinet across the living room, the red power LED of the stereo amplifier stared unblinkingly at him like a cyclopean eye. Setting the orb back down, he took up the remote control in its stead. He aimed the remote at the entertainment center. Zap.

A sea of sound once more immersed man and orb, changing both in ways too subtle to be immediately understood.

Piles of reports lined the back of Kyle's desk; a floor-bound stack leaned precariously against a crammed bookcase. Even today's mound of executive summaries, precisely centered on his blotter, was daunting.

Sweeping sandwich crumbs from the top report, he read the title: "Economic Repercussions of a Switch to a Fusion Economy."

Below that he found "Passive Infrared Analysis of the F'thk Anatomy," "Means for the Analytical Substantiation of Antimatter Power Systems," "On the Efficacy of the F'thk Visual Apparatus: a Follow-Up Investigation," and "Speculations on Interstellar Trade Modalities."

The top and bottom reports presumed that Earth and the F'thk reached a meeting of minds, and were light-years outside his area of expertise. He set those aside to review at home that evening. The middle three showed more promise.

Speed-reading its abstract quickly revealed that "Means for Analytical Substantiation" was an elaborate plea for replacing the replacement Gamma Ray Observatory. He snorted. He hardly needed a presidential commission to tell him that the fingerprint of matter/antimatter energy conversion was gamma-ray production, and that the atmosphere blocked gamma rays. The good news was that a substitute for the satellite lost in the *Atlantis* explosion might possibly, if money were no object, be quickly constructible from the lab prototype. The bad news was that such an orbital observatory, even more than its huge and ungainly forebear, would need the services of a massive booster—the shuttle—for delivery to space.

Oh, the irony of a grounded shuttle fleet when the Galactics came a-calling. The Russians weren't flying manned missions either, although in their case the stand-down was due to an ever imploding economy. He wanted *so* badly for Man to be a spacefaring race, even if only skimming the top of its own atmosphere, when dealing with the F'thk. Sans shuttle, the International Space Station had been vacated via its emergency lifeboat.

A fireball in a clear blue Florida sky returned, unbidden, to his mind's eye. One more horrible image, like the glowing streaks of the disintegrating *Columbia*, he knew he could never forget. He set aside the report, grabbing another for distraction.

The IR study of the F'thk was crisp and factual: just what he needed. Several conference rooms used for meetings with the aliens had, at the commission's direction, been instrumented with hidden infrared sensors. Satisfaction with the report faded, however, as he completed the introduction and moved into results. Computer-enhanced images from the sensor data revealed little more than sporadic hot spots in ambient-temperature bodies.

Since the visitors seemed equally energetic and equally clothes-free in all Earthly climates, this apparent cold-bloodedness was yet another puzzle.

The low-resolution pictures provided the only anatomical data he had—the F'thk consistently declined all suggestions that they provide biological/medical information. Kyle's rationale for the request, that such data were necessary to avoid any inadvertent endangerment of either species, was politely dismissed. H'ffl asserted full confidence in his guidance from the Commonwealth's scientists. The possibility of a biological incident seemed to amuse him. Beyond keeping their own knowledge to themselves, the F'thk also refused requests to be examined by X-ray, ultrasound, or any other active imaging technique. When pressed, they invariably answered, "Information is a trade good."

Flipping pages impatiently, Kyle encountered more excuses than derived anatomical data. The report ended with the predictable request for supercomputer time for additional image enhancement. "Approved," he scrawled, and tossed it into his out basket.

One down.

"Visual Apparatus" was full of minutiae about F'thk viewing angles and stereoscopic vision. He was about to add this tome to the out basket unread when his thumbing-through uncovered a section on separate day-and-night vision systems. "The dilation of F'thk pupils," he read, "indicates that the upper eye of each pair is optimized for day vision, the lower eye for night vision." He reached reflexively for his coffee cup as he began studying the report more closely.

The night-vision data was the result of one of Kyle's sugges-tions. The F'thk did not approve X-ray imaging—and certainly could carry sensors to tell if their wishes had been ignored—but planning could widen the range of achievable passive observations. After the surreptitious tripping of a circuit breaker, low-light video cameras in a rigged room had caught the pupils of F'thk night eyes dilating with extreme rapidity. Pupil dilation—substantially wider than occurred when lights had been dimmed for a view-graph presentation—was still in progress when the windowless room had become too black for the high-sensitivity CCD video-cams to function.

Faugh. The coldness of the coffee finally registered; he emp-tied the dregs into the potted plant beside his desk. Pouring a fresh cup from the brewer on the credenza, he wondered what was bothering him. Obviously, their night vision was suited to a moonless world . . .

Moonless. Was *that* the problem?

The text-search program needed only a few seconds and some keywords to find the transcript; K'ddl's words at the White House reception were as he'd remembered. "I do not wish to offend, but no F'thk would ever invent such dark nights or such a paltry number of moons."

He shut his eyes in concentration, a finger marking his place in the report. How likely was it for such ultrasensitive night vision to have evolved on a planet with several moons?

He didn't know, but that's why the commission had a biologist.

A delightful aroma—basil and rosemary? Kyle speculated—wafted down the State Department hallway. It was, happily, no longer considered necessary to fast in front of the aliens. One week into the commission's existence, a commissioner had fainted midsession. An amused ambassador, upon learning the cause of the commotion, insisted that the F'thk did not consider it rude for the humans to dine whenever they wished. The aliens themselves needed to eat only once for each of *their* days, about thirty Earth hours. Rather than impede progress by suspending meetings for meals, they would be happy to continue while the humans ate. Really.

A group of commissioners and F'thk strolled slowly down the hall toward one of State's many dining rooms. Kyle's stomach rumbled as they approached the food, though from nerves rather than hunger. He was, for the first time, deviating from the visitors' explicit wishes. His right hand, hidden in his pants pocket, fondled a tiny ultrasonic beacon; the gadget, when triggered, would pulse once at a frequency to which a previous test had shown the aliens unresponsive. The isolation of a suitable frequency had required some experimentation—it had turned out that the F'thk communicated among themselves by modulated ultrasound, using a language human scientists had made zero progress in analyzing.

The hall narrowed where two china closets had been retrofitted. Behind the wooden doors on both sides of the cramped

passageway were the newest and most sensitive ultrasound imag-
ers that money could buy. A F'thk named Ph'jk was in the lead;
as he entered the space between the hidden instruments, Kyle
squeezed the hidden signaling device.

It happened too fast to register. Ph'jk reared up on his hind
legs, lashing out with his front hooves at the right-hand doors.
K'ddl galloped forward, squeezing into the narrow space to shatter
the doors to the left. Within seconds, slashing claws and pounding
hooves reduced wood and electronics alike to splinters. Ignoring
the sparks and wisps of smoke rising from the wreckage, the
F'thk continued wordlessly into the dining room. Splintered wood
crunched beneath their hooves as they crossed the wrecked area.
Dazedly, the humans followed.

H'ffl set a claw, talons retracted, on Kyle's shoulder and squeezed.
"Information is a trade good," he said. "We trust you will not
attempt again to steal it."

Kyle wiped a swatch of condensed steam from his bathroom
mirror. The long, hot shower hadn't done much for his shoulder
or his mood; he scowled at his bruised reflection. A sore shoulder
was all he had to show for yesterday's escapade.

The ultrasound equipment had been ruined beyond hope of
recovery of any internal images of the aliens. Should've networked
the damn machines, he thought, hours too late. The data would've
been out of their reach before they had the chance to react.

Or maybe not. Over his first cup of morning coffee, he called
the commission staff desk to confirm his suspicions. Passive
sensors also hidden in the hallway had revealed three other
ultrasound sources to have been present: each of the F'thk had
apparently carried a jammer. It wasn't a *big* surprise: the immediate response proved that they'd been carrying detectors; why
not jammers, too?

He'd brooded all night for nothing. There had been no lost
opportunity to have spirited away stolen imagery by network
before the alien reaction. Sighing, Kyle headed to his office and
the staff's overnight report on the incident, at once eager and
reluctant to read what else he'd missed.

The private-sector commission members had largely disappeared with the opening session's TV lights—to return when the

cameras did. Glory came of being named to the commission, not in serving on it. Staffers were more than happy to fill in for the vacant members.

The latest gathering in the committee room resembled the colloquium of scientists, engineers, and policy makers he'd expected in the first place. For at least the hundredth time since joining the administration, he decided Britt was dumb like a fox. He was also, to Kyle's unspoken chagrin, sitting in today—bosses have prerogatives. So far, Britt had been a silent observer.

"Here's what we've got." Kyle gestured at nothing and no one in particular. "Clean, essentially limitless, fusion power, the technology for which they'll swap before they leave in return for downloads from our public libraries—if we've voted to join the Commonwealth. They will sell only to governments, who can then license fusion to power-generation companies. Their reasoning is that government control will minimize disruptions to the economy.

"Point two. If a . . ."

"Wait," called Darlene. "Why not license fusion just once, through the UN?"

Fred Phillips from Commerce rolled his eyes. "Give it a *rest*. The Galactics choose not to deal with the UN, and they don't want to talk about it. Besides, I like the precedent: we have far more to dicker with than most countries."

"And it doesn't strike you as odd that a galactic commonwealth, talking planetary membership, is practicing national divide and conquer?"

"Objection noted," interrupted Kyle. He agreed with Darlene, but knew no one else did. Majority opinion, led by Commerce, was that bypassing the UN eliminated a human cartel. Just shrewd business.

"Point two. If a majority of nations," he gave Darlene a warning look, "ask to join the Commonwealth, the F'thk say they'll submit Earth's petition. Membership, as far as any of us can tell, appears simply to regularize the trade relationship."

Krulewitch from MIT spoke without looking up from his palmtop computer. "I thought we were still being evaluated."

"We are." Kyle fidgeted with the laser pointer someone had left on the lectern. "The petition will be accompanied by their own report about our suitability."

"Then isn't the fusion-for-library-access trade a conflict of interest? And they won't let us send our own ambassador?"

"Yes, and no way. Not only can't we send an ambassador, we can't set foot on the landing craft, let alone the mother ship." Kyle rubbed his cheek ruefully. "I've asked for *that* privilege a dozen times. They always change the subject."

"Antimatter production?" asked Krulewitch.

"A flat no. K'ddl suggested that a species stuck on one planet shouldn't use the stuff." Playing the Galactic, Kyle changed the subject, ignoring the MIT physicist's knowing grin. K'ddl's answer rubbed salt in a still open wound. "Point three: lots of loose ends and seeming contradictions, none of them having any obvious bearing on whether this august body recommends a US vote for joining the Commonwealth."

He rattled off some of the more vexing observations. The apparent overconservatism of the mother ship's lunar parking orbit. The ducking of most questions. The unwillingness to let human biologists examine the F'thk. The inexplicably good F'thk night vision. The absence of trace toxins around the F'thk, despite the claimed toxicity of their food. The failure of air filters to capture any hint of the F'thk organic chemistry. The . . .

"They're playing countries off one against the next," piped in Darlene.

"Point four," called out an undersecretary from Energy. She gave a nasty edge to her voice.

Kyle set down the borrowed pointer. He paused to make eye contact with everyone in the room. "Three points are all. Trade is a good thing, and they know things we'd like to learn. Commonwealth membership would help us trade. The longer we study them, the less I, for one, understand them."

Britt Arledge spoke for the first time that session. "Then I should anticipate the full commission recommending an application for membership?"

Across the room, heads of commissioners and staffers alike bobbed yes. All heads but two: his and Darlene's.

What was so bothering him that he'd pass up the secret of practical fusion power? That he'd risk never knowing what marvels Earth and the aliens could next agree to share? Even if he *could* convince the commission to say no, what was his justification?

"Kyle?"

Feeling that he'd failed, but not knowing how or why, Kyle was reluctant to meet his boss's gaze. Instead, he found himself peering into the galactic orb that sat on the table in front of Arledge. Not sure to which of them he was speaking, Kyle finally and unhappily answered. He willed his voice to be firm.

"So it would appear."

CHAPTER 5

President Lauds Galactic Commission Recommendation
—*USA Today*

Protect Earth's Information Birthright
—yesterday's most popular dialogue on the
Modern Revelations News Group, *AmericaNet*

Chernykov Denounces Western Cultural Imperialism
—*Moskva Daily News*

Gustafson Quits Galactics Commission
—*Washington Post*

CLEANING OUT AN OFFICE, Kyle mused, wasn't the chore that it used to be. Those of his files that could be retained, he'd copied over the Internet to rented mass storage. He'd download them onto longer-term storage once he started at the new job.

His physical possessions fit in one box: favorite desk accessories, pieces of executive fidgetware, and framed photos of himself with dignitaries he'd met as science advisor. In the last category was a picture with Harold Shively Robeson, shot at Kyle's swearing in; it memorialized the first and last time he'd met the President.

On top of everything else, he set an orb. "What secrets do you keep?" he asked, gazing into its shimmering depths. Like everything else Galactic, it kept its opinions to itself.

The PalmPilot in his coat pocket chose that moment to chime, announcing an incoming call. The screen revealed the familiar face of his Russian counterpart. Ex-counterpart. "Hello, Sergei Denisovich."

"Good morning, my friend. I'm glad I caught you."

Kyle set the palmtop on the now-bare desk where its camera plug-in could capture him. "At least you're not a reporter."

"Still, I wish to know why you did such a stupid thing."

"Take a number, Sergei." The Russian waited silently for more of an answer. "Oh, hell, Sergei, why *not* tell you? There are too many things about the F'thk I don't understand. Most of the commission wanted to move now, locking up the secret of fusion; I wasn't ready yet."

"We simple Russian peasants are new to this democracy business, but don't people get to vote their consciences?"

"I did, by leaving the commission. It was pretty clear what the administration wanted." Kyle grimaced. "There are also rules about how much, and just plain how, a political appointee embarrasses the President who named him."

"Deciphering politics in Moscow is difficult enough; I'll leave you to sort out the rules in Washington." As the Russian spoke, the picture briefly broke up. When the image returned, Sergei was smiling sardonically. "Well, my friend, at least we will always have Canaveral. As to your future endeavors, I wish you luck."

They chatted a bit more, mostly about Kyle's imminent return to his pre-Washington position—he'd resigned as the presidential science advisor as well as from the commission—but the conversation never quite homed in on a real topic. Kyle wondered just why the Russian had called.

That mystery was replaced with a new one when, by then in his soon-to-be-vacated apartment, Kyle checked his e-mail. Judging from a timestamp, the bad transmission during Sergei's call had somehow registered as an incoming message—and it was all garbage, of course.

His mind would not let go the conversation. What an odd phrase: *deciphering politics*. Could this be an encoded message?

Like many Internet users, Kyle had posted half a pair of encryption keys to a public key-management server. Anyone could send him a confidential message by encrypting it with this public key; only Kyle, using his private key could decrypt it. He ran the "message" through his e-mail reader's decrypter and got different garbage.

This is foolishness, he thought—a diversion from the serious packing the DC apartment yet required. The Cold War had ended years ago; did he really suspect his Russian colleague of practicing intrigue? Still, their conversation nagged at him. *We will always have Canaveral.*

Academic cryptologists had decried the government-sanctioned encryption algorithm as breakable; cynics claimed that Washington wanted the ability to eavesdrop. Did Sergei share such fears? Was Sergei telling him that the Russians had broken the code?

Or was Kyle simply paranoid about a burst of static that had confused his comp?

A Web query revealed *ziplock* to be the hacking community's secret-key algorithm of choice. He downloaded an executable for the alternative privacy software from a file server.

Kyle was relieved when the key *Canaveral* failed to decrypt the message. He had no better luck with *Atlantis*, with any of the crew names, or with the date of the explosion. *Get a life,* he told himself; his self, instead, tried again with "Apollo/Saturn V" as the key. The ziplock decrypt program now revealed:

I don't trust the F'thk either.

P. A. Nevsky

Another Net search explained the vague familiarity of the alias. Prince Alexander was an early Russian military hero, dubbed Nevsky for his defeat of Swedish invaders on the banks of the Neva River. Alexander later reached an accommodation with the conquering Mongols, a deal with the devil that maintained a degree of Russian autonomy.

Was Sergei likening the F'thk, some Russian faction, or the West to the barbarian Mongols? Retrieving a morning headline that his news filter had culled for him, Kyle hyperlinked to the Russian president's polemic about spiritual pollution from encroaching Western values. Chernykov's speech blasted the very idea of F'thk using decadent Western culture to represent humankind to the Galactic Commonwealth.

Multimedia client software in his palmtop subverted to accept an e-mail message transmitted surreptitiously as static during an international video call—a capability that the Russian intelligence service surely didn't want known. The equivocal subtext about a compromised (but by whom?) public encryption system. The ambiguous alias. Russian nationalist hysteria.

The mind boggled.

Amid the expanding set of questions, Kyle clung to one certainty: a peer whom he deeply respected shared his own distrust of the F'thk.

In public life, one has contacts and associates. In politics, balloons drop by the thousands at nominating conventions and are otherwise unseen. In government, banners bear simplistic slogans writ large in standard fonts.

At Franklin Ridge National Labs, Kyle's once and future employer, the cafeteria brimmed with dozens of old friends, hundreds of balloons, and a mildly bizarre welcome banner obviously plotted by a fractal program. He wondered why he'd ever left.

Full of punch—spiked, his spinning head told him—and sheet cake, he let himself be led to his new office. The path chosen by Dr. Hammond Matthews, Kyle's friend, guide, and successor as lab director, began to look suspicious. "Hold it, Matt. We're heading for the director's office."

"Not so," Matt dissembled, nonetheless leading the way to Kyle's former office. Matt gestured at the door, which read OFFICE OF THE DIRECTOR EMERITUS. "The director, that poor, benighted bureaucrat, parks himself one aisle over. Some carefree researcher with a fat, unencumbered budget hangs out here." Kyle was seldom speechless, but finding this such an occasion, he threw open the door and went inside . . .

. . . Where he was even more surprised to discover Britt Arledge standing. Matt shrugged apologetically, and closed the door from the outside.

"Good man, that," began Britt.

Kyle pointed to a seat, then settled into the chair behind the

old, familiar desk. He could've taken another spot at the conference table; his anger led to the unsubtle reminder that he no
longer worked for Britt. "Miss me already?"

"I have work for you already."

Kyle had been in Washington too long to lose his temper with
one of the most powerful men in the administration. Lest that
temper escape confinement, he kept his answer short. "Oh?"

"Did you plan to spend some time here studying our F'thk
friends?"

Kyle spared the barest hint of a noncommittal nod.

"Then fifty million dollars of the black may prove helpful."

Black money: intelligence-agency funds. A lot of it, and from a
budget which by its very nature was subject to the most minimal
of oversight. He considered various possible answers before settling
for the simplest. "Thanks." As silence stretched on uncomfortably,
he added, still in a monosyllabic mode, "Why?"

"In case you're right." Arledge took a cigar from his jacket
before continuing; failing to spot an ashtray, he sniffed the cylinder longingly before putting it back. He climbed to his feet.
"Since I mean us to get fusion before the Russians do, I needed
America's best talent to find out."

The Russians again. Essential as news filters were, they had
their downside: when you were too busy to follow what was
happening, you didn't know to update them.

Wondering what, if anything, about the Alexander Nevsky message to mention, Kyle almost missed the subtext. Almost. "You
wanted me off the commission. You pushed." This time, he left
the *why?* unstated.

"I needed you here. You can't act nearly as convincingly as you
can storm off in high dudgeon. QED."

He should be furious at the manipulation, Kyle thought, but
somehow he wasn't: he'd rather be here than Washington. "Sometimes I marvel that you never ran for President."

Britt arched an eyebrow by an understated millimeter. "I didn't
have to," he said.

CHAPTER 6

Russia Protests U.S. Arms Sale to Ukraine
—*NBC Moscow Bureau*

Treasury Threatens Cutoff of Loans to Russia
—*Voice of America*

Nationalists Favored in Russian Federation Elections
—*CNN*

THERE COULD BE VERY few matters more pressing than interstellar visitors and their advanced technology, but a foolish humankind seemed to have found one: a return to nuclear madness.

Bellicose speeches and resurgent Russian nationalism were bad enough; now Kyle found himself immersed in a far scarier nightmare. As world tensions inexplicably climbed, the White House asked him to spearhead Franklin Ridge's round-the-clock research into a national-security disaster: the rash of failures in "national technical means," diplomat-speak for spy satellites. If, as everyone suspected, the Russians were killing the satellites, how were they doing it? And why?

And what would happen when, despite the nation's best efforts to build and launch replacements, America found herself blind?

Franklin Ridge National Labs nestled into a secluded and pristine fold of the Allegheny Mountains. The location was isolated but still an easy drive from many East Coast cities.

National crises do not recognize weekends, but Kyle took one anyway. The data made no sense. He needed an outside, fresh perspective, and he knew where to find it. And from whom.

Darlene Lyons had stayed on the Galactic Studies Commission when he'd left. "Someone," she had opined, "has to champion reality there." He remembered the words, and hoped that they would generalize to his new problem, as he rang the doorbell of her Georgetown duplex.

After a welcome hug and some pleasantries, he wound up perched on the front edge of a sofa, picking at crackers and cheese. He picked, as well, at words, unsure how much to say even as he reminded himself that he had invited himself over.

"Is there a scintilla of a reason for you to be here?" She studied him over a glass of Chablis.

Scintilla was the compartmented code word for the top-secret satellite investigations at Franklin. Startled, he almost spilled his own drink.

"So much for the theory that my innate charms brought you." Setting down her glass, she stacked a napkin with crackers. "Yes, I'm cleared for Scintilla. What about it?"

"You know that the spysats have been killed with X-rays?"

She nodded.

"A couple of the birds were grazed by the beam before getting fried. The final telemetry lets us approximate the power density of the beam as it locks in." He'd reached the part of the analysis that most upset him; he drained his glass and with a trembling hand poured a refill. "I don't believe that the Russians—or anyone here on Earth—could generate that beam. I think the F'thk are meddling."

Settling next to Kyle on the sofa, she laid a hand on his elbow. "We think so, too."

"The commission?"

"State." It was now her turn to look uncomfortable. "I don't have a code word to exchange for this one. Just keep it to yourself.

"According to H'ffl, the Galactics have their own factions. It's been centuries since the Galactics last discovered a new species possibly eligible for membership. For all that time, their Commonwealth has been evenly split between more-or-less authoritarian states and more-or-less democratic, individual-rights societies. That the nations of Earth are split between the two philosophies has thrown the Galactics for a loop: neither side feels comfortable about how we'd affect their power balance. Earth was almost not contacted for that reason.

"The F'thk are basically libertarian, in the individualist camp; that's why they came first to Washington. H'ffl has told several American diplomats, me among them, of his biggest fear: he has reason to believe one of his legation is an agent for an authoritarian species. He is not sure which, and he doesn't think it's important. What does matter is that the statists are determined to assure their side a majority—and they will do *anything* to avoid a defeat."

Kyle rubbed his chin thoughtfully. "So this alien spy is behind the nationalist authoritarian resurgence in Russia? They want to tip Earth's balance of power to tip their commonwealth's?"

"There's no direct evidence the Russian situation isn't a homegrown political phenomenon. It's far from uncommon for beleaguered parties in power, or those who want to assume that power, to look for a foreign enemy and play the nationalism card. The scary question is, will alien chicanery cause the Russians to do something foolish?"

"The Galactic authoritarians may win if the nationalists take back Russia. They avoid losing, in any event, if the Earth immolates itself."

"That's how it looks," Darlene agreed.

"How's the US commission stand on this? Other countries? Should we ask the F'thk to leave?" Which is not to say they would necessarily honor such a request.

"Won't happen." She shook her head. "Everyone's afraid that the last guy seen got the latest techie favor from them. So every country except the last one visited wants the F'thk to stay long enough to see *them* again."

"And every new stopover ratchets up the anxiety level that much more." He drained his wine, unable to see any escape from the dilemma.

✳   ✳   ✳

Hammond Matthews was a belt, suspenders, and Krazy Glue sort of scientist—his findings, however counterintuitive, were thoroughly tested before he ever verbalized them.

Matt sprawled the length of what had been, until recently, his own sofa in his own office. With a shoulder-length mane of blond hair, strong jaw, pale blue eyes, and absolutely no hint of a tan, Matt looked like a vampire beach bum. He wore chinos, a knit shirt, and sandals, his one suit and tie stored until the next Washington visitor arrived.

"Heart attacks," echoed Kyle cautiously. When he had asked Matt to search for interesting correlations with Galactic activities, he'd not expected medical coincidences.

"Heart attacks," confirmed Matt. "Every city hosting a Fellowship Station shows an increase."

"Unfortunate, but surely a natural enough response to the excitement. I was on the Mall, you know, when they came to DC."

"In every case, the pattern began days after the visit. Interestingly, pacemaker failures account for most of the increase."

Kyle caught the implication—he remembered the warning plaques on early microwave ovens. "Orbs don't emit microwaves, or any RF. Commission physicists monitored orbs from the day after I got my first. No orb has ever been seen to radiate anything."

"And I'll bet every one of those measurements took place inside a Faraday cage."

Of *course* the orbs were observed inside electromagnetic shielding. How else suppress . . . external signals . . . that could interfere . . .

Spotting the LED of enlightenment over Kyle's head, Matt climbed to his feet. "Let's step down to the radiometry lab."

Radiometry was a windowless room whose walls, floor, and ceiling hid a lining of grounded copper foil. With its metal door closed, the entire lab was a Faraday cage. Around the room, antennas of every description stood in storklike vigil. Orbs, in various states of disassembly, were everywhere—not that dissection had explained anything. ("No user-serviceable parts," he thought inanely.) In three corners, frameworks of two-by-fours covered with fine-mesh copper screening enclosed smaller test spaces for the conduct of precision experiments.

The workbench along the back wall supported a parabolic antenna aimed at an intact orb. A power cable snaked from the dish antenna's blocky base to a power supply on a lower shelf. Thinner signal cables connected several small dipole antennas arrayed around the orb and around the parabolic dish to a rack of instrumentation.

"We could approximate the carrier frequency from the sensitivity of pacemakers, but it was trial and error to find a signal coding to which the orb responded—if we weren't simply imagining things." Matt rested a hand on the test rig. "Courtesy of your commission's observations, at least we knew that the F'thk favor phase-modulated transmission. The control computer ran through twenty-odd thousand permutations before finding a pulse sequence to which the orb responded."

At Kyle's eye level on the instrument rack, the screen of a digital storage oscilloscope showed two flat traces: no signals in or out. Kyle took a deep breath. "Show me."

A mouse click triggered the beamcast; the lines on the DSO screen instantly mutated into complex waveforms. A bit of typing made the computer translate both phase-modulated signals into the more familiar format of binary pulse trains.

Whatever the orb had to say took lots of bits.

CHAPTER 7

"YOU'VE GOT FIFTEEN minutes," said Britt Arledge. "Since the world is coming apart at the seams, be happy for that."

The White House office was spartanly furnished and fanatically organized. For once, Kyle appreciated the obsessive order—it made it that much easier to spot the Galactic orb he felt certain would be present. He quickly spotted one on a bookshelf beside the room door.

He sidled to one end of Britt's desk, blocking with his back the line of sight between Britt and the orb, before taking from his pocket a folded sheet of paper. Raising the other hand to his mouth, he made the universal "shh" gesture.

Britt read the note without visible reaction. "You know, I feel like some coffee. Care to join me?"

They went instead, Kyle leading the way, to a previously arranged cubbyhole in the next-door Old Executive Office Building. The room had a table, two chairs, a PC, and *no* orbs. "Thanks for bearing with me."

"Telling me my office is bugged is a surefire way to get my attention." Britt sat on the edge of the table. "So who's bugging it, and how do you know?"

"The F'thk, that's who. And you won't like the 'how' any better. The orbs are recording devices."

"Which would mean that every officeholder of any significance in this town is bugged, starting with the President."

Kyle didn't care for the skepticism implicit in *would mean*. Instead of commenting, he popped a CD-ROM into the computer. The PC was Tempest-rated, specially designed to suppress the electromagnetic emissions that—in an ordinary computer—would allow skilled eavesdroppers to recreate the monitor image. On-screen, Hammond Matthews summarized a series of experiments upon orbs.

Every orb that the lab had tested showed the same behaviors. If immersed in an actively changing environment—people moving, music playing—the crystalline depths of an orb also changed quickly. When triggered by the proper microwave interrogation pulse, the stimulated orb had a lengthy response. The same orb, observed by videocam in an empty and silent room, changed its appearance very slowly; when interrogated, it had a short response. The experiment was repeated with consistent results using orbs labeled Washington, Tokyo, Moscow, Beijing, and London—units that Darlene had had embassy staff obtain overseas and ship home by diplomatic pouch. *Everyone* was being spied upon, whatever their political school.

Britt tugged an ear thoughtfully. "If I'm following, these devices are usually inert, passively recording the images and sounds that impinge on them. Only when they get this interrogation signal are they active."

"Right. The recording portion, the crystalline globe, needs no power. Think of it as very advanced, electronically readable film. The readout-and-reply portion in the base, beneath the bowl-shaped antenna, *is* externally powered—it takes its energy from a microwave interrogation signal. Now that we know to look, we've detected such interrogation signals. Orbs are routinely probed in and around all major national capitals—everywhere a 'Friendship Station' was left.

"Better, we can triangulate back to the origins of the triggering signals. Those sources turn out to be satellites. They're radar stealthed, which is why NORAD hadn't noticed them as part of the routine tracking of orbital space junk. They're also very dark, which makes them hard to detect visually even when you know where to look. Still, the satellites soak up a lot of energy from the sun. Infrared instruments on NASA satellites can spot these satellites easily."

"Can we be sure these aren't Russian or Chinese, or other Earth-originated satellites? Someone working with the F'thk?"

Kyle popped the CD from the computer. "There are no stealth launches—when something blasts off from anywhere on Earth our spysats know it. These birds had to have been deposited directly into orbit from space, not launched from this planet."

"Which brings us to more pressing issues, like the escalating mortality rate of our spysats."

"*Related* issues. We know instantly when our birds get fried, because we're in constant communication. We don't have such immediate knowledge of Russian satellites. It turns out, though, that their spysats are starting to tumble in orbit, as if out of control. More and more of their birds are acting just like our known dead ones."

The tiny room fell silent as Britt struggled to absorb the enormity of these discoveries. At long last, he shook his head sadly. "So the F'thk go from capital to capital spreading suspicions. With bugging devices by the millions spread across the great capitals of the world, they know what buttons to push, and they watch how we all react when our buttons *are* pushed. They're disabling everyone's spysats, which has us and the Russians escalating our strategic alert status—which keeps feeding the distrust. The Chinese don't trust either of us, and now they're on heightened alert, too."

"Yup, that pretty much sums it up."

Britt gave him a hard look. "So why, exactly, are you *smiling*?"

"I'm just glad to have friends in high places who share my sense of the danger."

The video, shot from a distance with a telephoto lens, was grainy and jerky. The voice-over, apart from the raw emotion in the narration, was unintelligible. Neither distraction diminished the horror.

The footage of the spectacular launch and even more spectacular explosion of a Russian Proton 2 rocket had been captured by an enterprising Korean journalist. Debris rained down on the sun-baked steppes surrounding the Baikonur Cosmodrome in Kazakhstan. Kyle could not see the enormous fireball blossom without recalling the *Atlantis*, without a lump forming in his throat.

At Britt's gesture, Kyle muted the sound on the CNN feed. An aide was whispering into the President's ear, something about President Chernykov. Moments later, the Moscow hotline connection was active and on speakerphone. The pleasantries were perfunctory and abrupt.

"Dmitri Pyetrovich, we had hoped that a joint scientific project would help to diffuse the recent tensions. Needless to say, today's fiasco will not contribute to this aim."

"Fiasco?" The booming accompaniment was probably a hand slapping an unseen desk in emphasis. "An *American* fiasco, I say. Your shuttle carried the first version of this satellite, and it blew up. Now one of our most reliable rockets carries a hurriedly upgraded lab model of the same observatory—and again there is an explosion. If you look to assign blame, look to your own people."

"My people tell me it was a launcher failure . . ."

"Your *spies*, you mean." Another background rumble punctuated the Russian's intense voice. "Our experts are still analyzing telemetry, and have released nothing."

President Robeson scowled at the speakerphone. "Calm down, Dmitri."

"*Don't* tell me to calm down. Judging from past incidents, the Kazakhs are likely to demand some sort of penalty payment from us for supposed environmental damages. The cosmodrome immediately suspended all further launches of the Proton 2 until they complete an investigation, which shuts down our commercial delivery business for heavy comsats." There was whispering in the background. "One of my aides wonders if you *wanted* this disaster, even arranged it, to favor your own aerospace companies and their launch-service businesses."

Accusations and veiled insults flew. Leaders of the two great nuclear powers growled and fumed. At last, the President had had enough. "I think we can agree continuing this conversation is not to anyone's advantage. But before we end the call, perhaps you will tell me this, Dmitri. Have your experts found anything surprising in the telemetry?"

There was impatient finger tapping, and an unseen Russian sighed. A new voice, that Kyle recognized as Sergei Arbatov, spoke up. "No. Nothing unexpected. It is all a mystery."

✳   ✳   ✳

"Damned Russians," snapped President Robeson for the benefit of the orb on his desk. "I need to stretch my legs. Walk with me." He stormed from the well-wired Camp David office, followed by Britt, Kyle, and a Secret Service retinue. Without further comment, he led them into the moonlit Catoctin Mountain woods. The house was soon hidden from sight by the trees. "Give us some space," the President told the chief of the protection detail. The agents faded into the woods, their attention turned outward.

"*Good* show, Kyle."

"Thank you, sir." His mind's eye kept flashing back to cataclysmic fireballs. "I wish I'd been wrong."

"But you weren't," said Britt. "You were right all along the line. The Galactics targeted the Baikonur launch, as you predicted. The arrangements were made by phone and Internet—and surely many of the relevant details were arranged out of range of the damned orbs—so your theory that they can monitor all of our electronic communications is apparently also right."

Kyle retrieved and began to fidget with a pine cone. "When the opportunity arises, thank Sergei." Sergei who had somehow expedited the launch. Sergei whose theatrical tone of resignation disguised the agreed upon code phrase: nothing unexpected.

For the Galactics had no reason to suspect what the conspiring human scientists now expected: microwaves. Steerable microwave beams from stealthy satellites, beams that converged on the Proton's fuel tank. Enormous energies focused onto the metal shell of the rocket, metal that instantly conducted the energy as heat to the liquid hydrogen within. Kyle pictured a sealed metal container of gasoline in a microwave oven. First, the liquid heated, expanding and evaporating, until the pressure burst open the container. The pressure-driven spray rapidly mixed with air, to be exploded by the first spark.

Nothing unexpected . . . but microwave-borne sabotage *was* expected. That meant the sensors Sergei was to have secreted on the Proton had, before the explosion halted telemetry, reported back in some innocuous guise the presence of strong incident microwave radiation. Russian-placed sensors read out by Russian telemetry equipment—the latest evidence would surely allay any doubts President Chernykov might have had.

"Dr. Gustafson. Sir?"

He shrugged off the reverie into which excited exhaustion

had taken him. A Secret Service women had emerged from the woods. "Yes?"

"Call for you, sir." She handed him a cell phone.

"Sorry, sir," he told the President. To the phone, he added, "Gustafson."

"Hello, pardner." The voice was Hammond Matthews's. They exchanged a few pleasantries and touched on some routine business, projects on which they didn't mind the Galactics eavesdropping. "Too bad you missed the barbecue."

"Was it big?"

A chuckle. "We had five grills running *hot*. You would have loved it."

Translation: five stealthed Galactic satellites with a line of sight to Baikonur at the time of the Proton launch had flared on infrared sensors. Which meant they were generating far more power than usual. Pumping out weapons-grade microwave beams, presumably.

"Sorry I had other commitments. But I need to run." He returned the phone to the agent, who disappeared back into the woods.

He brought his walking companions up to date on the final test and confirmation.

Robeson gave him a hard look. "This must be what happened to the *Atlantis*."

"Yes, Mr. President." He kept his voice flat. "They appear determined to keep us from making gamma-ray observations."

"I have my own observation to make," said the President. "There's a term for the situation where others attack your national assets, where they kill your citizens.

"We call it a state of war."

It would be a strange war, a conflict unlike any Earth had ever known.

The Galactics had yet to reveal a credible motive for their hostility. Like so much of what the humans *thought* they had learned about the F'thk, the aliens' behind-the-scenes hints were contradictory and apparently part of their inscrutable plot. Ambassador H'ffl had also confidentially told the Russians of the authoritarian and individualist factions among the Galactics—but in this version, the F'thk were socialists in the authoritarians' camp, worried about an anarchist mole in their midst.

The war against the aliens must also remain hidden, for no one could fathom why, if the Galactics wanted to destroy humanity, they did not simply *do* it. The gigantic mother ship orbiting the moon, regally indifferent to any direct communication from Earth, was never far from anyone's mind. Perhaps nothing but rationalization or a sense of squeamishness separated Earth from direct annihilation by the aliens—reticence that could give way to resolve if the humans were not seen to be playing their assigned roles. Earth would fight its war for survival as its antagonists had inexplicably begun it: through subterfuge.

And so the F'thk, and the vast majority of the people of Earth, would be encouraged to believe that great and foolish powers were edging ever closer to the nuclear brink . . . while the few human leaders and scientists in the know were riddled with doubts. How dangerously easy it would be for the *appearance* of imminent global warfare being so realistically maintained to become cataclysmic reality.

Unless and until that catastrophe occurred, Earth's best minds would—when their disappearance from Galactic orbs and compromised global communications could be justified—work to unravel the mysteries and to imagine any possible defense against the Galactic powers already revealed.

Silver light angled through the leafy canopy. As three men reached a small clearing, one paused. He glanced overhead to the full moon, his lips moving silently.

"What's that, Kyle?"

"A bit of poetry, Mr. President." He jammed his hands into his pockets. "I've always known that somehow, someday, I'd go to the moon. It's what drew me to physics in the first place. The day I met Sergei, moments before the *Atlantis* disaster, I told him I was sure that man would return there. The key to all this is the Galactics' mother ship—out there, circling the moon. If we're to succeed, *we* must go there."

"So what's the poetry?" asked the President.

Kyle tipped his head back, the better to observe the world that had for so long held his fascination. Feeling strangely like an oracle, he spoke crisply the words he had earlier been moved to whisper. "I'll come to thee by moonlight, though hell should bar the way."

" 'The Highwayman'? Unless you're an incurable romantic, that poem doesn't exactly have a happy ending."

Kyle's eyes did not leave the beckoning moon. "I'm an incurable *realist*. I'll do what I must, go where I must, to achieve a happy ending.

"And that's where I think it will be."

A FOOLISH SYMMETRY

CHAPTER 8

"A GENERALLY UNRECOGNIZED contributor to the worldview of the Krulirim," dictated Swelk, "is the symmetry of the Krul body shape." Outside her cabin a raucous comment, followed by bellows of laughter, defeated the computer's attempt to parse her words. She repeated the sentence. Immersion in her longtime studies was a distraction from brooding about the work she *should* have been doing—and from which she was so inexplicably barred.

Her latched door quivered from the impact of something heavy—or rather, some*one*, because he spoke. The complaint was drunken, slurred and indistinct, but the word "freak" was clear enough.

"The Krul body is commonly described as triform, as most of its components occur in threes. Within the largely spherical central mass, internal organs are triplicated. Three limbs, spaced equidistantly around the torso, are equally adapted for locomotion and manipulation. Each limb ends in a three-part extremity, which in turn bears three digits. Limbs, extremities, and digits are all opposable, providing three progressively finer levels of physical control. Sensory stalks near the top of the central mass are also triplicated, providing multiperspective audio and video imagery at all points in a full circle around the Krul.

"Despite the understandable descriptive focus on triplication, the effective symmetry of the Krul form, which favors no specific direction, is radial. So complete is this effective radial symmetry that a Krul observer does not and cannot locate a physical object solely by reference to her body. Distance from the observer may be so defined, but the second geometric parameter needed to localize an object within a plane requires a reference external to the body. The magnetic sense of the Krul provides this external reference, by defining a line between her and the nearest magnetic pole. An angle with respect to this line of external reference can then be combined with the bodycentric radial distance. . . ."

Nonreaction sometimes discouraged those outside. Not this time. Impacts continued to rattle her door, and yelling to scramble her dictation. The frequency of the interruptions showed it was once more open season on misfits. *How would those outside react,* Swelk wondered, *if told their successful adaptation to life on a spaceship showed* they *were freaks?* Most Krulirim could not function outside a planetary-scale magnetic field—the inconstancy of the shipboard artificial field, its orientation noticeably changing with every few steps taken, induced nausea and confusion.

Not well at all, she decided. She checkpointed the computer and tucked it into a pocket. Any work she got done today would have to be accomplished someplace more secluded. The same was likely true of any sleep she might hope for. Taking a deep breath, she flung open the door to run the gauntlet to somewhere hopefully quieter.

"Swelkie, you monstrosity. Weirdo. Abomination." Taking tones of voice into account, the taunts ranged from condescending affection, as one might address an ugly but familiar pet, to open hostility. The captain presumably intended no permanent harm to befall Swelk—she remained an occasional resource to the project from which she was so aggravatingly excluded, not to mention a paying passenger—but the crew, to whom her quasi-confinement had been entrusted, did not necessarily understand the intended limits to their abuse. The scientist within her recognized with cool detachment that they might lack the self-restraint to overcome ages of social conditioning and temper their mistreatments.

"Hello, Froll. How's it going, Brelf?" She was unable to extend all her placative greetings before the harassment began. *It's not personal, it's not personal,* she told herself silently. She dodged a flung partially eaten piece of fruit, only to trip over something thrust between her limbs. A delighted roar greeted the *splat* of her graceless landing, followed by gales of laughter as Brelf, ever the ringleader, dumped on her a cup of something pungent. The cackling intensified as Swelk slipped in a pool of the liquid while trying to stand up.

"So where are you going, beautiful?" Brelf's witticism set them all off to tittering.

"To clean up, I think." Her uncomplaining acceptance of their pranks seemed to satisfy them; they did nothing more as she struggled, with more care this time, to an erect position. They let her pass, content to guffaw at her clumsy progress down the corridor, her lame limb trembling, before returning to whatever drunken game of chance the sorry fact of her existence had so unjustly distracted them from.

Her lame limb trembling. My curse in a phrase, thought Swelk, limping to a quieter part of the ship. And if my disability weren't enough, they blame me for adding perhaps two three-cubes of years to this voyage. That reckoning was in Krulchuk years, of course, not ship's time, but whether a starfarer ever saw family and friends again depended on the passage of time on the home world. Most people did not leave home.

"Swelk!"

She pulled herself to full height, bearing most of her weight on the good limbs, aware that she still dripped soup. "Yes, Captain."

"My officers and I are too busy to deal right now with passengers. Why are you out of your quarters?"

Translation: too busy to deal with her. The shreds of wet vegetable sticking to her body were suddenly an asset. "A mishap, sir. I came forward for cleaning supplies from ship's stores."

"Very well." Captain Grelben leaned slightly. Balanced effortlessly on two limbs, he pointed down the hall with the third. "Find your supplies, get cleaned up, and return to your cabin." Dropping to all threes, he strode away. He disappeared into the officers' lounge, through whose briefly open door could be seen not only several officers but also the ship's other passengers. They were using the translation and cultural interpretation program she had trained, the expert-system software whose operations she had been too naively trusting to keep to herself.

In the blissful quiet of the storeroom, Swelk surrendered to anger and fear. Her body shook; her weak limb threatened to collapse of its own accord. She lowered herself, wearily, to the deck. The hard lump in her pocket reminded her that she'd come here to continue on her treatise, but she was no longer in the mood. It was *not* supposed to be this way.

It was not fair. It was not right. But when had Swelk's life ever been either?

CHAPTER 9

KRUL CAME IN only two kinds: perfect and mutants.

The race had had to advance from cave dwellers to a society rooted in science before radioactivity, the cause of most mutation, was discovered. They had had to develop interstellar travel to learn that the concentrations of radioactive elements in Krulchuk's core and crust were unusually high. By the time they knew enough to say "There but for the aim of an alpha particle go I," by the time medical advancements would have permitted prenatal correction of most mutations, selective infanticide had long been an unquestioned cultural imperative. Swelk was even sympathetic in the abstract to the custom, without which the Krulirim would never have cohered long enough as a species to *have* technology.

So abnormal newborns continued to be put out of their parents' misery. Swelk was doubly a freak, because, despite her flaws, she still lived. Swelk's father had been too resentful of Swelk's mother's death in childbirth to relinquish a living entity to blame. Once Father had sufficiently recovered from his loss to do the right thing, too much time had passed—the "civilized" fiction that Swelk had succumbed naturally to her birth defects was no longer credible.

Swelk seldom saw her father. Her nurse taught that when life gives you a *kwelth*, you make *kwelthor* stew with it. Swelk didn't care for stew, *kwelthor* or other, but she took the point.

So, she was a freak in an intensely conformist society, and nothing she could do would change that. Swelk picked her type of "stew": to be the objective outside observer of a society that lacked outsiders.

Over time, Swelk's personal journal overflowed with commentary about the society that, from her unique perspective, was closed and intolerant. Her restlessness grew with the volume of her private notes. Krulchuk became too confining: unwilling to offer her an opportunity, increasingly devoid of any even mildly interesting variety.

The more Krulchuk palled, the more the stars beckoned to her: new worlds, different societies, other intelligent species. Father gladly paid her fare—with luck the frontier or the rigors of travel would kill her off, or he himself might have passed on before the monstrosity's return. In the worst case, Swelk's return during Father's lifetime, her tour of Krulchukor colonies would still have spared him the embarrassment of her freakish presence for some three-cubes of years.

She realized after the first few planetfalls what only wishful thinking had kept her from extrapolating before leaving home. Krulirim brook *no* deviancy; ergo, transplanted communities differed little from the society of the ancestral world. If anything, the new societies were more orthodox, less accepting of differences, than the home world. On any worlds with the potential to support Krulchukor life, exotic biospheres were systematically weakened to make way for imported biota. Those sentients that had been discovered, none nearly so advanced as her own species, were quarantined and systematically looted of any worthwhile resources. Disdain and neglect combined in an unofficial policy of cultural destruction.

She cashed in her remaining tickets to buy passage on the first starship returning to Krulchuk. That vessel was the *Consensus*, a well-used cargo craft with a few cabins for passengers of limited means and corresponding expectations.

She knew no one aboard the *Consensus*, but that hardly mattered. Her nurse aside, and she had passed on, the Krulirim of Swelk's acquaintance mistreated her no less than did strangers. Few Krul ever encountered anyone as visually different as she; those exceptions lacked precedents for how to behave toward her. Deference to authority generally won out—her treatment generally depended on how authority figures treated her. Shipboard, the captain's impatience with and sometime ridicule of her were quickly adopted.

She gladly stayed in her room at first, organizing the extensive if disappointing notes from her travels. When her tiny cabin grew tiresome, she volunteered, notwithstanding her status as a passenger, to stand watches. Between stars, nothing ever happened on a watch, but someone was required on the bridge just in case. She expected no gratitude from officers spared the boring duty, nor did she receive any—she was content with a change of scenery and less confining surroundings in which to be shunned. And for the comparative peace ... Captain Grelben did not tolerate harassment when Swelk was on watch.

And that was why Swelk was the one to detect the radio signals from Earth.

The unexpected signals were at first faint and erratic, and Swelk did not doubt that any of Captain Grelben's undisciplined staff would have simply ignored them. She persevered. Coping with her handicap, and with those who would torment her because of it, had taught her patience.

The radio-frequency anomalies had progressed slowly from arguably a figment of her imagination to formless certainty—the *Consensus* was not traveling toward the unexplained broadcasts; rather the signals themselves kept getting stronger. Taking on more and more extra shifts, she had slowly learned to assign various patterns to different languages. Her puzzled analyses grew more focused, if still unproductive.

She had yelped in surprise upon determining the modulation scheme that converted some of the radio waves streaming past the *Consensus* into moving pictures. A bit more tweaking had added a synchronized sound subchannel to the moving pictures. Now she began to adopt the software she had trained across visits to several worlds to learning and translating the unknowns' communications.

Even as Captain Grelben acknowledged Swelk's progress, the discovery brought renewed cruelty from the crew. "Trust the freak to find more freaks." And these beings *were* odd by Krul standards, with separate limb-types in pairs: a bottom set dedicated to locomotion and a top set to manipulation. Their bodies moved preferentially in one direction, like Swelk's; their sense organs favored that side. By reason of her handicap and the shunning of her own kind, Swelk sometimes felt closer to the humans than to her shipmates.

And then, amid the ever-swelling torrent of signals, Swelk encountered what must have been educational material for the youngest of the aliens. It was elemental: basic symbols and acting out of their meanings, fundamental concepts repeated in endless variations. While the big bird never made sense to her, she came to recognize numbers, the sounds that went with letters, whole words. Her vocabulary grew. In time, other Earth television programs made sense.

And the more she learned, the deeper became her sense of wonder.

Swelk's discovery had for a time transformed the trip from mundane disappointment to the wondrous adventure of which she had dreamed.

She was not the only passenger on the *Consensus*, although she did not know much about the others. Their cabins were in the better-tended parts of the ship, while she had been exiled to what she suspected was a former closet in the crew quarters. The other passengers were somehow involved in the entertainment industry, she gathered. Popular amusement had no appeal to Swelk, the unvarying perfection of the actors just one more personal rebuke.

She was astonished when Rualf, the leader of the other passengers, took Swelk's part in an argument with the captain.

Swelk had become forceful for only the second time in her life. The first time had been to negotiate the terms of what she and her father both saw, for quite different reasons, as a voyage of liberation. This time she was arguing with Captain Grelben to divert the *Consensus* to investigate Earth.

Pre-spaceflight philosophers on Krulchuk had accepted without qualm or question the silence of the cosmos. Surely the Krulirim, who alone had overcome the universal tendency of species to mutate into oblivion, were the ideal and only intelligent race. Starflight had necessitated a redefinition of that uniqueness: the planets of many stars fostered life, and intelligence, or at least the use of language and tools, arose almost as often. Krulchukor superiority and—of course—centrality survived those discoveries, because the Krulirim remained in one way unique: their mastery of technology. When other intelligences obtained technology, it mastered them. Two three-squares of worlds were known where the dominant species once aspired to technical greatness and the stars; they had achieved only self-destruction and ruin. The causes varied—overbreeding, environmental devastation, genetic-engineering disasters, and, most frequently, nuclear immolation—but the effects, collapse and regression, were constants. And so the superiority of the Krulirim, and the perfection of everything about them, was vindicated . . .

One more supposedly intelligent species, argued the captain, meant nothing. It was of little interest, and even less cause for diverting the *Consensus*. These humans would only destroy themselves, while *he* incurred huge penalties for late deliveries, and his debts continued to pile up. Relativity slowed many things, but not the accumulation of interest.

"But they are right at the crisis point," Swelk argued, "perhaps *past* the crisis, if only barely. They speak of reducing their nuclear weapons, remedying their ecological excesses. If I am right, the Krulirim could have a companion advanced species."

Grelben, unlike his suddenly assertive passenger, equally monitored all directions at once. Nothing in his stance indicated that he was seeing the recovered television pictures from Earth, appearing on several screens on the bridge. Swelk nonetheless knew he *was*; the shiver in the spacer's body declared that what Swelk suggested was anathema. One deformed adult Krul on board was almost too much to bear—could any sane person consider normal a technologically capable planet that teemed with such deviancy? "We will *not* change our course, you—"

"Captain Grelben, if I may." Rualf glided onto the bridge with a grace Swelk could only envy. His entrance had surely spared the cripple a devastating insult.

"Of course, sir." The quick transition to deference was astonishing.

"Captain, I've overheard in the corridors a little about this curious discovery." Rualf's sensor stalks wiggled in an understated display of worldly amusement. "Would it be possible to hear a bit about it directly?"

"You heard the man," snarled the captain.

Swelk needed no encouragement: here, finally, was someone interested in her amazing find. Rualf and his company were widely traveled; perhaps she had lost faith too soon. Perhaps somewhere among the worlds of the Krulirim there *were* people with the creativity and imagination to consider new ideas. Maybe even people to whom Swelk could sometime explain her concepts of group dynamics and social organization.

She launched into an ardent exposition on the challenges of technological development, the crises certain technologies caused societies, the failure of Krulchukor explorers to find any peer-level species. She waxed eloquent that this new species, whose presence had become clear from its radio broadcasts, could yet survive this crisis and become equals. Krulchukor philosophers had long postulated that a self-destructive drive was inherent in all other races; she marveled at the rebirth in thinking and worldview that would arise once such Krul-centered thinking was disproven.

Swelk was too enthusiastic, too rapt in futuristic visions, to take notice of the subtle interactions of gesture and posture between captain and honored passenger. All that registered of her audience's reaction—an audience! what an unaccustomed concept!—was Rualf's spoken response.

"Young woman, you have discovered something extraordinary. I find myself intrigued. Perhaps you will allow me to discuss the matter in private with our captain."

Giddy with the unexpected courtesy, even praise, Swelk stammered her concurrence and limped from the bridge.

Rualf had had influence that Swelk could only envy. The *Consensus* was redirected, with the full support of all passengers, to investigate Earth.

CHAPTER 10

CAPTAIN GRELBEN BECAME harsh in enforcing Swelk's detention once the *Consensus* neared the humans' solar system. Detention was her term, not his; he merely made clear that she was unwelcome without invitation beyond the crew quarters. Rualf's coterie made similar feelings plain. Officers and passengers alike fell silent whenever she approached—and there was no possibility of sneaking up on beings who sensed equally well in all directions.

A life spent as an outside observer then served her well. She gleaned what she could from overheard bits of conversation, from changes to shipboard routine, from the general announcements that preceded and accompanied the ship's maneuvers. She knew, though no one told her directly, that the *Consensus* had stopped at Earth's moon, that still-mysterious preparations had been made there, that direct radio contact had been established with—in the crew's words—Swelk's freaks.

Rualf occasionally solicited her help in the translation or interpretation of a radio intercept while sharing as little information as possible: her "independent" commentary, he said, was invaluable. Rualf was always scrupulously polite; Swelk realized too late that the open-mindedness she had trusted was a sham, an example of his art. She remained clueless as to his interest in the discovery of the humans, *so* interested that he'd championed rerouting the flight he had chartered.

So, from many sources and with much deduction, she learned that her hopes had been realized. The humans had *not* let their technology destroy them!

Now, as the ship hopped from one Earth location to the next, the crew was content to stay aboard. Experiencing an alien culture had no attraction to normal Krulirim, nor was Earth itself hospitable: its sunlight was too hot and yellow, its thin ozone layer admitted unsafe levels of UV, its carbon-dioxide level was nonlethal but debilitating. On board at a landing strip or on board in a parking orbit—it was all the same to the able-bodied spacers. Her own requests to visit with the humans were rejected.

Something happened at those landings, though, something to which only the officers and *normal* passengers were privy. Rualf alone among the inner circle occasionally shared crumbs of news about the humans. The more robust *her* translation program grew from extended use, the more Rualf's sporadic comments tilted toward smug superiority about progress in some undisclosed grand scheme.

Swelk burnt with curiosity, outrage, and feelings of injustice. Before each planetfall she was escorted to her cabin, "So as not to be in the way, you understand."

Fuming in her tiny room yet again, she reached a decision. She opened her door. "Brelf," she shouted. "I have an offer for you."

The deckhand was off duty, which meant he'd be drinking or gambling. Probably both. Hearing his off-color stage whisper to his shiftmates, and their titters, she allowed herself a moment of satisfaction: she'd picked her words to encourage some amusement at her own expense. Brelf emerged from the crew galley looking satisfied with his cleverness, his buddies following. "What do you want, Swelkie?"

"Out of here, of course." To their laughter she added, "Any more time in this closet will drive me insane." She dipped her sensor stalks in a pout. "Trust me, that wouldn't be a pretty sight."

They roared in appreciation, the freak poking fun at herself.

"So here's my idea. I'm so tired of talking to myself that even a Girillian swampbeast would be enjoyable company."

Brelf flexed the digits of an extremity thoughtfully. "Well, Swelkie, that is an interesting suggestion. I'm sure you know that we have a couple of swampbeasts on board. Not just them; we have ourselves a whole Girillian menagerie, and a messy, ill-tempered bunch they are. Thanks to you and your humans, we'll be watching over the monsters for a whole lot longer before they get to the imperial zoo on Krulchuk." He tipped onto twos, sweeping the unburdened limb inclusively across the group of his mates. "Anyone here care to let Swelkie take their shift feeding the beasties?"

"And cleaning up their shit afterwards!" someone added, evoking more hilarity.

"What do you say, Swelkie? Are you so tired of your deluxe accommodations that you would do a little light cleaning for us?"

Success! Willing her voice calm, she flexed her shortened limb. "I guess I can use the exercise."

"Come along then, Swelkie," said Brelf. "Who knows? A swamp-beast may find even you attractive."

Swampbeasts turned out not to be the most stimulating companions Swelk had ever had, but neither were they the worst. Where Swelk's sidedness resulted from a congenitally deformed limb and the need to cope with it, swampbeasts were naturally bilateral in two different respects. There were three limbs on each side, each limb flaring into a large webbed appendage that distributed their weight over a broad area to keep them from sinking into their native muck. The eating end had a protuberance that held not only the mouth, but also the brain and many of the creature's sensory elements. The animals ate more or less constantly, and excreted almost as rapidly out the other end, an apparent trick to keep them well stocked with nutrients while minimizing the body weight to be suspended above the swamp.

She raked together their many droppings without complaint. The animals wouldn't care about her disapproval, and anyway, she had asked to be here. Every so often she would trade her rake for a shovel, emptying the dung into a standard bioconverter. The machine recycled the wastes, plus a dollop of fresh chemicals from ship's stores, into fodder as wholesome as could be found in any swamp on Girillia.

That was the theory, anyway. With Swelk's surreptitious adjustment to the bioconverter, the food was not quite that wholesome. She felt some minor guilt about her actions, the swampbeasts being aggrieved first in their capture, then in the mud-free artificiality of their confinement, and now in her treatment of them. Guilt or no, the feed they now received failed to agree with them. The cargo hold pressed into service as a zoo was awash with feces, fouler smelling even than usual. None of the crew objected to her taking as many caretaker shifts as she wished. Brelf and his pals found the outbreak of diarrhea hilarious. "Seeing Swelk makes even a swampbeast ill."

The stench served a purpose: it substituted for close supervision when she was out of her cabin. No one wanted to be near her while she took care of the menagerie. That, in the end, was her purpose. The *Consensus* carried four lifeboats, one of which was reached through the cargo hold that had become the Girillian zoo. The access hatches that led to the lifeboats were all monitored by sensors that reported to the bridge—but one cut wire guaranteed that the sensor to this lifeboat always reported the hatch to be shut.

She had unencumbered access to the tiny but complete spacecraft. One part of the lifeboat's equipment was a radio.

CHAPTER 11

HER FIRST UNCENSORED news made Swelk wonder if she had gone mad.

The broadcasts she had monitored most of the way to Earth had shown humanity resolving old grievances, de-alerting its missiles, reducing its weapons of mass destruction. Stepping away from the nuclear brink...

Since she'd been excluded from the broadcasts, which had not been a long time, much of that progress had been reversed. The latest reports made clear that tensions had ratcheted up again. The airwaves were full of threats and dangerous bravado.

An even bigger shock was the *other* story that dominated the human media: the visit of the Galactics. Other starfarers had arrived at about the same time as the *Consensus*. Earth was being appraised for membership in some interstellar commonwealth. Earth's evaluators were welcomed everywhere, lured by the promise of the Galactics' fusion technology to those nations that cooperated.

The Krulirim had had interstellar travel for generations, without encountering a people as capable as themselves—not even, until now, anyone as advanced as the humans. Some intelligent species had failed to exit the Stone Age. Those that had achieved higher technology universally reversed course, living pathetically amid the mysterious and often deadly ruins of their own former greatness.

The Galactic species touring and inspecting Earth bore no resemblance to any intelligent race known to Krulchukor science. A recognizable offshoot of an otherwise self-destructive race would have made some sense, would have been satisfying to her. That wasn't the case—the F'thk were totally unknown. If she couldn't account for this one species, what explanation could there be for the appearance of a whole multispecies federation?

And while the F'thk were all over the humans' news, she saw not one Krul.

How could it be that she'd overheard nothing, from anyone on the *Consensus*, of the supposed impossible: starfarers of a species other than their own?

In her confusion, she almost forgot to reemerge from the lifeboat to continue her zookeeper duties. The trilling alarm of her pocket clock saved her. She would surely have died of disappointment and curiosity if, deception discovered, she again lost touch with events on Earth. She programmed the lifeboat's computer to record selected topics and sources for her, then reluctantly returned to the cargo hold.

With renewed feelings of guilt, Swelk arranged for the unexplained ailment to spread to two other Girillian species. She needed lots of time unsupervised.

"Captain." Swelk tipped her torso toward Grelben respectfully, carefully keeping her bad limb behind her, out of his line of sight. Stretching the shortened limb this way was painful, but normals took hiding of her infirmity as a sign of respect.

Experimentation had shown that he was least antagonistic when they were away from the humans. They were in Earth orbit now. "May I have a moment of your time, sir?"

His olfactory organs wrinkled. "Make it quick. You stink of those foul creatures in the hold."

"My apologies, sir." The bastard: having paid for her passage, she was doing the work his crew found too objectionable. That was unimportant and by her own design; she tamped down the irrelevant thought, unexpressed. "I wondered about your contacts with the humans. Was I right? Does it look like they will succeed?"

"It does not seem so. In fact, they are moving quickly towards blowing themselves up." He flexed an extremity. The expression was thoughtful, yes, but also implied something else. Anticipation? "At least this bunch will be remembered better than most. We'll have records of what they accomplished and how it ended."

There was a time when Swelk would have accepted Grelben's statements without question. Growing up a freak, her defects a cause for comment by every passerby, she often hid herself away. Still, as unskilled as were her interpersonal skills, his comments failed to ring true.

"So we will do more than save copies of their own broadcasts?" The two eyes turned toward her narrowed in momentary suspicion, then relaxed. Though Grelben's inability to see Swelk as an equal served her purposes, she fumed inwardly. Underestimating the freak was a too-common reaction.

"Rualf's troupe is making additional recordings with their own equipment. We may also be able to save some human artifacts."

"Then I guess we're doing everything we can." His eyes narrowed briefly again before once more rejecting the possible double meaning.

That her words could have a double meaning—despite not knowing what that second denotation could be—was a chilling confirmation of her darkest fears.

The hastily programmed data filter had worked well: Swelk's next visit to the lifeboat was rewarded with an eye-popping collection of television intercepts.

The presence of the Galactics changed the bigger picture. It would be tragic if the humans, so close to achieving maturity, self-destructed, but her bigger dream was intact. The Galactics, wherever they came from, had obviously attained social maturity. Here was companionship for the Krulirim. Here were alternative body forms, and intelligences who would have no reason to disparage what to them would surely be Swelk's very minor differences.

More than anything, she ached to visit the Galactic mother ship. The human media seemed every bit as fascinated with it as she; telescopic views of the habitat-sized vessel were backdrop to many news broadcasts. The lifeboat's computer did the conversion from human units of measurement: the spacecraft waiting in orbit around Earth's moon was enormous, as large as Krulchuk's own third-largest moon. The object's perfectly burnished surface, bristling with countless antennae and hatches, made plain that this was an artificial structure.

The human media seemed never to tire of covering F'thk visits to Earth's cities. Those visits, she first thought, came in approximate order of political importance. Coverage of Earth's other major story, the slide toward nuclear war, corrected her impression. The F'thk ship was frequenting, in approximate order of destructive capability, the capitals of Earth's declared and suspected nuclear powers.

An insistent alarm recalled her again to her duties at slopping the animals and hosing down feces-covered decks. "Just one more video," she promised herself, resetting the timepiece to extend her stay briefly. It was a good decision: the next item in the queue was coverage of the initial F'thk visit to a city called Teheran.

Unlike the Galactic mother ship, the F'thk landing ship was of a scale with which Swelk could identify. Using individuals in the welcoming crowd for scale, she decided that the F'thk vessel was somewhat smaller than the interstellar passenger ship on which she had begun her grand tour. That vessel, the *Unity*, was her standard of reference; shuttle-crew hostility had kept her in her cabin on approach to the in-orbit, about-to-depart *Consensus*.

The F'thk gave speeches. Dark-skinned humans with facial hair gave speeches. A nondescript Hovercraft deployed from the ship to deliver a kiosk of some sort to an Iranian park. The F'thk spokesperson operated the machine, extracting and distributing ceremonial objects of some sort. She fast-forwarded: long after the dignitaries left, masses of people queued up for the souvenirs.

Her alarm chimed again, and this time she dared not wait. She closed the lifeboat behind her and returned to the unaccustomed physical labor that made so much possible for her.

Though the knowledge had been slow in coming, Swelk had learned to recognize Rualf's correct manners as a manifestation of his art and a disguise for his contempt. Now Swelk would test her own skills of deception. The next time the actor summoned her to discuss a bit of intercepted video, Swelk was sensitized for any evidence or clues, no matter how veiled.

She tipped her sensor stalks one way after another, as if the flat image would reveal new information from the various perspectives.

Play the fool. "I recognize the human behind the desk. He is often in the material you show me. Who is he?"

"The leader of their most powerful subdivision. He is called the President."

"And these others?"

"Advisors of the President. Now listen." Rualf repeated the video.

She listened carefully to the recording, then asked for a replay. "This subdivision, this country, feels threatened by another called Russia. Those sound like alternative nuclear-warfare strategies under review."

"Certainly," said Rualf, his tone indicating impatience. Belaboring the obvious was not why he deigned to deal with her. And if nuclear-strike planning was under way, then the horrible crisis that Swelk dreaded could be almost upon the humans.

"My question, Rualf, is this: why would they broadcast such stuff? Detailed planning for an all-out war is surely meant to be secret."

"This is not from a broadcast," Rualf conceded.

"I am astonished they would discuss these matters in front of visiting Krulirim, or allow you to record them."

Rualf was silent for a long time; Swelk wondered if her probing had been too overt. Boastfulness eventually defeated caution. "These are not matters they would care to discuss in front of outsiders." He whistled sharply in amusement. "Did you hear what I said? In *front*. I've been dealing with these absurd creatures for too long.

"Never mind that, you *are* right—and since you recognized this isn't a human video, I may as well make it easier to view." He adjusted a control, changing the presentation to 3-D, then rewound toward the midpoint of the recording. "Here. See that crystalline sphere in a bowl on a metallic base on the President's desk? We give those spheres out as gifts all over Earth, especially to the decision makers. The images we are watching are from another such globe elsewhere in his office.

"It's a passive audiovisual recording device. Periodically we scan their major cities with steerable microwave beams. The microwaves provide momentary power to the devices to upload whatever they've recorded."

Rualf misunderstood her dumfounded look. "I'm not surprised

that you never encountered these gadgets. We use them all the time in making 3-V films, but moviemaking is the only way I've ever seen them used."

She *had* seen such objects, however. The surreptitious Krulchu-kor bugging device was one of the souvenirs manufactured by the Galactic Friendship Stations and distributed by the F'thk.

CHAPTER 12

SOMEHOW SWELK MAINTAINED her composure long enough to complete the conversation with Rualf. She limped to her cabin, too attentive to her own thoughts to take notice of the crew's taunts.

The F'thk were distributing bugging devices, which Rualf implied were Krulchukor technology. Data from those devices were being exploited by the officers and other passengers of the *Consensus.* Conspirators, she decided was the correct and much shorter term. Either the conspirators were in league with the F'thk, or the conspirators *were* the F'thk. In either case, what could possibly be the purpose of the conspiracy?

Dropping wearily onto her sleep cushion, she could not decide which theory was the more unimaginable. Of all the group she now labeled conspirators, none but Rualf could for any length of time disguise his repugnance for her deformities. Their distaste was equally plain for the alien intelligences previously discovered by the Krulirim. How could they possibly be cooperating with the F'thk? Look at their attitude toward the humans. It all seemed so psychologically unlikely.

But the alternative was not physically possible. How could the F'thk *be* Krulirim?

And yet, how could the F'thk *not* be the Krulirim? The human media showed no other aliens.

A gurgling stomach reminded her that she had missed the last two meals. Swelk dug through a stockpile of prepackaged rations she kept in her room, her company in the galley of the *Consensus* seldom being appreciated by her shipmates. What a delightfully uncomplicated pleasure: to pick some food and eat it. So few of the concepts swirling through her mind were ever simple anymore. Certainly, none were pleasant.

The practicality of her task brought a fresh perspective. There was at least one variable that she could eliminate, with no subterfuge required. She called up the ship's library and located a picture of the ship in which she sat chewing.

Despite her suspicions, she almost choked at the hologram that appeared. Either the F'thk landing ship was the *Consensus*, or the F'thk had found its clone.

No clone: some of the broadcasts stored in the data banks of the lifeboat were real-time reports of F'thk landings. Timestamps for those recordings matched what Swelk knew to be landings of the *Consensus*. Even physical locations matched.

Everything was consistent . . . and everything inexplicable. And what, if anything could or should be done about it?

"You have *got* to help me, Rualf."

The entertainer peered dubiously at Swelk. She had just been quite useful in interpreting one of the odder broadcasts from Earth. "Help you with what? If you refer to your issues with the crew, sorry—I will not get in the middle of that."

A dip of her sensor stalks suggested, *You can't blame me for trying.* The shrug was a deception, something for Rualf to reject so that a lesser request might be granted in consolation. "I suppose not. I need distraction, is all. There is a great deal of nuance to Girillian dung, at least for someone with my level of expertise, but I have almost exhausted the possibilities."

"What did you have in mind?" His stance conveyed guardedness.

"You and your friends, your troupe. You make movies, correct?"

"Of course." The posture relaxed. He knew all about dealing with fans. All fans were odd—their strangeness was just not usually so visually evident.

"Well," she tipped toward him respectfully, "I've never actually known anyone in the entertainment field. I wondered if you had recordings of some of your troupe's films that I could borrow to view in my room."

"Wait here." He popped into his cabin, returning with a standard computer storage cube. "Enjoy."

"Oh, I'm sure that I will find your work *very* interesting." He did not seem to take note of the potential difference between interest and enjoyment.

The swampbeasts had come to trust Swelk, *humphing* in welcome when she arrived, hanging their heads sadly when she left. The show of affection deepened her guilt without altering her resolve—and caused her to shift the food tampering to another pair of creatures. So far those large limbless crawlers showed no signs of eliciting her sympathies.

She limped from cage to tank to stall, cleaning up the various messes. Despite her eagerness to see what new uncensored information awaited in the lifeboat, she took pleasure in her task. It was nice to be appreciated, even if only by a swampbeast. She stroked their fur carefully with a long-handled brush, bringing forth more contented *humphs*. Even the hold's smell was becoming familiar.

Or was it abating? That would be bad, stench being the main guarantor of her privacy. Steeped in shame, she synthesized fresh batches of nutritionally deficient animal fodder. For good measure, she spilled some feces near the hold's main door, to be sure to track some into the corridor later.

The lifeboat computer kept selecting more broadcast material than she had the time to review. She sampled and skimmed, without obtaining answers to what was, in her mind, the biggest question: why did the *Consensus* pretend to be what it was not?

Swelk whistled softly to herself in amusement: the beasts she tended were always themselves—and the only beings on board to enjoy her presence. If the humans did not destroy themselves, would she be allowed to establish a relationship with some of them?

A foolish notion, but it suggested another. The conspiracy she suspected, its form still obscure, its purpose unknown, seemed too much for her alone to uncover. There were, however, countless humans. Did any of them have doubts? If such could be found, could she and they somehow help each other?

She reconfigured the lifeboat's broadcast search to select information on anyone who had expressed skepticism about Earth's interstellar visitors, then returned to her duties in the hold.

Without enthusiasm, Swelk accessed the index on Rualf's data cube. It turned out to contain three-squared and three movies. Searching them for clues, to exactly what, she could not even guess, would take a while.

Sooner started, sooner finished. She told the computer to run through all the contents in storage order. Most of the actors she recognized from shipboard encounters, not only Rualf: the same group, as typical for Krulirim, had worked together for a long time. That did not mean that she could put names to them; many of the troupe ignored her.

She fell asleep to the quiet drone of the third film. Like the stories that had preceded it, this movie involved a perfect character who had lapsed into the slightest bit of individuality, becoming unhappy and stressed as a result. Even Krulirim were not as variety-free as these films suggested. Creativity and exploration require initiative, even if the common culture chose not to recognize it. What boring drivel . . .

Sleep was a vulnerable time for any Krul, slumber's sensory shutdown in such utter contrast to normal awareness in all directions at once. No one could sneak up on one of her kind—except in her dreams.

Krulchuk was a planet with active plate tectonics, its interior kept hot by the slow decay of an overabundance of thorium and uranium. Without that internal energy source, Krulchuk would have been inhospitable to life, as far as it was from its sun. Without the high background radiation, the evolution of its unlikely life would have been much different. And without the constant upwelling of magma, first driving the continental plates apart and then reuniting them in tremendous convulsions, and the attendant shifts in oceanic circulation, Krulchuk would not have experienced regular cycles of ice ages and warming.

Multicellular life arose soon after one such breakup of a temporarily unified mega-landmass. The continents that resulted drifted separately for eons, each a laboratory for evolution, before they next crashed together. The distant ancestors of the Krulirim were suddenly in a fight for survival with the offspring of a different path: bilaterally symmetric creatures. The trilateral ultimately prevailed; the bilateral disappeared without a trace until Krulchukor science discovered the fossils of the vanquished monsters.

A few scientists whispered that a random metabolic mutation within the trilateral phylum better suited them to Krulchuk's next ice age. Their theory, that trilateralism itself was not inherently superior, remained controversial.

Whatever had caused the great die-out of the bilats, their fossils were an immediate sensation, instantly recognized by some primitive underbrain survivor of that dawn-of-time struggle. The unnatural beings that sometimes appeared to Krulirim in their vulnerable dream states suddenly were *of* nature, and more frightening than ever.

Rualf's character howled dramatically in another overacted film. The emoting disturbed the dozing Swelk, who opened one eye in reflexive curiosity. She shrieked herself, suddenly alert. It took several deep breaths to slow her pounding hearts.

She had wakened during a dream sequence in which Rualf wrestled with a monster from his inner mind. A horned and fanged bilat, its talons and the corners of its mouth dripping gore, a creature to whom the term *nightmarish* truly applied.

Rualf vanquished his inner beast, enriched by the recognition that it symbolized his less than perfectly social ways. As the film ended, the actor sought out the communal embrace of his neighbors. Big surprise.

Credits rolled. There was a prominent credit for robotic effects. Her first reaction had been that the bilat was a computer-generated graphic. A robot made sense, though: the creature and Rualf had been so entangled in their fight.

A robot. Swelk rewound the film to the dream sequence. The monster seemed to be a cinematic amalgam, a composite of the scariest old fossil finds and the director's imagination. "Enough movies for now," she told the computer. "Does the ship's library have an encyclopedia?"

"Yes."

"Show me an overview of extinct Krulchukor bilats." Text and an image appeared instantly. "Scroll." Midway through the article she encountered a skeleton that her imagination easily fleshed out.

Add two pairs of eyes and it was a F'thk.

CHAPTER 13

SWELK GOT NO MORE rest that sleep-shift, her mind lost in a haze of odd findings and vague suspicions. So what did she *know*? That the so-called F'thk were robots controlled by the starship's performer passengers, with full cooperation of the officers. That the "symbols of galactic unity" the F'thk distributed everywhere were audiovisual bugging devices. That she was excluded from whatever the F'thk, and the Krulirim behind them, were doing.

Why these things should be true was a mystery, but as her mind grappled with the few hard facts, an unsettling theory took shape in her mind.

Testing that theory would require taking a big risk.

The product of a conformist species, Swelk had wondered if her revised Earth news filter would find any skeptical humans. She need not have worried. Her handicaps and social isolation made her more individualistic than any Krul whom she knew— but the cacophony of human viewpoints exceeded her ability to comprehend.

Once governmental pronouncements and mainstream networks were excluded, Earthly theories about the F'thk knew no logical bounds. Speculations ranged from the imminence of a supernatural catastrophe, if she correctly understood this English word "apocalypse," to an equally delusional expectation that the F'thk had crossed the light-years looking for fresh meat.

Then again, end-of-the-world scenarios weren't so bizarre: nuclear tensions increased wherever the F'thk visited. Catastrophe, if not from paranormal causes, was an increasingly realistic prediction.

Still, she did not see how the hysteria in the alternate channels helped her. If she *could* contact any of these hysterics, she saw no reason why she *would*. They, like she, were on the outside of whatever was happening, trying to look in.

It did not help her sense of hopelessness that most Earthly information was beyond her reach. In the time it had taken the *Consensus* to reach Earth—a few months of relativity dilated ship's time, several years of Earth time—the humans had migrated much of their information infrastructure from analog to digital technology. What the humans called their Internet apparently brimmed with information. The lifeboat computer had not been designed to interoperate with human networking protocols, alas, and she lacked the skills to expand its repertoire.

So the latest query had put her into noise overload. What she sought might not exist *anywhere* in this ocean of information. With little hope of success, she asked the computer to look again, this time saving only broadcasts with demeanor like several calm news readers that she identified *and* that expressed concern about the F'thk.

"What do *you* want?" Grelben grumbled.

"A word with Rualf," answered Swelk apologetically. Long gone were the days when the captain let her be alone on the bridge. She had waited to contact the actor until she knew he was here.

"It's not a problem, Captain," Rualf said soothingly. "I will talk with her."

She launched into a prepared speech about a recording he had once shown her. The new interpretation was not urgent; she sidled as she spoke until she was leaning against the horizontal working surface at the front of an unoccupied console. The underside of the ledge was her target.

Her deformed limb was near the workstation. The infirmity made most people uncomfortable; they tended not to look in its direction. For once, she welcomed their distaste. With two good limbs and the rim of the ledge to support her, she used the obscured limb to take a blob of sticky putty from a pocket between her body and the console. The blob was loosely wrapped in plastic sheeting to which the adhesive did not cling well.

Swelk flattened the blob against the underside of the ledge. The plastic, which peeled off silently, was returned to her pocket. She removed a spare pocket computer, which she pressed deep into the putty. The weak extremity cramping from such unaccustomed fine-motor activity, she stretched sticky stuff around the edges of the computer, the better to secure it.

"Are you about done?" asked the captain. "We have work to do here."

"Almost, sir." Her real task complete, she brought to a conclusion her rambling discussion with Rualf. "I'll be tending to the Girillian animals, if you need me."

Neither suggested that such a consultation was likely, which was fine with her. She hobbled to the cargo hold, where she had left her usual pocket comp. Her call to the hidden unit on the bridge went through silently, because she had disabled its speaker.

" . . . A house in Vrdlek City," declared Rualf's voice. Expensive property.

"I prefer something in the desert," responded Grelben. "Perhaps shorefront on the Salt Sea."

Swelk bobbed her sensor stalks in relief. Her improvised bug worked.

The search program in the lifeboat computer was goal seeking. When the main channels that it monitored failed to locate information to Swelk's newly stringent specifications, the set of frequencies audited was expanded, then expanded again.

Swelk found herself reviewing a segment recorded from a history channel, puzzled that the computer had selected this. Mid-interview she understood. The biography was of a famous scientist, who had ended her career as an inspirational teacher. Her most infamous student, it seemed, was a Kyle Gustafson, "the former presidential science assistant and resigned chairman of the American Commission on Galactic Studies." The camera lingered momentarily on an image of two men.

One man she knew from Rualf's spying device: the President. And that leader's science advisor had resigned in an undisclosed disagreement over the F'thk?

"Computer. Find out all you can about this Kyle Gustafson."

"What do you think, Stinky?"

The male swampbeast *humphed* contentedly. He pressed his head against the one-time broom with which he was now regularly groomed. Both swampbeasts, tentatively Stinky and Smelly, *loved* to be brushed between their nostrils. It was hard not to like creatures who took such joy from Swelk's ministrations.

Humph wasn't much of an answer to her question: why interact with humanity through the F'thk? The easy explanation was xenophobia: use of what she now recognized as robots to avoid direct dealings with the odd aliens. That seemed wrong—nowhere on her travels had she encountered Krulirim using robots to interact with previously discovered intelligent species.

She considered herself an expert in cultural variation, what little there was, among the Krulirim. Entertainers were one such variation. Certainly their willingness, even desire, to be personally visible, to be the focus of attention, was outside her people's mainstream. Rualf's troupe was clearly at the center of contacts with the humans—the F'thk were their robots.

Smelly *flumphed* in impatience. She also wanted to be groomed. "Almost your turn, baby." What advantage did the F'thk offer over direct interaction with the humans?

Smelly lowered her head to butt Swelk. The impact could have been much harder—it was only a request for attention. She patted her oversized charge affectionately. "Big beastie. What a big . . ." She was suddenly reminded of a fact that familiarity had obscured—the swampbeasts loomed over her, as they towered over any Krul.

As humans would tower over any Krul.

The robots called the F'thk, however, were taller than nearly all humans. The F'thk "eyes" were very near the tops of their un-Krulchukor heads. There *was* an advantage to using F'thk rather than Krulirim to interact with the humans, and one that would appeal to the troupe.

Assuming the F'thk "eyes" were camera lenses, an unobstructed view for image capture.

"If a human group *did* spot one, surely it would be attributed to its enemy."

Swelk stiffened. She had been resting in an acceleration couch, sipping absently on a high-energy drink from the lifeboat's emergency stores. "Return to the start of that conversation," she ordered the computer. "Display text version."

Most bridge chatter turned out to be irrelevant, giving her hope that what she feared about this conversation was all in her imagination. Still, she believed that the inconclusiveness of her spying meant only that the most interesting discussions took place in another cargo hold of the *Consensus*, part of the ship to which the entertainers had free access but from which she was barred. There, presumably, could be found the controls for operating the F'thk.

"Enemy" was one of the keywords with which she screened for anything useful. After a momentary pause, a screen filled with text. She scanned past the pleasantries as Rualf joined Grelben on the bridge.

Rualf: Are our satellites all in position? Can they see in sufficient detail?

Grelben: Yes and yes. (impatient tone) As I said they would.

Rualf: And the humans do not know?

Grelben: Your people listen to the Earth recordings, not mine, but I would not think so. The satellites we deployed are radar-invisible; it would take very bad luck for the humans to physically see one. If a human group *did* spot one, surely it would be attributed to its enemy.

Rualf: Stupid freaks. (laugh) Lovely monstrosities.

Swelk read on, in fascination and horror. There could be no doubt: a conspiracy against the Earthlings *was* under way. Much about how the plot would unfold remained clouded, but its purpose was clear—and what she had most feared.

Rualf put it best. "Close-ups from our satellites of missile launches and nuclear destruction. Intercepts of Earth's media as they scurry in panic. Recordings from our bugs of their final moments." A gleeful laugh. "Yes, the humans respond well to their cues. When they blow themselves up, what a fine and *profitable* movie we will make of it."

"I've been counting on it," said the captain.

*   *   *

Light-years from any authorities, Swelk had never felt so alone. Her species' at-best benign neglect for their less accomplished fellow sapients was awful enough. That was nothing compared to what she had discovered: the planned genocide of the humans in the name of profit.

And she had led the plotters to Earth.

She shut herself into her tiny cabin, clutching the sleep cushion with trembling limbs, smothering moans of despair in the bedding. Her sensor stalks slumped in abject misery against her torso.

What a fool she was. What arrogance to have thought herself a capable observer of Krulchukor culture. Now her ignorant presumption would destroy the most advanced civilization her people had ever encountered.

No.

She willed her limbs to relax, opened her eyes, focused her mind. Shame solved nothing. Realistically, nothing she could do aboard this ship would change anything.

She had to get to Earth.

CHAPTER 14

THERE WAS A CLUE, but she was too excited to notice. That carelessness almost cost Swelk her life.

Animals once more fed and groomed, she had returned to the lifeboat to check on the latest data search. There was a wealth of information about Kyle Gustafson, his education, his career history, sessions of the American commission on the Galactics.

The newest file was a video of the American president in loud telephonic argument with his unseen Russian counterpart, trading accusations about the recent midlaunch explosion of an American scientific satellite aboard a Russian rocket. So trivial a cause for so high-level an argument: the relationship between the countries must have become very strained. Kyle Gustafson took no part, standing silently in the background, but his height and reddish hair made him stand out.

Gustafson's mere presence had a staggering implication: his principled resignation had not separated him from his nation's leader. And *that* must mean Gustafson's concerns about the Galactics received some level of consideration within the American government.

As a loud boom echoed in the cargo hold, she realized she had failed to make a more pressing deduction. "Unlock this door!" shouted Captain Grelben.

She *should* have wondered why this material had been located by her query. Like the war-strategy session that Rualf had shared, a shouting match between national leaders was unlikely to be waged in public. Which suggested that the meeting that so interested her had *also* been recorded secretly by one of Rualf's spheres . . .

The shock of realization almost froze her. She had neglected to limit her last request to current broadcast intercepts, and her query must have enlisted the *Consensus*'s main computer. It was easy to guess what had followed: security software spotting the unauthorized data access and tracing the request to the lifeboat's computer, an alarm sent to the duty officer, a call to the captain, the realization of the lifeboat's proximity to the zoo that she tended without supervision.

"Swelk, you freak. Open this hatch *now*." A loud bang. Animals bellowed in confusion.

Cultural genocide was her species' horrific norm. *Physical* genocide was not. If the captain and Rualf had done half what Swelk now suspected, she could never be allowed to speak with the authorities on Krulchuk. Keeping her ignorant had been, in a crude way, a kindness—it preserved the option of letting her live. Discovery of Swelk's investigations eliminated her continuance as a viable outcome.

At least the plotters had made one small mistake: coming straight to the cargo hold in a rage without first looking up the hatch-lock override code.

Not that her actions demonstrated better forethought. "Lifeboat. Break communications with the *Consensus*." What next? Wasn't she trapped as surely as her swampbeasts? No, although she would have been had the *Consensus* been on the ground. "Can you launch without the cooperation of the main computer?"

"Yes. That is one of my emergency modes."

The pounding and shouting stopped. That meant no one expected her to open the door and someone had gone for the code. She had only seconds—terminals were all over the ship.

"Can you take me to Kyle Gustafson?" The off-limits information whose access had endangered her could also save her.

"Not with certainty. His current position is unknown, but the upload does include his residence and work locations." Swelk wasn't surprised: she had assumed the main computer had been tapped into the Earth's Internet.

She'd have to take the chance.

An unseen hatch crashed against a wall; she heard extremities slapping the cargo-hold floor and oaths of disgust at the animals' smell. A short hall connected the lifeboat bay to the cargo hold; a quick glance showed her that corridor hatch was ajar.

"Emergency departure. Close airlock. Launch."

The lifeboat and its automation could get her down to surface, but she would be stuck where she landed—if she got that far.

She could only hope the confusion aboard the starship equaled her own. Her few preparations for escape to Earth suddenly seemed more fantasies than plans. "Lifeboat. No communications with the *Consensus*, nor with any of its lifeboats." Her mind's eye pictured a sudden windstorm in the ship she had fled, air streaming from the cargo hold into space through the suddenly gaping lifeboat bay, until the corridor hatch was sucked shut. Poor swampbeasts! "Was anything big blown from the ship?"

"No."

At least her hasty exit had probably not killed anyone.

What could they do beyond following her? She had a moment of panic on recalling the anti-spacejunk defense, then wondered if it would require reprogramming to fire at something moving *away* from the ship. That was pure speculation, but since she could do nothing about the laser, she might as well assume her theory was correct.

They would track the lifeboat all the way down, and there was nothing she could do about it. Still, observation of an escape attempt was something to which she had given thought: they could not see through clouds, and radar would not reveal what she did on the ground.

It was night in the United States. "Computer, show a weather map centered on Gustafson's home. Indicate nearby safe landing areas." Luck finally favored her; the whole region was clouded.

A landing site selected, she turned to other preparations. There wasn't much time.

The lifeboat broke through a dense bank of fog shrouding the forested and weathered peaks of the Allegheny Mountains. Landing radar and the onboard computer had delivered her with precision between two parallel ridges; the ship settled rapidly into a narrow valley. Gustafson's house was one valley away; the Franklin Ridge

National Laboratory, to which Gustafson had returned in official disfavor, and the nearest town, were two valleys farther. The human's likeness, printed from one of the files whose download had exposed her, was in a pocket of the fresh garment she had taken from the lifeboat's stores.

She was belted securely into a padded couch, a squishy bag strapped into the seat next to her. Many shifts spent tending to her Girillian charges had cleansed her of all squeamishness; she doubted she could otherwise have gone through with the ploy with the sack. The bag was filled mostly with materials produced on the way down by the lifeboat's bioconverter. The synthesizer itself, portable of course, was in one of the tote bags she had prepositioned in the airlock for her upcoming quick exit. Without synthesized Krulchukor food, she would starve in a few days—assuming she lasted that long.

"Landing in three-squared, three-squared less one . . ." A console display showed an uneven surface rushing to meet her. Radar reflectivity supposedly proved that the lumpiness was vegetation. She would know soon, one way or another.

She struck with a thump, sliding and bumping along the uneven surface. A landing limb hit something hard. The skid snapped; the ship tipped and went into a roll. The craft finally jolted to rest, its leading edge crumbled around the bole of a tree.

"Open both airlock doors." She may as well confirm reports that Earth's air was breathable. Two doors cycled open; the rough landing had not damaged the lock mechanisms. She released her belts. In standing, she almost collapsed to the deck. The hard landing had badly bruised one of her normally good limbs.

This was taking too long. "Status?"

"Another lifeboat just launched."

One deduction of which Swelk was certain: she would not be chased by Krulirim. They had to expect her to abandon her lifeboat; her pursuers would have to leave their own craft. She took comfort that no human broadcast had *ever* shown a Krul. Surely they would not reveal themselves now.

And a lifeboat in pursuit, not the *Consensus*—appreciated, if not surprising, news. She had guessed the bigger ship would not dare to land in this rugged terrain. Launching a lifeboat had meant delay to retrofit teleoperation controls. While she had never seen a F'thk in person, she had watched videos of them among humans—few of the big robots could fit in a lifeboat.

The emergency stores included flares. She ignited one now, shoving the lit end into a drawer packed with flammable supplies. The fire blossomed, heat scorching her weak-limb sector as she hobbled to the open airlock.

Swelk looped the straps of two supply sacks around her torso. She couldn't make good time across the rough ground balanced on only her two strong limbs, especially with one now injured, and her foreshortened limb could never have supported that much weight. And now that crippled extremity had another problem.

The lifeboat had ripped a scar across the valley floor. She remained for two three-cubes of paces within the path of destruction, lest the bulging sacks she dragged leave too obvious a trail from the wreck. The fire grew hotter and brighter as she turned toward the alien woods. A sickening smell followed her. Then the flames must have reached the main fuel tanks, not emptied by the short trip from low Earth orbit. Her last thought, before light and sound and blast overwhelmed her, was a mixture of doubt and hope.

Would the stranger whose picture she carried come, or would she have to find him?

CHAPTER 15

ANOTHER DAY OLDER, but not visibly wiser.

Kyle Gustafson sat on his porch, his rattan chair leaning against the fieldstone front of the house. A vague yellow glow, barely discernible through the fog that overhung the mountains, was the only evidence of what the calendar declared to be a full moon. The telescope that he would otherwise have been using lay idle on its tripod.

He was contemplating—no, be honest: brooding about—the moon, around which circled the enigmatic mother ship of the equally mysterious Galactics. The enemy. On a clear night he could stare endlessly through the telescope at the great vessel, the unsubtle embodiment of science and technology far beyond Earth's own. Under the threat of that behemoth, humanity dared not even let it be known that a danger had been recognized. What could keep the aliens, were their indirect destruction of mankind to be foiled, from simply doing the deed themselves?

Key American and Russian space assets, including strategic early-warning satellites, kept dying. Individual F'thk explained confidentially that a Galactic faction was illegally assisting the other human side. The aliens hinted at a balance-of-power crisis within their commonwealth, and how humanity's competing authoritarian and democratic philosophies could affect that balance, should Earth be admitted. It was a plausible story for why

F'thk factions would meddle on Earth—but the stories didn't jibe. And, oh yes: the pretty souvenir orbs that the F'thk distributed everywhere, supposed "symbols of galactic unity," turned out to be spying devices. No wonder the F'thk, in their whispering campaigns, knew just which geopolitical buttons to push . . .

So the few people in the know play-acted the descent into nuclear madness, posturing for the benefit of the ubiquitous Galactic orbs, ever wondering whether today would be the day when an overstressed bomber pilot or submarine captain or missile-silo crew turned pretense into cataclysmic reality. Perhaps the aliens had already tired of waiting—the tactics that had almost brought the US and Russia to war were being tried now in Pyongyang, Islamabad, New Delhi, Beijing, Teheran, and Tel Aviv.

The *crack* of a sonic boom demanded his attention. He turned toward the sound, in time to observe a bright spark break through the low clouds and sink into the adjacent valley. From the light of the . . . exhaust? flames? . . . it did not *look* like an airplane, but he'd gotten only a glance. By the time he heard the crash, he was inside, dialing 911.

He had already plunged into the woods, flashlight in hand and cell phone in his pocket, when an explosion lit the sky.

At one level, the situation was clear enough, if tragic: crashed vehicle, fire, explosion. A sickening smell, not quite burning meat and gasoline, hung over the area. There was no sign of survivors, and the blaze was far too intense to let him approach the wreck. At least the forest was too wet to spread the fire. Judging from the violence of the detonation, he was almost certainly too late to help, but he half loped, half slid down the slope as quickly as he dared.

His cell phone chirped, but all he received was static. Not a surprise, here on the valley floor. If the call were from the rescue squad, they could follow the light of the fire. They were clearly on the way—the sirens were growing louder. After reaching his house, they would have to hoof it in, as he had.

What *was* he looking at? The burning craft no more resembled a plane up close than it had shooting across the sky. A F'thk vessel? He pivoted slowly, absorbing the whole terrible scene, a wide irregular gouge marking the craft's final careening course.

Trees swayed and branches bowed in the wind. Flames danced

and twisted, spurted and died back. Light and shadow swirled around the valley in total confusion.

There! Perhaps twenty yards away, at the edge of the trees, something totally out of place caught his eye. It could have been the flames and odor operating on Kyle's subconscious, but his first impression was of an old charcoal barbecue grill somehow scuttling along on its three legs.

The sirens stopped; an emergency team would be over the crest and here in minutes. It looked like there was someone to be helped—and it was no F'thk.

The alien stood its ground as if pinned by the beam of Kyle's flashlight. The barbecue-grill comparison wasn't bad, even with a closer look. The limbs were jointed, though, unlike the tripod base of a grill, and the articulated . . . hand? foot? . . . at the end of one limb wore what could be a bandage. Three short stalks rose from the top of the torso.

Two sacks slumped on the ground nearby. The alien murmured softly, the sounds unintelligible—and a bag spoke. In English. "Are you . . . Kyle Gustafson?"

He was shocked, both by the question and that it sounded like a F'thk. A F'thk would *not* fit in that bag. A speech synthesizer and translator, then. "Do you need help? Why are you here?"

"Are you . . . Gustafson?" it repeated insistently.

"Yes." What was going on?

"Turn off . . . your light," ordered the alien. "Don't let . . . them see you."

He knew nothing about this species of Galactic, but judging from its harsh rasping and the pauses in the synthesized speech, it was gasping for breath.

Shouts of encouragement from the emergency team were getting closer. Beams of their flashlights shone over the ridge. He dimmed his flashlight and hurried to his unexpected visitor.

Trembling, the alien settled onto the ground. It pointed down the valley, in the direction from which its wrecked ship had arrived. The suspected bandage had a dark splotch, from which, as he watched, a large drop plopped. "They're . . . coming." A sonic boom soon proved it right. An intact version of what lay burning nearby broke through the clouds. "The F'thk."

"Do you need help before they get here?"

"I will . . . be fine. Don't . . . let F'thk . . . find me."

"But *why*?"

More tremors wracked the creature's body. Its sensor stalks dipped. "Keep . . . telling your . . . self it's . . . only a . . . movie."

CHAPTER 16

KYLE HAD ONLY SECONDS to make a decision, and he decided. The alien had sought him out specifically, and it must have a reason. He had to trust that it was a qualified judge of its own medical condition.

He carried the exhausted alien deep into the woods, walking always toward his flame-cast shadow, until the blaze ceased to light his way. Striding alone back toward the fire, he snapped occasional branches to discreetly mark the path. He made another trip with the bags of supplies.

The alien hidden, he walked parallel to the edge of the trees for a while, before switching his flashlight back on to emerge from the woods near the wreck. He called out a greeting to the rescue team that was scampering down the slope. The roar of a second spacecraft landing drowned out what could have been awkward questions.

Two F'thk emerged, shutting the airlock behind them. F'thk were difficult enough to tell apart in good lighting, as far as Kyle could tell differing only in slight variations of skin tone. He had no idea whether he'd met either in his days on the commission. The new alien's warning fresh in his mind, Kyle did nothing now to call attention to himself.

Easily seven feet tall, the F'thk towered over the human

emergency squad. Both stood closer to the flame than the humans, even the protectively suited firefighters directing sprays of foam from canisters lugged over the ridge.

"How many were on board?" asked a firewoman.

"One." The F'thk who spoke did not directly face the wreck or the woman he answered. It wasn't being impolite—that was the F'thk way.

It's only a movie, the exhausted alien had said. A hallucination, surely—but if it were true, what a view the F'thk had. Behind Kyle, someone whispered, "It smells like burnt meat. I don't think the pilot made it out."

The F'thk also had acute hearing. "We will soon know," said one. Eventually the other added, "A terrible mistake. This lifeboat was ejected accidentally during routine maintenance."

Implausible on its face, but not impossible—like so much about the F'thk. Of course Kyle knew something the F'thk didn't know he knew: about the injured Galactic hiding in the woods.

Under a sea of foam, the fire flickered out. A F'thk clambered aboard, charred wreckage crunching beneath his hooves. The fire-fighters exchanged glances: it was still *very* hot in there. They did not take into account its full-circle vision. "Do not be concerned. My kind are very heat-tolerant for short periods."

Several rescuers shone flashlights through the open hatches. Much of the cabin had been burnt beyond recognition. A shape-less, incinerated mass was still belted into what looked like an acceleration couch. The seats were far too small, and of the wrong shape, for F'thk. "Crispy critter," someone muttered.

The F'thk on the still smoldering lifeboat removed the pre-sumed charred remains of his missing fellow. If it or its com-panion mourned his/her/its death, they kept those sentiments to themselves.

Then, as quickly as the F'thk had arrived, they were gone.

much of the emergency rations on board were the biomass it converted."

From what Kyle had told her, the robots had returned to the *Consensus* with "her" burnt remains: a perfect genetic match. Into the sack of synthesized tissues had also gone the garment she had worn onto the lifeboat, stained with Girillian feces. Grelben and Rualf would want to believe that she'd perished in the lifeboat, her body mangled and burnt beyond recognition in the crash. Swelk had made it as easy as she could for them to hold that belief.

Color slowly returned to Gustafson's face. "I think you should explain why you came here."

Swelk's host drank cup after cup of coffee, once she convinced him, on the basis of his first serving, that the strong odor was not offensive. Mildly odd, perhaps. She contented herself with tap water and a snack fresh from the converter.

Both were, for the moment, talked out. After comparing notes, each knew far more than before their meeting—and far less than they needed to know.

Keep telling yourself it's only a movie. What a concise explanation for the enigma that was the F'thk. What an indictment of Krulchukor ethics: that nuclear devastation of Earth and millions of human deaths were acceptable special effects for Rualf's film.

Any possible course of action was unclear. Krulchukor technology was advanced far beyond Earth's, beginning with fusion power, artificial gravity, bioconverters, and robotics. And the starship drive, of course. To Kyle's dismay, Swelk had only the vaguest idea how the drive worked. Her interests were in social, not physical, sciences. She thought she remembered once hearing that the drive tapped the base-level energy of a vacuum.

But she also brought good news . . . or if not good *news*, an upbeat inference. The Galactic mother ship, that so unresponsively and impressively orbited the moon, beyond human reach, could not possibly be what it appeared. Like the F'thk, it must be a prop, something improvised during the lunar stopover of the *Consensus*. A radar buoy embedded in a holographic projection, Kyle theorized—extremely impressive, and nothing humanity could reproduce, but *not* real. A special effect.

If Earth's scientists could prove there were no miles-across enemy vessel, it would mean mankind had only to deal with

CHAPTER 17

SWELK RESTED ON a soft platform, her wounded limb freshly bandaged. The bed was in luxurious contrast to last night's trek over the mountain ridge to Gustafson's house. Her scientific detachment proved to be something of an abstraction: clinging to an alien—even the man she had sought out—took a constant effort of will. The experience of dealing intimately with Smelly and Stinky had again served her well.

One of her good limbs held food freshly synthesized in the portable bioconverter she had dragged from the lifeboat. Its preprogrammed capabilities included a full menu of Krulchukor cuisine.

"A useful gadget," her host said now. Kyle sat in a chair watching her. "Don't leave your home planet without one."

He did not realize *how* useful. "Given an organic sample, it can convert almost any biomass to any other." She raised her bandaged limb, which still throbbed. "Such as skin, bone, muscle, and blood." She did not know the meaning of his sudden pallor and loud swallowing, so she continued. "My former shipmates would not rest until they found me, and any humans thought to have spoken with me could have been at risk."

"So you cut off your finger as a template for the synthesizer?"

Bit her digit off—there was no time to hunt for a knife. "And one spacecraft . . . and the *Consensus* was still in the habit, from time to time, of landing.

And anything that came to Earth, Kyle said, humanity had a chance to handle.

A helicopter was on its way. When it landed, Swelk would allow herself to be zipped into a duffel bag. Kyle would carry her aboard, and both would be flown in secrecy to the presidential retreat he called Camp David.

A small number of American and Russian officials already knew that the F'thk were not what they seemed. No more than a handful, Kyle had assured her, would be told that the F'thk were the teleoperated puppets of the xenophobic Krulirim—or that one very special, very brave Krul had defected to Earth.

One very frightened and guilt-wracked Krul, *she* would have said.

"Can I bring you anything?" He asked that a lot, and thanked her often for coming, as if *he* owed *her* something.

Swelk channel-surfed as they waited. The television evoked a simpler time, when knowledge of the humans had been hers alone, solitary and naively content on the starship's bridge . . . a time *before* she had brought here the threat of destruction. She stopped at the image of magnificent, giant creatures. "What are those?" The English translation came, muffled, from the other duffel in which were packed her few belongings.

"Elephants."

"I should like to see elephants, sometime." And nurture them. Who will take care of Stinky and Smelly?

"When it's possible, I will be delighted to escort you." A mechanical *thp-thp-thp*-ing sound intruded. "Swelk . . . our ride is almost here."

Swelk limped to the gaping duffel. Shunned by her own kind; now to be hidden from most of his. Humanity remained in terrible peril from her acts, the information she brought offering perhaps insight but no help. Incredibly, she felt . . . *happy*. Something had changed for the better. What?

Keep telling yourself it's only a movie, she had told Kyle. She had known humans had movies, but seen very few. Her quote now to Gustafson from one of his country's greatest films was unintentional but apt.

"This could be the beginning of a beautiful friendship."

LAST ACTS

CHAPTER 18

"CHIEF OF STAFF in the side pocket!"

A startled Britt Arledge, urbane elder statesman and confidant of the President of the United States, turned toward the unexpected shout. Rolling along parallel to the laboratory floor, at about his waist level and seemingly immune to gravity, was a basketball-sized, mottled white sphere. The orb submerged without impact into his torso before vanishing.

"Join me in my office and I'll explain." Kyle Gustafson led the way out of the crowded lab, past electronics racks and grinning technicians. He ignored his former boss's dour expression until they were behind a closed door. "The so-called Galactic mother ship is like that demo."

"A cue ball with glandular problems? *This* is why you urgently summoned me from the White House?"

"Not a pool ball, a hologram." Kyle perched on a corner of his desk. "It explains a lot."

Britt found a chair. "Not to me."

"From the day the Galactics arrived, I've never liked the explanation for their mother ship parking in a lunar orbit. A safety precaution, we're told, because it's antimatter-powered. Being a big prop, meant to intimidate us, is a much more credible reason for putting it where we can't easily examine it."

Britt crossed his arms across his chest but said nothing.

"If the aliens, as they claim, do react antimatter with matter on their ship, it would produce telltale gamma radiation. Gamma rays don't penetrate the atmosphere, so to maintain their lie they can't allow high-altitude gamma detectors. That's why, shortly before announcing their arrival, they destroyed the space shuttle carrying a new gamma-ray observatory to orbit. That's why they exploded the Russian rocket with the backup instrument." Kyle waved off an objection while Britt was still formulating it. "No, I haven't confused an inability to measure with proof there is nothing to *be* measured. We've surreptitiously flown gamma-ray detectors on weather balloons. The data we can collect that way are nowhere near as good as the lost observatories would've gotten, but we've seen *no* unexpected gamma radiation from the moon's vicinity."

"Anything else?"

The untimely on-orbit deaths over the past few months of older, less-capable gamma-ray-sensing satellites was only circumstantial, not conclusive. "Recall what we've learned from Swelk." He glanced reflexively at his office safe, wherein sat a copy of the CIA's most recent eyes-only report on the alien's ongoing debriefing. "You know I've been perplexed by our observations of the F'thk. It's no wonder I've been confused by their 'biological' indications . . . Swelk says they're robots. I'm convinced that the mother ship, like the F'thk, is a special effect. Swelk said the starship from which she escaped spent time on the moon before coming to Earth. That's a ship we *know* exists—we have the cracked runways to prove it. A lunar stopover gave them the opportunity to set up lasers to project the hologram—like my cue ball, only much larger. Of course the Krulirim need lots of lasers, and big ones at that, to simulate a mother ship orbiting the moon."

"Of *course*."

Kyle winced at the sarcasm. "You disagree?"

"I'm unconvinced. Say it is an enormous hologram. Why would a hologram be visible to radar?"

Kyle nodded. "It wouldn't. But the Krulirim could have easily put a radar buoy in orbit around the moon, a buoy around which the hologram would be centered. The buoy would dynamically generate a radar echo in response to any incident radar pulse."

"And this buoy, naturally, would be visibly obscured by the hologram." Britt stood.

Such a buoy, even unobscured, would likely be too small to be seen from Earth, even by the Hubble. Kyle kept that complication to himself as an unnecessary distraction. "It's not as if we lack evidence. We know the aliens destroyed the Russian's Proton launcher, and how they did it. The manner of that rocket's destruction matches everything we know about the *Atlantis* disaster. We know the aliens are filling our cities with spying devices. And an ET defector, looking nothing like the 'official' F'thk emissaries, practically landed in my yard. *She's* proof."

"I concede alien hostility, and I don't forget for a moment it was your skepticism which led us to that fact. But none of the evidence relates directly to the mother ship. Maybe it has great shielding, or the antimatter reactor is shut down for maintenance. Maybe the ETs *are* lying, but only about using antimatter. Proving or disproving such ideas is more in your bailiwick than mine.

"I'm going to propose an alternative scenario, one drawn from the skills *I* use every day." Britt met Kyle's gaze. "It's a much simpler explanation than yours. We have only Swelk's word for it that she was defecting.

"Did you ever consider that she may be lying?"

A riddle wrapped in a mystery inside an enigma . . . Winston Churchill's description of Russia fit the baffling Galactics at least as well. And the mad scientist for whom she was waiting.

Darlene was a career diplomat and the senior-ranking State Department representative to the American commission that routinely coordinated with the Galactics. None of that experience had prepared her for cloak-and-dagger operations. That Kyle was no more plausible than she to play agent only deepened the mystery.

Searching the crowded Metro parking lot, Darlene's head swiveled to and fro in a manner she felt sure must somehow look furtive. Per Kyle's odd request, she wore a head scarf and large-lensed sunglasses.

A nondescript boxy sedan pulled up to the region of curb labeled "kiss and ride"; the passenger-side window slid down. The mad scientist was behind the wheel. "Can I give you a lift?" Kyle asked.

Darlene got in and removed her scarf. "Government license plates. A motor-pool vehicle?"

"Swapped for my car inside a mall's covered parking garage.

Any overhead observers are *very* unlikely to know where I am."
The clearly implied watchers were Galactic. He merged expertly
into the heavy traffic streaming from the commuter lot.

"And per your invitation, which you so interestingly and oddly
had FedExed, I'm meeting you at a station that required me to
change trains in an underground Metro stop. That makes my
whereabouts equally disguised." She tucked the scarf into her
purse. "Where are we going that's so secret?"

He pulled onto a highway, heading northwest into rural Maryland. "Let's just say a pleasant drive in the country."

"A few days ago a Galactic lifeboat crashed and burned near
your house. Now you're playing spy. I doubt those situations are
unrelated."

"We'll see."

She twisted her neck to examine a loosely closed box on the
backseat, a container from which emerged scratching sounds and
soft thuds. "What's in there?"

"Kittens for a friend. She's from out of town, and misses her
own pets." He pointed to a sunlit wooded hillside aglow in red
and gold. "Check out those leaves." He turned onto a shoulderless
two-lane country road. She gave up with a sigh, silently admiring
the fall foliage until after almost thirty minutes Kyle pulled into
a small graveled lot.

Behind a low, hand-stacked fieldstone wall, amid a sea of fallen
leaves, sat a picturesque white farmhouse. The sign dangling by
two chains from the crosspiece of a wooden post declared, simply,
VALLEY VIEW—1808. She guessed that was the construction date
rather than an address.

Valley View could have been a bed-and-breakfast . . . except
for the four alert-looking men who paced nearby. One watched
the new arrivals, one studied the road, and two peered intently
into the nearby woods. From the corner of an eye she saw Kyle
observing her, a slight smile on his face. Wondering how she'd
react to a B&B?

The crash of the Galactic lifeboat could not have been kept
secret. A whisked-away survivor was another matter. She turned
to Kyle. "A CIA safehouse, I presume."

Swelk was sunken deep into what she'd been told was called a
beanbag chair, the single piece of Krul-friendly furniture in the

house. There were engine noises outside. Footsteps in the front hall revealed that one of her guardians—or were they captors?—was striding down the front hall. The unseen door opened with a squeak. The mutters of human conversation were too faint for her pocket computer to translate.

Perhaps only a change of shift. Leaving one stalk to monitor the entrance to her room, her attention and two sensor stalks remained fixed on the flat-screen television that hung on the wall. The only signal source was something called a DVD player. There was little else to do between questionings. Her lack of access to Earth's broadcasts and its Internet shouted distrust.

Knowing what her people were doing, she could not fault her hosts for their suspicion.

"Kyle!" she yelped in delight as her new friend entered, box in hand. She struggled out of her hollow in the beanbag. A human female accompanied Kyle, her eyes opened wide.

"Swelk, this is my friend and colleague Darlene Lyons, from the American State Department. Darlene, I'd like you to meet a *real* Galactic."

Standing, the chimerical alien rose only to Darlene's waist. Its torso was a flattened black spheroid perched atop three spindly legs. No, make that *limbs*—the appendage Swelk had extended in greeting was as much an arm as a leg. It had a clearly prehensile end, suggesting a cluster of three opposable hands, each with three opposable fingers. Three objects vaguely suggestive of untrimmed rubbery celery stalks protruded from the top of the body. Two stalk tips seemed to be studying her. "I am pleased to meet you," said a box on the counter, speaking moments after the ET emitted a burst of vowelless and incomprehensible sound. "I am called Swelk, from the Krulchukor ship *Consensus*."

She dropped in shock into a nearby chair, rationalizing that it was diplomatic to come closer to the little alien's level. Kyle, thankfully, interceded to bring her quickly up to date. Swelk's defection and the intentional destruction of her lifeboat to cover her escape. The xenophobic tendencies of the Krulirim. The long-extinct fossil species from Krulchuk serving as the prototype for the tall centauroid robots presented to humanity as interstellar emissaries: the F'thk. The giant mother ship orbiting the moon a mirage meant to intimidate. The movie company aboard the

Consensus, conspiring to provoke nuclear war as the ultimate special effect.

Her mind whirled. "So there is no Galactic Commonwealth?" she finally managed.

"Not known to my people," answered the alien's translator.

Over the alien's head Kyle quizzically raised an eyebrow. The alien's third eye stalk could surely have seen the gesture, but would the ET have understood it?

His hopefully subtle signal was unnecessary. It had become clear that the F'thk were lying . . . why should she not be as skeptical of this new alien? Swelk's whole species was until now undisclosed.

Squealing, Swelk flexed a sensor stalk toward the cardboard box Kyle had set down. A coal-black kitten, not yet grown into its ears, was bursting through the flaps. Arching its back, the cat fluffed up its fur and hissed at the alien. "What's *that*?" yelped the translator.

As Kyle tried to calm the feline, Darlene worked scenarios in her mind. That the Krul was being truthful was only one possibility. Ostensibly friendly F'thk had privately told Darlene and other human diplomats that the many-specied Galactic Commonwealth was riven by factions. If that much of the F'thk story were true, Swelk could be an agent, planted by one side. If so, to what end?

"It's a baby animal, a young cat." Kyle offered a sack of kitty treats to the alien. With his other hand he stroked the kitten soothingly, as Swelk now cautiously extended an extremity. The black cat sniffed daintily, then licked the offered treat. A loud purring began.

If Swelk were telling the truth, the aliens *could* be vulnerable when their single starship landed at one Earth city or another. But if she were lying . . . then the ship they might attack would be a mere landing craft from a miles-wide behemoth in lunar orbit. What retribution would the ETs exact?

And if there were, after all, a Galactic Commonwealth, a sneak attack on its emissaries was likely, at a minimum, to disqualify Earth's application. Without pretending to understand the interspecies politics of the supposed Galactics, Darlene could understand some aliens opting for the familiar. Maneuvering the humans into discrediting themselves could be an easy way for one faction to maintain the often-comforting status quo.

Kyle released the kitten; as it sidled toward the alien, still holding a treat, a second kitten, this one a gray tabby, scrabbled from the box. With a manipulation no human arm could have duplicated, Swelk's extended limb extracted and extended another morsel without dropping the sack or the piece already being sniffed by the black cat. "What are they called?"

"You can name them," answered Kyle.

He hadn't brought her here to play with the kittens, cute as they were, nor had he lightly disclosed what must be an *extremely* closely held secret. So why *was* she here? As an unofficial second opinion, perhaps. As different as were their professions and interests, she and Kyle shared what she considered a healthy dose of skepticism (which, Darlene had good reason to suspect, her Foggy Bottom associates more often considered an annoying contrariness).

The respect was mutual, and the opportunity for a career diplomat intriguing. She scooped up the curious tabby, for which the antiques-furnished salon was entirely unprepared. "Swelk, I'd like to learn all about your people."

CHAPTER 19

FROM DEEP WITHIN a beanbag chair—Kyle had now brought one for most rooms of the building, Swelk watched two more curious and dissatisfied visitors leave. Humans under stress, she knew from both intercepted movies and her short time on Earth, paced to and fro. Krulirim in like circumstances also moved, in their case—naturally—always in circles.

Swelk's present immobility was willed. Her lame leg always ruined the perfection of her loops; she'd endured enough ridicule about her deviancies to have learned long ago how not to evoke more. Seething though she was in unexpressed frustration, a fragment of her mind laughed at the foolishness of maintaining self-discipline in front of the bilateral humans.

"May I join you?" asked Darlene Lyons from the doorway. She was at the house much more often than Kyle.

Why bother, thought Swelk. So far today she had failed dismally to answer questions about the engines of the *Consensus,* the numbers and capabilities of its antimeteor lasers, and the range of its lifeboats. Of the lifeboats she had known only that the reach was less than interstellar. She had abruptly ended the last session, about "military capabilities," when she realized what motivated the two men's inquiries: a possible assault on the *Consensus.* Despite Swelk's abuse by its passengers and crew, thoughts of revenge had not motivated her hasty departure.

"Of course," Swelk waggled two digits in feigned welcome. The gray tabby, now named Stripes, leapt clumsily onto the beanbag chair. It toppled against her, and almost immediately fell asleep. The fuzzy little thing, all legs and ears and impossibly soft fur, could not have been more different from a Girillian swampbeast—and the kitten reminded Swelk achingly of her abandoned charges. She would *not* cause them more suffering. "But I won't help Earth attack my former shipmates."

Darlene's cheeks reddened, a reaction whose meaning Swelk could not penetrate. "I have no desire to become a radioactive extra in a Krulchukor movie. What would you propose we do?"

Swelk's sensor stalks drooped in sadness and shame. The passengers and officers of the *Consensus* were eager to sacrifice the most advanced race her people had ever discovered. Would the plotters accept disappointment, meekly heading home if their plans were widely disclosed ... or would they find new means to produce the same result? Rualf's special-effects wizards had already produced the robotic F'thk and the illusion of a gigantic moon-orbiting mother ship. Did she dare gamble they could not find a way to goad any Earth country into attacking its national rival? From newscasts Swelk had surreptitiously watched in her lifeboat hideaway before her escape, it seemed that counterstrike after counter-counterstrike would inevitably follow the first hostile launch.

And what if the filmmakers' attempts to fool Earth into a photogenic self-destruction *did* fail? Would Rualf and Captain Grelben, their dreams of vast wealth dashed, lash out at Earth in anger and disappointment? Swelk felt certain that an unsuccessful attack on the *Consensus* would draw an enraged response. Either way, as the morning's earlier visitors had made her realize, she simply did not know what danger the Krulchukor ship represented. There was no doubting from the humans' questions that they were concerned.

And *she* had led Rualf and Captain Grelben here. The exile's sensor stalks collapsed in withdrawal. The suddenly limp tendrils lay draped across her torso, obscuring her vision and muffling her hearing.

"Swelk!" called Darlene. "Are you all right?"

Swelk roused herself with a shake, her sensor stalks snapping painfully erect. "I am far from all right, but I have only myself to blame for that.

"And as for your previous question, I have no idea what we should do."

Kyle watched Swelk watching the kittens from the comfort of the beanbag chair she had towed into the dining room. Blackie and Stripes—*there* were two unimaginative names...were all Krulirim so literal?—were tussling for no obvious reason, their tiny mouths opening repeatedly in meows either silent or too high-pitched for him to hear. From time to time a cat forgot what she was doing and pounced on the disheveled fringe of the oriental rug on which they played.

The little alien had two sensor stalks pointed at her pets; the third was time-shared between Kyle and routine scanning of the room. One needed little time with Swelk, he thought, to deduce where the ET's attention was focused. He glanced at his wristwatch and sighed inwardly. His impatience was unfair, and he knew it. One debriefer after another grilled her most of the day, every day. He had to allow her an occasional mental break.

Those feelings of tolerance did nothing to expand the hours in Kyle's day. Well, he hadn't grown up with pets for nothing. After a while, he took the laser pointer from his pocket, waving it to make a jiggly red dot beside the kittens. They immediately stopped wrestling to chase the spot around the room. The hunt became a stakeout at the hall-closet door beneath which the laser dot had vanished. They were likely to stay there, staring at the gap under the door, for some time.

With the kittens quieted down, he tried to get Swelk back to business. "I'd like to talk some more about the bioconverter."

Success: she favored him now with two sensor stalks. "What else is there to say? I put organic material in. I take different stuff out."

"How does it work?"

"Here is the On-Off button. I can pick what I want made from the list in this display, or insert a sample here. I speak how much I want. Raw material, when needed, goes into this chute. Anything it can't use is emptied here. Food is deposited in the final compartment." She flicked, three times, all the digits of one limb. He took it as a sign of annoyance. "I have told you, and others, all of this before."

The day was overcast; the illumination from the window was gloomy. He pointed at the chandelier over the dining-room table.

"Would you mind if I turn on the lamp?" Standing without waiting for an answer, he was surprised at the response he got.

"I do not like your lights. They make me jumpy."

"All right." He sat back down. Kyle knew people who got depressed in the winter from too little sun. There was even a medical name for the condition: seasonal affective disorder. In Swelk's case, of course, the ambient light wouldn't improve with the months-distant lengthening of the days. Renewed sympathy for the solitary alien washed over him. He tamped down the feeling—what Earth needed now was information. "I understand the controls for the bioconverter. My question is different. What happens inside to make it work?"

The alien hesitated. "Chemicals are broken apart. The pieces are recombined into new chemicals. Maybe there's a computer inside to control it."

Foiled again. Kyle's certified-evidence-free theory was that the bioconverter employed nanotechnology: self-replicating molecular-sized machines to manipulate atoms and molecules. Nanotech was conceptual at best in some of Earth's cutting-edge labs; any clues to its practical implementation could be priceless. The darker side of Kyle's speculation, if he could substantiate it, would be a whole new reason to fear the possible wrath of the Galactics. Imagine flesh-eating bacteria with attitude . . . .

Quit it, Kyle. It seemed he would be getting no hints from Swelk. Alas, her failure to answer these sorts of questions implied nothing about the truth of her story. How many people did he know without a clue how, say, their TV or refrigerator worked?

Speaking of refrigerators, and probably why he thought of one, he wouldn't mind a cold soda. Retrieving a can would provide a few minutes in which to exorcise his frustrations, since the safehouse was presently without a functioning cooler.

No one had seen a way to tell whether Swelk's bioconverter or computer had undisclosed capabilities . . . such as communicating with the ship from which she had, or claimed to have, defected. Even if her story were accepted—personally, he believed her—the danger would remain that hostile Krulirim could eavesdrop through her stolen equipment.

One of the few things he truly *knew* was that F'thk spying devices, the Galactic orbs, used microwaves. That Swelk's gear, *if* it had a communications mode, also exploited the electromagnetic spectrum, seemed like a good bet to take.

In terms of suppressing radio-based communications, stashing the alien in an existing radiometrics lab would have been ideal—but it would have sacrificed secrecy and discretion. Instead, the isolated one-time farmhouse had been hastily "remodeled" before Swelk was moved in and her debriefing begun in earnest.

The farmhouse's walls were newly spray painted with an electrically conductive pigment. Rolls of fine copper mesh lined the attic floor and cellar ceiling. Copper screens now covered all windows and doors. Everything was interconnected and grounded. Kyle had personally tested and blessed the finished product: an unobtrusive electromagnetic shield.

In the greater scheme of things, it was a small matter: a too casually draped dropcloth had let some of the sprayed conductive paint drift into the guts of the refrigerator. Plugged back in after the alterations were finished, the motor, obviously shorted out, had fried itself. It appeared that the owner previous to the CIA was one of those frugal fools who used pennies as fuses.

"I'm going to the trailer for a soda," Kyle told Swelk. "Can I get you anything?"

"I will stay with water from the kitchen tap."

The back door banged shut behind Kyle. The Airstream trailer to which Kyle now headed sat discreetly behind the house. Originally deployed as a communications station—the safehouse's shielding also blocked the agents' cell phones—the motor home was now most prized for its tiny refrigerator. He waved at an agent behind the house on a cigarette break, got a Coke, and returned.

"Sorry for the interruption." Blackie and Stripes were still waiting for the "mouse" to emerge from the closet. "About the bioconverter again, how is it powered?"

Swelk had gotten a glass of water during his absence. She had to climb to the counter to operate the sink. Instead of answering, she and her computer traded untranslated squeals. Finally, her computer said, "The translation program does not have the word I want. Maybe your technology does not have this capability. Some of the material I feed into the bioconverter is used to make the electricity. The energy is stored in something like a battery."

It sounded like a fuel cell, although a much better and more flexible design than any Kyle knew. That itself was interesting, but another opportunity had just presented itself. "Does your computer have notes about how the bioconverter itself works? Maybe even a design?"

More squeals and whines. "I am sorry. No."

Had he imagined a pregnant pause after "sorry"? Or was Swelk short of breath, as so often happened? She'd told him that Earth had more CO_2 than home. "Why not?"

Swelk's sensor stalks dropped. Body language for regret? Or for evasion? "I was unprepared for my escape." Pause. "I left the *Consensus* when my spying was discovered. My computer was mostly filled with movies." An even longer pause. "Sorry."

Another plausible explanation . . . for another aggravating roadblock. Britt's skepticism had one more data point of support.

"Cold War II: First Casualties!" screamed the headline.

A well-read *Washington Post* had been left on the table of the NASA conference room in which Kyle waited for Britt Arledge. Goddard Space Flight Center, in Greenbelt, Maryland, was a short drive from the White House—and the sprawling, campuslike complex had several electromagnetically shielded labs for the routine assembly and checkout of scientific satellites. A get-together here offered reasonable assurances against Galactic eavesdropping without drawing alien attention to Kyle or the federal lab at which he officially worked. Proximity to the District was simply a bonus.

Despite the inch-tall banner, details on the clash were sparse. There had been a brief but deadly dogfight over the South China Sea between Russian fighters based in Vietnam and carrier-based American fighters. Accounts differed, of course, as to who had fired first. Moscow claimed its planes had been on a routine exercise, and their approach to the carrier task force was no more sinister than hundreds of similar events over the years. Washington said a targeting radar had been detected.

What *was* clear was that three SU-22s and two F/A-18s had been splashed. Two pilots, one Russian and one American, had failed to eject. Both were missing and presumed dead.

"Dirty business, that."

Kyle looked up at the sound of Britt's voice. "That it is." The wonder was that more incidents, and more deaths, had not occurred as the tensions between the United States and Russia kept rising. It was, to the very few who knew, a simulation of a nuclear crisis ... but that pretense of hostility could turn real enough at a moment's notice. Too many nerves were stretched taut. Too many weapons could be loosed on a moment's notice.

He flung down the newspaper he'd been studying. Given what Swelk had told them, did Earth's nuclear powers need to continue the disaster-prone deception? He was trying to work that through in his own mind. "We'll be meeting down the hall."

Nodding, Britt followed Kyle along a road-stripe-yellow corridor to the shielded privacy of a cavernous, multistory satellite-assembly lab. Hands clasping the steel-pipe railing of a catwalk, Kyle felt free to speak his mind. "Is the President prepared to tell the Russians about our defector? We need to stop the madness before something even worse happens."

Britt's nostrils flared slightly, as visible a sign as he ever gave of disagreement. "I'm not yet convinced that she *is* a defector, and not an agent. Why are you?"

It was the debate they kept having. Nothing in Swelk's ongoing CIA debriefings had revealed any inconsistencies in her story, nor had the little ET shared anything irreconcilable with Kyle or Darlene. A large part of that consistent story, unfortunately, was wide-ranging unfamiliarity with her species' science and engineering. That an intelligent member of a modern society could be ignorant of its technologies—Britt cheerfully admitted that he was without a clue how a radio worked and what kept a plane in the air—settled nothing.

The more cynical CIA debriefers went further, speculating that the very absence of minor loose ends in Swelk's story suggested a fabrication. Kyle thought he'd squelched that insinuation, as a groundless extrapolation to the aliens of a human foible. Who was to say all Krulirim didn't have a flawless memory for detail?

This was no trivial difference of opinion; humanity's future teetered on the fulcrum of the choice they must soon make. Kyle's knuckles were white from pressure as he fought to control his emotions. "No amount of contradiction-free interrogation is going to overcome your doubts. Ironclad proof of her story, if Swelk is telling the truth, is on the *Consensus* ... which, as you know, the ETs won't allow us aboard." The few attempts to hide bugs on the aliens or their equipment had been met with uniform failure and angry F'thk denunciations. The President himself had banned further attempts as too dangerous.

"And yet," Britt flashed a momentary smile, "you asked that we get together."

"True." Kyle extracted two glossy sheets from the manila envelope that he'd carried tucked under an arm. Each page bore an image of the moon, its cratered landscape unmistakable. "Take a look at these."

Britt's eyes switched back and forth between pictures. The tiny time-stamps in the corners of each differed by only milliseconds. "They're the same scene, right? The left one shows much more detail."

"The higher-resolution shot is an optical image. The other is a computer reconstruction from a reflected microwave pulse." Kyle suppressed an urge to discuss just how much computation had been required to generate the latter image. "We adopted technology used to predict the stealthiness of airplane designs without having to build them first."

He took back the images before handing over a third. The new picture showed the supposed Galactic mother ship. Less than half a hemisphere was visible, the rest an inky blackness. A similarly divided lunar landscape provided a dramatic backdrop. "Sunlight is striking from the side, obviously."

Britt tapped the photo. "What's this dark spot?"

"Good eye—it's a shadow."

"Of what? It must be something big."

"A hangar. Their utility spacecraft, the ones that never land on the Earth-visible side of the moon, emerge from and return to that bay. Most of the time the door is closed." One of the just-mentioned auxiliary craft was also in the image. Kyle was aware, although the still frame didn't support the knowledge, that the smaller vessel had just exited the hangar.

Britt looked at him shrewdly. "But you claim not to believe in this mother ship. Swelk says it doesn't exist."

"That hangar for the auxiliary craft would be a thousand-plus feet deep. We can calculate that depth from the geometry of the shadow." The previous microwave observation had shown craters much shallower than that. With a flourish, Kyle offered a final image. "Now look at this."

This computer-reconstructed microwave image, its timestamp again well within a second of its optical analogue, did not show any auxiliary craft. And the Galactic mother ship appeared only as a featureless sphere.

CHAPTER 20

The American and Russian navies today separately announced the apparent loss of a submarine in the North Atlantic. Few details, and no official theories as to the cause or causes of the incidents, are available. French and Spanish seismologists recorded events in the region consistent with underwater explosions. Deep submergence rescue vehicles are being rushed to the area by the two navies, but hopes for any survivors are slim.

The frigid state of relationships between these nuclear powers, and the proximity of their lost submarines, suggest that the disasters might in some way be linked. This is an inference about which spokespersons of both sides declined comment.

—BBC News Service

THEY WERE SOUNDED OUT, nominated, haggled over, and finally agreed upon in the most casual of contexts: huffed conversations between joggers; "chance" encounters of smokers in the shadow of the Pentagon; a tête-à-tête between parents at a kids' soccer match; walks in the woods surrounding Camp David; a half-dozen other innocent-seeming meetings in venues previously confirmed to be free of Galactic orbs and potentially compromised Earthly comm gear. The disappearance for even a few hours of the principals—the President, the director of the CIA, the secretary of defense, the secretary of state, the national security advisor—could trigger who knew what response from nervous Russians or inscrutable aliens. The five who were now gathered, in the most rustic of surroundings, would hold the debate their principals could not.

Kyle had volunteered his sister's remote Chesapeake Bay cabin. Darlene had driven from the District with him; the others arrived soon after, two in separate cars and one in the motorboat now bobbing alongside the cabin's rickety pier.

The dragged-indoors picnic table around which they met, a tarp covering the carved doodles of Kyle's young nieces, had never seen such august company. Erin Fitzhugh was a CIA deputy director, the terseness of her official resume implying a long history in covert operations. USAF Lieutenant General Ryan Bauer—former B-52 pilot, Gulf War veteran, ex-director of the Ballistic Missile Defense Organization—was presently on staff to the Chairman of the Joint Chiefs. Kyle was a widely respected physicist and the director emeritus of Franklin Ridge National Lab; more important, he was the one-time (and still unofficial) science advisor to the President.

Darlene's credentials, she felt, were the least impressive. A long-time foreign-service officer and now a deputy undersecretary of the Department of State, she was here to represent the diplomatic perspective. Britt had assured her that no one had *ever* considered holding this summit about the aliens—which was all that the invitees had been told about the gathering's purpose—without the first diplomat to see through the facade of F'thk good intentions.

The President's chief of staff was the final member of the small group, there to direct discussion of the still-undisclosed topic and report back to his boss. Of all the participants, Britt had the highest public profile. Official Washington thought he was down and out with this fall's virulent strain of flu.

Kyle was indulging some odd urge to play host before the discussion kicked off. As Darlene gave him a hand in the kitchen with cold sodas and salty snacks, Bauer and Fitzhugh rehashed the North Atlantic incident. The working theory was an undersea collision between the Russian attack sub that had been trailing an American boomer—ballistic-missile sub—and the American attack sub too closely following the unsuspecting Russian.

The details didn't parse at first—Darlene's job at State dealt with human rights and fostering democracy, not arms control and nuclear deterrence. A chill washed over her as, through whispered consultations with Kyle—a presidential science advisor's purview certainly did include nuclear matters—she came up to speed.

Dissolution of the USSR had removed several outward-looking land-based radars from the Russian missile-defense network, gaps that became ever more troubling as the Galactics systematically destroyed early-warning satellites. In predictable parts of every day, the Russians were effectively blind to submarine-launched missiles along two narrow corridors. Attack subs like the one the Russians had just lost sought to find and secretly track the American boomers. In case of hostilities, destroying a boomer before it launched would scratch twenty-four ballistic missiles, each with up to twelve nuclear warheads. American attack subs, in turn, silently stalked their Russian counterparts, ready to pre-emptively take out a Russian hunter. The vulnerabilities created by the Russian blind spots made hair-triggers inevitable . . . and incredibly dangerous.

The doomed subs had followed a boomer into one of the Russian blind spots.

"We've *got* to step back from the brink," Darlene blurted from the kitchen. "We're too close to disaster."

The national-security pros exchanged a look that said, "ama-teurs." Erin Fitzhugh cleared her throat. She was more one of the guys than most of the guys. "We and the Russkies have half a century's practice at dancing on the edge. Now, whenever our tensions show signs of leveling off, the F'thk, or Krulirim, or whoever the bug-eyed monsters are, turn their attention to the less experienced nuclear powers. Would you feel any safer if the damned ETs were working their magic on the Pakistanis and the Indians? Israelis and Iranians? *I* sure as shit wouldn't—their command-and-control systems are all bad jokes."

Pretzels flew as the diplomat undiplomatically slammed a tray onto the picnic table. "Are you saying the Atlantic incident was staged?"

"All *too* real," interrupted Britt. "Entirely real, and for the rea-sons Erin has articulated. We don't dare encourage the aliens to put more effort into manipulating the less seasoned members of the nuclear club. And unless we keep the military in the dark we can't hope to keep secret our knowledge of concealed ET hostility. So the operative question is, when, if ever, do we take on the aliens?

"That, ladies and gentlemen, brings us to the purpose of our meeting. The President is considering telling President Chernykov about our alien defector."

Stripes, who had been pouncing alternately on her sister, the fronds of a fern rustling in the draft from the fireplace, and her own tail, skidded to a halt with a sudden confused expression. After a moment of whatever passed for consideration in her young brain, the kitten skittered off in the direction of the nearest litter box. She thundered up the worn wooden stairs making noise in total disproportion to her size.

Swelk almost hoped the kitten would be too late. Tending to the Girillian menagerie had begun as a ploy; caring for them had become ennobling. She yearned to regain that quiet satisfaction of being needed. There was a flurry of unseen digging noises, and then Stripes returned at full gallop to the salon. With a leap and a midair twist the cat was off in pursuit of something only it could see. Swelk waggled her sensor stalks in amused confusion . . . the thing Kyle called a poltergeist baffled her translation program.

With thoughts of him, her momentary good mood vanished. The human to whom she felt closest had not stopped by in two days. And it was not only Kyle—none of her most frequent visitors had come by. Even an alien newly arrived could tell from the demeanor of her guards that the substitute questioners were of lesser status than those who had disappeared.

What Kyle and the others were doing, she could not imagine.

"It seems clear-cut enough to me," said Kyle. He didn't entirely feel that way, but the other summiteers were erring in the opposite direction. "Either Swelk is a defector or she's not. Which do we believe?"

Everyone began animatedly speaking at once, stopped, then all started up again. On the next random retry, the ex-spy got the floor. "The ET could be a real defector—and delusional. She could be entirely sane and sincere, and unaware that she's been filled with disinformation. She could be lying through whatever she uses for teeth, for reasons fathomable only to celery-eyed monsters, and still reveal . . . with whatever encouragement is appropriate . . . incredibly valuable information. We need to understand her motivations to have any hope of making sense of anything she tells us."

From nowhere came a memory of Swelk dangling a scrap of yarn above leaping kittens. "Delusional? A secret agent? Erin, have you ever actually *met* Swelk?"

"No, by intent." Fitzhugh impatiently flicked a potato-chip crumb from the table. "My people have. I talk to them; I read their reports. I'm objective. It's the *professional* way to handle supposed defectors, even when the stakes aren't so high."

Ryan Bauer popped open another Coke. "It's just too convenient that nothing in Swelk's story can be confirmed—short of what could be a suicidal attack on the F'thk vessel. She claims she's some kind of outcast and dilettante social scientist, excusing her not knowing anything helpful. The lifeboat she came down on is melted slag. Her computer can't be experimented with, because it contains her translator. Her so-called bioconverter can't be fiddled with because that would put at risk her food supply." He rolled his eyes. "Could the little monster's story *be* any more convenient?"

"Oh, *please*," Darlene snapped. Beside her, Britt's head swung back and forth, like a spectator at a tennis match. And just as unuseful.

"Excuse me," said Kyle, stunned by the unexpected disbelief. Swelk had specifically sought him out. Was he too close to, too influenced by, the little ET? "Maybe we can approach the problem another way. The most critical of Swelk's disclosures, whatever her motives, is the nonexistence of the mother ship. If we can corroborate *that*, if we can be sure there's 'only' the so-called F'thk vessel to handle, her story would be valuable."

Ryan shoved back his chair, its legs grating against the floor. "Come *on*, Kyle. Small telescopes see it. Radar shows it."

This time, Kyle had six copies of the images that had *almost* convinced Britt. He passed the prints around the table without explanation, letting the pictures tell their own story.

"Holy crap," reacted the CIA exec, her eyes bright. "The microwave and visible-light images don't match." Ryan, nodding in agreement, looked chagrined. The USAF Space Command could have made the same observation . . . weeks ago.

"Why haven't we seen a discrepancy before?" asked Darlene. "I know the mother ship has been scanned by radar."

"Radar's ordinarily used to locate and identify an object, not to create a detailed image of it," Bauer explained. "What Kyle's showing us took a *lot* of computation. Why bother when it was so plainly visible to telescopes?"

Kyle rapped the table confidently. "The reason, my friend, is because our defector *said* there could be no mother ship. I'm saying the optical image is a hologram, and the featureless glob must be the echo of a radar buoy we can't see."

Darlene, for some reason, refused to catch his eye. What was going through her mind?

She didn't give Kyle long to wonder. "You *know* I like Swelk. I trust her, too. That said, the stakes are too high to go with my gut. Like Reagan famously said of the Sovs and disarmament, I think we have to 'trust, but verify.' "

Dar was the *last* person he'd expected to object. "What other explanation is there?"

She tipped her head, tugging a lock of hair in reflection. "I defer to every one of you about technology. Without knowing much about tech, though, I can concoct another explanation for what we're seeing. Kyle, you've explained before that the aliens have radar stealthing. Their satellites that upload recordings from the souvenir orbs, the satellites that we watched destroy that Russian rocket . . . *they* were stealthy."

"Go on," encouraged Britt.

"So imagine for a moment that Swelk's account isn't true. Whether she's purposefully lying or has been filled with disinformation, someone, in this scenario, wants us to believe her. They *want* us to mistakenly conclude that the mother ship is fake." Darlene swept a hand grandiloquently over the pictures, her words tumbling out in a rush. "Couldn't they enable a stealth mode on their small craft? Then those smaller spaceships would be seen visually but not by radar. Isn't it at least possible that a real, physical mother ship could use a stealth mode to prevent a true radar reflection *and*, whenever pinged, emit a synthesized signal that matches a featureless large blob? Wouldn't those stratagems also explain your observations?"

Scientist, general, and spy master exchanged surprised glances. Erin Fitzhugh found her voice first. "If you ever get tired of working at State, there's a spot for you at the Agency."

Discussion continued—of Swelk's debriefings, of analyses of her salvaged equipment, of the international dangers posed by recent F'thk secretive whisperings—but the decision-making part of the meeting had ended. Whatever their opinion of Swelk, no one could be certain her story was true. There would be, for now, no disclosure to the Russians of her arrival and claims. Unwilling themselves to recommend a desperate attack on the F'thk ship, they dare not risk influencing the Russians to try.

Would they be ready to share, Kyle wondered, before a nuclear miscalculation obliterated them all?

CHAPTER 21

STINKY *HUMPHED* WITH satisfaction, leaning into the push-broom that now served as his brush. Swelk groomed the swamp-beast with long, smooth strokes, quietly pleased at the glossiness of his leathery skin. As Swelk worked, Smelly butted her head, first gently, then insistently, against her. "Your turn is ..."

Smelly's importuning was not simple impatience for her turn. Swelk plummeted, only then realizing they had all been suspended in midair. Stinky and Smelly shrank as she plunged, until only their fading fearful trumpeting remained. A recess of her brain noticed without explanation that the animals had not fallen.

She shuddered awake, intertwined digits rigid with fear. Bellows of unseen swampbeasts filled her mind. After forcing her digits to relax, to unlace, she tried but failed to stand. Visions of terrified swampbeasts overwhelmed her as she toppled, overcome by dizziness.

The nightmare did not surprise her—as much as she already loved the kittens, she missed the swampbeasts terribly. For the intense vertigo, however, she had no explanation.

Blackie and Stripes tumbled into the room, curious, perhaps, at the unexpected nighttime noises from Swelk. She preferred to think they had come to console her. As the exile stroked their soft fur, she could not help but wonder, What is wrong with me?

❋　　❋　　❋

It was not yet 9:00 A.M., and four new pies were already cooling on the counter. The kitchen sink overflowed with mixing bowls, measuring cups, and utensils Kyle couldn't name. Hours before the Thanksgiving turkey would go into the oven, his seventy-year-old, gray-haired, stooping mother kept bustling.

Britt had more or less insisted he take a break. "Juggling knives blindfolded while riding a unicycle at the cliff's edge isn't instinctive behavior. A few months of it gets to most people. You should take some time away." To Kyle's rejoinder that he didn't exactly work for Britt anymore, the politician had answered, "Then accept it as advice from a friend. You're fried. Go away for a few days." So here he was.

He'd offered to help Mom and been refused. He'd been shooed away when he started to wash dishes without asking. He'd proposed in vain that she sit for a while. With Mom it could've been a gender thing; he suggested that she save the potato peeling for Carol, Kyle's sister, whose family was due around noon. Nothing worked. Dad no longer tried; he was in the den reading the morning paper.

Fine. Kyle knew from whence came his own stubbornness gene. "Say, Mom, you mentioned a scrapbook? I thought I'd take a look." The *St. Cloud Times* was generally hard-pressed to find a local angle to national, let alone interstellar, affairs—they had covered Kyle's stint on the Galactic Commission with (to Kyle) embarrassing fervor. Mom couldn't get enough, and had the fat binder full of yellow-highlighted clippings to prove it. She'd brought it up repeatedly since his arrival last night, undeterred by all changes of subject. He *knew* she'd sit beside him on the parlor sofa whenever he picked up the scrapbook—and she did. As he leafed through it, he caught from the corner of his eye a self-satisfied smile. Maybe he wasn't the only one smug about an exercise in applied psychology.

Living as he did at the epicenter of events, none of the main articles were surprising. The sidebars were more diverting. Upstate Minnesota was not without its share of cranks—two had accosted him at the Minneapolis-St. Paul Airport, and the F'thk arrival was all the proof they needed. That no facts tied the newcomers to supposed UFO sightings and alien abductions seemed not to matter.

The important thing was that Mom was off her feet. He proceeded to read, slowly.

✳   ✳   ✳

The 7-Eleven was mobbed. Not only was the convenience store the closest approximation to an open grocery this Thanksgiving Day afternoon, but it was half-time in a tied Cowboys-Vikings game. Two men in line ahead of Kyle wore Vikings caps with soft stuffed horns. As inane NFL headgear went, he preferred Green Bay cheesehead hats. He kept the opinion to himself.

He looked randomly around the store, killing time. A full head of white hair, glimpsed in an overhead security mirror, caught his eye. Was the stranger watching Kyle? The man began study-ing his boots self-consciously as Kyle turned toward him. With a shrug, Kyle shuffled to face the checkout counter again. Thinking, *This would be easier if I were Swelk*, he glanced over his shoulder at the dairy case's glass door. The somehow-familiar reflection peered back at him, the guy's expression a mix of brooding and expectation.

Hell, after many years out East, Kyle was a Redskins fan. He stepped out of line.

His observer was short, maybe five-six, with a gaunt face dominated by a hawklike nose and piercing eyes. Up close the man's hair was a pale, pale blond, not unusual here in Outer Scandinavia. Dark brown, almost black eyes *with* that hair were. "Do we know each other?"

"Um, no." Uncomfortable grimace around the chewed butt of an extinguished cigar. "Anyway, you don't know me. I feel I know you, Dr. Gustafson."

"Oh. Media coverage of the commission. My fifteen minutes of fame." It didn't explain why Kyle thought he *did* recognize this guy. "Sorry to have bothered you. I'm sure you have people to be with today."

As grief flooded the stranger's face, Kyle realized why the man looked so familiar.

"This will only take a few minutes," shouted Darlene over the keening of the air popper she'd brought from home. The loud whistle of the appliance's blower was soon punctuated by the rat-a-tat salvoes of exploding corn kernels. Melting butter sizzled in a pan on the stove top. Darlene warmed to the familiar sounds and scents. What could be more normal than movies and popcorn?

The venue was far from normal: Thanksgiving in a safehouse

with a fugitive ET. The microwave-free kitchen seemed to predate the Eisenhower administration. Cooking involved a freestanding gas range that would be used that evening to reheat the CIA-provided holiday dinners. The agents would eat, in ones and twos, at their convenience. They were invariably polite to Darlene, but at the same time intensely clannish. If she bothered with a reheated meal, she figured it would be eaten with Swelk.

Swelk lacked holiday expectations, and in any event she would synthesize her own dinner. The usual feedstock for her bioconverter was pizza crusts and leftover takeout Chinese. So, as the popcorn popped, Darlene was "cooking" for, and feeling sorry for, only herself. Her folks, God bless them, were on a cruise. Fail to make it home for three years running, and suddenly there's an expectation. She couldn't say why she'd declined Kyle's invitation to Minnesota.

On second thought, she could: confusion over what, beside professional, her relationship with Kyle was supposed to be. Darlene wasn't seeing anyone at the moment, nor did she care to. Her last relationship, with a partner at a cut-throat DC law firm, had ended badly when he forgot how to leave the go-for-the-jugular attitude at the office. Not that a covert war against interstellar aliens and the approach of Armageddon put one in the mood for a social life . . .

She had to laugh as Stripes sauntered into the kitchen from the hall. White markings around the kitten's eyes gave her an expression of permanent surprise. Cats for Swelk—sometimes Kyle's instincts were dead on. She valued Kyle as a colleague and thought they were becoming good friends. Unfortunately, his Gobi-dry humor and flirtation-impairedness had her at a loss about *his* intentions. Who knew what signal she'd have sent by going to meet his family? She'd think about sorting it out in a few months if civilization still existed.

Plastic popcorn bowl in one hand, a warm Diet Coke in the other, Darlene backed out of the kitchen, bumping the door open with a hip. "Ready to start . . ." she began. She turned to find Swelk splayed out on the dining-room floor, twitching. The din from the air popper had clearly obscured the thud of the ET hitting the planking. Nothing muffled the crashes of her bowl and soda can. "Swelk! What's wrong?" Two agents burst in from the hall as she spoke.

"I don't know." The computer took forever to translate. "I suddenly could not stand on all threes. The room was spinning around me." Swelk arose shakily, her second utterance put more quickly into English. "Whatever it was, it is going away."

The delayed translation was scary, bringing to mind slurred speech. Did Krulirim have strokes? "Is there anyone we should call?" That any human physician could treat the alien was implausible, but Darlene couldn't bear not acting.

"Yes." Sensor stalks bobbed in amusement, involuntary tremors marring the wry waggle with which Darlene had become familiar. "My doctor is unfortunately light-years away." In the awkward silence that followed, tremors subsided into mere tics.

"Ms. Lyons?" asked an agent economically.

"I don't see what we can do," she told the guards. One shrugged. They left. "Swelk, maybe we should skip the movies." A whiff of buttered popcorn rose as she cleaned up the worst of her mess. One species' aroma was another's toxic fumes. "Does this smell bother you?"

"It was not the smell." The digits of an extremity clenched momentarily in Krulchukor negation. "Make more, if you would like. As to the movies, it would comfort me to watch."

"Okay to the movies. I'll skip the food."

At Swelk's command, a hologram formed over the dining-room table, projected by the alien computer. Indistinguishable Krulirim milled about a packed circular room, as writhing spiders scrolled around the bottom of the image. Opening credits? Captions for Swelk's benefit, Darlene decided, as the translator intoned, in a voice unlike what it used for Swelk, "The Reluctant Neighbor."

She watched from a slat-backed Shaker chair, rapt but unhappy. Fascination with the alien film was understandable. Ditto her unhappiness with Swelk's unexplained episode.

She knew she was overlooking something of extreme importance. But what?

The rolling pasture was bleak and windswept, its dormant grass brittle beneath Kyle's shoes. The flapping wings of a crow breaking cover made the only sound. Then it was gone, and stillness returned.

He was a good mile from pavement. How stupid was he to let embarrassment bring him here? Too late he'd realized why the man at the 7-Eleven looked so familiar: a press photo in Mom's scrapbook. Andrew Wheaton's wife and son had disappeared, and he blamed the F'thk. That the Galactics hadn't appeared for another two months seemed unimportant.

"The farm breaks even," said Wheaton finally. A weather-beaten red barn was just visible in the distance behind him, past a stand of pin oaks. "Most years. With my night job at the airport we made . . . I make . . . ends meet."

"Twin Cities?" asked Kyle.

"St. Cloud Regional. I'm a baggage handler." He tapped with a scuffed boot tip at a tuft of grass. "Bunches of pilots radioed in about an unidentified light that night. The tower people talked all about it, but radar didn't see nothing."

An evening star? Venus appeared in the evening sky that time of year. Ball lightning? A small plane whose radar transponder was out of order? Several things could explain a mystery light in the night sky.

"The house was empty when I got there." A gust of wind stirred the farmer's pale hair. "Tina's car was in the drive. House lights was on. Junior's sheets was rumpled, so he'd been to bed. Dinner dishes was only half done. So they was home at around eight, same time the pilots seen the thing in the sky."

Kyle jammed his hands into his coat pockets. He felt sorry for the man, but how did that help? His body language must have conveyed those doubts.

"I drove home through snow. The only tire tracks at the house was from my truck. I found footprints, though. From boots, I mean. Their coats and boots were gone." Wheaton stared at a low area in the meadow. "They walked here, I think to check out the lights. They didn't come back."

"What did the police say?"

"Snow covered everything before the cops got here. They didn't believe me about the footprints. Said maybe a friend drove them away. Said maybe they left before the storm started, so that there'd be no tire traces under newer snow.

"They asked, did I beat them? Bastards. Changed their tune some when they couldn't find Tina and Junior nowhere. Now, they think I did it." He jerked his coat zipper up an inch. "Bastards," he repeated.

"It?"

"Think I killed 'em. Cops dug up a bunch of the farm. Didn't find nothing." A tear rolled down the farmer's cheek.

Jeez. Kyle didn't know how to respond. He studied the depression which Wheaton had indicated. Today was a day for déjà vu. First Andrew, and now the dip seemed familiar. Nothing grew here in November, but the dry grass in spots of the hollow was stunted and sparse. Kneeling for a closer examination, the ground's cold wicking through his jeans, the thinness of the grass was explained: the earth from which the few blades grew was compacted, like a dense clay. The word "clay" also teased his memory.

How these observation helped, if at all, eluded Kyle. All that he felt certain of, somehow, was that the despondent farmer had done no harm to his wife and child. "If you don't mind, I'll have the area checked out."

Wheaton nodded. He kept his face carefully composed, as though afraid to hope.

Walking back to his car and Andrew's pickup, Kyle recalled what Andrew had bought at the 7-Eleven: a turkey TV dinner and a six-pack. He could do nothing about the lost family, but he *could* address that sad and solitary holiday meal. "I hope you'll join me at my folks' house for Thanksgiving dinner."

CHAPTER 22

THE BLACKENED BLOTCH that marked Swelk's landing site dominated the view eastward from Krieger Ridge. Kyle had paced out the scar, and it was fifty yards wide at its narrowest. The only visible irregularities at the opposite end of the valley were three reddish patches that more suggested than presented themselves. Grass didn't grow well in those spots, and the clay-tinted earth peeked through.

In the Midwest, where Kyle had grown up, soil was *black*. Years after settling in Virginia, its red soil sometimes still caught his eye. These particular red areas, which together defined an acute isosceles triangle, had lodged themselves in his subconscious: they marked the landing site of the second F'thk lifeboat, that had followed Swelk. The three landing skids had borne the entire weight of the lifeboat, tamping down the ground underneath.

Kyle tore his eyes away from the photographic blow-up of the valley near his home. The time for speculation was past. It was time instead to see if he were imagining things.

Hammond Matthews jotted numbers onto a whiteboard. His annual winter beard, begun at Thanksgiving, was almost neat. By Easter, when he'd next shave, he would look like a mountain man . . . except for the white socks and sandals. Past and present lab directors were alone in the eavesdropper-proof confines of the shielded radiometrics lab.

Matt finished with a John-Hancockesque flourish. "The top number is a measurement: the weight of the charred remains of Swelk's lifeboat. Middle pair of numbers: upper and lower bounds of weight estimates for the F'thk lifeboat that followed her. The estimates derive from soil compression under the marks of the landing skids, just like you suggested. Measured wreckage weight falls nicely inside the bounds of that calculation, so the approximation method seems valid." Matt pantomimed a drum roll. "Last two numbers: the same range computation for the similarly configured compression marks in the pasture in Minnesota." He didn't bother stating the obvious: these numbers were *also* consistent with a landing by a F'thk lifeboat.

The result was only what Kyle had expected—and yet it was shocking in its implications. He crossed the room to the insulated carafe of coffee. Even a percolator or a hot pot would interfere with the lab's sensitive instruments. He was less interested in a refill than the opportunity to face away from his collaborator and good friend. Need-to-know sucked.

"Kyle, buddy?"

"Yeah." He studied his cup.

"Compared to what we do for a living, tracing whose property your samples came from wasn't much of a challenge. Neither was running a Web search on the name Andrew Wheaton. Can you guess what I'd like to know?"

Kyle turned. "How a F'thk lifeboat could land in Minnesota two months before the mother ship arrived. What the F'thk have to do with the Wheaton family disappearances. Why the F'thk would be snatching humans."

"Yes, to all of the above, although those questions are way beyond my pay grade." Matthews retrieved a paper scroll from a file-cabinet drawer, unrolling it across a desk. It was a world map, sprinkled with hand-drawn red circles. Most of the scribbles were in the US and Russia. "No, what I'm wondering is how many of these other UFO sightings in the past year also show evidence of F'thk presence."

With its window cracked to let out steam, the safehouse bathroom was freezing. Darlene showered quickly with the water turned to full heat. She ran out of hot water within minutes.

The bathroom mirror was covered with condensation when

she got out. Unfortunately, the one outlet in the bedroom she'd adopted was nowhere near its mirror. Shivering in her robe, she used her hair dryer first to clear a spot on the befogged mirror and then on her hair. She gave up on the job as soon as she achieved nonsopping wet.

Hair damp and pulled back in a pony tail, she bounded down the stairs for a mug of hot tea to wrap her hands around. Guards were talking softly on the front porch as she rounded the corner to the kitchen.

Swelk was spread-eagled on the kitchen floor, her limbs quivering.

"Again? What happened?" Her only answer was the dipping of stalks: a shrug. Why the hell weren't the agents ever around when this happened? Darlene knelt beside the alien, all thoughts of the cold forgotten. Eventually, as the twitching subsided, Darlene helped Swelk back to her feet. "What can I do?"

"I was suddenly dizzy. I do not know why." Wobbly on two limbs, Swelk braced herself with the third against a cabinet. "What can be done? Nothing like this has ever happened to me."

"Are you eating enough? Would you know if something were missing from your diet?"

"My food is fine. At least my equipment tells me so." Swelk fell silent, and seemed to withdraw. "I do not know what is happening. When I sleep, I dream of falling. When awake, I sometimes do fall."

"I wish there was some way I could help."

Swelk pointed upward. She could not get herself a drink without climbing onto the counter. It appeared she was too unsteady for the ascent. "If you would pour me a glass of water, and watch a movie with me, I would much appreciate it."

Inside what was, after all, a summer cabin, the howl of wind and the drumming of rain were loud. The storm, passing up Chesapeake Bay, was expected to become New England's first nor'easter of the season. No one had arrived at *this* crisis-team meeting by boat.

Whether because of the noise, or the inexplicable air of distraction from Fitzhugh and Bauer, Kyle found himself nearly shouting. "Guys, it's really quite clear-cut. We know from direct measurement what a Galactic lifeboat weighs. We know what indications it leaves behind at a landing site. There are *five* confirmed landing sites, each corresponding to an unexplained disappearance. The implication is that aliens kidnapped these people to figure out what makes us tick. What we're scared of. One more way to know how to push our buttons."

"Are all the sites in the US?" Britt polished his eyeglasses with his tie as he spoke.

"Yes, but that might be because we've only looked at suspected landings here. Scoping out prospects in Russia will take resources I don't have." Kyle looked pointedly at their CIA and DoD reps, but they avoided his gaze. Time again to suggest more information-sharing with the Russians? As he opened his mouth to propose it, Erin Fitzhugh's pager beeped.

"Hot shit!" yelled the CIA deputy director as she scanned the short text on the pager screen. Moments later, the general's pager burst into a short fanfare. Reading his own message, Ryan, too, broke into an out-of-character, ear-to-ear grin. They high-fived across the table.

"Good news?" asked Darlene dryly.

"Big time." Erin Fitzhugh interlaced her fingers and ostentatiously cracked her knuckles. "*Big* time. The Israeli Air Force just bombed the crap out of a hole deep in the Iranian desert."

Kyle's stomach lurched. Wasn't this just another step down the slippery slope to disaster? "War in the Middle East is somehow *good*? I thought our plan, such as it is, required keeping the visible tensions between us and the Russians."

"That's still the plan," said Bauer. "There's no chance of watching CNN out here, is there? Damn. Anyway, 'Hot shit,' as Erin so amusingly put it, is dead on. We were all but certain the Iranians had a surreptitious nuclear program. Our best evidence, though, was that they had only enough weapons-grade uranium for two or three bombs. There's radioactive fallout downwind of the air strike."

"So Iran is now probably nuke-free," Darlene filled in the blank. "With Israel's nuclear capability the world's worst-kept secret, the Iranians are much more likely to behave."

"Game, set, and match," agreed Fitzhugh.

Fine, then, it was good news (presumably cryptically conveyed) ... but only to the extent of extinguishing *one* of the fuses the aliens kept trying to light. And how many deaths had even this single victory cost? "It's the *Krulirim* we have to stop. The landings and kidnappings all predate the F'thk broadcast announcement and the appearance of the mother ship. These landings and abductions before the arrival of the so-called F'thk ... surely they substantiate Swelk's story."

Britt stood at a window, peering out over the Bay. The storm was receding. "Backs it up, yes. Proves it, no. You'd like me to conclude that because the F'thk arrived before we saw the mother ship that the mother ship cannot be real.

"You can't certify that the mother ship wasn't, for example, lurking behind the moon where we couldn't see it. You can't know that the mother ship didn't just arrive later than the F'thk, that the vessel we deal with wasn't a scout.

"The Israelis put out one fire for us. With good luck, and good planning, we can douse a few more." Britt turned toward the table, hands clasped behind his back. "I can tell you for a fact, the President will not sanction an action as desperate as an attack on starfaring aliens until he has absolute proof the mother ship doesn't exist ... or absolutely no alternative."

With *bad* luck, they'd all soon glow in the dark. Kyle took a deep breath. "Understood. I believe there is a way to determine, once and for all, whether the mother ship is real. We'll have only one shot at the test, and—you won't like this—the experiment *must* involve the Russians."

As the silence stretched, he suddenly realized that Britt, Erin Fitzhugh, and Ryan Bauer were grinning. Britt gestured at Erin.

"Oh, we trust the Russians right now," she said. "Iran is a Russian client, and guess who gave us the lead to locate the Iranian nuclear-weapons factory."

CHAPTER 23

THE GALAXIES WERE unimaginably distant, their violent, slow-motion collision unleashing equally unfathomable energies. Millions of years later, the tiniest fraction of that energy streamed past Earth. Ironically, after traveling so incredibly far, the X-rays produced by that intergalactic encounter were absorbed by Earth's thin skin of atmosphere.

"Your request surprised me, my friend." Sergei Denisovich Arbatov stood beside Kyle in the cluttered astronomic-studies lab at the University of Helsinki. Sergei's hairline had receded shockingly in a few months' time. Could stress do that? Some things hadn't changed: the twinkle in the Muscovite's eyes and, despite the onset of winter, his trademark deep tan. "NASA has several instruments capable of observing the object you selected. Your failure to comment why I would be interested also intrigued me." The personal delivery by the American ambassador of Kyle's letter might also have engendered some curiosity.

There was a time when research satellites were operated by large teams of technicians from gleaming control rooms arrayed with phalanxes of consoles. Such extravagance for mission control now applied mostly to manned space flights—of which there were none, with the shuttle fleet grounded and the Russians broke—and bad sci-fi movies. An entry-level workstation with Internet access to a steerable antenna sufficed. The PC on the dented wooden lab bench was, just barely, adequate.

Tarja Nurmi, the instrument controller there to assist them, half sat, half leaned on the lab stool in front of that PC. Her back was to Kyle and Sergei. Her tattered and too-large sweatshirt was incongruously emblazoned with a Virginia Tech seal. Her pale blond hair, common enough in this corner of the world, brought Andrew Wheaton guiltily to mind. The grim confirmation Kyle could provide—that the site of his family's disappearance *had* seen an alien landing—would do Wheaton little obvious good, while possibly endangering Earth's underground resistance.

Focus, Kyle directed himself sternly.

The names the young astrophysicist had been given for her visitors were aliases. If she wondered why, in a world possessed of a ubiquitous Internet, those guests insisted on observing in person, she made no comment. Language differences didn't stop her—she and the Russian and French coprincipal investigators for whom she usually toiled all communicated in English. Those co-PIs were ticked off and several time zones distant, fuming at the unexplained preemption by Rosaviacosmos of their long-scheduled viewings. Sergei, as science advisor to President Chernykov, had arranged the retasking of the Russian space agency's orbiting X-ray observatory.

Surely the Russian had analyzed Kyle's unexpected request before doing so. The American briefly inclined his head toward the Tarja's back. *I must be discreet.* "Yes, we have X-ray instruments in orbit. None has this exact viewing angle just now." The need to use a Russian satellite was actually fortunate. It should make Sergei much less likely to question what—Kyle fervently hoped—they would soon see. He was not about to verbalize why exactly *now* was so important, or that the biggest supercomputer at Franklin Ridge had number-crunched for days to identify this not-soon-to-be-repeated opportunity. "Are we ready, Tarja?"

"We're locked on now." With casual grace, she moused open a new window. A scatterplot popped onto the PC monitor, colored dots richly strewn across a black background, the many hues representing X-ray frequencies invisible to the human eye. The small blinking square at the window's exact center enclosed the blazing dot that was tonight's target. In the lower-right corner, a frequency-vs.-energy histogram summarized the radiation from the crashing galaxies. In the lower left, a real-time clock counted in milliseconds.

A large circle dominated one side of the window, part glowing crescent and the rest a lightlessness interrupted by a faint dusting of pinpoints. "The big disk is the moon, of course." The young Finn tapped the screen. "The crescent is what Earth sees right now of the sun-facing side. We're seeing directly reflected solar X-rays. What appears to be the dark side of the moon is blockage by the moon of the sky's X-ray background."

Sergei frowned. "Why are there *any* spots on the dark side?"

Tarja yawned and stretched before answering. Fair enough: it was 2:37 A.M. by local time. "Sorry. Those stray dots on the dark side come from the scattering of solar X-rays from all around the solar system. Reflections from planets and asteroids."

"Will the clock stay on-screen if you zoom in?" asked Kyle.

"It can." She yawned again. "Sorry." She keyed a new scale factor and the window was redrawn. The targeting square and the dot it encompassed lay near the dark edge of the moon.

Kyle crouched over Tarja's shoulder. The clock display, reading out in Coordinated Universal Time, was scarcely a minute from the instant he'd memorized. Forbidding himself to blink, he watched the dot creep closer and closer to the moon. A side of the targeting box kissed the limb of the moon, slid over the moon. Sergei, on his right, exhaled sharply seconds later as the multigalactic dot abruptly winked out, eclipsed by the moon.

"Get what you needed?" Stifling yet another yawn, she handed them diskettes containing the session's observational data.

Before the American could overcome his own sympathetic yawn, Sergei replied. "Yes, my young friend. We have." Tapping Kyle on the shoulder, the Russian added, "Perhaps it would be best if we took a walk."

The campus grounds were dark, deserted, and bitterly cold. The deserted aspect of those circumstances was good. "Interesting that you answered Tarja for me, Sergei." Kyle's breath hung in front of him.

Sergei hunched his shoulders against an icy gust. "You were very specific as to when a fairly unremarkable astronomical object must be observed. Such insistence, it makes one ponder."

The stars sparkled like diamonds. The crescent moon they had so recently "seen" by its X-ray reflection shone down with a cold white light. "Were your musings rewarded?"

"I had to wonder, as perhaps young Tarja would, were she more awake, why one would schedule an observation certain to be interrupted. Could it be, I asked myself, that I'm not here to see what my friend *said* he wanted to show me?" An eddy of snow swirled past them. "Was it only a coincidence that you wanted to look so near to the moon?"

"Go on." Did Sergei *really* know, or was he bluffing?

"There is something important in the vicinity of the moon."

Kyle scrunched his neck, in a vain attempt to shelter more of his face and head within his upturned collar. And he'd thought Minnesota was cold.

"Exactly on schedule, the edge of the moon hid our celestial X-ray source. But *that* eclipse was not what you brought me to see, was it?" Sergei grasped Kyle's coat sleeve. "More interesting, I think, is that our observation went uninterrupted *until* the moon blocked our view.

"It is time, *tovarich*, to explain why you expected the Galactic mother ship to be transparent to X-rays." The glaring political incorrectness of that Soviet "comrade" showed just how overwrought Sergei was. "And does such transparency mean, as I believe, that there is no mother ship?"

CHAPTER 24

ROOSEVELT AND CHURCHILL held several secret summits in the depths of World War II. Less often, both met with Stalin. It was assumed that the Axis Powers had spies in all the Allied capitals, but the leaders still managed to sneak away and meet.

Kyle searched for solace in that imperfectly remembered bit of history. Alas, the one war-time conference he knew by name was the infamous, arguably failed Yalta. He hoped that catastrophic encounter wasn't an omen.

He was one of a handful of Americans in the summit delegation. A Russian contingent of similar size was across the table. The table in question resided in a private estate an hour's drive outside Ankara. As far as the rest of the world knew, this was a gathering of oilmen to discuss new pipeline routes for Caspian Sea crude. The cover story excused secrecy amid tight security.

Also as far as rest of the world (and, hopefully, the aliens) knew, President Robeson and his senior advisors were on retreat at Camp David . . . but when Marine One, the presidential helicopter, had returned to its base in Quantico, Virginia, the summiteers were on board. A low-key motorcade that had to have made the Secret Service cringe took the entourage to the general-aviation section of Dulles International Airport outside Washington. Their Russian counterparts arrived in Turkey by equally circuitous, and, it was hoped, confidential means.

The room had been swept for bugs by the protection details of two presidents. Sergei, whom Kyle was glad but unsurprised to see, accompanied him on another inspection. This was one meeting most definitely *not* staged for hidden observers. Completing their rounds, they eyed the sumptuous buffet left by their absent host. Kyle hurried to his seat, pausing only to fill a mug with strong, muddy Turkish coffee. No time would be spent coddling the jet-lagged.

"Dmitri Pyetrovich, how are you?" began President Robeson. Dark bags beneath his eyes belied a light tone.

"Fine, fine." President Chernykov impatiently waved his interpreter to silence. A former KGB apparatchik, his English was excellent. "You, me, the bug-eyed monsters, we are all great. Is merely a vacation of old friends." The cigarette trembling in his hand underlined the sarcasm.

"I take your point, Dmitri. We cannot be out of the public eye for long, and we have much to do."

"I hope we can agree on something *to* do."

Kyle summarized America's findings, Sergei from time to time interjecting corroborative data from the Russian investigations. Kyle tried to be brief, but there were enough new players in the two delegations that much give-and-take was required. When he at last retook his chair, utterly drained, he was hopeful that the gist had been successfully conveyed.

The Galactic orbs, those supposed symbols of peace and unity so freely dispensed by the F'thk, were spying devices. The systematic destruction of the satellites each nation relied on for detecting ballistic missile launches, losses that gave credibility to the innuendoes spread by the aliens on their travels. The many peculiarities of the F'thk visitors. The anomalies of the mother ship: none of the expected gamma radiation, its complete lack of detail when viewed with microwaves, its transparency to X-rays. Human disappearances at sites marked by the signs of a F'thk lifeboat landing—often months before the announced arrival of the aliens. And the *pièce de résistance*: the alien defector whose shocking explanation—"it's only a movie"—explained every known fact.

A movie intended to climax in the nuclear self-annihilation of Earth.

Chernykov's expression grew uglier and uglier. None of this

could have been new to him, but the succinct totality was intense. "Damn these aliens. Damn them. I want to *strike*. Enough, I say, of science projects." He snarled something in Russian.

General Mikhail Denisovich Markov, Chernykov's military advisor, sat ramrod straight in his chair, looking ill at ease in his civilian clothes. A jagged scar angled down his left cheek. He reddened at his president's words.

"Who speaks today about how we will destroy these evil creatures?" said the American translator. Something in the delivery suggested a serious toning down of Chernykov's comment.

A muttered Russian response. Chernykov cut off the translator. "My military feels we cannot attack. The once-proud Russian armed forces cower from a movie company on a rundown cargo ship."

Kyle's fingers dug into the padded arms of his chair. This was no time for macho crap. Britt might later tear him a new one, but Kyle had to speak. "This *movie company* has a starship at its disposal. They have a fusion reactor. I've seen their incredibly powerful masers—microwave-frequency lasers—destroy a space shuttle. We know they can fry satellites with X-ray lasers. Swelk, our defector, says the starship uses lasers to blast space junk. If they can vaporize objects hurtling at them at an appreciable fraction of light speed, do you think anything we launch at them can matter? We damn well *should* be afraid of attacking."

His words tumbled out, faster and faster. "Suppose we attack and do succeed? Will the fusion reactor blow up? Will the stardrive, about which we haven't a clue, explode? How big a crater will be made if that ship does go boom?"

Chernykov, his upper lip curled, studied faces turned ashen at Kyle's outburst. "I thought we had come here to prepare to *act*. They have blown up your shuttle *Atlantis*. They have cost each of us one of our finest submarines. Will you ask them, 'Please, go home now'?"

What of the five crew on that shuttle, or the *hundreds* on those subs? The never-distant image of the fireball above Cape Canaveral blossomed anew in Kyle's mind. How many millions had to join them? A hand was suddenly squeezing Kyle's forearm. A warning from Britt . . .

"Dmitri." President Robeson's voice oozed calm reason. Kyle had learned over the past few months that the icy calm masked bottled anger. At whom this anger was directed was not obvious. "We concur on the need to act. That agreement leaves many questions. What are the aliens' vulnerabilities? How can we exploit such weaknesses? When and where can we strike?"

"This is better, Harold. Please tell me more."

"General Bauer will explain, Dmitri."

Ryan went to the head of the table. "Dr. Gustafson raises pertinent points about the complexity of an attack on the aliens."

Chernykov frowned but held his peace.

"The aliens' laser weapons would be a factor in any attack on the ship in flight. We must assume, as the good doctor suggests, that the ETs can acquire and destroy targets quickly. Our bombs and missiles would be nothing more than slow-moving space junk, easily killed."

A burst of Russian words stopped Bauer. The American translator rendered Markov's interruption. "Certainly, General, the starship must handle an occasional meteor. Would it handle many targets at once? Perhaps we can overwhelm their defense with a massed attack."

Bauer's forehead creased in thought.

This was madness—but could he raise *another* objection without being escorted from the room? Kyle began drumming on the table; as people looked his way in annoyance, he managed to catch Sergei's eye.

"Quite ingenious," said Sergei, taking the hint. "Still, I hope you will indulge a physicist's view of the problem. Our fastest missiles go only a few kilometers per second. In CIA debriefing notes I have been shown, this Swelk claims their ships approach light speed. As you know, the speed of light is three hundred *thousand* kilometers per second. That's how fast their ship overtakes space junk that's more or less stationary. At even one-hundredth that speed—which rate they surely exceed, or else a trip between even the closest stars would take centuries—they are accustomed to targets moving orders of magnitude faster than anything we can fire."

Britt leaned forward. "Dr. Arbatov, I don't follow you. You discuss the speed at which their ship travels. The issue relates to their ability to counter a massed attack by our missiles."

"Excuse me. I will make the point more directly. Imagine the alien starship overtaking a pebble in space at a thousand times the speed of our rockets. They must spot it, track it, shoot and destroy it, all in an instant. May not their defenses handle each slow Earth-fired missile, one by one by one, each with ease?" He smiled disarmingly at the American general. "Your fine navy has Aegis cruisers that can shoot down missiles traveling at hundreds of miles per hour. How many hang gliders must an assailant deploy to overwhelm an Aegis cruiser?"

Swelk came awake with a whimper, the world whirling around her. At least the spinning tended to stop after her eyes had been open for a while. Why could she not sleep soundly?

Guilt, loneliness, a fault in the bioconverter on which her life entirely depended . . . she had many theories. Perhaps confinement. Perhaps nothing more than the intermittent bonging of the angular ugliness that Darlene called a grandfather clock. A recess of Swelk's mind insisted it had recently heard four bongs.

Climbing shakily to an erect position, she began to prowl yet again what little she was allowed to experience of her adoptive world. The only humans around this late were her guards, outside on patrol or else in their trailer. Enough moonlight filtered through the curtains for her to forego Earth's unpleasant artificial illumination.

Four rooms upstairs, four down. Compared to her cabin on the *Consensus*, these chambers were luxuriously spacious, but there was no denying her situation. She had traded her own kind's open hostility for the less obvious, but no less real, distrust of the humans.

She was not allowed outside the building. What little news she was given of Earth's peril—due, she could not help reminding herself, to her own gullibility—was highly selective. Her many questions were deflected with polite evasions. And Kyle, the human to whom she had fled in hope and guilt and desperation, had disappeared without explanation.

Blackie stirred at the soft sounds of Swelk's approaching tread. The kitten stretched languorously, rubbing one eye with a forepaw. She tipped onto twos, using her lame limb to scoop up the yawning kitten. The kitten burrowed herself into the complicated three-way juncture between the limb's extremities and broke into a loud purr. That gentle rumble, pressed against the deformity that so defined Swelk, was ineffably soothing.

If only the humans' distrust could be so readily overcome.

*   *   *

Cooler heads prevailed and declared a recess. While most of the summiteers attacked the breakfast buffet, Britt and President Robeson disappeared into the estate's richly paneled, high-ceilinged library. When they reappeared, the President had an index card in his hand. After a final glance at his notes, Robeson cleared his throat.

"The president," and Robeson nodded at Chernykov, "made a comment earlier that we did not pursue. That remark was something like, 'Can we ask them to go home?' It was an idea expressed in the heat of debate, and perhaps we did not give Dmitri Pyetrovich's observation the attention it deserved.

"We are all outraged at the deaths the aliens have caused. Having said that, revenge is seldom a wise basis for policy. Our prevailing interest, I submit, is the avoidance of future losses . . . most particularly prevention of a nuclear war. Our scientific folks," and he saluted Sergei and Kyle with a glass of ice water, "have done us a great service. It is time to focus our minds on 'the man behind the curtain.' May not these Krulirim illusionists, like the great and terrible Wizard of Oz, bow to reality? They have been found out!"

Explaining the simile to the Russians took longer than the whole speech. As that got sorted out, Kyle marveled anew at watching a master politician at work. Crediting Chernykov with wisdom for what had been biting sarcasm . . . what a slick way to let the Russian gracefully distance himself from suicidal attack plans. Not for the first time, Kyle wished he had absorbed a fraction of the people skills to which Washington had exposed him.

"I apologize, Mr. President, for my unfamiliar reference. Your mastery of English and of our culture are such that I sometimes forget where you are from." Robeson removed his glasses, peered through them at a window, then wiped them vigorously with his handkerchief. (A premeditated moment of quiet, Kyle suspected, for the Russian to take in the flattery.) "The point, I hope, remains valid. We have known for months the aliens' purpose: incitement to nuclear war. For all that time, if I may be allowed another theatrical figure of speech, we have been afraid not to be seen playing our parts. The aliens, we told ourselves, want to destroy us. The owners of that awe-inspiring mother ship could certainly obliterate us if we did not cooperate. Our best theory for the curious indirection of the obvious alien hostility was fastidiousness: their consciences would be cleaner if, in the end, we blew ourselves up.

"But things have changed. Our understanding has changed, thanks to a courageous Krul from whom we now know what is truly going on, thanks to rigorous scientific research to verify what Swelk has told us. There is only the one spaceship that flits from country to country, stirring up trouble. They incite us to self-destruction not from any intent to work indirectly, but because only *self*-destruction serves their purposes.

"So I return to the Dmitri Pyetrovich's insightful question." Robeson, who had been pacing, halted across the table from Chernykov. "If they are told their cinematic goal will not, and cannot, be achieved, may they *not* simply go home?"

The atmosphere in the conference room, all morning so gloomy and foreboding, suddenly changed. As only Nixon could have gone to China, only this American president could propose accepting their losses from the aliens and moving on.

Despite exhaustion, jet lag, and incredible pressures, Robeson cut an imposing figure. Kyle could not help but recall his amazing biography. Marine captain and decorated Vietnam vet. Crusading state's attorney, fearlessly pursuing organized-crime families in New Jersey. Trustbuster in the Department of Justice. Two-term senator with a passion for national-security policy. Still early in his first term as President, making headway fulfilling a campaign promise of military reform.

Yes, it was a speech that only Robeson could have made, and he had done so masterfully.

Aw, crap! thought Kyle. Here we go again.

For fear of eavesdropping, all personal electronics had been left outside the conference room. Deprived of his PalmPilot and Net access, Kyle couldn't hope to get the quotation exactly right—and it was probably by Anonymous, anyway. The essence of the line, in any event, was crystal clear. "Every complex problem has a solution that is simple, obvious . . . and wrong."

You haven't lived until the presidents of two nuclear powers scowl at you. But having done so, could you then live *long*?

Britt, with characteristic poise, asked only, "What's on your mind, Kyle?"

Here goes. "It's possible the Krulirim will go home if we ask. Before their arrival they had no reason to wish Earth ill. That said, there's a small voice whispering in my ear."

He'd just seen a politician at work, flattering Chernykov. "One of my flaws, I freely admit, is the tendency to view everything through the lenses of science and logic. In my early attempts to influence government policy, when you first brought me to Washington, I relied too rigorously on logic. I also crashed and burned far more often than I succeeded. A very wise man"—okay, Britt, recognize yourself here!—"eventually got through to me. I now occasionally know enough to ask, 'Can the other guy afford to live with my logic?' What worries me at this moment is how unclear it is that the Krulirim can afford to just leave.

"To be brief, I wonder . . . will Swelk's former shipmates accept the risk that what they attempted here will remain secret? Is that a gamble they can afford to take?"

Doubts were appearing on faces around the table, including, he was relieved to see, on the faces of both presidents.

"I'm trying to imagine how the conspirators may see their situation. Must they not be asking themselves, Will we ever be held to account for our actions? What if another Krulchukor ship were to discover Earth? If humanity refuses to obliterate itself, how soon until Earth's starships are visiting our worlds?

"What if humans and other Krulirim do meet? Our aliens killed the crew of the *Atlantis*. They've presumably killed all the people they kidnapped, before their splashy public arrival, to better understand us. They're responsible for yet more deaths, beginning with the submarine catastrophe. We have film of their ship at sites across our planet. We have by now millions of the orbs and a wrecked lifeboat from their ship: technology whose origin they can't refute. In short, the plotters can hardly deny trying to stampede us to self-genocide."

"Even if we do nuke each other, some records may survive." Britt spoke with his eyes shut, deep in thought. "And survivors may still speak with future visitors. And that means . . ."

" . . . And that means," completed Kyle, "there's a very real risk—whether we blow ourselves up or not—that the ETs planned all along to utterly obliterate humanity before leaving our solar system."

✶   ✶   ✶

"Depend on it, sir," Samuel Johnson is said to have remarked, "when a man knows he is to be hanged in a fortnight, it concentrates his mind wonderfully." The summiteers outside Ankara, eye-to-eye with the extinction of humanity, found their attention wholly focused. That convergence gave birth, at last, to a terrifying plan possessed of but a single virtue—no one saw any reason why the plan was *necessarily* doomed to failure.

Which wasn't to say a failure wasn't likely.

Attempting to destroy the starship was too risky. Ignoring the starship and hoping it would depart in peace was likewise too risky. And that left . . . capture.

Commandos would strike the next time the starship visited a Russian or an American city.

CHAPTER 25

"I THINK I MISJUDGED you." Ryan Bauer, a water tumbler full of ice and amber liquid in his hand, flung himself into the captain's chair across from Kyle. "In a fingernails-across-the-blackboard sort of way, you're all right."

The borrowed private jet, most specifically *not* designated Air Force One, was plushly carpeted and richly appointed. There were no flight attendants aboard, in the interests of the trip's secrecy, but the Cessna's pantry came stocked for major partying. With the summit over, and serious attack-planning impossible until they got home, the passengers were taking advantage. "You'll turn my head, General. Or is it the bourbon speaking?"

"Scotch." Ice cubes tinkled as Bauer downed a healthy swig. "But in a good cause."

"Okay." Kyle had no idea where this was going.

"You're all right," the flyer repeated. "You have a good head on your shoulders and an insane willingness to speak your mind."

"So what good cause does the Scotch support?"

"My willingness to step onto a plane." Laughing, he nabbed a jumbo shrimp from Kyle's plate. "Not what you expected, was it."

"Most pilots actually like airplanes."

"It's not that." Bauer leaned forward conspiratorially. "You understand these things. I'll gladly fly after the Tea Party."

Tea Party was the code name for the as-yet unscheduled assault on the starship. What Kyle failed to grasp was what he supposedly understood. "Excuse me?"

"Beam weapons." Bauer expropriated another shrimp. "The lasers on the moon use visible-light frequencies, so that we can see the hologram. They took out the *Atlantis* and that Proton with microwave frequencies. The early-warning birds are being fried with X-rays. Why X-rays, do you suppose?"

"Because the atmosphere blocks X-rays. If the aliens had used microwaves, like they did with the *Atlantis*, we and the Russians would have had a better chance to see what was really going on, instead of automatically blaming each other for the saticide. Some of those downward-stabbing microwaves could have been detected on the ground. We don't have beam weapons in space, and neither do the Russians . . . as far as we know, anyway."

"Saticide. I like that. Hafta suggest it to someone at the Pentagon." Bauer admired the spectacular alpine scenery rushing by far below. "Swelk's ugly friends have lasers that are far too tunable for my liking. Now, whenever I'm flying, I feel like a sitting duck."

Tunable lasers. Microwave beams tuned to an excitation energy for liquid hydrogen had exploded the fuel tank of the *Atlantis*. X-rays from the same alien satellites continued to destroy Earth's satellites. The leisurely pace at which Earth's satellites were targeted had been a mystery. Since Swelk's defection, Kyle had come to believe it was plot-related. Film plot, that was. Rualf, no friend of Swelk's, presumably wanted his bugs to capture plenty of suspenseful scenes in the build-up to Armageddon.

"Kyle, buddy. Are you with me?"

Tunable lasers. How separated were the excitation frequencies of liquid hydrogen and jet fuel? They were surely much closer together than microwaves and X-rays. "Sadly, Ryan, I *am* with you . . . but maybe you're not worried enough. Why limit your misgivings to attacks on the jet fuel in planes? What about petroleum pipelines? Natural-gas storage tanks? Hell, what about ordinary everyday gasoline?"

"Yeah, you're all right." Bauer downed another healthy swig of scotch. "Planning for Tea Party just got a whole bunch more complicated."

"How so?"

"Because," said Bauer, "you may be right. We and the Russians had better plan to attack all the alien satellites at the same time commandos storm the ship on the ground."

The F'thk ambassador trotted briskly up the ramp into the gaping airlock. As was his custom, H'ffl was the last of the delegation to come aboard. He stood in the airlock, gazing serenely over six hundred thousand smiling Pakistanis, until the outer door thumped shut.

Ridiculous two-sided creatures.

"Helmet, clear. Unit, off." The effect of Rualf's first command was to give him a view of the cargo bay. The robot through whose cameras he had been seeing remained in the airlock. His second command put the robot itself into its idle mode. Stiff from spending much of an Earth day inside the teleoperations gear, he cautiously disengaged his limbs from its delicate controls. With a squeal of delight, he freed his sensor stalks from the restrictive helmet. All around him, members of the troupe were extracting themselves from their own equipment. They all moved like Rualf felt: clumsy and stiff from long confinement.

It was night shift by ship's time, and he strode grandly through the mostly empty corridors to the officers' mess. Control of a F'thk required precise motions of the digits; flexing and stretching and moving boldly felt wonderful.

His mood was far from the euphoria the strutting suggested. The humans, in a display of sly animal cunning, continued in their stubborn refusal to destroy themselves. The Pakistani junta, the true subjects of this visit, were not progressing toward an attack on India with nearly the speed Rualf would have liked. At least the generals had rounded up a good crowd of extras.

How long until the captain's still good-natured rumblings of impatience turned serious? How long until the captain insisted on a return to civilization? Or could Grelben, his ship heavily mortgaged even before the interstellar detour, afford to go home without his cut of this film?

"No rest for the wicked," he announced to no one in particular. It was an Earth expression learned from one of the first freaks they had abducted The expression amused Rualf greatly. The freak, of course, was long beyond amusement. He changed direction on impulse, deferring his snack to go instead to the bridge.

"How was . . . Islamabad?" asked Grelben. The question was a courtesy; his attention was mostly on a maintenance console.

"Fine, Captain. Very interesting." Rualf reared onto twos to thoughtfully flex the digits of his third extremity. "Could I have a word with you in private?"

"Take over," Grelben told a junior officer. "I want a report by shift's end on the status of the environmental system. To Rualf he added, "Come to my cabin."

They walked in silence to the captain's quarters. Inside, Rualf admired the hologram of a Salt Sea shorescape. "Beautiful scenery. I understand why you want to acquire property there."

"Which implies completion of our little project here. I hope what you want to discuss is the imminent completion of our undertaking."

Rualf tipped toward the captain in an insincere show of respect. "I've been thinking about that happy day. With their many shortcomings, the humans could fail to do a proper job of self-destruction. I can envision a situation where we have all the recordings needed for a three-square of movies—but a few survivors still retain some technology."

Grelben trained two sensor stalks on him. Inside the small cabin, such direct scrutiny was a frank, almost rude, stare. "Are you saying your plan is not working?"

"Of course not." If it *were* true, he would not say that. "We set out to capture scenes that we could not invent, and we have those. I could make terrific films now."

The staring eyes narrowed shrewdly. "I remember bold promises of nuclear destruction. Special effects that you have yet to produce."

"I will." Rualf was confident the F'thk could goad *some* humans into a nuclear exchange, which would suffice for the movie. That said, only the Russians and Americans had the capacity to do truly global damage. For reasons that remained unclear, and despite his best efforts, the Russian freaks and the American freaks kept recoiling from full-scale warfare.

The worry gnawing at Rualf's gut was devastatingly simple. What if Swelk had been correct about the humans' potential?

The *Consensus* could not leave behind an unobliterated Earth. Krulirim were long-lived, especially those who, like his troupe, did much relativistic traveling. Until the destruction of the space shuttle and the subsequent abandonment of their space station, the Earthlings had been, if just barely, spacefaring. How long, if they did not destroy themselves, before they became starfaring?

His kind had freely pillaged the worlds of the primitive species they came across—but the savages were never overtly harmed. An encounter between humans and another Krulchukor ship or a Krul-settled world could be disastrous.

There had to be a plan to destroy Earth if the freaks refused to follow his script.

"So why did you want to see me?" Grelben had stopped staring, if only long enough to pour himself a drink.

"It occurred to me we have an option. We are closest to success with countries having smaller stockpiles of nuclear weapons. Hostilities between two such countries will give us almost everything we could hope for. We may want to consider leaving once that kind of war happens. It could get us home sooner." Time to see what the captain was made of. "But it would require us to do a little cleanup."

Grelben stoppered his flask. His penetrating gaze returned to Rualf. "Some fumigation?"

Great minds, it appeared, thought alike. "That's right."

"I like to clean up after myself." The captain waggled his sensor stalks in amused satisfaction. "I happen to have given some thought to how it could be accomplished."

The strip-mall restaurant boasted, using the verb loosely, an eclectic mix of Chinese wall hangings, a bar filled with brass fixtures and potted ferns, and art-deco furniture. It was shortly after six o'clock on a Saturday evening, and not quite half the tables were occupied. The Hunan Tiger evidently wasn't the first eatery to occupy this location. It was unlikely to be the last.

Amid the ebb and flow of diners' conversations, Kyle had an epiphany: *I need to get out more.* Two men in a nearby booth looked away in embarrassment as he caught them eyeing him. He shrugged and smiled—his fifteen minutes of fame again. Or they were staring at Darlene, which would have combined bad manners with good taste.

"We won't be talking much shop tonight." Darlene had been scarfing down rice noodles; she pushed away the half-empty bowl. "What were you thinking, suggesting this place?"

"That it would be nice not to talk shop for a change." And that this was the calm before the storm. He refilled their tea cups, awaiting her response.

A brief smile chased away an even shorter flash of surprise. "Yes, I'd like that."

"So what's your story?"

"More a vignette than a story. I'm from Iowa. Mom taught French in high school; Dad, German." She quit talking as the waiter delivered their egg rolls, and didn't resume when he left.

Ah, a fellow Midwesterner *and* an only-in-the-workplace extrovert. No wonder he could relate. "Therefore you became a diplomat to prevent another European war?"

She had a nice laugh. "I'm told the French were the aggressors in this case."

"Go on."

"In my own understated way, I rebelled—I studied Spanish. That led me to Latin American history. I don't have the patience to teach, so here I am."

He spooned duck sauce onto his egg roll. "If you don't have patience, why doesn't working in government make you *crazy*?" He canted his head thoughtfully. "Or has it?"

She'd just begun a snappy comeback when his cell phone chimed. *Very* few people knew this number. "Hold that retort."

If the summons wasn't unexpected, its timing was. He waved over their sullen waiter. "Please cancel the rest of our order." To Darlene, he explained as much as he could in public. "We have to get back to town."

"We're not ready." Ryan Bauer's tone carried conviction. "Most of North America is covered, in theory. The Russians tell me the same about central and eastern Europe. Hawaii and most of Russia east of the Urals are still hanging out there. And last I heard, a few people live in Africa, Latin America, most of the European Union, China, India."

The crisis team had reconvened at Britt's urgent summons. Wind rattled the cabin windows; the sky was forebodingly gray. Today's agenda had only one topic: how soon could the *Consensus* be assaulted? Britt didn't like the answer he was getting. Or rather the nonanswer. "Ryan, that's irrelevant. I asked about the starship."

"Britt, you've seen Kyle's study. Their weapons satellites can kill an airliner within a minute. We know they routinely scan our cities with low-power beams. That's how they do a readout of the infernal orbs. A frequency tweak and a squooch more power, and the same scans will explode cars instead. What would that do to, say, London or Rio or Tokyo?" Ryan thumped the table. "Our strategic defense labs are all in-country, not surprisingly. Same with the Russians. Those labs are where the experimental beam weapons are. To have a prayer of protecting anyone else, we need to deploy, and in secret, to other spots around the world."

A Franklin Ridge study sat in front of Kyle. His lab had done its usual beyond-thorough job. Bauer, if anything, was downplaying the potential disaster. Urban sprawl routinely engulfed once-isolated refineries and natural gas tanks. And natural gas had become the fuel of choice for small, city-sited electric power plants. These new plants were everywhere, run by factories and electric utilities alike. Estimated casualties of a microwave strike from enemy satellites: tens of thousands per city, almost instantaneously.

"I said, how soon, General?" Britt's voice was icy.

"Britt. Since we've started down the path of reviewing our vulnerabilities to the satellites, it'd help me, at least, to finish that." Darlene had read the study, too. Erin Fitzhugh nodded her concurrence.

"Five minutes," begrudged Britt, bending only slightly to the unusual display of unanimity. Bad news as yet unshared peeked out from his eyes. "Then I expect a number, Ryan. And it better be measured in days."

"Five minutes," Bauer agreed. "Very discreetly, I've had the best analysts at BMDO"—the Ballistic Missile Defense Organization—"look into this. Keeping the enemy satellites from doing who knows what means engaging them the moment we reveal ourselves."

"Engage them how?"

"Any way we can, Britt. We have experimental ground-based ABM and ASAT, antiballistic missile and antisatellite, laser weapons. So do the Russians. Those can engage enemy satellites that are reasonably close to overhead. We have some mothballed air-launched ASAT missiles, launched from F-15s. Those can be deployed overseas, but that will take a little time. The Russians have tested a space-mine system. That basically put bombs into orbit, bombs that are exploded when their orbits approach a target. And we can improvise weapons, fitting ballistic missiles with infrared sensors. The ET targets are stealthed, but they can't help radiating excess heat that we can see."

A thunderclap shook the cabin. Seconds later, a sloppy mix of rain and sleet began pelting the roof and walls. Britt stared downhill at the wind-whipped bay. "I remember Sergei's glider analogy. Can ASAT missiles accomplish anything, or are they more for our consciences? I won't delay for symbolism."

"Oh, we'll accomplish something. I guarantee it." Bauer shook his head sadly. "We'll draw their fire. If we're really lucky, the commandos will penetrate the starship and get the aliens to call off the satellites, before they've done real damage to civilian targets."

Megadeaths were riding on one roll of the dice. Kyle took a deep breath. "Britt, the Russians agree with the plan of deploying rudimentary civil defense before the raid. You *know* that. What's going on?"

"You have to specify your Russians. President Chernykov, yes. Your friend Sergei, yes. The ultranationalists, no." Britt turned away from the window and the storm. "The Russian ambassador brought a dispatch to the White House this morning. It's about yesterday's gangland shoot-out in Moscow."

The story had merited two paragraphs in the morning's *Washington Post*: cops and robbers and a warehouse fire. "I don't get it," Kyle said.

When had Britt ceased looking distinguished and begun looking *old*? "It had nothing to do with the Russian Mafia. The nationalists learned Chernykov's government leaked the site of the Iranian nuclear-weapons depot. They were furious at the betrayal of a long-time Russian ally.

"Bottom line, there was a coup in the works. The fire was to cover up the real story—a botched raid by the Interior Ministry police. Chernykov thinks he can suppress the story for maybe a week. He hasn't trusted the nationalists' judgment enough to bring them in on the real aliens situation." He raised an interrogatory eyebrow at Erin Fitzhugh.

"The Agency doesn't trust them either," she answered. Britt's news was apparently not a surprise to her. "Russia's sacred destiny, restore the glorious empire of the golden communist era, yada yada yada. I wouldn't trust the nationalists with Swiss Army knives, let alone nukes. Problem is, the military and internal-security forces are riddled with sympathizers."

"Thanks, Erin," said Britt. "Dmitri was advising the president, in an act of incredible statesmanship, that he may not be able to retain power much longer, at least not without entrusting the nationalists with the truth about the aliens. Possibly as little as two weeks.

"The Consensus is scheduled to visit Washington in six days. That's how long, General, you have to get prepared."

Kabuki theater, ballet, and medieval passion plays.

Darlene sank with a sigh of quiet contentment into her favorite chair. A cup of tea sat beside her on the end table. She hadn't been in her own house much these past few months. Only rotten weather and the twilight finish of today's crisis meeting on the Bay had brought her home tonight, instead of driving another two hours to the safehouse.

Indian Devadasi temple dancers and Chinese shadow-puppet theater.

Diplomats spent hours politely observing the traditional dramatic arts of other countries. At the start of her career, that had included countless—and endless—*zarzuelas*, the Spanish variation on opera. Sadly, understanding the dialogue and lyrics made opera even more artificial.

Aboriginal storytellers banging clapsticks and drums.

At the zap of a remote, the gas log in the fireplace lit with a whoosh. The flames appeared twice—directly, behind the fireplace's tempered glass doors, and again reflected from her big-screen TV. The television was off . . . she'd had it up to *here* with visual entertainment.

Her long-last-at-home serenity was evaporating. Guess who wasn't in the defense/spy circle? Guess who wasn't Britt's protégée? Now take a wild guess who was tasked to watch movies?

Despite years of on-the-job desensitization and her initial enthusiasm, the Krulchukor films were grinding her down. Earth's covert resistance had *so* few members—how had she wound up in such a meaningless and unproductive role? This was like too many overseas assignments, when she'd been the sacrificial diplomat nodding through some lavish cultural extravaganza the ambassador had refused to attend.

She tucked herself into an afghan. How many movies had she watched so far with Swelk? Six, she thought, but they all blurred together. Swelk had started her with *The Reluctant Neighbor*. Pausing the holographic film every few minutes to ask questions, re- and rere-watching scenes to catch stuff she realized she'd missed, training herself to recognize alien cinematic conventions . . . that first movie had stretched itself out over twelve hours. Kyle had asked her to describe it, and the best she could come up with was "Victorian comedy of manners meets film noir." Then came *Circle of Friends*, ten and a half hours, and *Strength in Numbers*, ten. The movies weren't getting shorter, but she was acquiring some facility at reading a Krul's body language. The new skill reinforced a conviction that Swelk was telling them the truth.

So? If she accepted the concept of a world-threatening hostile theater company, it wasn't much of a stretch to believe that the one Krul she had met could act.

Darlene eyed the heap of mail a neighbor had been regularly bringing inside. She couldn't bring herself to look at it. What came next? Oh, yes. *Revenge of the Subconscious*. She'd had high hopes for that; it contained, Swelk had advised, the dream sequence based on extinct Krulchukor monsters. Even a human could see the resemblance to the once enigmatic F'thk. Darlene had once more found herself believing the little ET.

And again that movie was a predictable morality play. Conformity is good; individuality is an aberration. Fit in, get along, understand the other Krul. Empathy, empathy, empathy.

Darlene found herself on her feet, hunting for a snack. Her milk was two weeks past its expiration and lumpy; she returned the cereal to the pantry and heated canned soup. The movies were rich with nuanced relationships and subtle societal cues, replete with hints of cultural structure she was only beginning to notice. They were invaluable as social commentary, but it was *so* hard, when viewing them so intensively, to get past the boringly consistent moral.

Going Home had made Swelk cry—at least weeping was how Darlene understood the collapse of Swelk's sensor stalks into overcooked-pasta flacidity. The title alone, given Swelk's situation, was enough to make Darlene's eyes mist. The ET had no expectations of ever seeing home again. Dammit, she *liked* Swelk, but her job did not allow her to trust the alien.

Darlene returned to the den and its cheerful fire. She couldn't even remember the name of one movie. She had to tell herself she did good for the cause at the team meetings—she couldn't see what she accomplished as a film critic. Or did she even delude herself that she contributed in the group? She hadn't been brought to the big meeting with the Russians.

Flickering flames, familiar surroundings, comfort food . . . she plopped back into her arm chair. Cultural force-feeding not-withstanding, she really did know her immersion in Krulchukor social structures and conventions was invaluable. It had to be, didn't it?

Think, woman.

She found a memory instead of a thought: Kyle dismissing her plot summaries as "Chick flicks on steroids." Real helpful.

Or was it?

"It's only a movie." Those were among Swelk's first words to Kyle. Only a *Krulchukor* movie. A movie directed by Rualf, as were, supposedly, all the films Darlene had been lamenting. What sense did the coming apocalypse make as a Rualf film?

More, even, than *Revenge of the Subconscious*, the film in which humanity was unwillingly starring would have spectacular visual effects. Wide distribution of Galactic orbs finally made sense—no self-respecting Krulchukor movie could get by on explosions. It needed pathos. Heads of state and *their* orbs would be vaporized when the missiles hit . . . but the troupe could continue scanning orbs in the countryside. Plenty of poignancy and social interest as chaos and fallout spread.

It was a stunning insight. Shivering, Darlene reclaimed the afghan earlier cast aside. She *knew* there was something else here, some other implication waiting to be recognized.

When it finally came to her, she actually clapped her hands in glee.

Britt was the product of old money and a multigenerational tradition of public service. His mother was a past national-society president of the DAR. A deep social chasm separated the landmark Arledge mansion from Darlene's humble home.

When enlightenment struck, well past midnight, she didn't hesitate to drive over. Time truly was of the essence.

"It's all right, Bill," Britt told the Secret Service agent who answered her knock. Instead of the silk pajamas and velvet smoking jacket she'd envisioned, her host wore a plaid flannel shirt over cargo pants. She must have looked surprised. "And I put them on one leg at a time."

He led her into a sitting room, then cut short her nervous visual search. "No orbs in the house. No gadgets in this room that could possibly be tapped. Daily bug searches. What can I get you to drink?"

"Nothing, thanks." Darlene was glad he had a fire going. His burnt real logs. She stood by the hearth, arms outstretched to warm her hands. "You know that tea party we're planning for a few days from now?

"I think I know an easier way for the partygoers to get in."

CHAPTER 26

RUALF RAPPED CONFIDENTLY at the cabin door behind which, he had good reason to suspect, the captain was asleep. One extremity of his raised limb held an ornately carved flask; a second extremity clasped matching goblets.

"What is it?" Grelben's voice was groggy and abrupt, as if to disprove the cinematic convention that all ships' captains woke instantly.

"I have good news, Captain." Excellent news. Long-awaited news. "And some vintage *k'vath* to toast it."

The door swung open. Grelben's posture of annoyance vanished as he noticed the near-legendary label on the bottle. "Come in."

"It has been a long road." Rualf carefully decanted two servings of the foaming green elixir. "Here is to the next road. To the road home, and wealth at our journey's end."

One eye widened in curious suspicion. "You seem to be leaving out a few details."

"May I use your computer?" Receiving a grunt of assent, Rualf continued. "Intercepts file for the American president. Conversation tagged 'almost there.'"

The hologram that leapt into being featured two familiar humans. The office where they met was, as if a parody of Krulchukor perfection, oval in shape. "The President and his chief advisor. Watch."

"This must be held in absolute confidence, Britt," said the

President. He sat behind a massive desk, his image clearly captured by an orb. A scrolling ring of text interpreted the facial expression and stance as denoting extreme levels of tension and weariness. Swelk's artificially intelligent translation program continued to learn. "There's something I need done that requires the utmost discretion. You'll get lots of opposition, but I trust you to make it happen anyway."

"Of course, Mr. President."

The President waved one of his freakish upper limbs. The translator called the gesticulation dismissive. "It's just us, Britt, and we've no time for formality."

"Fine, Harold. What is this about?" Curiosity and worry, speculated the text caption.

"Art and history. It's about culture. It's about preserving our heritage."

"I have to say, Harold, this is rather mysterious."

"Watch," interjected Rualf. "I could not have scripted this moment in a million years."

The President swiveled his chair to look out the window behind his desk. The orb lost its direct view—but the leader's strong profile and haunted expression were captured perfectly in reflection on the glass. Behind and through that image could be seen a towering stone obelisk. Robeson's reflected chin trembled. "In a matter of days it all ends, Britt. The somewhat-sane Russians are losing control. The lunatics who are taking over will hit us with everything. We'll defend ourselves. Between us, we'll reduce it all to so much radioactive rubble.

"There must be something left to remember us by. Something to teach the survivors—if nuclear winter doesn't kill everyone—that once we were great."

"Visually, that is just perfect." Rualf pointed into the hologram. "That tall monument, whatever it is. It reaches to the sky like a satiric symbol of the potential these poor ill-fated creatures did not live to fulfill." He savored his use of the past tense, considering the humans' doom already determined.

The presidential aide had recoiled in shock, settled heavily into a chair, then recovered his wits. "What do you want me to do? What *can* I do?"

"Gather—very discreetly—some of our national treasures: art, archives, artifacts. Have it taken for safekeeping somewhere unlikely to be bombed." The President spun back towards his confidant. The interpretive subtitle announced: great sadness. "But on the remote chance I'm too pessimistic, you *must* do this behind the scenes. Worse than the panic publicity would cause is the probable interpretation by the Russians. They could misinterpret that we were evacuating our cities in preparation for our own first strike. I don't want to goad them into launching."

Britt rocked in his chair. "There are always museum exhibits on tour between cities; some of those should be easy to waylay. And I've read that much of any museum's collection is not on display, but warehoused or in labs for study. It should be possible to quietly pack up and move some nonpublic parts of collections."

"That sounds excellent." The President's lips briefly curved upward. The translator advised: feigned good cheer. "Maybe a few of the most precious items on permanent exhibit, like the Constitution and the Declaration of Independence, can be withdrawn under pretense of doing some restorative work."

"I'll do what I can, Harold."

"I depend on it, Britt."

"Freeze," commanded Rualf. "This is what was missing." To Grelben's puzzled gaze, he added, "It was going to be a good film—but not artistic. Not *important.* Our audience had no reason yet to really care about the humans. But *this* . . . this striving against all odds for immortality. How can the audience not *love* that?"

Grelben grunted. "I leave such matters to you."

As you should. Keeping his self-approval to himself, Rualf struck a dramatic pose. "You know what would be even better?"

"What?"

"An ironic success. Imagine the F'thk rescuing a few human trinkets. I see the humans, as they die, taking comfort that some of their artifacts have been removed from Earth to preserve their memory." Rualf was overcome with the majesty of his artistic vision. "I *love* it."

In a tumultuous scene, the Krul heroine overcame her aspirations of personal fame. Her family embraced her. Credits rolled. Music swelled. At least Swelk called it music . . . the repertoire of the Krul's translation software did not extend to cross-species harmonic substitutions. Darlene's private description for the film's audio accompaniment was the enthusiastic stirring of a large bag of broken glass. The soprano counterpoint suggested that the mixing was performed with the bare limb of the musician.

Despite the predictability and aural assault, Darlene could not help but smile. In a flash of synergy, or serendipity, or gestalt, or epiphany, or . . . her insight was multicultural and by rights ought to be known by a hundred names. Earth had been plunged into danger to produce a film—and the filmmaker's artistic sensibilities would prove to be his undoing and Earth's salvation. There was a symmetry here that she couldn't get over. God bless these awful movies.

It would have been perfect to share her discovery with Kyle, but he was off helping strategize the upcoming attack on the maser satellites. It felt *so* good to know she was truly contributing. She could even watch the alien movies now without wincing.

As if reading Darlene's mind, Swelk asked, "What did you think of that show?"

"I enjoyed it," Darlene lied tactfully. Now could she unobtrusively redirect the discussion? She thought she saw an opening by which Swelk could validate her thinking. She wasn't after a sanity check so much as a fine-tuning. "I was taken with the emotional wealth of the final scene. It seems like Rualf likes to end all his films with an intense personal climax like that." Did the translator handle tones of voice? Darlene didn't know, but just in case, she made an extra effort to sound casual. "Am I correct in remembering that we're watching a complete collection of his works?"

"So I was told." Blackie and Stripes dependably fled the vicinity of Krulchukor music. Now that the film was over, the kittens were back. Swelk, sunk deep into a beanbag chair, now devoted an entire limb to each pet. Each kitten was on its back, stomach bared, purring loudly at the massaging of nine digits. "Rualf, unlike his heroine, continues to appreciate attention. I would be very surprised if he omitted any of his films. At the least, these must be the movies of which he is most satisfied. Why?"

"It occurred to me to wonder about the movie Rualf is now making. Worldwide ruin and destruction don't seem to give Rualf the type of ending he always goes for." Darlene strove for nonchalance. "I'm no expert on Krulchukor cinema, but it seems the new film is"—what term had she used with Britt? Oh yes—"dramatically deficient. It lacks personal realization."

"I see." The atonality of the translation implied anything but understanding.

"Here's a crazy thought." Hopefully *not*. Hopefully this thought was entirely sane. At Darlene's urging, Earth's one shot at surprising the aliens relied on this idea. She forced a casual laugh. "I don't know why I'm even thinking about this. It's not like Earth's interests lie in the structure of Rualf's film. I'm just reacting to watching so many of his past projects.

"Wouldn't the movie be more consistent with Rualf's approach if humans did something altruistic before the end? If, before they perished, they made some noble gesture? If they acted—of course, tragically too late—for the betterment of all?"

"It would indeed. That finale would almost certainly appeal to Rualf. But the artistry of the film is hardly Earth's biggest concern." Swelk paused in her ministering to the kittens. "Or am I wrong? Have circumstances become so dire that *you* seek immortality in a great film?"

"Hardly," said Darlene. She was feeling pretty smug at the confirmation the little Krul had provided. "My fondest hope is that Rualf never finishes his film."

The secretary backed silently from the Oval Office, leaving a grim President alone with his visitor. Behind that visitor, a galactic orb high on a bookshelf saw all. "Welcome, Ambassador H'ffl. I appreciate you coming on such short notice."

Rualf peered out through the camera lenses of the F'thk robot. "Please, Mr. President, have a seat. I prefer to stand, but there is no reason for you to." A standing robot did not tire, and it had an excellent filming angle. He did not continue until the human retreated to the chair behind his desk. "Now what is this matter of great sensitivity mentioned in the radio message?"

Enigmatic muscular twitches played across the human's face. ("Unhappy and worried," interpreted a text window in Rualf's helmet). "This is a hard matter of which to speak."

"Pardon me, Mr. President, but the tensions between America and Russia seem to be escalating. Human politics are not my field of expertise, but to an outsider the situation looks unpromising. I fear this is not the time for delay. If I can be of service, I hope you will speak plainly." Orbs and intercepted communications showed preparations for war increasing *so* rapidly, finally, that the H'ffl robot had been delivered in a lifeboat. Rualf had been unwilling to delay meeting with the President until the next scheduled visit to Washington of the *Consensus*.

The President's face contorted ("grieving," read the interpretation). "Things aren't very promising to an insider, either." He opened his mouth as if to say more, then closed it. The sad expression continued.

Did *no* human ever make things easy? Rualf would have thought the appropriate course of action obvious. Clearly he had been on this awful world too long, if he seriously expected reason from the natives. "I apologize in advance for the suggestion I am about to make. My words will seem to imply a lack of confidence, when perhaps all will work out for the best." The robot tipped its head in mimicry of a human gesture of confidentiality. "What I am considering skirts the limits of my authority." He paused again, hoping the human would make the conceptual leap. The scene would be more dramatic if the human made the proposal—whatever hints Rualf made to get there could be edited out.

"No need to apologize. Some new thinking is very much needed." The President briefly squeezed his eyes shut ("struggling for the proper words"). "Can your people stop our madness? We seem powerless to stop ourselves."

"How? By threatening harm to you or your adversaries? Coercion would not only be wrong, and against everything for which the Galactic Commonwealth stands, but surely also futile. Why would our threat be more of a deterrent than your own evident plans to harm each other?" Rualf zoomed in as the robot spoke, capturing a tight close-up of the President's face. The human leader closed his eyes again in thought and sorrow.

A moment later, those eyes snapped open amid an interplay of facial muscles Rualf could not understand. ("He has reached some decision?" guessed the caption.) "Mr. Ambassador, I believe you *can* help. Help us in the event of the worst. We could destroy ourselves, destroy our world. If that happens, I would die happier knowing that a small part of what we accomplished will be remembered."

Thank you! These humans at least had *some* sense. "You have much of which to be proud. I can promise you that even if the worst does happen your story will be remembered." *Now, you slow-witted bilat freak, actually make the offer.*

"That is good news." ("Increased decisiveness.") There was a dramatic pause—too long a pause, but that would be tweaked in editing. "I want to go a bit further. I would like to send with you a sample of our achievements. Pieces of our art, selections of our finest thought."

Success! Rualf made the robot nod its head in humanlike agreement. "I understand. A sad plan, but perhaps a prudent one. Yes, I would be willing to do this." Playing to the orb he had the robot add, "All will be enthusiastically returned if we are, happily, too pessimistic."

"I wish this fine old house could be saved, or the great monuments of this wonderful city. They can't. Most of our finest treasures are impossible to save." President Robeson studied the room as he spoke, as if trying to memorize it. He straightened in his chair in resolve. "Anything too visible cannot be taken without being noticed. Notice would bring panic. Panic would be misinterpreted by the Russians as a pre-attack evacuation. I will do my duty to defend and avenge America. I will *not* trigger her obliteration."

Rualf somehow contained his glee for long enough to complete the transaction. A landing by the *Consensus* could hardly be disguised, and the President insisted there be no big deviation from past routine that could raise Russian suspicions, but still some unique arrangements were necessary. The trusted aide whom the orb had seen assigned to gather America's treasures was now brought in to coordinate the details of a circumspect transfer. This Britt person thankfully had a mind for details—what he now proposed was workable.

The coming scene took shape in Rualf's mind as plans were finalized, and it was a thing of poignant beauty.

Andrew Wheaton chewed on an unlit cigar, debating whether he was going to do this. The scrap of paper in his hand had the unlisted cell-phone number of Kyle Gustafson, information wheedled from the scientist's mother. The Gustafsons, who had welcomed Andrew to their Thanksgiving dinner with open arms, were the salt of the Earth. Andrew was a lot less certain what he thought of their son.

Dirty dishes filled the sink. Crumbs and stains covered the table in front of him. Tina would have been disappointed—she kept the little farmhouse spotless. He choked back a sob. If Tina was here he would not be thinking about this call.

Would Kyle talk with him? The man had been nice, at least. But the cops had been nice too, at first. Then they had laughed behind their hands at the UFO nut. Then they had as much as accused him of killing his own wife, his own son.

Was Kyle Gustafson any different? Andrew had dared to hope so. After he'd shown Kyle the field, people had come to the farm. They took samples from the pasture, did a survey. But then . . . nothing.

Kyle had left a business card with a phone number—but he never answered the phone. Sometimes an assistant, a young-sounding man, picked up. He took messages, even returned calls. The young man was polite, but he knew nothing. "Kyle will call back when he can."

What did he expect, anyway? Tina used to tease Andrew for buying tabloids. The "big" newspapers didn't understand about aliens, only the tabloids did. A tear ran down his cheek. Did Tina understand now? His gut told him that she was gone.

Was there anything he could do? He had thought and thought—and there was something. But that something made sense only if he had abandoned hope. He looked again at the scrap of paper in his hand. At his last hope. He dialed.

"Hello?"

"Dr. Gustafson, this is Andrew Wheaton."

"Hi, Andrew. I didn't know you had this number."

Didn't want me to have it. "I told your mom I had to reach you." When no comment came, Andrew continued. "I need to know what your people found."

"Andrew." There was anguish in the voice. "There's nothing I can tell you. I'm sorry."

His guts felt like someone had reached in and squeezed them. "Nothing to tell? Or nothing you want to tell?"

"I'm sorry," Gustafson repeated. "Sincerely. Andrew, I have to go."

Tina had sewn the blue gingham curtains over the kitchen window. She'd cross-stitched the samplers decorating every wall. Andrew Junior had colored the crayon drawings pinned to the corkboard and magneted over most of the refrigerator door. "I'm sorry, too," he whispered.

The alien devils . . . soon *they* would be sorry. He would see to it.

CHAPTER 27

THE COASTER CLUNG to Kyle's glass of ice water, suspended by a film of condensation. Then gravity had its way; the coaster fell to the floor.

Drink coasters were a concept with which Swelk was unfamiliar. The unexpected noise made her drop her glass. It shattered. She shuffled in confusion.

"My fault. I'll take care of that." Kyle started picking the largest shards from the puddle, pausing to shoo away the kittens, who had come to investigate. They were in the safehouse's dining room, Swelk's favorite room. If he had to guess, based on his woefully inadequate grasp of Krulchukor psychology, that was because of the large oval table. It was one of the few curved pieces of furniture in the house.

Darlene, who'd been about to leave after her own visit, stuck her head in the door. "Blot that with a towel. I'll be right back." She returned pushing a vacuum cleaner, its power card trailing behind her into the front hall. She flicked on the handle-mounted switch.

Swelk collapsed, her legs convulsing. Her sensor stalks went rigid.

Kyle lunged for the cord and yanked. As the plug whipped into the room, Swelk's seizure was already fading. Her squeals of protest were untranslatable. "Swelk, what can we do?"

Darlene dropped the vacuum's handle. "Not again."

"Again!" snapped Kyle. His eyes remained on the twitching alien. "What the hell does *again* mean? You've seen this before?"

"Seen, no. Well, sort of. Twice I've been in another room when Swelk had some type of twitching episode. I was never right there when it happened, and I saw *nothing* like this. The first time, a pair of agents saw her right after, too." Her brow furrowed in recollection. "Swelk made it sound like vertigo. I know she's mentioned waking up dizzy."

"I . . . I am . . . am fine," the translator stuttered. The alien climbed back to her feet and walked shakily to the nearest beanbag chair. She dropped heavily, rustling the plastic peanuts inside. "That was horrible . . . whatever . . . it was."

She had dropped like a stone when the vacuum cleaner started. The kittens had bolted at the same time. Was it the unexpected racket? "Swelk, it's important that we isolate the problem. If you agree, I'd like to turn this"—he pointed at the vacuum cleaner—"on for a moment. We need to see if the symptoms return."

Swelk clasped her extremities, all the digits interlaced. From within the hollow of the beanbag chair, she said, "At least I cannot fall from here."

He plugged the vacuum cleaner back in. The switch was still on; the motor restarted with a roar. Swelk's limbs spasmed. He pulled the plug, and the fit began immediately to subside. "I guess we won't be doing much vacuuming."

Darlene impaled him on a dirty look. "What can we do for you?" she asked Swelk.

What was going on? "Swelk, what were you doing when the earlier episodes struck? What was happening around you?"

"Maybe some water, Darlene." The ET's sensor stalks bobbed. "In an unbreakable container, if there is one." She chugged most of a glassful before answering Kyle. "I wasn't doing *anything*. Standing in this room, waiting for Darlene."

He exchanged puzzled looks with her. "Dar, do you remember what you were doing?"

Her eyes closed in thought. "The first time was before one of

Swelk's movies. I was getting popcorn. The other time, I'd spent the night. It happened the next morning while I was showering."

Showering wasn't terribly noisy, and the only shower in the safehouse was upstairs. Kyle pinched the bridge of his nose in concentration. Hmmm. *Getting* was a rather all-purpose verb. "Were you popping the corn?"

"Uh-huh."

"In the little microwave oven in the trailer?"

She shook her head. "The microwave stuff has too much fat. I'd brought an air popper from home."

I see, said the blind man, as he picked up his hammer and saw. "The second time, did you dry your hair?" To her puzzled nod, he added, "With a hair dryer?"

"Well, yes."

Vacuum, air popper, hair dryer . . . what they had in common were electric motors. More precisely, if not per the everyday usage, electromagnetic motors. Swelk had mentioned once that the safehouse's electric lights made her jumpy. The radiation from household wiring was *tiny* compared to the E-M noise the vacuum cleaner's motor emitted.

"Kyle, what are you thinking?"

He recognized the impatient worry in Darlene's voice. "It's okay. Give me a second." If electrical appliances were the problem, why had there been so few incidents? He ran a mental inventory of modern conveniences. This old house had been chosen for its isolation, not its features. Its heat came from radiators, the circulation driven only by hot water rising and cold water sinking. The water was heated by an oil burner—no motor required. The rarely used stove burnt propane. The refrigerator and its big motor, entirely by accident out of commission. No bathroom fans. The guards came and went in shifts, so there generally wasn't showering—or, more important, hair drying—going on. The original landline phone, with its electromagnetic ringer, was out of service, which was easier than guarding it.

There was a moment of uncertainty as he recalled Swelk had a television. He'd once lost a college assignment by carelessly leaving a computer disk on a TV. His doubts receded as he remembered what set she had. To accommodate the old house's tiny rooms, the CIA had followed Kyle's advice and gotten an expensive wall-mounted model like the one he owned. The upscale unit had an LCD flat screen: real low-voltage stuff. Not a CRT with big coils.

This *had* to be important.

Flickering lights triggered seizures in some epileptics. How did flickering magnetic fields affect Krulirim?

Swelk was very proud of her studies. Kyle strained to remember something in a debriefing report, something from the Krul's personal research notes. Something about Krulirim orienting themselves by reference to the home world's magnetic field.

Hmmm. Earth's magnetic field was excluded by the safehouse's shielding. Was *that* why Swelk often woke up dizzy?

"Ladies, it will be for the best if I remove this vacuum cleaner." He'd happily bet an arm and a kidney that Swelk—or any Krul—couldn't tolerate fluctuating magnetic fields, at least at some frequencies. The sixty-cycle hum of standard wall current must be one of them. It would be a simple enough experiment at Franklin Ridge to measure the field strength of the appliance that had so instantly incapacitated her.

With the crisis a mere two days away, was it too late to exploit this discovery?

"General Bauer is unavailable. Would you care to leave a message?" The aide at the other end of the connection sounded bored. If he recognized the caller's voice or remembered having taken four messages from Kyle already that day, he disguised it well.

"No, thanks." There wasn't time for this nonsense, not with the Tea Party imminent.

Kyle hung up and redialed. When Britt's secretary wouldn't put him through either, he asked for voicemail. He had painful familiarity with the politician's total recall—anyone who had ever worked for Britt did. Today Kyle was counting on it. "Britt, I'm going to recite some numbers. What I've just learned is equally important. I *must* meet with the Mad Hatter. *Now.*" Kyle had invented that alias for the leader of the raid, but Britt would surely crack the code.

He rattled off numbers in twos, each pair the month and day he'd first discussed with Britt some key finding about the aliens. The revelation that Galactic "unity orbs" were spying devices. The discovery that the mother ship was transparent to X-rays. The confirmation that "F'thk" lifeboats had been at abduction sites, long before the aliens' overt appearance. "He *must* meet me at my funny friend's place. Please acknowledge."

Hanging up, Kyle left Franklin Ridge for the safehouse, to do the thing in the world he was worst at . . . waiting.

Why was Darlene so nervous?

Swelk stared out a dark window, miserably alone. Inside the safehouse, only she and the kittens were awake; Darlene, who was spending the night, had gone to bed. Krulchuk's day was roughly three-cubed and three Earth hours in length, and Swelk was far from adapted to her new planet's speedier rotation.

Recently, Krulchukor movies seemed to fascinate Darlene. The diplomat probably understood Krulirim better than any other visitor, but that insight came from experience with only one Krul and one small film collection. Darlene did not know how many human entertainments Swelk had viewed: a lot. Human broadcasts had led the *Consensus* to Earth. The lonely Krul had watched many more hours of Earth's television than the entirety of Rualf's library. Counting the guards, Swelk's experience with humans included more than two three-squares of individuals. She was a far better interpreter of humans than the other way around.

Why was Darlene so nervous?

Trees outside the window swayed. The house creaked. A kitten scratched enthusiastically at her litter box. A beanbag chair rustled as Swelk shifted her position. Darlene was more immersed than ever in Rualf's movies. The human's excitability had intensified after a discussion about the actor's artistic sense, after that odd conversation about whether Rualf would prefer to end the filmed destruction of Earth with some human act of altruism.

Swelk dismounted from the chair to pace in imperfect circles. Darlene had been agitated by those cinematic insights, but had tried not to show it. And why the recent shift in mood to nervousness? Swelk understood worry in anticipation of impending doom—but not disguised expectation. In the nighttime stillness, bedsprings squeaked. Darlene was also restless.

Excitement at how Rualf would prefer to end the movie? Did that suggest a human intention to influence the filming? But Rualf wanted to film an epic disaster, so why would the humans care about the details? What did Darlene imagine as the act of human altruism?

Swelk paused midcircle. Whatever this dramatic act might be, its purpose was to bring Rualf to film it. Was Rualf being tricked? Scenes from human entertainments flooded her mind, scenes she did not totally understand, from contexts foreign to her. Soldiers, criminals, imaginary monsters ... all were unfamiliar concepts imperfectly grasped. A large part of that incomplete understanding was a preference for ambush. Violent, surprise, deadly attack.

Was a subtle appeal to the filmmaker being used to lure the *Consensus* into danger? Was Darlene's interest in Rualf's films focused on constructing an irresistible scene? Almost certainly, yes. Less clear was how Swelk felt about this. How had she imagined this would all end?

But killing was wrong, no matter by whom.

Her interrogators had resigned themselves to a steadfast refusal to answer direct questions about vulnerabilities of the *Consensus*—while continuing in convoluted ways to collect data. It was as if a tacit bargain had been struck. They amassed information that could be used in an attack ... but she could believe, or rather delude herself, that she was not responsible. Swelk enabling Darlene to understand and entrap Rualf was as much a betrayal as would have been revealing any weakness of the ship.

Well, she *was* responsible—and she could not bear it if the resolution of her mess caused the deaths of her one-time shipmates.

Alone in midnight darkness, Swelk knew her existence as a solitary Krul was doomed. In *Revenge of the Subconscious,* which she had recently rewatched with Darlene, Rualf confronted a flawed aspect of himself. His character had become a loner, attempting to be complete unto himself. He had naturally failed.

Now she had to vanquish *her* inner monster.

There was an outburst of mewing and thuds: playful tussling by Blackie and Stripes. Much as she loved the kittens, the image that came to mind was of larger, much more docile creatures: Stinky and Smelly. She could not endure the thought of harm to those innocent beasts.

Crossing the hall, she reared up on twos to pound on Darlene's closed door. Without waiting for an answer, Swelk entered. The cold moonlight streaming into the room made Darlene, seated on the edge of her bed, look ashen. Her hair was matted and tangled.

"I know an attack is planned on the *Consensus*. Proceeding

means destruction, for you, for the Krulirim, or probably both.
I want to avoid that suffering. I want to help.

"But it must be done on my terms."

Snow flurries swirled around Kyle and his visitor. "If this
diversion costs me one casualty, I will personally rip out your
heart and feed it to you." Barrel-chested, with arms thicker than
Kyle's thighs, Colonel Ted Blake's soft-spoken threat was entirely
believable. Blake was livid at being summoned from Delta Force's
base at Fort Bragg a day before the attack on the starship. His
commandos were en route to Washington as they spoke.

They were in the woods that abutted the safehouse, on whose
sagging porch Kyle had awaited Blake. He brushed aside a low
branch. "I understand your concern, Colonel."

"Oh? Whose lives are you personally responsible for?"

The whole planet's, but he didn't suppose that answer would
be well received. "Colonel, I know for a fact neither you nor
any of the Delta Force has met a Krul. Don't you want to know
something about your opponents?"

"Don't tell me my business," said Blake. "*I* know for a fact that
you have no military background. Now give me one good reason
why I should even be here, or I'll be on my way."

Kyle exhaled sharply. Here goes. "When we go inside, I'll stay in
the foyer. You go through the doorway to your left and back into
the dining room where Swelk will be. Keep your eyes on her. What
you need to see will happen as soon as I hear you say her name."

They returned to the safehouse, Kyle signaling with a finger
raised to his lips that the agent at the door was not to speak.
Inside, Swelk and Darlene could be heard talking. As Blake turned
left, Kyle took an electric razor from his coat pocket. He plugged
it into the front-hall power outlet. When Blake said, "Swelk, I
presume," Kyle clicked the switch to on.

There was an immediate thud, followed by a drumming against
the wooden floor and shouts of dismay from Darlene. Kyle turned
off the razor. The drumming quickly faded. He clicked the razor
on; the spastic beat resumed. He switched off the shaver a second
time, this time unplugging it.

When Kyle entered the dining room, Darlene was hovering
anxiously over the still-prone Swelk. He shrugged apologetically
to them both.

Blake's glower had been replaced by shrewd calculation. "Shall we continue our hike?" asked Kyle. An agent handed him a backpack as they left the safehouse.

"What you just witnessed, Colonel, was the aliens' biggest weakness. Swelk was instantly disabled by the electric motor in my razor."

"Explain."

"Members of her species orient themselves by reference to the planetary magnetic field. Any electric motor, not just the one in a razor, converts an alternating current into an alternating magnetic field. The electromagnetic part, called the rotor, pushes magnetically against a stationary permanent magnet, the stator. As you know, wall current alternates at sixty cycles per second. I just inflicted on my friend a sixty-times-per-second reversal of her sense of direction."

"So she had extreme vertigo."

"Right," agreed Kyle. "But more than that. You saw her twitching uncontrollably. If you listened closely, you might also have heard that her computer immediately stopped translating her words. Swelk was shouting something, but while the motor ran that speech was unintelligible." The computer itself was unaffected, continuing to translate, or at least to make alien-sounding noises, in response to Darlene's English.

"Couldn't your ugly little friend be play acting?"

"She had no warning of what I did, and her response surely *seems* involuntary. That aside, it turns out the house surveillance system recorded prior incidents." Once Kyle had been told of Swelk's previous episodes, he had known to look. Darlene, who had been unaware of the hidden cameras, no longer showered there. He dug in the backpack. "Hence this videocam."

They stopped beneath a towering hemlock. Blake accepted the videocam and pushed the Play button. In the preview screen, Swelk stood in the dining room, a date and time appearing in tiny digits in the display's corner. Moments later, Swelk collapsed. Kyle handed over a second videotape. The new image showed Darlene in the kitchen, overseeing an air popper. The date and time matched Swelk's collapse on the first tape.

"Check these." Kyle offered two more tapes. Once more Swelk was stricken, now concurrent with Darlene's use of an electric hair dryer.

"Maybe it's the noise, not the motors." Probing curiosity had replaced hostility.

"Nope. A razor heard across the house is quieter than Swelk's own translator. I made an audio tape of a popcorn popper and played it back on a cassette recorder. That made her ill at ease, because the recorder itself has a small motor, but how loudly I played the tape made no difference." They resumed their walk. "When I converted that same tape of popper noise to MP3 format and ran the file through an electronic player, Swelk didn't react at all."

"You're saying we can disable the ETs with a big electric motor near the starship."

The safehouse was no longer visible through the trees, but a clearing had come into view. A windswept field in Minnesota rushed to mind, the meadow from which Andrew Wheaton's family had been abducted. "No, the ship's hull would surely shield them. But if we can get an airlock open, penetrate that shield . . ."

"My guys know all about penetrating things, and we're not restricted to kicking down doors." Blake's smile was frankly predatory.

"There's a fusion reactor in that ship, which will be in the heart of metropolitan Washington. The last thing we want to do is to make it go boom."

"I don't think they're going to respond to the Delta Force ringing the bell, even if all we're carrying is razors."

"*Swelk* knows how to get us in." Kyle ignored an outburst of protest. "She deduced from her questioning that an attack must be imminent."

Blake swallowed an oath. "You trust the little monster?"

"That's exactly what I propose to do: trust her. *If* we bring her, she promises to share the airlock keypad code that will let us into the ship."

"Bring an enemy to the raid." Blake was incredulous.

"Bring a defector. An *ally*. That's what I sincerely think she is. Every fact in our possession confirms that she is. If I'm right, her help will be invaluable, in operating the onboard systems after we take over the ship, in interpreting anything the crew says."

"And if you're wrong?"

Kyle swallowed hard. "I'll be very sorry. You see, I'm going to be in the lead truck."

CHAPTER 28

RUALF SAT AMID a ring of displays, analyzing camera angles. The ship's hull was studded with sensors. The President was in the Oval Office, ready to watch a closed-circuit television view of the ceremony while, unbeknownst to him, an orb observed him. Rualf shouted final directions to the troupe as to where their F'thk cameras should stand. They wriggled into the robots' control suits.

Show time.

The outer door of an airlock cycled open. The ramp descended. The robots trotted down the incline and arranged themselves in an arc that faced a quintessentially human building: a hideously ugly box with huge doors. It was meant, obviously, as housing for the freaks' simple aircraft. Today it held instead a collection of Earth's primitive arts and crafts.

As always when the *Consensus* visited, the humans diverted their airplanes to other airfields. No humans were yet in evidence. That was good—the starship had visited Washington often enough that curious crowds no longer rushed to meet it. And an intimate ceremony befitted Rualf's sense of aesthetics.

A short door inset in an aircraft-sized portal swung open. The American delegation exited. As the humans approached across the concrete, Rualf whispered orders to position the robots into a slightly different configuration.

"Welcome back to Washington, H'ffl." A silver-haired human extended an arm in greeting. "Please accept the President's apologies for his unavoidable absence. He felt his presence would draw too much attention to this meeting."

The text window in Rualf's helmet provided an unnecessary reminder: Britt Arledge. H'ffl reached out one of its arms, gravely performed the human ritual. "It is good to see you again, Mr. Arledge. Please tell President Robeson that we understand."

"It would be a much happier occasion if we were about to join the Galactic Commonwealth. But that is not to be." Arledge peered directly into one set of H'ffl's "eyes": a perfect close-up. "The people of Earth have foolishly shown ourselves too immature. Perhaps the steps we are about to take are unnecessarily cautious. I pray that is so . . . but I dread it is not."

"The F'thk share your hopes and fears," lied Rualf. "We accept your treasures in trust, to show with honor across the galaxy, and, we hope, to return to you someday."

"Our cargo vehicles are loaded." Arledge pointed to the building that housed Earth's trinkets. His head bobbed in some signal, in a grotesque parody of the articulate fluency of which Krulchukor sensor stalks were capable. "So let us begin."

With the abundant energy from a spaceship's fusion reactor to run bioconverters and maintain an environment, stranded Krulirim could hope to survive in almost any solar system long enough to be rescued—if their need for recovery could be made known. That was why the *Consensus*, like most spaceships, carried amongst its provisions a collection of emergency buoys, and why its computers held directions for fabricating more. Standard practice, upon arrival at an unpopulated solar system, was to pre-deploy some buoys in case of later need.

The buoys were essentially freestanding interstellar signaling stations. That purpose required the ability to generate and store energy, to receive from a marooned crew the specific details of the call for help, to convert those specifics and that accumulated energy into coherent microwave pulses, and to aim the message pulses precisely at a distant target star. Each buoy was a solar-powered satellite, with a powerful onboard computer, a remote-control interface for programming by the presumed stranded crew, and precision sensors for aiming.

Point that powerful maser downward at planetary targets, rather than across interstellar distances, and the buoy was an enormously destructive weapon. The *Consensus* had ringed the Earth with two three-squares and three of such weapons.

Grelben straddled the squat padded cylinder that was his command seat. Displays encircling the bridge showed a panoramic view of the landing site and the unfolding of Rualf's climactic scene. Other displays updated him regularly as to which masers had a line of sight to this airport. Parking a few buoys in synchronous orbit would have eliminated that tedious task, but the humans had that near-Earth region filled with their own satellites. Keeping his buoys secret had meant putting them in inconvenient orbits, where they could not hover over a fixed terrestrial location. Keeping the satellites secret had also required making them invisible to radar, and grafting radar-canceling mechanisms to the buoys had made his hybrid devices sporadically unreliable. To be certain of killing a target, he had to assign several buoys.

He periodically glanced at the unfolding ceremony. "Some of my people's greatest accomplishments await within those trucks," a gray-topped human was saying. Grelben wondered whether these Earth mementos could somehow be sold—as movie props and souvenirs, of course, not as real artifacts. There would be time to sort that out on the long trip home.

"And now we commit our treasures to Earth's new friends . . ."

The *Consensus* had never landed this near to buildings—he had always insisted on wide separation, the better to escape from potential surprises by an emergency launch—but Rualf's "artistic integrity" for this scene dictated a cozy, confidential setting. *Can we move this along?* fumed Grelben to himself. He felt exposed down here.

Alas, the onboard lasers could only fire forward, since in space the ship was only at risk from junk overtaken in flight. So here he sat, watching anxiously in all directions for he knew not what, tracking the buoys as they orbited in and out of line-of-sight. If a threat did materialize, and none ever had, he would have to select a target, pinpoint its location, and uplink those coordinates to a satellite. It was also hard to know in advance with what maser frequency to strike. Ship's sensors would monitor his target for scattered energy; if too little energy were being absorbed he would have to reprogram the attack frequency.

Yes, he would have been *far* happier with what had become a routine landing: in the center of a human airfield, far from any possible hazard. Grelben had no reason to doubt that the humans, who had never in any way threatened his ship, had no intention of making trouble today. Rualf kept assuring him that the humans were entirely intimidated by the light show made manifest near Earth's moon. The freaks *should* be overawed by it, even if the main cause for fear and dread had yet to be manifested. But it would. . . .

From the shadow beneath a retractable passenger walkway, Andrew Wheaton surveyed the idle runways of Reagan National Airport. A Baltimore Orioles cap, bought that day as camouflage, shaded his eyes. His FAA ID tag from St. Cloud Regional dangled from his coat zipper. He ambled to the traffic noise from the nearby George Washington Parkway, trying to project a casualness he did not feel, onto the deserted field. The top of the spaceship peered over a line of hangars.

Chewing an unlit cigar, he sauntered to the fuel depot and a row of parked tanker trucks. With air traffic diverted for the aliens' visit, the drivers had the afternoon off. In Andrew's pocket was the heavy ceramic ashtray he'd taken from a workers' lounge. He threw the ashtray through the driver's window of the end tanker. Reaching through the shattered glass with a gloved hand, he unlocked the door.

Andrew had rewired the farmhouse twice; hot-wiring an ignition did not faze him. The truck was already rolling when someone burst from the depot to check out the noise. The watchman receded rapidly in Andrew's rearview mirror. Cold wind spilling through the broken side window whipped the cap from his head.

Those F'thk bastards who had stolen his family would now pay.

A cargo van, supposedly the first of many, approached the awaiting starship. Kyle was the van's passenger. His heart pounded as they started up the ramp into the gaping airlock. F'thk watched silently from the concrete; others of the robots awaited in the airlock itself, to assist with the expected unloading.

"Ready?" Col. Blake drove one-handed, his other hand resting on the parking-brake lever. He was of the "I won't ask my men to do anything I wouldn't do" school. Oddly, Blake saw no inconsistency in hinting Kyle was a few beers short of a six-pack for accompanying him.

What would Blake do if I answered no, wondered Kyle. They were nearing the top of the ramp. "Let's do it."

"Okay." The commando slammed on his brake pedal and yanked the emergency brake lever. They squealed to a halt with the van's tail hanging out of the airlock. "Sit tight." The advice was unnecessary. The F'thk in the airlock were being torn apart by a hail of bullets from hidden snipers—and from the Uzi Blake had retrieved from the glove box to fire through the windshield. The same fate befell the more exposed robots on the ground. As if in slow motion, the outer airlock hatch clanked impotently against the reinforced van. "Go, go, go."

They flung open their doors. The control panel was right where Swelk had said it would be, its buttons labeled in spidery characters reminiscent of the keypad on her computer. Familiarity was not enough; two human hands did not begin to have the dexterity of the nine fully opposable digits at the end of a Krul limb. Grinding his teeth, Kyle tried again and again to press precisely the sequence of key clusters he had memorized.

It didn't help that Blake, who was applying plastic explosives to the inner hatch, kept bumping into him. One way or another, they were going to get inside, because only a crew held hostage could disable whatever doomsday devices they had deployed.

"Take off!" screamed Rualf. The edge in his voice came partially from simple desire for instant obedience, but mostly from irrational terror. The rich data stream from the robotic control suit gave an illusion of reality that while normally a convenience had without warning become a near-death experience. Rualf had just suffered the tearing apart of H'ffl's body and the final spasmodic misfirings of dying sensors. "Grelben! Get us out of here."

From the computer in Rualf's pocket came a shouted reply. "I *can't* take off. The outer door is jammed, and the ramp is designed not to retract with the airlock open. I have someone trying to override the interlock. And these freaks you promised would never attack? They radioed a demand for our surrender."

With shipboard sensors Rualf saw that all the outside robots were down. A camera viewing outward from the airlock showed two busy humans inside and more vehicles converging. Only the inner airlock hatch separated him and his troupe, all struggling to extricate themselves from the teleoperations suits, from their assailants. The hatch suddenly seemed a very flimsy and inadequate defense. "Grelben! Use the satellites. Blast them."

"Blast what? Our own ship?" came the angry answer. There was a pause. "Maybe I can use the masers on nearby buildings, or parked airplanes, to create a diversion. Get ready to drive out an unblocked airlock and tow the . . . oh, shit."

"What!?" Rualf was finally free of his suit. Fleeing the cargo bay, he could not put from his mind the humans at the airlock controls. How could they possibly expect to find the command sequence? As he waited for the zoo hold's inner airlock hatch to cycle, he interrupted Grelben's cursing. "What's wrong?"

"Get a Hovercraft out *now*." The captain's voice was grim. "The buoys are under attack."

With a liquid hum, the airlock controls finally responded to Kyle's inputs. "Back inside the van." There was no way to know what might come at them through the hatch he'd been so eager to open. On the rear deck of the van was a gas-powered, seven-thousand-watt, electric generator. Several multioutlet surge protectors were plugged into the generator. From the surge protectors, in turn, hung two vacuum cleaners, a leaf blower, a belt sander, a kitchen mixer . . . pretty much every motorized appliance in Kyle's house.

"Fire in the hole." He mashed down the generator's On button. As the engine roared to life, he and Blake began switching on appliances. The noise was deafening. As he stepped down from the van's side door, the inner airlock hatch *thunked* into its fully open position. Krulirim writhed and thrashed on the deck, some with limbs entangled in unrecognizable equipment. The thunder of the portable generator masked any sounds the aliens may have been making.

Just as Kyle was thinking, *Victory*, he was jerked roughly around. He lip-read, rather than heard Blake's words. "We have a problem."

✳   ✳   ✳

The overcrowded trailer in which Swelk anxiously waited was ripe with an odor she did not recognize. Despite every effort to keep out of the way, she was bumped and bruised. The humans stretched, contorted, and strained to look past one another at the instruments and display panels lining the trailer's walls. Darlene tried to report status occasionally, but the cacophony of speech rendered the translator mostly useless.

It grieved Swelk that the humans still distrusted her. The trailer doors were secured by a keypad device. The irony that she had revealed the keypad code to the *Consensus* was not lost on her. What was lost on the people streaming in and out of the trailer, however, was that a Krul saw in a full circle—she was in no sense "facing" one of the walls of instrumentation as were her human companions. She had already espied the code that would let her exit. That knowledge was of no practical use—this trailer was the only enclosure in the vicinity shielded against Kyle's impromptu magnetic weapon.

A cheer rang out. Swelk quivered, though the reaction must be only nerves. Actual exposure would have incapacitated her. Kyle must have succeeded in opening the airlock door. *Please be all right. Please be all right.* Images of her shipmates, of the Girillian menagerie, of Kyle alternated in her mind. She was not certain for whom the wishes of safety were most fervently intended. *Please be all right. Please be . . .*

The mass of people in the trailer had fallen suddenly, ominously silent.

Truly awful violin music screeched from the Walkman cassette recorder Andrew Wheaton had brought to the airport. Wild clapping greeted the end of the tune. "That's *great*, sweetie," Tina encouraged. "Play it again for Mommy?" Andrew laughed through his tears, remembering what Tina had later admitted—she'd had no idea what Junior had played.

"Thank you, Mommy," answered a voice as sweet as the music was tortured. Screeching resumed. Tina's *again* was the single clue this shrieking was related to the earlier "tune."

Andrew brushed away the tears, but left the tape, the final recording of lost wife and child, running. Swinging the stolen tanker truck around the end of a row of hangars, the alien ship loomed before him like a beached whale. The truck had fishtailed coming out of the curve; he eased up on the gas, lining up on one of the vessel's landing legs. He patted the photo of the three of them he'd taped to the dashboard.

Then he pushed the gas pedal to the floor.

He was astonished to see puffs bursting from the concrete. Moments later, the tanker lurched, its rear dragging. People were shooting at him—or at his tires, anyway. Were there troops here to protect the murdering devils? The truck swerved and swayed as he fought to control it. One of those swerves revealed a ramp leading into the ship. Newscasts often showed the outer airlock hatch open at the top of a ramp.

A low armored truck, a "high mobility vehicle," sped from a hangar, rashly trying to cut him off. There was no need to see if that driver truly was suicidal—better to sweep around and charge up the open ramp. Another Humvee raced up parallel to him. He didn't hear these shots either over Junior's playing, but his windshield filled with holes. The wind of his forward motion pressed against the weakened windshield. The glass shattered, countless shards stabbing him in the chest and face and arms.

He patted the St. Christopher's medal that dangled from the rearview mirror, and once more the photo. "See you soon."

The ramp was directly in front of him.

Either the roar of the portable generator or the boom of the backup explosives was the commandos' cue to race across the tarmac from hangar to starship. No part of the plan involved a tanker truck—but one was nonetheless barreling toward them.

Kyle couldn't make out much detail at this distance. The tanker driver had pale hair, dark eyes, and a cigar in his mouth. Then it hit him: Andrew Wheaton. Kyle never doubted that the grieving father and husband meant to crash into the ship. Blake's soldiers were at a loss, unable to stop the tanker and unwilling to risk setting it afire as it sped toward their objective.

Could he deflect the tanker? Keep it from climbing the ramp? Kyle gestured; Blake followed him back to the van. The generator weighed nearly 250 pounds; grunting, they shoved it out the van's side door onto the airlock floor. Electric cords yanked loose; Kyle threw appliances from the van. "Plug it all back in!" he screamed into the sudden comparative quiet. He jumped into the driver's seat and threw the van into reverse.

CHAPTER 29

GROANING, KYLE CRAWLED away from the heat and flames. After a few painful yards, he was grabbed under an arm by Ted Blake, who half dragged, half carried him from the hell that had erupted. Blake left him propped against a hangar wall, goggling at the raging inferno. He had by sheer good luck rolled behind the wrecked van, and been sheltered from the worst of the fireball.

What did this all *mean?* After his leap from the speeding van and the explosion, he couldn't think straight. Of one thing he was certain: Wheaton was dead. How many Krulirim had the man taken with him?

Darlene appeared from somewhere. "Kyle!? Are you all right?"

He failed miserably in an attempt to smile, but vomited noisily without effort. "I've been better." Still, his mind was clearing. The airlock he had with such difficulty opened was engulfed with flames, entirely impassable. And apart from the flames, the ship *looked* funny. It was at an odd angle; a landing support must have been snapped by the blast.

The fire and explosion had surely incinerated the generator and his sorry collection of appliances. Swelk always recovered quickly after a electric motor was switched off. If any Krulirim survived, maybe on the opposite side of the ship, they would be recovered by now.

What would they be doing?

✳   ✳   ✳

For time without measure, the deck fell from beneath Grelben. The walls spun around him, receding into infinite space. He somehow floated and fell simultaneously, limbs spasming. When the sensation faded, he pulled himself onto his command seat. Bridge displays showed F'thk robots littering the concrete, mostly torn to pieces. On other screens, a human ground vehicle racing toward the deployed ramp. The inner airlock door had been opened during his incapacity. His ship was exposed! Before he could engage the remote-hatch override, the onslaught of vertigo resumed. He toppled from the seat, limbs entangled.

The explosion that rocked the *Consensus* penetrated even the chaos into which he had once more been plunged. The mysterious disorientation stopped, but his still-quaking limbs refused at first to function. A searing wind burst onto the bridge, tossing the duty crew like leaves. The bridge displays went blank; his dazed mind needed a moment to deduce that the hull cameras had protectively retracted. It was an automatic mechanism, normally triggered by the heat of an atmospheric entry. Hull sensors reported a soaring temperature. As bodily control returned, he slapped the audio reset on the alarm panel; its many flashing lights told him everything that he needed. Fire suppressant sprayed from nozzles in the ceiling.

"Brelf, you're on damage control," he snapped at the first live crewman he saw. His attention remained fixed on his ship's defense. "Rualf, report. Rualf." There was no response. The alarm panel revealed a raging fire in the cargo hold where the troupe worked. It seemed impossible that anyone there had survived.

Communications with the robots ran from the incinerated controls in the hold to the ship's radio center to antennae in the hull. The high-gain antenna dishes, like the exterior cameras, were retracted and useless. One antenna, however, was molded into the hull itself. That configuration made the antenna necessarily omnidirectional, dispersing energy with profligacy in all directions, but his immediate needs were short range. With that antenna he broadcast to the robots. He couldn't control them with bridge equipment, but he needed to see through their sensors.

Only three robots responded, and their images came from close to the tarmac. Just one view showed the ship—and that picture made him knot his digits in rage and fear. Amid billowing black smoke, flames licked hungrily at the *Consensus*. The ship had tipped, its stern flattened where it had struck the ground.

More and more lights glowed on the alarm panel. "Captain," called Brelf. "Fire is spreading throughout the ship. Most controls are damaged, unresponsive. The drive . . ."

The crewman did not need to complete his thought. Without the interstellar drive, nothing else mattered. They were marooned, at the mercy of the freaks whose extinction he and Rualf had conspired to cause. Without access to the high-gain antennas, Grelben could not even control the satellite weapons. They were without hope, he thought.

But not without options . . .

Images of the *Consensus* in the grip of flames looked down at Swelk from three walls. Her view of the command-trailer instrumentation was suddenly unimpeded. Darlene had been the first out the door; others, to whom no one had bothered introducing Swelk, soon followed. She cringed the first time after the explosion that the door opened, but the horrifying dizziness did not strike. The fire must have destroyed Kyle's weapon.

The soldiers who remained had eyes only for their equipment . . . while *her* vision, as always, went in a full circle. No one was watching her. She had either been forgotten in the excitement, or the humans had excessive trust in their locked door. She tapped out the key code that unlatched the trailer door. A hinge squealed as she pushed against the door. As she jumped out, one of the uniformed men in the trailer lunged at her. He crashed to the trailer's floor, half of his torso hanging outside—but caught her by her belt. She tore loose, but the pocket in which she kept her computer ripped. The computer fell to the pavement just outside the hangar. There was no time to stop for it. She screamed as she ran, "I must help. I must help." Those giving chase gave no signs of having understood her.

An eye aimed antimotionward, toward the hangar, saw Kyle. He was bloody, agitated, and screaming. The evidently unbroken computer translated, "Don't shoot." Not waiting to see if that advice would be taken, she fled toward the *Consensus*. She ran no faster than the men in pursuit—an unlame Krul would have left them far behind—but with her three-limbed ability to veer instantly in any direction, she was much more agile. She could

also see them coming, from whatever bearing, and her shortness made her hard to grab. She dodged and bobbed, unable
to outpace them, but—however precariously—at liberty. Bright
red trucks raced toward the *Consensus*, sirens blaring. From the
hangar came the shouted words, anguished even in translation,
"I'm sorry, Swelk. I'm sorry."

Reaching the ship, she found she was more tolerant of heat
than the humans. She stood near the blaze, panting in exhaustion, for the moment beyond the soldiers' reach.

Through the flame-filled airlock came the panicked bellowing
of the swampbeasts.

Swelk had run here impulsively, unable to stand idly by when
the only Krulirim within light-years were imperiled. No, be
realistic . . . the survivors would all *die* if they did not get out.

Another terrified howl rang out. Despite the roar of the fire
she knew it was Stinky. His renewed call was joined by his mate.
As flames billowed from the open airlock, Swelk realized, *Something inside is fanning those flames.* She galloped around the hull,
sticking close to the ship where the soldiers could not follow.
A *second* airlock was wide open; she could feel the draft of air
being sucked into this hold by the raging fire. This hold's ramp
was unextended, but the landing foot's collapse brought the entry
within reach. She clambered aboard.

She found herself inside the zoo hold. Her Girillian friends
screamed in fear, hurling themselves again and again against their
cages. Fire suppressant streamed from nozzles overhead. She ran
between the pens, unlatching doors. The heat seared her lungs.
"Get outside!" she screamed at a Krul she found fallen but stirring beside a cage. Soot-covered, he was unrecognizable. Whether
the disorienting weapon or the explosion—or perhaps both—had
downed him she could not tell. "Out the hold airlock."

Ignoring her own advice, Swelk limped deeper into the ship.
Two crewman stumbled by her, bleeding, dazed, purposeless. "To
the zoo hold," she called as she pushed on. Flickering emergency
lights guided her to the bridge, through corridors ever thicker
with smoke.

She arrived, finally, gasping for breath, at the command center.
Still bodies littered the room. Only one Krul worked purposefully:
Captain Grelben. He toiled feverishly at a console, so rapt in his

duties that he did not at first see her enter. He ignored the alarm panel that glowed from top to bottom in the purple blinkings of worst-case disaster. "Captain. Come away."

"Swelk." His voice was cold. "I trust we have you to thank for our difficulties." A coughing fit interrupted him. "It does not matter. Your freaks are doomed."

Predestined in his mind to fail, because of Krulchukor prejudice? Or condemned by his plans, by some twisted revenge the captain still strove to inflict? "Captain. There is still time to get off the ship. We can live here. The humans are good people." The smoke was choking her. "Will you let them find their own way?"

Grelben reared up on twos, sweeping the third limb through a broad arc. It somehow encompassed the death and destruction on the bridge and throughout the ship. A hacking convulsion deep in his torso made him wobble, his upraised limb tremble, ruining the grand gesture. "*This* is their way. *Death* is their way. So run away, mutant, but it will do you no good."

"Before I am done, you and your disgusting freaks will experience death on a scale beyond your wildest imaginings."

Kyle pressed a bloody cloth to his head. Darlene sat beside him, her back, like his, braced against the hangar wall. Fire trucks were spraying foam on and around the ship. They had had some success containing the blaze, but the flames leaping from the *Consensus* itself were growing. Blake's men ringed the ship from a distance.

"Not bad for an amateur." Blake, who looked as spent as Kyle felt, was on his feet and in complete charge. Several of the Delta Force stood nearby. Whether the compliment referred to Kyle's efforts or Andrew Wheaton's suicide attack was unclear. "You'll be pleased to know the weapons satellites are inactive."

"That is good news." Kyle's tone belied his words. Swelk had gone into the burning ship. Could she possibly survive?

"So are we safe now?" asked the colonel. "Is it over?"

"I don't know. Even if the aliens are dead, there are systems on board we know nothing about." Kyle tried to think past his pain and worry. The Krulirim had an interstellar drive, artificial gravity, bioconverters—incredible technologies he did not begin to understand. How could he possibly say whether the fiery destruction of such equipment would release uncontrolled forces? That was just one of many reasons why the plan had necessarily been *capture* of the ship. *Quit it,* he told himself sternly. *Don't waste time on useless speculation. What can you usefully contribute?* "They have a fusion reactor. You can think of it as a controlled thermonuclear bomb. The biggest danger may be the reactor blowing."

"How big a problem are we talking?" Blake was amazingly matter of fact.

"We have no way of knowing. If they're good engineers, though, there will be safety shutdowns." Kyle's head throbbed as secondary explosions wracked the starship. "Be happy for one difficulty we don't have. Swelk knew that their reactor fused helium-three. If they'd used hydrogen isotopes, like our experimental fusion reactors, we'd have faced an enormous explosion. Think Hindenberg, but much bigger—even without a nuclear event."

A commando had appeared at Blake's side. "Sir, you should see this. It was found on the tarmac near the command trailer."

This was Swelk's pocket computer. No sooner had Kyle recognized it than it spoke. "Captain. Come away."

"Swelk," answered a second voice. "I trust we have you to thank for our difficulties. It does not matter. Your freaks are doomed."

"I remember," whispered Darlene. "Swelk had hidden a pocket computer on the bridge. That's how she determined what the plotters were up to."

"Right." Kyle tried to recall everything he'd learned or surmised about Krulchukor computing. What he called Swelk's computer was more—it was also a communications device. All such computers on the *Consensus* were wirelessly networked. The Krulchukor magnetic sense was indifferent to radio frequencies, just as human eyes were indifferent to ultraviolet light. And with inner *and* outer airlocks doors open, the ship's wireless network must now extend onto the airfield. They were near enough for the device hidden on the bridge to network with the unit Swelk had dropped—a unit still set to translate to English.

"Before I am done, you and your disgusting freaks will experience death on a scale beyond your wildest imaginings."

"Congratulations, by the way,"

Swelk felt the captain's scrutiny. She was covered with burns, oozing fluids from countless scrapes and burns. "For what?"

"For a successful escape. For surviving this long." Grelben seemed indifferent to the state of the alarm panel, where lights were increasingly switching from crisis purple to an even more ominous Off. Panels and consoles around the bridge sprayed sparks. He coughed, choked by smoke, fire suppressant, and unknowable fumes. "For the cleverness of your bilat friends."

"System integrity at risk. Redundant equipment failures. Safety shutdown of reactor in three-cubed seconds." The ceiling speakers crackled and hissed.

"I could override the shutdown. It would turn this side of the continent into a large hole."

"No! Do not do that. You *must* not do that!"

"Why not?" Grelben whistled in amusement at her. "This ship was *everything* to me. Look at it now."

"The humans should not suffer for what I have done. I brought us here." Her thoughts raced, even as she felt her body succumbing to the heat and toxic gases and injuries. "If you want someone to blame, it should be me." She had been *so* proud of herself for spotting Earth's broadcasts. She had done everything in her power to convince him to bring the *Consensus* here. That Grelben had agreed for his own dishonorable reasons did not mitigate her responsibility. The depth of her presumption stunned her. How arrogant it had been to undertake a personal exploration of Earth rather than report her findings to the authorities on Krulchuk. Pride blinds the eyes, her old nurse liked to say. Swelk's pride had caused all this.

"Safety shutdown of reactor in two three-squared seconds."

"I blame you. You do not need to doubt that." A rumble deep in the ship made his words hard to hear. "What say you? Would you like to go out with a bang?"

"Captain, *please* let the reactor shut down safely." Her hearts pounded in fear, in guilt, in dismay. The mass murder Grelben envisioned was, like Rualf's stage-managed war, almost too large to grasp. One way or another, she knew she was dying, and another extinction also clutched at her. "Let the crew escape. I lived here—all it takes is standard bioconverters. They can live here, too. You can live here."

"Safety shutdown of reactor in three-squared seconds."

"A captain without his ship? I do not think so." He clenched all the digits of an extremity in violent negation. "Nor will, I think, sane Krulirim follow your example."

She had to keep him talking. A few more seconds, and the shutdown would be complete. Amid so many crashed systems, the reactor could not possibly be reactivated, to become once more a threat. "Let that..." A wave of smoke erupted onto the bridge, gagging her. She hacked and coughed, unable to speak. Would she fail, in the end, simply from an inability to get out the words? With a violent rasp, she spit out the pitiful remainder of her argument. "...be their decision."

"Safety shutdown of reactor in three seconds... two... one."

"Get out of here," coughed Grelben.

"Reactor shut down. Plasma has been vented."

Swelk groped through smoke-obscured corridors as fire crackled within the walls. Had her feeble words in the end swayed the captain? Whatever the reason for his forbearance, she was grateful. But she could not forget his taunt: *Nor will, I think, sane Krulirim follow your example.*

Could she not avoid the guilt of the whole crew's death? *Revenge of the Subconscious* flashed into her mind. Was *she* not the monster? She lived apart from her people—of necessity, she always told herself, but was that entirely true? Did she relish her uniqueness? There was no denying that her personal actions had brought a shipload of her kind here. Brought them to a world of bilats, who—however justifiably—were now slaughtering the Krulirim. She *had* to convince the ship's survivors to escape with her.

Swelk turned from her path toward the zoo hold to save her people.

Grelben tripped and fell over a body in the almost impenetrable smoke, the impact knocking the wind from him. Inhaling reflexively, his lungs filled with noxious fumes. He retched repeatedly crawling through the murk for an emergency respirator.

Limbs weak and shaking, he regained a secure position on his command seat. He removed the breather from his mouth. "Status comm." His rasping voice was no longer understandable. "Status... comm," he repeated with exaggerated enunciation. The hologram that formed was too attenuated by smoke to be read. "Flat... screen... mode." He leaned toward the display, bending a sensor stalk until it almost touched the flat surface. Comm remained, in theory, operational. He could send a message with any antenna he did not mind losing in seconds to the flames gripping the hull. "Command . . . file . . . 'Clean . . . Slate.' "

Sucking oxygen again from the respirator, he recalled with amusement Swelk scuttling to what she considered safety. The mutant believed she had dissuaded him. Well, in a way, she had. She had convinced him that the quick death of a fusion explosion, for her and those who had abetted her, was too kind. So there had been no need to keep the reactor hot while he finished his other business. "File . . . open." A deep breath from the respirator. "Send . . . file."

"Help me up." Kyle's unaided attempts at verticality were feeble. "Hurry."

Blake grabbed his outstretched arm and tugged. "You should be seeing a doctor. From our minimal acquaintance, though, I sense you're not big on taking advice."

Kyle ignored him. "Dar, help me out to the ship."

"Sergeant," bellowed Blake. He waved to a woman in a Humvee. "Drive my friends."

Darlene helped him into the low-slung truck, and seconds later, out again. They joined the soldiers who surrounded the wreckage, and the fire crews who had contained the blaze. They made no attempt to douse the ship itself. Kyle could not find fault with their decision not to endanger whatever firefighting mechanisms were built into the vessel. "This is too reminiscent of the night I met Swelk. Her death in the flames of the very ship she had successfully escaped . . . it's so awful. I can't help but picture Rualf laughing mockingly."

"Convincing the captain to let the reactor shut down . . . she saved our lives, the lives of untold millions. She really is a hero."

"I know."

He could no more stand still here, baking in the intense heat of the fire, than he'd been able to sit and watch from across the concrete apron. He started limping around the ship; Darlene followed in silence. There was a second open airlock. Through heat shimmers and smoke he saw motion within. Survivors? Were they afraid to come out? "Hand me Swelk's computer. Come out. You will not be harmed." The computer emitted the vowelless noise with which it always spoke to Swelk—at a low volume that could not possibly be heard inside the ship. "Computer, maximum sound level." It babbled back, no louder than before. "Computer, as loud as possible." Repeated paraphrasings had no effect.

What else could he try? Yelling. Perhaps it would translate louder if he spoke louder—and so it did. "Come out! You will not be harmed!" The Krulchukor equivalent, a vowelless eruption, burst forth. Moments later, two metal containers were flung from the open airlock.

"Don't shoot!" hissed Kyle to the startled commandos. The devices were clones of Swelk's bioconverters. The translation of these words, hopefully, was too soft to be heard inside. "Come out!" he screamed again.

Rualf struggled to remain upright, dazed by the latest explosion to rock the *Consensus*. Smaller blasts sounded throughout the ship. Smoke thickened even as he marveled, stupefied, at the disaster. The hatch into the heart of the ship flapped between half- and full-open, its motorized mechanism thudding in abrupt reversals, unable to respond to fire both inside and out. With a spectacular tearing sound, the machinery stopped.

A gale whistled through the hold, sucked through the gaping airlock and stoking the spreading blaze like a bellows. The open airlock . . . that was his only hope of escape. He had a vague recollection of someone telling him so. Had one of the crew, or of his troupe, already come through here? No—whoever it was had gone *into* the ship. Some foolish hero type. He stumbled, limbs still quivering from what must have been a human weapon, toward the lock.

An impossibly loud feminine voice shouted from outside. "Come out. You will not be harmed." Had humans learned to speak like Krulirim? How could that be? Somehow, the thundering voice was familiar.

Swelk!

The Krul who had gone past him, gone deeper into the ship . . . it was she. *She* was the reason the humans knew to stage a scene he could not resist filming. To bait a trap. The impossibly loud command, doubtless synthesized by Swelk's computer, nearly paralyzed him with fear. What would the humans do to him if he fell into their power?

A wave of coughing came over him. He was dead if he stayed here.

But if he were the only survivor . . . the humans would not know he was the one responsible for directing their photogenic self-destruction. He waded through smoke to the interior hatch with its broken motorized controls. The hatch that had inconveniently frozen half open. There was an access panel beside the controls; he flipped it open to get at the manual crank. Wheezing, he worked until the heat-warped door was fully shut—then he jammed the mechanism. The wind whistling inward from the lock, due to fire-fed suction into the ship, died abruptly as the hatch slammed shut.

Time for his escape. He groped toward the beckoning airlock, low to the deck where the air was slightly fresher. Fodder, animal shit, the Girillian ferns they had started synthesizing for the animals to shit on . . . stuff was piled everywhere, and more and more of it was burning.

He was forgetting something. Escape to what? *He could not survive without Krulchukor food.* These beasts ate synthesized food, surely. Behind a cage he spotted what must be bioconverters. Gripping with one limb the handles of two heavy synthesizers, he dragged them, awkwardly, to the airlock. He flung them outside, and went for more.

"Come out!"

Something monstrous emerged from the smoke, as though summoned by the imperious demand. A bilateral head on a thick neck towered over him, like a ghost of the F'thk. Rualf had just recognized it for a Girillian creature when it knocked him over. Massive hooves pressed him into the metal deck. Agony washed through him—but to lose consciousness now was to die. As he tried to lever himself upright, a Girillian carnivore ran over him. It was smaller than the first animal, but its feet were studded with talons. Rualf collapsed, screaming, to the floor. Thick smoke filled his lungs.

As Rualf lay quivering, limbs splayed, bleeding and coughing, battered and bruised, apparition after apparition burst from the smoke and flames. The biggest were deep within the hold, as if herding the rest. He sprawled, helpless, as creature after creature stomped and slashed him, each encounter inflicting new anguish.

The last thing Rualf ever saw was the huge flat foot of a swampbeast descending upon the center of his torso, directly over his sensor stalks.

*   *   *

The commandos flinched as a six-legged creature leapt from the open airlock. Only that moment of surprised nonrecognition saved the animal. "Hold your fire!" yelled Kyle. As Swelk's simulated voice reverberated from starship and hangars, he searched for and found on the computer what he hoped was its microphone. He covered the aperture with his thumb. "Hold your fire!" Muffled, the repetition went untranslated. He'd seen such a creature before—in a hologram projected by this very computer. "It's a zoo animal. There may be more."

Animal after animal appeared out of the smoke and flames. They retreated in confusion from burning ship and human building, lost and confused, huddling together. If the Girillian menagerie included predator and prey—and Kyle was almost certain from Swelk's tales that it did—the xenobeasts were too overwhelmed to care. He'd never quite believed the stories of terrestrial predators and prey fleeing peacefully side by side from forest fires—now all skepticism vanished. "Call the National Zoo. We need game-keepers, pronto."

"Swampbeasts. They're beautiful." Darlene's voice was quietly awestruck. She pointed, quite unnecessarily, at two magnificent, web-footed animals that stood about eight feet tall. They were the last to emerge from the airlock now impenetrably thick with smoke.

She gently took Swelk's computer from Kyle's hand. Walking slowly toward the knot of shivering animals, she crooned, "Smelly. Stinky. Smelly. Stinky." The computer repeated something after her, softly. The swampbeasts pushed forward. Bowing their heads, they approached cautiously, eyes wide and staring. They brushed their enormous heads against Darlene's outstretched hand, then settled to their knees beside her.

Swelk's computer did not translate "humph," but that was okay. They understood what it meant.

Swelk coughed and spat, splattering a smoke-blackened clot of blood against the bulkhead. The clot sizzled. Despite the fire-suppressant sprays, fire was everywhere. Her skin was blistered. Her extremities had been so repeatedly scorched that she no longer felt them.

The initial fireball had burst through the open hold where Rualf and his troupe had been working, killing everyone. She had no idea why the hatch to the ship's interior, never unlocked when she was aboard, was now wide open. The ship's corridors had channeled the fire and blast, catching most of the crew at their posts. The draft from the second airlock had deflected the fireball from parts of the ship, sparing the bridge from the worst of it.

And saving her Girillian friends.

She had explored the *Consensus* from end to end, and there were no survivors. She omitted Grelben from her tally. He would surely refuse to leave the ship. Captain's prerogative. Captain's curse. Captain's penance, too, she considered, still unable to wish upon him, or anyone, death in this manner.

She had been lost repeatedly in the smoke, been saved more than once by providential discoveries of emergency respirators. Their capacity was limited, and she'd left a trail of empties behind her on her trek. She finally found her way to the hatch that led to the zoo hold and safety.

The entrance was shut and inoperative.

Frantically, she tore open the access panel to get at the manual override. The crank stuck after a quarter turn. Crying in frustration, she tugged and tugged. It would not budge.

The corridor grew ever hotter. Gagging, Swelk limped to the cargo hold where the fire had begun. The flames there remained impenetrable to vision, let alone passage. She could not get off the ship. She turned inward, stumbled to the bridge, feeling herself roasting.

"I did not expect to see you again." The captain was slumped across his command seat, his limbs and sensor stalks limp. A command console behind him flashed insistently.

Swelk could not see the console—the flashing was an alarm of some kind, she assumed—but its light pulsed luridly through the thick, billowing smoke. "No Krul should die alone."

Grelben winced at her words. "You are a better Krul than I give you credit for." When she did not comment, he added, "You are a better Krul than many of us.

"Let me show you something. Look closely; the outside sensors burn off in seconds when I expose them." A gagging fit interrupted whatever explanation he was trying to make. He gestured at a flat display. "Section . . . three . . . two . . . two . . . camera . . . on."

Swelk peered through swirling smoke into the little display, flat like a human television. A sense of warmth, totally unrelated to the fires ravaging the starship, suffused her. The Girillian animals, her friends, were wandering on the airfield. There was no mistaking the two who were settled calmly beside Darlene: Smelly and Stinky. As the swampbeasts extended their long necks to be touched, the image dissolved into a blizzard of static.

"Sorry, Swelk. That's my last outside sensor."

They sat—together—in companionable silence until consciousness faded from them.

Except for smoke and hungry flames, all that moved on the bridge of the *Consensus* was the text still blinking on the command console.

Clean Slate acknowledged.

THE LAND OF DARKNESS

CHAPTER 30

THE GARMENTS AND SKIN colors varied with the architectural backdrops, but the scenes were otherwise depressingly alike. Seething seas of humanity: fists shaking, faces contorted in anger, mouths agape in angry chanting. Desecrated flags—usually American, with a scattering of Russian. Hand-lettered signs—always in English—denouncing the two great nuclear powers. Uncle Sam in effigy, hung or aflame or trampled underfoot.

Why isn't anything Russian ever hung in effigy? wondered Harold Robeson. *An effigy bear, maybe? Hal, isn't there something more productive you could be thinking about?*

There was a hesitant tap. His secretary was befuddled by his blowing off a long-scheduled confab with a key senator, for no apparent reason other than navel gazing. "Yes, Sheila."

A mass-of-black-curls head poked through a barely ajar door into the Oval Office. "Secretary McDowell to see you, sir."

Nathan McDowell, the secretary of state, was a short, pudgy fellow, his acne-scarred face dominated by a plug nose and a scruffy goatee. He evidently went out of his way to find ill-fitting suits, which he then had professionally rumpled. The contrast of his dishevelment with his ten-steps-ahead thinking could not have been starker. "Mr. President."

They were alone, *old* friends who'd met as Marine lieutenants in Nam. The formality was ominous. He pointed at a chair. "Take a load off. What's up, Nate?"

Ignoring the invitation, Nate studied the muted monitors. "Basking in the appreciation of our fellow citizens of Earth?"

"I never expect appreciation, but is holding down the stupidity so much to ask?"

"Not stupid, Hal, only ill-informed. Reacting to dashed hopes." His friend paused, hands clasped behind his back, watching the chanting mobs. "Do you know how many billion people on this Earth live in grinding poverty? How many have yet to use a phone?

"The arrival of the Galactics was a big deal to them." McDowell gestured at the screens. "In some ways, more than for the advanced countries. These people are taught—with some justification—to blame the major powers for colonialism and Cold War proxy wars, for the banking panics that periodically crush their economies, for global warming. The Galactics stood for *hope*. They promised new wonders for *Earth*. The poorest on our planet had the most to gain, while the envied, and sometimes hated, First World was revealed in its technological shortcomings.

"Now we and the Russians have taken all that away."

"What hope?" Robeson pounded what had once been Teddy Roosevelt's desk. "Dammit, Nate, the aliens were genocidal. We and the Russians, the ones being reviled in Cairo and Beijing, in Caracas and Lagos and wherever, we saved the world from megadeaths, to be followed by radioactive fallout and maybe nuclear winter. We suffered hundreds of casualties stopping it all."

"So we say." McDowell raised his hand. "Don't shoot the messenger. If you're a subsistence farmer or sweatshop worker in a Third World hell hole, would *you* believe aliens came from another star to meddle in human politics?"

"You think we should have revealed the aliens tried to destroy us for their movie?"

"Despite being the truth, that is even less believable. What's our evidence? Shot-up F'thk robots just prove the aliens were wise not to leave their ship in person. Swelk's debriefing videos? Since her responses came from a translator gadget, anyone skeptical will 'know' the tapes were dubbed." Nate shook his head. "How many Americans believe the Apollo landings were staged? No, the Krulirim first-level deception—that balance-of-power issues in their Galactic Commonwealth made Earth expendable—remains our best bet. There are lots of countries whose politicians were part of the F'thk whispering campaign."

"Do these fools think *Atlantis* blew itself up, that our early-warning satellites spontaneously fried themselves? Why, in God's name, do they suppose we attacked the aliens?"

McDowell finally settled into a chair. "You *know* why, Hal, unpalatable as it sounds. For very good reasons, we and the Russians mock-waged Cold War II. For our gambit to succeed, that mutual hostility had to be believable—and it was. We have the casualties to prove it. You can't expect everyone to suddenly believe we were kidding.

"Details vary from version to version, but here's what most people, including Americans, think. The Twenty-Minute War was our misguided attempt to turn Cold War Two hot. Radioactively hot. Benevolent aliens did their best to protect Earth from our folly, downing our missiles and slagging launching sites. In retaliation, or to disrupt the alien meddling, we killed the ETs we could reach. The other aliens, those aboard the moon-orbiting mother ship, left in disgust."

Robeson jammed his hands into his pockets—the President can't be seen plopping his head wearily into his cupped hands, not even by his oldest confidant. Too bad. "If the aliens are the heroes, what do the rioters think holds us back now? We have plenty of missiles left."

"They think," said McDowell, "we came momentarily to our senses. And that they'd better keep our minds focused." A muted screen changed scenes, from the humanity-filled Tiananmen Square to the besieged American embassy in Jakarta. "Or that the quasi-coup in Moscow cooled things down."

Robeson shivered. It had been *so* close. Dmitri Chernykov had failed in the first requirement of an officeholder: knowing how secure was his grip on power. He was supposed to have had another few days before the nationalists made their move. "Will their new coalition hold?"

"Nam was simpler, wasn't it?" McDowell was standing again, holding a Marine Corps-era snapshot of them he'd taken off a bookshelf. "Ending a firefight unshot and uncaptured meant things were fine." He put back the photo. "My Russia experts say the power-sharing pact *may* be stable. The nationalists in

the coalition seem fervently to believe the credible disinformation about a shooting war. In their eyes, Chernykov is a hero for
lobbing nukes at us. That said, near-immolation is a bit scary.
They're content to let things simmer down. America, goes the
current thinking, knows better now than to try pushing around
Mother Russia."

"Meaning Chernykov must pretend belligerence. It keeps getting
better." Robeson took a bottle of spring water from the well-
concealed mini-refrigerator. "Something for you?"

"Got anything harder?" To Robeson's glance at a clock, Nate
added, "It's late enough in London."

"What did the Brits do now? Don't tell me *they* don't accept
the truth." Robeson splashed liquor into a glass. His reach for
the water carafe drew a frown; he delivered the scotch neat.
Something *bad* was coming.

"To paraphrase a former occupant of this office, it depends
what your definition of 'accept' is. Recognize the validity of our
data, yes. Believe what we say transpired, yes." McDowell took a
long swallow. "Understand why they weren't party to the deliberations? Show willingness to come to terms with their exclusion?
Not . . . a . . . chance."

Flashes of color outside the Oval Office window caught his eye.
The first was his visiting three-year-old granddaughter, who had,
she'd proclaimed at breakfast, dressed *herself*. He had to laugh.
Brittany had on lime-green pants, a maroon-and-gray plaid shirt,
and yellow sneakers. A broken kite dragged and bounced behind
her. His daughter and two Secret Service agents tagged along. He
tore his eyes away. "Go on, Nate."

"It's more than the Brits. France, Germany, Canada, Japan . . . pick
your loyal ally. They're all outraged." Another swig. "As a diplomat,
I understand. Not consulting a long-time partner is bad enough.
They don't much like the explanation: we considered telling them
what was really happening an unacceptable security risk. They
can't handle that, for the best of reasons, I grant you, we flat-out
lied to them." McDowell drained the glass. "*I* lied to them."

"No more than did I."

Nate stared into the empty tumbler, looking *old*. At long last
he said, "The difference is, you were elected."

"No." The suggestion was too horrible to consider. "You're not
resigning."

"Yes, I am. America's best friends have a real problem with us. We've lost credibility, and only something dramatic will show our contrition. They want proof of our remorse." McDowell poured a refill. "It's for the greater good."

"Your resignation is not accepted. I need your help, Nate."

"Then take it. My considered opinion is I'm expendable." McDowell waved at Brittany, skipping past the window again. "I have grandkids, too. You'll be doing me a favor."

"I didn't become President to sacrifice my friends." In meaningless symbolic atonement, Robeson's thoughts continued. At that instant, he truly *hated* his job.

"But you will." McDowell's smile was worldly-wise, as if reading his mind. "I don't recall the Constitution making you the planet's guardian, either—but you are."

"Pour me a shot," Robeson said. They both knew that meant, "Yes."

The spring day was delightful. Only a few high clouds scudded across a blue sky. Flowering trees were in full bloom; the air was thick with pollen; the gentle breeze was warm. Elementary-school students streamed by, teachers and parental escorts shushing and herding.

Nuclear war and alien Armageddon alike seemed as unreal as snow.

"Great place," said Kyle. He sat beside Darlene on a bench at the National Zoo, the new Girillian habitat before them. That exhibit's popularity was in no way reduced by complete ignorance where Girillia *was*. The snaking queue of tourists extended well past the sign that read: THREE HOURS WAIT FROM THIS POINT. The adjacent Panda House, home of the zoo's famous Chinese great pandas, was for the first time in Kyle's knowledge without its own line.

"Lovely." Darlene brushed an errant lock of hair from her eyes. "Swelk would've approved."

Nearby, an elephant trumpeted. A swampbeast—almost certainly Smelly, Kyle thought—boisterously *harrumphed* back. Not a day had passed since the near-apocalypse at Reagan National that he did not think of Swelk, but visiting her charges here was especially wrenching. "I made a promise, the day we met. She was channel surfing at my house while I made arrangements for her. She asked to see elephants."

"It's not your fault, Kyle."

"She specifically sought my help. If not my fault, then whose?" As close as he and Dar had become in their grief, the silence stretched awkwardly. Kyle found himself studying the faint lunar crescent, scarcely visible in the day sky. "I don't know that Krulirim ever wear shoes, but I keeping waiting for a huge boot to drop."

"They're *gone*, Kyle. All gone. The hologram of the mother ship disappeared—you *know* this—while . . . while the ship was burning. The satellites they left behind are inert."

He understood the catch in Dar's throat: she could as accurately have identified that instant as just before Swelk's death. Delta Force surveillance cameras had captured the brief appearance amid the flames of an antenna. Much analysis later, he knew the dish had been aimed at the moon. *Something* had been transmitted: the mother ship had vanished seconds later. "In a way, I wish we had been better able to hear those last exchanges on the bridge." And in a way, that would have made their helpless witnessing of Swelk's death yet more painful . . . even though it seemed she passed away entirely at peace. "Whatever the reason—the crackling flames, or Grelben and Swelk coughing from the smoke, or overheating of the hidden computer through which we eavesdropped—so much that we heard was garbled, incomplete.

"What was in the file 'Clean Slate'? Steps to reverse however much of the damage they could? Or some sort of doomsday device?" Despite the balmy weather, he shivered.

"Kyle, you'll drive yourself crazy." She squeezed his hand. "Why don't we go see the girls?" Dar had adopted Swelk's kittens, now eight months old.

He squeezed back. "I'd like that." *And I like you,* though he wasn't prepared to explore that feeling. He didn't think she was quite ready either. But there would come a time . . .

Strolling together to the subway station, Kyle tried hard not to stare up at the ghostly moon. On that lifeless world, so central to the aliens' deceptions, he somehow knew Earth's future would be determined.

CHAPTER 31

The legendary courtier Damocles is said to have reveled at a royal banquet, oblivious to the sword suspended above him by a single hair. Humanity, in celebrating its escape from the plot of hostile Krulirim, may be as recklessly unobservant as was Damocles. Like Damocles, extreme peril hangs, unnoticed, just over our heads and beyond our reach.

> —excerpt from "The Continuing Danger
> from Krulchukor Artifacts"
> (Classified national-security briefing to the President)

THE SWORD OF DAMOCLES was a later conceit. The comparison with which Kyle first vocalized his resurgent dread was less elegant, and far less flattering to his species.

Inch-thick salmon steaks, crusted with black pepper, sizzled on the grill. Mesquite smoke rose from a bed of perfect red-hot coals. Chirps and warbles filled the air. An ice dam collapsed in the chrome bucket in which a champagne bottle was chilling for the meal, the melting cubes settling with a lyrical tinkle into new positions.

If only things were as idyllic as they appeared.

"I like it." Britt's sweeping gaze encompassed the old fieldstone house, the rough-surfaced redbrick terrace framed in massive weathered timbers, the ranks of pine and mountain ash and dogwood in full flower that graced the nearby hillside. Kyle's other guests were at that moment hiking up that steep slope. "Very calming."

"Thanks, boss." Kyle expertly flipped the salmon as he tried to imagine a segue into what was bothering him. Darlene had succeeded, at his instigation, in drawing those other guests, the balance of the erstwhile crisis task force, from earshot. The more time he spent with her, the more glaring were his own rough edges. How would she—had she known—bring this up?

He needn't have worried.

"We've been colleagues how long?" Britt nibbled on a deviled egg. "This is my first time here. And, no offense, you're an every-silver-lining-has-a-cloud sort of guy . . . not to deny that your annoying pessimism all too often turns out to be annoying realism. In short, you're the last member of our merry band I'd expect to host a victory party. What is this *really* about?"

Still unsure how to begin, Kyle pondered the salmon sizzling on the grill. "It's like shooting fish in a barrel," he blurted. "And we're the fish." In plain English, that was the unnerving conclusion of weeks of confidential research.

Darlene, Erin Fitzhugh, and Ryan Bauer emerged into the clearing on the crest of nearby Krieger Ridge. From where they stood, the burned-out site of Swelk's arrival remained evident. All recognizable fragments of the lifeboat had long ago been taken to the Franklin Ridge lab. Good job, Dar: they'd be away long enough to cover the basics.

"Would you mind elucidating, Kyle?"

"The Krulchukor weapon platforms. They're orbiting over our heads, beyond our reach. They're quiescent, but we can't know what may set them off again." Now that the topic was broached, icy calm settled over him. He was as certain of this analysis as any work he'd ever done. "Ever ask Ryan about his fear of flying?"

"Care to pick up the pace? I imagine you arranged our friends' absence to speak alone with me. They'll surely be back for dinner soon."

Guilty as charged. "The masersats have been quiet since the destruction of the *Consensus*. We've taken that to mean the starship controlled them. No starship, no threat. But that was only inference. People at the lab have been poring over the records from that day. We can't interpret the radio signals from the *Consensus,* but there is no obvious time correlation between messages and maser blasts. We witnessed several smooth hand-offs of attack roles as Earth's rotation took some satellites out of line-of-sight of their targets. And we now know the masersats didn't all stop shooting at once." Kyle suppressed an irrelevant twinge of cognitive dissonance at calling the tactical transfers hand-offs. Krulirim did not exactly have hands.

"And this means?"

"It suggests that the satellites have autonomous capability. That worries me. And we can see from Swelk's translation program, and dealings with the F'thk robots, that Krulirim have better language-understanding software than humans. Natural language understanding is one of the largely unmet challenges of artificial-intelligence research. The observations all confirm Swelk's claims of widespread AI usage at home, technology far beyond anything we have."

A wind gust riffled Britt's hair as he thought. "Then why did the masersats stop firing? What would make them start again?"

"Now I'm drawing my own inferences. There might have been multiple causes for the halt. First, we were attacking the masersats as best we could. We probably damaged or destroyed a few. Meanwhile, and second, some masersats might just have hit all their preprogrammed targets. Before stopping, they'd already destroyed our and the Russians' experimental ground-based ABM/antisatellite laser facilities. They'd obliterated the International Space Station"—thankfully abandoned since shortly after the *Atlantis* disaster—"and far too many other satellites. They'd nailed dozens of ICBMs in flight, missiles we'd retasked as antisatellite weapons, then fried the silos those rockets launched from." Kyle scowled in remembrance of the casualties.

"Point three. The masersats are solar-powered. Even one microwave blast uses lots of stored energy. Infrared observations during the assault suggest some masersats were temporarily drained. They would have had to recharge before they could fire again.

"The Krulirim didn't expect our ambush. My hypothesis is that the masersats were in an automatic self-defense mode. Once they hit all preprogrammed targets"—like, presumably, the innocent, sitting duck of a space station—"and once we stopped providing targets of opportunity by firing at *them,* there was nothing obvious left to shoot at. Who knows what activity, what overheard radio chatter, AIs on the satellites might interpret, or misinterpret, as threatening? Who's to say under what circumstances they can self-designate new targets?"

Kyle rushed on. "And we still don't know the meaning of 'Clean Slate.' Or what the Krulirim did on the moon. We *must* go there, we have to."

Britt's beer stein shattered on the patio. Kyle stared. His boss never lost his temper.

"No." Widened eyes revealed Britt's self-amazement. "Kyle, there are limits."

"But we don't . . ."

"I said, no. Do you honestly believe Nate McDowell wants to retire right now? Do you understand what happens when a billion overseas consumers boycott American corn and fast food and computers and movies?"

Kyle's other guests crossed a glade halfway down the hill. Whatever he'd done wrong, he had to make amends. Quickly. He did a mental rewind. "A moon program isn't affordable?"

"Not politically. Not economically." Kneeling, Britt began to collect bits of glass. "I apologize for my outburst."

"It's all right." But it wasn't. How dire were circumstances? *Take* something *when you can't have everything.* The advice that popped into his head could have come from Britt's years of mentoring, or Dar's more recent influence. It wasn't his normal approach to problems.

"Britt, excuse *me.* Forget I mentioned the moon, and we'll get back to certainties. The aliens eavesdropped on us by satellite. Their software translated and interpreted what they overheard. And our most optimistic projections say we disabled fewer than half the masersats."

Erin, Ryan, and Darlene made known their imminent return in an outburst of laughter. Erin Fitzhugh roared the loudest, no doubt relishing her own raunchy joke. A grinning Ryan Bauer followed her from the woods, waggling the beer emptied during the brief hike. Darlene appeared last, looking sheepish.

"Enjoy your meals, folks." Britt straightened, a cupped hand holding a carefully arranged mound of glass shards. His confident manner belied his earlier, unwonted anger. "It looks like we have work yet ahead of us."

*   *   *

Darlene blushed at another peal of laughter, as Britt, Ryan, and Erin made their ways to their cars. She made a production of dumping paper plates and plastic utensils into the trash—it kept her back to the hall from which Kyle, having escorted the others, would reappear. As she dawdled, crunching gravel marked the departure of vehicles.

"Thanks again for the help." Kyle had stopped in the doorway. "For the side dishes *and* getting me time alone with Britt."

Damn that Erin Fitzhugh. Darlene began scraping serving bowls. "My pleasure."

"Leave those. That's above and beyond the call of duty. You've got a long drive, too."

She puttered a little longer at the sink, until she felt her face was no longer red. Frantic scratching at the patio door gave her a good excuse to turn. She'd brought the kittens for the day. "Mind if I let in Blackie?" Stripes was already ramming around inside.

"Sure." Pregnant pause. "On the back forty before dinner . . . why all the cackling?"

She was a trained diplomat, and she could surely spin, digress, or weasel her way out of any admission. But this wasn't work; maybe she'd play it straight. Wiping damp hands on her jeans, she swiveled to face him. "How shall I put this? Erin speculated somewhat colorfully about the . . . closeness . . . of our friendship."

"I can imagine how delicately she made the suggestion." Kyle grimaced. "If you don't mind my asking, Dar, what was your response?"

She hadn't dignified Fitzhugh's gibe with an answer. Darlene crouched to scratch Blackie between the ears. The kitten was a gangly teenager now. Swelk loved the cats—and she'd never see them grow up. Darlene fought back tears.

Life was too short to always play it safe. They kept skirting the edge of a deeper relationship, and then shying away. As Erin would have said, screw this. "I defended your virtue."

"Ouch! You sure know how to hurt a guy."

Saying nothing is an old ploy for making the other person say more. She said nothing for a long time. The moon peeked over the ridge, cool silver light streaming through the patio doors.

"And you said nothing I didn't deserve." He crossed the room and kissed her. "The moon is beautiful tonight. Let's sit outside for a while."

CHAPTER 32

IN HIS HEART OF HEARTS, the campaign that began at Kyle's barbecue was Project Swelk. Not only, he liked to think, would his friend have approved, the private name also befit the plan having three stages. The plan's final part, however, was something best unarticulated . . . at least for now. His reticence left unchallenged Ryan Bauer's proposed code name: Project Clear Skies.

Today was a big day in the execution of Phase One.

Kyle sensed the weight of the mountain, deep within whose bowels the command center was burrowed. It wasn't claustrophobia, which had never afflicted him. No, his awareness of the vast bulk of Cheyenne Mountain manifested itself in feelings of safety. Easily a billion tons of rock separated him from the masersats—reassuring despite his conviction that today's activities could draw no hostile attention here. The imagery he so eagerly awaited was being collected by passive sensors scattered around the globe. Much of the comm link from each telescope and instrument to these underground warrens traversed buried, military-use-only—which was to say, supposedly untrackable and unhackable—optical fibers.

If you're so confident, Kyle, why is that gigaton of shielding overhead so comforting?

He was in a VIP viewing area, whose glass front formed the top half of the rear wall of the space control center. Fingering his tie nervously—he was in a suit; his three companions were Air Force officers, and in uniform—Kyle scanned the tiers of workstations below, and the men and women laboring intently at their terminals. An enormous, flat-screen display dominated the front of the control center. The screen showed a world map, overlaid with the ground tracks of orbits of interest. Bright spots on the ground tracks marked the current positions of specific satellites. All but one orbit shown was for alien weapons platforms. The side walls held lesser, but still impressively large, displays. Those were currently blank.

Space Control, one of six major operations in the NORAD complex, kept tabs on everything in near-Earth space. Satellites operational and otherwise, spent upper stages of rockets that had launched those satellites—and debris from rockets that had exploded in the attempt, tools dropped on manned orbital missions . . . all in all, there were thousands of objects to be watched. NORAD did not reveal just how small an item it could detect, but they did, from time to time, warn NASA and commercial satellite owners to tweak a mission's orbit because a bit of space junk would otherwise pose a hazard.

There was an intercom button in the frame retaining the wall of glass. Bethany Johnson, the brigadier general commanding the 21st Space Wing, with responsibilities including Cheyenne Mountain Air Force Station, pressed it. "Five minutes. Look sharp, people." She was a wiry black woman of average height, with wide-set eyes behind wire-rimmed glasses. Johnson had none of Bauer's ex-pilot, good-ole-boy swagger; she'd risen through Air Force ranks on the unglamorous logistical side until Space Command began offering operational opportunities to women. Her demeanor conveyed endless determination. Releasing the button, she turned to Kyle and Ryan Bauer, her guests. "Any requests for the auxiliary screens?"

"Can you project our wayward satellite and the target?" Kyle asked.

"Absolutely, optically and in pseudocolored IR view. No radar, of course . . . by your rules. We wouldn't want to risk your AIs, should they be real, knowing we're watching." This *particular* masersat was visible to radar, although it hadn't been before the Twenty-Minute War. That this bird appeared on radar was one more reason to believe it was out of commission. Johnson nodded to her aide, who whispered urgently into his headset mike.

The side screens came alive. On Kyle's right appeared an unmanned spacecraft of obvious human design: gold-foil-covered (except for its solar-cell wing) and boxy, with nozzles and instruments and antennas jutting in all directions. The telescopic image was blurry, details lost to atmospheric shimmer. A picture-in-picture shot rendered the same satellite as imaged by infrared sensors. The computer-generated colors were indicative of incident sunlight absorbed by the satellite and reradiated, and of heat generated and emitted by internal operations. The satellite jittered and tumbled, the flames from random firings of attitude jets unmistakable in the IR view. Only in close-up were the tumbling and corkscrewing motions visible; at the coarse resolution of the front screen, the satellite's blue track was arrow-straight.

"Thanks," said Kyle. The left screen showed another spacecraft, whose flowing curves screamed of an alien origin. The hull had paired bulbous sections, suggesting the segmented body of an insect. The sections struck him as subtly mismatched, as though dissimilar machines had been fused. Whether that perception had any validity, he couldn't begin to guess. But forget guessing—the operation culminating today was part of a systematic process. In due course, if all went according to plan, an artifact like this would become available for dissection.

And Captain Grelben's plans? If Kyle had miscalculated, today's actions would trigger dormant Krulchukor AIs. The *Atlantis* fireball came unbidden to his mind's eye. Packed jumbo jets were as vulnerable to masers. Was it wiser to let sleeping weapons of mass destruction lie?

The Krulchukor satellite also tumbled slowly. Its wings, presumed power-generating solar panels, met the hull at quite different angles. "The masersats don't all look bent, do they?"

"Only a few are asymmetric; the irregularities that do occur all differ," said Ryan. "Best guess is it's battle damage. The laser probably wasn't on one spot long enough to sever a strut, just to soften it. And check out the IR view, how the bent wing's surface radiates heat so unevenly. I'm guessing our Russian buddies melted some solar cells."

That would be before another alien satellite slagged the Russian ground-based ABM laser. They were rehashing familiar facts, running out the clock. Kyle's stomach churned. His head swiveled from image to image: target and probe.

"Colonel," said Johnson to her aide. "Three minutes to closest approach. Would you do a synopsis for our guests?"

"Yes, sir!" Arnold Kim, a Korean-American with close-cropped gray hair, towered over his commanding officer. "General Bauer, Dr. Gustafson, we'll start on the main screen. You see seven parallel tracks, running pole to pole." On the display, those tracks tipped about twelve degrees to the north-south axis—the effect on the ground track of Earth's rotation. "Each orbit has three enemy satellites, equally spaced, appearing on their track as colored dots. The orbits are also evenly separated; that's one every fifty-one and change degrees of longitude. All twenty-one satellites circle at the same altitude, about twenty-three hundred miles. Every spot on Earth is in sight of several weapon platforms at all times."

The scenario was familiar: VIPs visit from Washington, and the attention-starved assistant belabors the obvious. Killing time was one thing; missing the action—even though everything was being captured for replay—was another. The translucent timer superimposed over Antarctica decremented below two minutes. "I've got it, Colonel. Green dots for satellites believed to be disabled, like that one." Kyle pointed. "Red dots for enemy satellites thought still to be dangerous." As the next encounter will be . . . if we get that far. "Yellow for the birds we're unsure of. That includes the three that have never been seen to fire, presumed defective."

"Yes, sir." The tone conveyed disappointment at thunder stolen.

Ryan Bauer glowered disapprovingly at Kyle. Too brusque, interpreted Kyle. By way of amends, he tossed out a question for which he needed no answer—and for which the reply should be brief. "But the blue track, Colonel, on the intersecting path across the alien orbits?"

"Our innocent, helpless visitor, sir."

"Sixty seconds." The advisory came over the intercom, presumably from someone in the control room beneath.

Kim whispered again into his mike. Sensors monitoring the satellites panned back; the spacecraft now appeared together in the side displays. Both spacecraft tumbled, the boxy one also jittering about seemingly at random. It defied mere human abilities to extrapolate whether a collision would occur—although, on the world map, the blue and green dots had merged. A text window popped up in a corner of the close-up, the value thus revealed dancing up and down without leaving the vicinity of ninety percent. The inset infrared view of the alien craft stayed cool—there was no sign of masers preparing to fire.

"Thirty seconds." The numbers continued to bounce, but the trend toward 1.000—certain collision—was unmistakable. "Twenty seconds . . . fifteen . . . ten."

The human satellite zigged once more, impelled by yet another seemingly random firing of an attitude jet. The spacecraft suddenly diverged; the numbers dropped in a blur towards zero. To whistles and claps and cheers of approval, in the viewing gallery above and the control room below, blue and green dots on the big screen separated.

Kyle extended a hand in congratulations to their relieved-looking host. "Well done, General."

How many alien weapons still functioned? Were those that had survived potentially hostile? What might induce an attack? Without answers, it was impossible to know whether the Krulirim were, from beyond the grave, still capable of trapping mankind on Earth. Space missions that had come to seem routine could now provoke truly frightening retribution. From the *Atlantis* explosion to the destruction of underground missile silos, the dangers of a space-based siege were all too apparent.

Today's maneuver had probed one of the masersats whose behavior had changed since the Twenty-Minute War. It tumbled along its path, where before it had maintained an orientation toward Earth. Its looping course was slowly deviating from the orbit it had once precisely shared with two other alien satellites—unlike those neighbors, it no longer performed the occasional maneuvers that would compensate for the perturbations from solar wind, lunar drag, and slight irregularities in the Earth's mass distribution. Its presumed solar wings no longer pivoted to track the sun, sharply diminishing the amount of solar power it could be accumulating. Observed by ground-based infrared sensors, it exhibited far less variability in heat distribution than most other alien satellites. And it had lost its one-time invisibility to radar.

If this satellite was, in fact, irreparably damaged, it ought not to respond to a flyby. With luck, none of the undamaged masersats would notice a flyby of this derelict, or if they did notice, consider the close encounter reason to react. The challenge, when the stimulus most likely to provoke an automated attack was a missile launch, was to somehow approach their prey.

Kyle's insight had been that launch would be avoided, if (and it was a big if) an already on-station spacecraft could be repurposed. With Ryan Bauer's ungentle prodding, Space Command offered a spysat. It was higher than most surveillance platforms, put there to test technology for observations from heights unreachable by the primitive missiles of rogue states.

The earthly concern that had motivated the expensive orbiting test bed now seemed quaint.

The spysat had been launched scant months before the arrival of the *Consensus*, with fuel for a five-year mission. It was owned by the National Reconnaissance Office, the supersecret agency whose very existence remained classified throughout the Cold War. No doubt not having paid for the satellite made it easier for Space Command to offer it up.

Kyle's scheme involved far more maneuvering than the NRO's mission planners had had in mind—but he didn't object to spending onboard fuel profligately. What mattered was that the spysat's orbit was about right, that its instrument suite included an IR sensor, and that the manufacturer had a good simulation program for modeling the satellite's response to engine burns.

The wide separation between masersats gave ample opportunities to send signals, without fear of detection, to human-built satellites. Soon after Kyle's barbecue, a new navigation program was beamed to the spysat. Two days later, the satellite's attitude jets began firing erratically. Fuel sufficient for eighteen months' normal orbit-tweaking was burnt in seconds, sending the spacecraft tumbling wildly and slightly raising the apogee of its orbit. From time to time, its onboard controls seemed to have some success in regaining stability, in reorienting the solar panel so that the batteries could be recharged—and then the sporadic engine firings would resume.

The episodic engine burns, however unconventional, were not random—but, it was hoped, observant AIs would infer equipment failure from the satellite's haphazard course. Eighty-six and a fraction orbits later, the wobbling satellite, its fuel half gone, had barely missed a Krulchukor satellite showing every appearance of inoperability.

"Phil Davis here is the wizard who coded the navigation program." The gangly lieutenant was one of the officers General Johnson invited to the viewing gallery after the rendezvous had passed safely. His blue eyes, beneath a single caterpillar-like brow, darted about the room.

"Excellent job, Lieutenant." Kyle gestured at the side display still showing the initial target. The human spysat had receded from this view. "Brilliant programming." Praise only made the young man's nervous ocular motions increase. Kyle sighed inwardly: his words were sincere. "Did you have any questions, Lieutenant?"

Davis glanced at his feet. His scuffed shoes, however unmilitary, evidently instilled confidence. "Yes, Dr. Gustafson. I was given a navigation problem to solve, under rather odd constraints. What, exactly, were we hoping to accomplish?"

Short, and to the point. "We were gathering data. Your calculations"— Kyle had in mind the probability estimate that had briefly overlaid the scene—"showed a very high likelihood our wobbly bird would impact the alien craft. If a functional AI were watching, don't you think it would've gotten the masersat out of the way before our last-moment zig?"

Cocking his head, Davis considered the alien craft. "A working AI *and* control of its own propulsion. It's much the worse for wear."

"I concede that ambiguity, but the larger conclusion is unchanged. In the Twenty-Minute War, we clobbered this thing enough that it can't defend itself. That raises my confidence about other masersats we thought disabled."

There was a soft knock, a pause, and the door swung partway open. A steward backed in, tugging a squeaky-wheeled cart laden with soda cans, bottled water, an ice bucket, and a cookie platter. He left as unceremoniously as he'd entered.

"Healthier than my usual celebratory libations. Thanks, I guess." Bauer grabbed a Coke. "So, Lieutenant. Will the next bit go as smoothly?"

The attention of two generals and a presidential advisor, plus, for all the junior officer knew, the fate of human civilization on his narrow shoulders . . . Davis broke into a sweat. A quaver in his voice, he pointed at the main screen. The timer still floating over Antarctica decremented toward the next mission milestone. "Thirty minutes, sir, and we'll know."

The commandeered NRO satellite continued its seemingly random attitude-jet firings. Pitch, yaw, and roll slowed dramatically, without altogether stopping. With no obvious indication of being under control, it reduced its tumbling enough for onboard sensors to reestablish with precision its orientation and position. Every few seconds it took a fresh IR reading of a remote patch of the southern Pacific.

The satellite likewise gave no overt indication when the message for which it waited was received. It was scanning for a large fire, unmistakable to its infrared sensor. The nonexistence of that oil-slick blaze was unambiguous—and an absence could not be correlated by a hostile AI with subsequent events. The nonrecall authorized the spysat to execute the next routine in its uploaded navigational program: rendezvous with a second orbiting alien artifact.

The new target was armed and presumed extremely dangerous.

Through the fiber-linked, surreptitious eye of a telescope far from Cheyenne Mountain, the hurtling spysat was seen to perform a series of brief attitude-jet firings. Pitch, yaw, and roll largely damped out. The men and woman in the VIP viewing room, all spectators at this point, stared at the wavy, grainy image. The main parabolic antenna on the spacecraft spun three times around its mounting post.

Three rotations meant "target acquired."

"Well done, again, Lieutenant." Bauer slapped the embarrassed young man on the back.

"Now it gets interesting." Kyle studied a side screen. This masersat's wings looked identical; both were tipped to catch the maximum sunlight. In the infrared view, stripes on the spacecraft rippled and flowed, like a beast languorously flexing its muscles.

The spysat on his left had resumed its manic tumbling. Infrared revealed more seemingly ineffectual engine firings. Sensors caught a flurry of heat bursts, longer at first, and then trailing off to sputtering. In the end, the solar panel pointed straight down to Earth, twenty-three hundred miles below. *It sure looked,* thought Kyle, *as though the probe halted its spin with the dregs of its fuel. Here's hoping any AI on the target agrees.* In truth, the tanks remained one-third full.

The countdown timer on the map display forecast rendezvous in six minutes.

"What's next, Lieutenant?" Bauer perched on the edge of the viewing room's oak table.

Davis gulped. "More waiting."

A red spot bloomed on the masersat's IR image, and the estimated collision probability plummeted. "That hot spot's no maser," said Bauer. "What happened?"

"It's moving," answered Kyle. "Now to answer the big question: was it sidestepping a suspect visitor? Or was it a coincidence, an ordinary orbit-maintenance maneuver?"

The spysat they did not dare to radio so near to its target obeyed its programming—and the absence of an at-sea fiery abort signal. Its engines sputtered anew, and its path changed. The collision probability climbed. The two craft came close enough to be viewed on the same screen.

On the spysat, fuel pumps toiled. Safety interlocks in the original software had been overwritten from the ground, allowing pressure to mount behind closed fuel-line valves. Other unorthodox reprogramming had retracted the heat-dumping radiator panels. Streaming sunlight, unfiltered by atmosphere, drove heat into the seemingly crippled satellite. Heat seeping into the fuel tanks raised the temperature of the contents, and the pressure of the vapors within.

The masersat pivoted toward the approaching spacecraft. Reddening of the IR image revealed waste heat from torrents of power being routed. "Weapon charging." Kyle spoke more to unclench his teeth than in expectations of conveying information. "*Something* on board learns fast . . . maneuvering once didn't help, so it's preparing more active measures."

"Funny thing." Ryan's eyes gleamed. "We can learn, too."

The spysat's earthward-hanging solar panel served as an impromptu anchor, the gravity gradient holding steady the satellite's orientation. Solar heat continued to flood in. When fuel-tank pressures exceeded a preset level, the onboard computer opened the valves.

Overpressurized fuels gushed into the attitude jets' combustion chambers. No spark was needed—monomethyl hydrazine and nitrogen tetroxide ignite on contact. In such over-spec quantities, that ignition was spectacular indeed. A fireball erupted, its IR image painfully bright. (*This bang is* our *doing!* thought Kyle. *See how you like it.*) The explosion turned the NRO's expensive satellite into tons of shrapnel.

IR sensors flared. Fragments blazed as they were blasted by the maser. But too many pieces were headed toward the masersat, from too close . . .

The Krulchukor satellite twitched as the wave of debris struck. Holes gaped in the solar panels and hull. The IR view flashed and sparkled, as metallic shards shorted out circuitry. Then the whole room flashed crimson—the catastrophic discharge inside the masersat of stored energy meant to be pumped out through the masers.

When tearing eyes could again focus, *no* satellites were on-screen.

Kyle steadied himself against a wall. His heart pounded. The only change to the situational map was two dots removed. No alarms meant no retaliatory strikes. "The bad news is, we've confirmed the masersats have the capacity to act independently."

"The good news is, we can still, at least sometimes, out-think them."

Eighty-seven days later, a barrage of reprogrammed ballistic missiles, launched in a synchronized attack from safely submerged American boomers, overwhelmed the eleven Krulchukor satellites thought most likely still to be functional. The other ten remained gratifyingly inert.

In condemnation of American unilateralism, sixteen nations and the European Union recalled their ambassadors to Washington. Overseas corporations, bowing to public outrage, cancelled high-profile orders for American passenger jets, oil platforms and pipelines, pharmaceuticals, and supercomputers. The immediate human toll: another eighty thousand badly needed jobs.

As a longer-term consequence of the Second Twenty-Minute War, the space control center at Cheyenne Mountain started tracking thousands more bits of orbiting space junk.

CHAPTER 33

THE HELICOPTER *thp-thp-thpped* its way across the Los Padres National Forest. The heavily wooded park was lush and green, the jagged gash of the San Andreas fault unmistakable as the chopper raced over it. Spectacular scenery and engine roar alike conspired to preempt conversation. The burly, ruddy-faced pilot, in any case, wasn't terribly talkative.

Kyle peered past his reflection at the countryside sliding by beneath. The trip from Los Angeles to Vandenberg Air Force Base was, as the crow rolled the flat tire, roughly 150 miles. The view from the aptly designated scenic highway would have been superb. In a simpler world, he would have loved to have driven, Dar beside him, sharing breathtaking vistas of coastal mountains and rocky shore.

Of course, in a simpler world, a mission this dangerous would never have been conceived.

While he yearned for the impossible, he could hope that the roads to VAFB not be clogged by misinformed protesters, nor half the world's weather disrupted by El Niño. The same climatological phenomenon that kept this forest so verdant had his wife leading a State Department delegation from Indonesian drought zones to Peruvian flood plains. The squall line barely visible to the west, far out over the Pacific, might or might not be another manifestation of El Niño. Would weather delay today's launch?

Obstruction by natural causes seemed *so* unfair. Wasn't it enough to face the technological superiority of the Krulirim?

The taciturn Air Force captain flying Kyle over the protesters pointed at something to the south. One of the Channel Islands? A ship? A noncommittal answering grunt seemed to satisfy her. It was just as well Kyle wasn't driving; the scenery had already lost his attention. He could not keep his mind off his problems.

The *world's* problems, Dar would have insisted, not *his*. The point of semantics made not a whit of difference. For five years, Kyle's had been a lonely voice, often the *only* voice, championing today's mission. For five years, he'd kept all doubts to himself— there were enough advocates for inaction. For five years, he'd awakened each day wondering if this were the day a growing deficit, or international hostility, or political expediency finally overwhelmed his tenacity.

And for five years after the fiery destruction of the *Consensus*, the flotilla of alien satellites circled overhead. Had they been a part of Clean Slate? In theory they had been neutralized . . .

As the helicopter began its final descent to the VAFB airfield, Kyle again rephrased his thoughts. After five years of preparations, he was about to test theory with six people's lives.

Tantalizingly just beyond humanity's reach circled three failed-in-orbit masersats. These inert satellites had gone untargeted in both Twenty-Minute Wars. The first time, that omission had reflected expediency—more obviously dangerous targets had drawn Earth's fire. By the second conflict, leaving alone these three satellites was a matter of strategic calculation.

Phase Two of Clear Skies aimed to retrieve one of those nearly intact artifacts.

A space shuttle could take a masersat on board— if it could climb far above its four-hundred-mile altitude limit, and if it could achieve polar orbit. Two extraordinarily *big* ifs. Raising the shuttle's altitude meant refueling it in orbit. Refueling meant somehow lofting large amounts of fuel into space in a vessel with which the shuttle could mate. Flight-testing a large-capacity space tanker could hardly be done in secret.

Nor could the preparations be hidden for a new shuttle launch site. Populated regions north and south of Florida precluded initiating polar missions from Cape Canaveral. Another coastal location was required. Somewhere, should the worst again happen, with ample empty ocean to its south. Someplace like Point Arguella, California—which, not coincidentally, lay within the borders of Vandenberg AFB.

All this activity by a reinvigorated American space program—and involving a launch site within a military base—was anathema to the international community. In a world that believed—or, as in Russia's case, where *realpolitik* favored pretending to believe—that benevolent aliens had left behind orbiting guardians, renewed astronautical ambitions by the slayers of those masersats were intolerable.

But protests, worldwide boycotts, and the grinding recession notwithstanding, after five arduous years of preparation, it was finally time to execute Phase Two.

When, finally, the weather held and the Navy drove a flotilla of seagoing protesters from the restricted seas off Point Arguella, when at last the first manned mission ever to launch from Vandenberg AFB rose on a bone-jarring, ear-shattering, column of fire . . . it was tremendously, awe-inspiringly, and blessedly anticlimactic. Kyle exited the massively blast-proofed Launch Control Center as soon as it was safe, gazing southward until the last faint speck of a spark disappeared. The contrail twisted and tore as the winds along its length assailed it.

"Way to go, *Endeavor*!" Ryan Bauer gave Kyle a congratulatory slug in the shoulder. The general had become a fixture at Space Launch Complex Six (SLC-6, "Slick Six" to the locals). "I can't tell you how good that feels."

Kyle couldn't argue. But still . . . "That was the easy part."

"What is it Britt says about you? Every silver lining has a cloud."

"I should have been on board! I could have been. Plenty of payload specialists have been shuttle-trained in two months—I could have afforded that." But the President had nixed it, for "national security" reasons. *Damn* it.

"What payload would you have overseen, besides a stomach full of butterflies?"

"A head full of insight about Krulirim." A seagull fluttered to a landing by Kyle's feet. "How many of the crew have that background?"

"None—which is why you're *here*. Should this mission fail, we'll need more than ever what's in your head." Bauer grabbed Kyle's arm, turning him until their eyes met. "Leading isn't always done from the front. Trust me: I know what it's like to order others into battle."

"Hopefully, it won't come to battle." Kyle swallowed hard. "But there's plenty of risk even if the masersats stay dormant."

The cabin cruiser bounced and shuddered, bludgeoning a path through high seas. Darlene for the umpteenth time patted her sleeve. The Dramamine patch was still on her arm, and still unequal to the task. With each wave crested, the boat and her stomach fell out from under her, to return an instant later with a bone-jarring impact. The worst of the storm, supposedly, was now pummeling Mexico.

"I said," yelled Roone Astley, the ambassador to Costa Rica, "the weather is much better." It was his boat, and he stood with maddening assurance on what Darlene considered a bucking deck. He motioned to starboard. "The sky is getting lighter."

Another lurch of the boat sent her reeling. Astley caught her before she fell. The bite of breakfast she'd foolishly taken rose threateningly in her gorge. Yes, the sky was brighter, which only made more horrifying the view of the shoreline they were paralleling. The tropical downpour whose trailing edge continued to lash the boat had stalled for three days over the narrow Pacific coastal strip. The rain-saturated mountainside had come rumbling down in two.

They were nearing one more village washed away by mudslide. Except for the occasional stone chimney, nothing but snapped tree trunks at odd angles emerged from the muck. Pounding waves had churned the encroaching mud into an enormous stain stretching hundreds of yards into the ocean. Objects that thankfully could not always be identified bobbed in the darkened sea. Many were corpses, already bloating from decomposition. It was hard to imagine anyone surviving the disaster. With the houses buried, she couldn't begin to guess what the population had been. Hundreds, surely. And they'd passed a dozen such tragedies already. "This is horrible," she said. "You know I have emergency funds to release. What else can the US do?"

Astley paused for a staticky announcement from the marine

radio before answering. "What the Costa Ricans urgently need is emergency supplies and logistical support. They're getting some from the EU and Japan. I doubt they'll take such visible aid from us."

The hull slammed into another wave trough. Darlene staggered. "Another government still officially enraged at us? Have we made *no* progress?"

"We're still the murderers who drove away the Galactics, and with them the secret of free fusion power." He throttled back briefly, for reasons she was too landlubberly to understand. "They'll take our money, of course, if we give it privately."

The worst thing was, this immense, slow-moving tropical depression wasn't an isolated event. This year's El Niño phenomenon was the worst in years. As America's goodwill ambassador, she'd been traveling from catastrophe to catastrophe for weeks. Drought and uncontrollable forest fires in the western Pacific, storms in the eastern. How had her country fallen so low in the world's esteem that accepting American disaster relief was an embarrassment? And knowing what she did about the aliens . . . the rage against the US was *so* unjust.

The Krulirim! Her watch confirmed a belated, jet-lagged recollection of the date. Today was Kyle's big launch. Guiltily, she wondered how the end of Clear Skies was going.

NASA practice for the shuttle was to separate the orbiter from its external tank when the pairing reached ninety-seven percent of orbital velocity. In a fuel-wasting maneuver, the manned orbiter aimed its tank, just before that decoupling, for a dramatic splashdown in the Indian Ocean. The logic was to safely dispose of the tank rather than have them accumulate in orbit.

This was an Air Force mission, and the start of a new practice. The now nearly empty tank stayed with the orbiter all the way into a circular orbit at an altitude of 150 miles.

"Target on visual," drawled Major Tara "Windy" McNeilly, the *Endeavor*'s laconic pilot. Closed-circuit TV gave the ground team a pilot-eye view of the dartlike fuel carrier being overtaken by the orbiter. The waiting tanker—basically an unmanned and stripped orbiter replete with fuel—had been launched from Slick Six weeks earlier. It had been parked in a higher orbit until needed, then lowered in preparation for *Endeavor*'s launch. "Ten klicks."

In simpler times, the first manned launch from Vandenberg and the first shuttle to carry its ET into orbit would have been enough experimentation for one flight. For today's mission, the novelty had just begun. Minute by minute, hour by hour, tension built. The spacewalk to attach radio-controlled attitude jets to *Endeavor*'s about-to-be-jettisoned external tank. (Built-in thrusters would have required extensive ET modifications and unmanned shuttle test flights—time Kyle was reluctant to spend.) Remotely piloting the tanker to *Endeavor*'s now-separated ET. Docking, refueling, and undocking—and repeating that dangerous maneuver until it was routine. Rendezvousing again with the partially refilled ET (no human spacecraft could carry a full ET's worth of liquid hydrogen and liquid oxygen into orbit). Mating *Endeavor* with its refueled ET . . . remembering throughout how the botched docking of a much smaller resupply capsule had almost killed everyone aboard the late, lamented Russian *Mir*.

"Piece of cake," said McNeilly as she completed the final docking. She unbuckled and floated free in the small cabin, making microgravity bows. Colonel Craig "Tricky" Carlisle, her restrained mission commander, waited until the disconnect valves in both orbiter and ET reopened before flashing thumbs-up. A middeck camera showed four more beaming faces.

The expressions in mission control were equally happy. Kyle found an unused mike, then shot a questioning look at the capsule communicator, who nodded her go-ahead. "I suggest you folks get some sleep. Your next stop is going to be really interesting."

Two astronauts floated free, the orbiter having backed off to a distance that made tethers impractical. Puffs of compressed gas from the backmounted MMUs, manned maneuvering units, nudged them closer and closer to their quarry. The black, vaguely insectile masersat absorbed most of the illumination from their helmet-mounted lights.

"It's as we expected," said Major Anson "Big Al" Buckley. "The wings are covered in a repeating pattern, a grid of squares connected by fine lines. It sure looks like a solar-cell array."

"Agreed." Major Juanita Gonzalez, a woman of few words, was cursed with the unavoidable astronaut-corps nickname of "Speedy."

Thousands of miles away, Kyle overcame the urge to scream

with impatience. Solar cells weren't today's issue. "Can you fold the wings?" CAPCOM relayed the question. The masersats could not have exited the cargo-bay airlocks of the *Consensus* unless the struts folded—nor could one fit aboard *Endeavor* with its wings extended.

"Negative on that. No visible hinges, buttons, switches, or cranks." On the telephoto view broadcast from the *Endeavor*, only a tiny gap appeared between Buckley and the satellite. From the camera's frame of reference, the astronaut was floating on his head.

"I'm stumped," admitted Gonzalez. "I'm clueless how the twenty-seven-toed buggers fold the wings."

The spacewalkers tried a few tentative pushes and shoves, to no avail; the wings did not budge. "Okay, propose we go to Plan B."

CAPCOM looked to Kyle and Ryan Bauer for approval. Kyle triple-checked the IR view of the screen. Just solar heating, as far as he could tell. He nodded. "Roger that, Speedy."

On *Endeavor's* video, the astronauts were seen to deploy small, shiny tools: cordless power saws. Gloves and bodies conveyed a trace of electric-motor whine into the spacesuits, to be picked up by helmet mikes. Plan C, if needed, involved small shaped charges. "Here's luck for a change," said Big Al. "These spars cut like butter."

Not entirely good luck . . . Kyle had hoped to use a spar stub as a grappling point for the orbiter's robot arm. The stumps sounded too soft for that purpose, which took them to Plan B-and-a-half. Gonzalez jetted slowly around the alien artifact, trailing double-insulated braided steel cable. The astronauts snugged the loop loosely about the masersat's waistlike indentation with a sturdy metal ratcheting clamp. Strong brackets with heavy-duty knobbed posts were secured under the cable, and the clamp ratcheted until the cable was taut. The spacewalkers jetted back to the waiting shuttle, each with an alien solar panel in hand.

"All set," said the mission commander finally. It meant the spacewalkers were back aboard and the wings stowed in the cargo bay. It meant Evelyn Tanaka, the only civilian aboard but NASA's unchallenged master at operating the shuttle's robotic arm, was ready to reach out and make history. It meant "Windy" McNeilly was set for another close encounter. The orange-insulated cable and chromed brackets made the waiting satellite far more visible than on initial approach. "Houston, six votes here for loading up this bad boy and doing a boogie on down."

All eyes were on Kyle. "Lots of ayes here, too, Commander."

Forty minutes later, with the long-sought satellite securely locked into a cargo-bay cradle, Kyle allowed himself to truly believe this was going to work.

Darlene clung to the railing, the gale streaming the remains of her breakfast away from the boat. Foul taste in her mouth aside, she felt better. That was not the same as feeling well.

Several embassy marines had accompanied the ambassador; one left the cabin to check on her. She couldn't recall his name. "Can I get you some water, ma'am?"

Sky, sea, and mud-covered land . . . everything was gray. Something caught her eye. Not far behind them, a pier stuck out to sea. The jetty, like the village that had once owned it, was mostly buried in mud, but the last twenty feet or so were uncovered. Huddling on the end of the pier was . . . something. "Do we have binoculars?"

"Yes, ma'am." He returned quickly with a pair. "Here."

The binoc view only amplified the apparent motion of the boat. Ignoring her nausea, she swept the glasses along the shore. There! A child of uncertain age was trapped on the end of the pier, clinging desperately to a piling around which her arms scarcely reached. Between crashing waves, the girl waved frantically. Her mouth gaped, but Darlene could hear nothing over the roar of the sea. She handed back the glasses. "Sergeant. Watch that jetty." She half ran, half slid into the cabin, to see if the ambassador could, somehow, rescue the child.

The cursing that erupted behind her made plain, before the boat had scarcely begin to turn, that the storm had claimed one more victim.

CHAPTER 34

ONLY KYLE'S FEET were outside the shadow of the beach umbrella, and that exposure was by choice. He was planted in a beach chair, toes digging into damp sand whose moisture was sporadically replenished by swirls of mild Caribbean waters. An unopened novel rested on his lap.

Reading was the last thing he felt like.

Darlene's chair and his shared the umbrella. Beneath the wide-brimmed straw hat that covered her face she murmured in her sleep. She was the reason he was here. She badly needed a vacation, and the only way to get her on one was to go himself. Globe-trotting hadn't worn her out, it was her itinerary: disaster after catastrophe after cataclysm. He tried to share her worries, her sadness, but talking wasn't enough.

What was the world coming to when lolling on the beach with a beautiful woman was a duty instead of a delight? Sipping a piña colada, he tried to get interested in his book. What part of his frustration, he wondered, came from knowing he may as well be here as at the lab? Specialists needed the first crack at the recovered masersat. He'd only have been in their way.

Maybe he did belong on the beach: Project Clear Skies was over. (*But not Project Swelk,* his inner conniver rebutted. Kyle had yet to dare articulating the unsuspected step three.)

Aside from Dar's murmuring, all that could be heard were

seagulls and lapping waves. They had a long stretch of St. Croix shoreline to themselves. Not many Americans could afford vacations these days, while former friends took their tourist euros, yen, and rubles elsewhere.

The utterances muffled by Dar's hat became whimpers. Her limbs twitched. Damn it! Kyle was neither mind reader nor gambler, but he'd have bet big bucks she was reliving that moment off Costa Rica. The one tragedy that, unfolding before her eyes, personified the many deaths for which she'd tried to extend America's often-rejected concern. That poor girl! How long had she been trapped at the dock's end, only to drown with rescue within sight?

And poor Dar, watching helplessly as it happened.

With a flash of déjà vu, the azure sky once more blossomed with remembered flames. Of the many deaths for which the Krulirim were responsible, none obsessed him like the five men and women on the *Atlantis*. He could no more have saved them than the doomed submariners or silo crews. The difference was he'd experienced the shuttle tragedy at first hand, and that it was of a scale he could viscerally understand. He understood Dar's grief, all right. The next time she cried out, he had an urge to join. He threw his book in frustration.

"Drink, mister?"

Kyle turned. The crockery on the boy's tray glistened with condensation. Cherry stems, cocktail umbrellas, and plastic straws peered over the rims. "A colada. Bill it to room 412."

"Two, please." Dar sat up and removed her hat. "I woke myself up." She shouted herself awake many nights.

"No, I disturbed you, hailing this young fellow." The lad kept from his face any reaction to the white lie as Kyle accepted two brimming drinks.

She waited for the boy to continue his rounds. "Not unless your voice rose an octave and you were whimpering."

"You've got to lighten up on yourself." He handed her a beverage. "No, really."

"Physicist, heal thyself."

Touché. He drew a long sip through his straw. "We are a sorry pair, aren't we?"

"Speaking of being sorry ... I apologize in advance if this offends you." Holding her mock-coconut vessel at arm's length, she exchanged grimaces with its ceramic face. "We finally have the"—she glanced around furtively, although no one on the beach was in earshot—"item. It will be studied. Maybe it's time to apply that same focused attention to climate issues. Global warming. El Niño. Improved weather forecasting."

"The same focused attention" meant, *Change what you're doing. Kyle, tackle a problem that's certain.* She knew he knew. He leaned over and kissed her. "I really love you."

That didn't mean yes.

"UN SecGen demands custody of stolen Galactic guardiansat." Kyle ripped the clipping with its screaming headline from a corkboard. He hurled it, wadded and torn, into a trash can. What would the UN do with the artifact if they had it? He pictured it behind glass in a museum.

Before letting that happen, he'd swipe it *again.*

"Like a patient etherized upon a table." If Hammond Matthews had noticed his colleague's fit of pique, he gave no sign. It was Friday, and Matt wore scientist casual: jeans, T-shirt, white socks and sandals.

The outbuilding devoted to the study of the captured masersat was uncharacteristically empty. *It's amazing,* thought Kyle, *what fifty bucks of pizza can accomplish.* He would join the mini-thanks after his private viewing.

The "patient" spanned a line of lab benches. It was twenty-some feet long, and the canvas tarp draped over it revealed only gentle curves and the hint of a waist. "Try not to disturb it."

"We're doing our best."

The metaphor Kyle truly favored was too discouraging to express, a comparison that had first come to him as the charred, twisted wreck of the starship was trucked to Franklin Ridge.

The aliens had fusion power, an interstellar drive, and artificial gravity. How far ahead of human technology were they? Swelk said they'd had space travel for many Earth centuries. Still, a species as tradition-bound as the Krulirim surely discouraged the heresies that begat scientific revolutions. For the sake of argument, imagine they were *merely* one century ahead of humans.

A hundred years ago, Earth's cutting-edge technology was vacuum tubes and biplanes. No jet engines or rockets. No quantum mechanics, which meant no transistors or integrated circuits. No computers or fiber optics. What would the best scientific minds of 1907 make of, say, a half-melted space shuttle or Boeing 777? What beside wings and a tail would make sense?

Negativism was a vice Kyle refused to indulge. He flipped back the tarp to uncover the familiar insectile shape. To his surprise, the satellite gave no evidence of having been opened. Except for strips of masking tape, it looked untouched. He felt the surprise on his own face. "But the wings came right off."

"Watch." Matt grabbed a portable electric heater with a pistol grip—an industrial-strength hair dryer. It started with a roar, heat shimmers rising from its nozzle. He directed hot air toward the stump from which had once sprouted a solar-wing spar. After a few seconds, a gap formed. The stump divided very near the hull, suggesting the hinge that had eluded the spacewalkers. Gripped in an insulated glove, the hinged joint swung freely. "No, wait." He waved off Kyle. After the area cooled, he straightened the spar and reheated it. The seam disappeared. Wiggling the stump showed the junction had returned to its former rigidity. "Works every time, at exactly the same distance from the hull."

Shape-retaining alloys were found in expensive eyeglass frames and golf clubs, but Kyle had never heard of a material that remembered and reformed seams. "How'd you find this?"

"We wanted to get inside. There were no bolts to undo, no seams to unweld. Rather than cut at random, and damage who knows what, we did an ultrasound scan. It showed seams. The hull material feels," he rapped, "more like plastic than metal, so someone mentioned thermoplastic. We tried heating the lines from the ultrasound image."

Aha. "The tape on the hull marks heat-activated seams."

"This is why you're paid the big bucks." Ignoring Kyle's humph, Matt began heating the waistlike indentation between the main hull sections, rocking the satellite to reach completely around. "Everyone comments these sections don't look like they belong together." A space opened as he spoke. "Things are often as they seem."

Kyle pried gingerly at the newly opened gap with asbestos-coated gloves. The hull sections parted, only a few wires linking the halves. Every satellite he'd ever seen was jam-packed, its parts tightly interlinked. "Okay, one side has the phased-array antennas for active radar cancellation—stealthing. The other side has wave guides for the maser. Any guesses?"

"In a minute." Matt unrolled a paper scroll, weighting the corners with empty coffee mugs. The printout appeared to be an ultrasound image. "The other grafts are less obvious, but *four* pieces make up this baby. Look here," he tapped, "and here. You can see two smaller modules also spliced in. Like the radar section, there aren't many connections to the main body."

"Any idea what this means?"

"Yeah. Swelk told you the starship was a commercial freighter. She traveled with a film company. So why did the Krulirim have doomsday weapons?"

"We've all wondered." The question drove Ryan Bauer *nuts*.

"Here's our best guess," said Matt. "Imagine you're on the interstellar equivalent of a tramp steamer. You have no weaponry, but signaling equipment must be *very* powerful to reach between stars. Say, comm masers." He rummaged in a cabinet drawer and found some candy. "At this rate, there won't be any pizza left. Now there's no reason to hide comm masers, but the aliens wanted these hidden. Their plan wouldn't work if we'd seen them frying the *Atlantis* or the early-warning birds. So what could they have carried that would hide comm satellites?"

"Radar buoys?" guessed Kyle. "Handy for returning to places one's already checked out. Only you reprogram the buoys to beam the opposite signal of whatever they sense."

"So we think." Matt popped a handful of candy into his mouth. "Say they've improvised a stealthed weapon. How is it aimed? The star sensors used with a comm maser wouldn't track a shuttle in flight." He tapped a small circle on the printout. "See this little guy spliced into the maser section? We hope to prove it's an IR sensor, interfaced to the onboard computer."

"What's this graft?" Kyle pointed on the scan to another hull alteration. This section had its own antenna; a few wires connected it to the main electronics section. His question elicited only a shrug. "Well, *I* have a thought. It looks like an independent, much lower power, microwave subsystem. Maybe it was used to read out the damned orbs. Swelk said the recording equipment was from the troupe's supplies."

"Makes sense."

His on-the-beach feelings of redundancy were largely confirmed. Matt's team was making tremendous progress. "Now the big question. Why did it stop working?"

By way of reply, Matt aimed a penlight. "What do you see?"

Kyle pondered. Fat wires leading from the two small grafts and the radar section ended in an ill-shapen metallic glob. Near that clump was something blocky whose only familiar features were a connection to the solar-panel stump and what looked like a "heat pipe" for transporting thermal energy to an external radiator. On a human satellite, the greatest source of heat was the main power supply. The blocky thing had a small scorch on an otherwise featureless and unused metal connector. He burst out laughing. "You just can't get good help these days."

"Yup," agreed Matt. "Bad power connections. It would seem a sloppy soldering job has given us our best chance yet to understand these guys."

I would've thought it impossible, thought Darlene, *to be lonelier than the sole noncelebrant at a party. Now I know better.* Being that lone noncelebrant's spouse was *much* worse. The intimate setting, an antique-filled sitting room in the White House Residence, only emphasized Kyle's withdrawal. She nursed a piña colada—she'd become enamored with them in the Virgin Islands—while chatting with the rest of the team. In a gathering of five, there was no disguising Kyle's silent sulking.

Britt said the President would be by to extend his appreciation, "for a job well done." *For a job two-thirds done,* Kyle had muttered, not that his principled dissent or his odd choice of fractions now mattered. Nor did it improve his mood that even she, however reluctantly and diplomatically, disagreed with him. As one of the team, she couldn't paper over *this* difference of opinion. Sighing, she again sampled her drink. The White House bartender was second to none.

The ringing of fine crystal got everyone's attention. Britt was wielding the silver spoon. "Everyone? A moment of your time, please."

"That ship sailed five years ago," said Erin Fitzhugh, drawing a laugh.

"Fair enough." Britt set down his champagne flute. "And since I, too, want to thank you all for your heroic efforts, that reminder is entirely apt. Darlene, Erin, Kyle, Ryan—the order of that list being alphabetical, mind you—your country owes you a debt of deep gratitude."

Darlene at best half listened to Britt's valedictory speech, brooding still on the fallout in her personal life of the group's unresolved rift. Despite every appearance of victory, Kyle wanted America to stay its course in a dogged quest for scientific certainties.

She didn't know how the mother ship had been projected. She didn't *care*. The key thing was, it was gone. That, and that the masersats were neutralized—for which Kyle deserved full credit. They had in hand, finally, one of the orbiting weapons—again thanks to him. With his own lab showing just how kludged it was, continued anxiety about alien threats was no longer tenable. *Sorry, hon, we have more pressing problems.* Like mending fences with the ingrate rest of the world. Like ten-plus percent unemployment. Like climate disasters. *Could I,* she wondered yet again, *interest him in global-change research? How rotten a wife would I be to try?*

"The President will be here in a few minutes, to add a few words."

She set down her glass, shaking her head no, when an attentive steward started her way. She'd be driving home. All she could do for Kyle tonight was let him drink freely.

The President entered. "Everyone, thank you for coming." Robeson circulated, shaking the men's hands and embracing the women. "What you accomplished, for country and planet, is exceptional. That so much had to be done in secrecy—and *was* done despite the approbation of the uninformed and unappreciative—makes those deeds all the more noteworthy. You have my complete respect and admiration.

"The dissatisfying part of our circumstances, I don't need to tell you, is the world's lack of understanding. That, my friends, makes the next point so difficult. It's surely far harder for you."

The President's gaze, which had been sweeping from face to face, locked now on Kyle. *This will* really *hurt,* thought Darlene.

"The campaign you orchestrated assured our victory. But in any war, especially one of subterfuge and deceit, an early casualty is truth. Suppression of the truth, our focus on the alien artifacts, and our custody of those artifacts, continue to estrange America from other nations.

"In a televised address Monday evening, I will announce completion of our program of alien study. The alien satellite and wrecked starship will be released to international investigation, under UN stewardship. I will also cancel the remaining satellite-recovery missions."

"Mr. President," Kyle blurted. "What about Clean Slate?"

"I'm sorry, Kyle. I know your concerns are sincere. That said, it's been a *long* time. Maybe the aliens tried something, and it did not work. You convinced us, rightly, that we had to understand the threat hanging over our head. Despite economic pain and world condemnation, we followed the course you laid. And maybe the alien captain was simply messing with our heads. The fact is, there is no credible evidence of an alien threat. So now—"

"But Grelben didn't know Swelk had bugged his bridge." Kyle couldn't contain his frustration. Darlene cringed—you don't interrupt the President. You certainly don't use that lecturing tone with him. "Grelben couldn't have been speaking for our benefit."

"So *now*," repeated Robeson, "it's time to move on, to enjoy such modest rewards as are in my power to bestow. I have many friends in the private sector, for those looking to make a change. And you'll have a sympathetic ear for new challenges you may aspire to in the executive branch." Robeson winked. "I won't mind if you avoid positions requiring Senate confirmation."

"Respectfully, sir." Kyle was nothing if not persistent, thought Darlene. Sometimes maddeningly so. "We haven't checked the moon yet, although the aliens spent time there. We need a lunar program."

That remark earned Britt a presidential glower: *He's* your *protégé.* Britt read the dirty look the same way she did. He took Kyle's arm and steered him into a corner. Their whispered conversation was unintelligible but intense.

Darlene joined Kyle as soon as Britt left, standing so that to face her, Kyle remained facing the corner. Behind him, by the hors d'ouevres table, Ryan and Erin compared notes animatedly—about Kyle's near meltdown, surely. Britt and the President were in another corner having their own one-on-one. "Honey, a boss once advised me, 'The third time I tell you something, I *really* mean it.' Wasn't there a third 'no' about a lunar program long ago?"

"I've lost count." He had the decency to look embarrassed, perhaps realizing he had pushed too far. "I'm getting another drink. You want a refill?"

"No, thanks. What about the President's gracious offer?" Diplomat 101: when an issue is irresolvable, change the subject.

"Outplacement assistance?" He mimed deep thought for about two seconds. "Astronaut doesn't require confirmation." His answer was too loud to have been only her benefit.

Britt, thankfully out of Kyle's line of sight, extracted a twenty-dollar bill from a coat pocket and handed the money to the President.

Darlene would have given Britt long odds on that bet.

"Hi, Chuck," Kyle called to the bored-looking guard. Hammond Matthews, ambling at his side, waved a greeting. They tried to exude nonchalance: the visiting VIP and the lab director on a casual walk-by inspection.

"Greetings, Docs. Too bad you're working. It's a beautiful weekend." He pointed at the note taped to the glass door clicking shut behind them. "I haven't seen the computer geeks. Can I call the help desk for you?"

"No, thanks. It won't take long once they arrive." Matt's smile stayed internal until they rounded a corner. "No time at all." The advertised network upgrade was entirely fictitious.

"Your secret plan for assuring our privacy is a sign on the door?

Matt mashed his thumb onto the fingerprint scanner beside the lab door. "The note's a memory jogger for anyone coming by despite the well-publicized scheduled maintenance. Their ID card won't get them inside today."

The lab had been stripped in preparation for the masersat's arrival; weeks later, the room still looked barren. Odds and ends, however—soda cans and coffee cups, small tools, digital meters, misplaced cell phones, open tech journals left facedown, wire scraps—had proliferated everywhere. Five computers remained on despite the purported network upgrade, their monitors flashing screen savers. Amid chaos striving to reassert itself, the masersat awaited.

Beneath its tarp, the satellite gaped open. "You have the parts?" asked Kyle. Getting a nod, he unsoldered four electronic components. Whatever those devices did, components with like surface markings—parts codes, they hoped—were in every Krulchukor pocket computer.

Matt jotted a discrete number with a fine-point marker on each liberated item. It wouldn't do to get confused which parts came from where.

Eleven not-entirely-destroyed computers had been recovered from the *Consensus*. Not one functioned. All had, presumably, been damaged by the fire. Swelk's computer worked—but its memory was filled with alien movies. While Swelk's was their only operational alien computer, it was too precious to tinker with. This could be their last chance to repair the other computers. Who knew *what* information those contained?

Of course, few of the computer components and none of the masersat parts *appeared* broken. Kyle imagined a 1907 engineer faced with an inoperative modern computer. If the only electronics I'd ever seen used vacuum tubes, what sense could I make of integrated circuits? Would ruined chips even look damaged? Heat can destroy electronics without melting the parts.

Which reduced them to crossing fingers and swapping components.

He tried not to consider the many permutations of parts substitutions ahead, as he soldered scavenged, same-labeled parts into the satellite. Whatever the international monstrosity that eventually arose to examine the masersat . . . if and when they got their act together, and actual research resumed . . . he'd eventually suggest that *they* try chip substitutions. Perhaps by then he'd have an online tutorial explaining everything.

Life was never that cooperative, though, was it?

CHAPTER 35

"HI, STINKY. Yo, Smelly." Boggy vegetation squished beneath their slowly shuffling, broad webbed feet. Good. Swelk had fretted about the unnatural metal decking her friends suffered aboard ship. The animals chewed contentedly on synthesized sludge, massive jaws sliding and grinding in a totally alien motion. Despite widespread suspicions that Krulchukor bioconverters employed nanotech, no one—certainly not Kyle—would endanger the Girillians by opening one for inspection. "Do they brush you guys enough?"

"Perhaps you could give the other guests a chance, sir." A zoo guard politely indicated the serpentine queue behind Kyle. Plenty of tourists were glued to the railing, but, Kyle guessed, none spoke so familiarly to the main attractions. "This exhibit is quite popular."

He moved along rather than argue. Seeing Smelly and Stinky was how he communed with his dead friend. He loved the cats, but associated them more with Dar. He drifted through the rest of Girillia House, murmuring as he went. None of these critters had bonded like the swampbeasts with Swelk; none affected him as deeply.

He found an empty bench. *Swelk,* he thought, *at least* one *puzzle that had us stymied is solved.* That reflection yielded a bit of solace he'd sought unsuccessfully in Girillia House.

The computer Matt had repaired with masersat parts might—in

twenty years? More?—lead to amazing breakthroughs. It wasn't a cookbook for fusion or interstellar travel, but it offered clues: operating procedures and detailed parts inventories. The recovered files, in Kyle's belief, held more promise than the charred starship surrendered to UN custody.

The *how* of the mother ship holo-projection had gnawed at him long after the *fact* of the hologram became obvious. Why would the aliens have such equipment with them? Discovering the masersats to be cobbled-together devices had only deepened the mystery.

But now, extrapolating from newly recovered Krulchukor files, he had an answer.

The alien star drive, its physical principles still maddeningly obscure, was inoperative deep within a star's gravity well. Starships used solar sails to exit solar systems—sailing conserved He3 for interstellar travel. In settled solar systems, big laser cannons rapidly propelled starships to where their drives could engage. In low-tech solar systems (which, in practice, meant any system not colonized by Krulirim), shipboard emergency gear included kits to build laser boosters. Seed a convenient, sunlight-drenched, silicon-rich asteroid with nanomachines. Wait a bit for semiconductor lasers, and the solar cells to power them, to grow. *Voilà!*

The moon's surface was one-fifth silicon by mass. Without an atmosphere, solar energy was abundant on the dayside.

If Swelk's translator had correctly converted units of measure, an emergency booster kit would expand into an about-kilometer-squared patch. An individual laser was a silicon structure only millimeters in size, but a full-grown booster contained billions. Inventory records showed several kits had been taken from ship's stores.

The evidence was entirely circumstantial, but Kyle was *sure* he finally understood the mother-ship trick. Just as Grelben's engineers had kludged masersats from onboard equipment, they, or perhaps Rualf's special-effects team, must have hacked into the booster-kit software. Change the aiming logic to track a moon-orbiting radar buoy instead of a receding starship. Add an animation model of the movie-prop vessel to be projected. (Model, as well, the occasional holographic auxiliary ship going to or from the mother ship—an effective bit of misdirection.) Schedule the hand-off of projection duties from laser patch to laser patch, to compensate for the moon's rotation and to mimic the mother ship's purported orbital path. For a species with centuries of computer experience, he guessed the reprogramming was a snap.

Memories of Swelk occupied his walk to the Metro station and the subway ride itself, reminiscences intermingled with hopes for a new beginning. In a West Wing waiting room, he tried to focus on the latter.

"Sorry, I'm running late. Crisis *du jour.*" Britt had appeared in the doorway. "Much simpler than crises *we've* handled. Come in. Can I get you something?"

"Water, thanks."

"Carl, two Perriers." Once the earnest intern nodded acknowledgment, Britt led the way to his office. "How's my favorite diplomat?"

"Fine." He took a chilled bottle. "Busy." A workaholic, not that I'm entitled to criticize.

Britt draped his suit coat over a chair. "It's ominous when you get terse and tongue-tied on me. What now?"

"Good news, actually." Kyle took a photo from his shirt pocket. "Matt's team repaired a recovered Krulchukor computer. Unlike Swelk's, it *wasn't* filled with movies and a translation program." They'd have been out of luck, though, without Swelk's computer to translate for *it.*

Britt raised an eyebrow. "After all these years, they fixed it. Interesting."

Admit nothing. "Good things come to he who waits."

"We'll let that lie. What's on your always active mind?"

Had there been an emphasis on "lie"? "It was a crewman's computer. The maintenance files should be *very* helpful in recreating Krulchukor technology. Case in point." Kyle explained the mother-ship illusion. "It's nice to know why the mother ship was off in lunar orbit."

An intercom buzzed. "Your next appointment is here, sir."

Britt picked up the photo. "For someone bearing good news, you don't seem happy."

Nothing would be gained by citing the maddeningly vague reference in a recovered file to Clean Slate. Nor would reasserting his unshaken conviction of dangers lurking on the moon accomplish anything. Every suggestion over the years of a lunar program had been rebuffed. Krulirim were patient. They had to be—interstellar voyages lasted years.

Why was he the only one who believed Grelben's plans could be years in preparation?

None of this prevented Kyle from doing his damnedest to be prepared. "Dar predicts the President will give the computer, too, to the UN. Our favorite diplomat implies I'm bitter."

Britt clasped his hands, fingers interlaced. "If, as I think likely, she's right, then what? Can I lure you into the District more often?"

"No, but with a good excuse." They had arrived, at last, at the reason for his visit. "I'd like to accept the President's offer of a job referral."

althed. If such an object existed, and popped up out of nowhere,
ely it would be an alien artifact. Spoiling the moonlight . . . Clean
te couldn't be anything simultaneously so huge and so petty,
uld it?

"Heads up."

Kyle turned toward the call and saw a can of Coke lofted his
y. He bobbled the catch. "Thanks, Matt. I clearly need the
feine."

"What'd I miss?"

"Can't be a solar problem and doesn't look like something in
ice blocking the light." That left the moon suddenly absorbing
it it had once reflected. That left the subject matter of a third
l, whose virtual caption read: LUNAR SURFACE. The big obser-
ories only confirmed what Kyle, with his amateur telescope, had
ided minutes after the mysterious fadeout: the moon's surface,
er than darkening, looked unchanged. Optical telescopes and
ar pinging alike detected no change to the moon.

"Infrared." Matt whapped his forehead with the heel of his
d. "Matt, you dummy. Ellen! Do we have before-and-after IR
ages of the full moon?"

"I'm on it." Ellen started typing feverishly.

"*Not* dumb, Matt. Sleep-deprived, probably. Brilliant, certainly."
was almost five in the morning. Almost time for his chopper
e to Washington, to try to make sense of this for the Presi-
t and an emergency cabinet meeting "If the moon is suddenly
orbing more sunlight, it'll be hotter."

"Here's before," called Ellen. "It's an archival shot from the three-
ter IR telescope facility up on Mauna Kea." A new display window
ned on the wall devoted to lunar-surface findings, showing a
y-scaled disc with occasional dark splotches. The gray-coded key
firmed the predominant lightly shaded areas were around 140°C.
dark patches, in the shadows, were as cold as -170 °C.

"What about a current IR view?"

"The file is downloading now. Go figure—the Internet's slow
ight." Ellen rubbed her eyes wearily. "Got it."

et another window popped up on the wall, and Kyle's eyes
ped open with it. The surface of the moon was getting *colder*.
he details were far from clear, but at that instant Kyle knew
t Clean Slate had to be. It was worse than anything he had
r imagined.

CHAPTER 36

DARLENE'S RIGHT LEG dangled from the freestanding hammock,
her bare foot inches above the patio brick. The hammock was
nevertheless swaying, Kyle's longer leg rocking them gently. Her
head rested on his shoulder. Blackie was curled up and purring
on her lap. A mild breeze was blowing, moonlight was streaming.
"Explain again why we hardly ever do this?"

He kissed the top of her head. "Because, Madam Undersecretary,
you're usually off gallivanting around the world."

That was a half truth not worth debating. She swigged some
no-longer-cold beer rather than respond. The past few months, he
was in Houston as much as she was gone on her own, more varied
travel. The President, true to his word, had gotten Kyle a shot at a
payload-specialist berth on an upcoming NASA shuttle mission. The
payload for whose calibration, operation, and, if need be, repair, Kyle
would become responsible did upper-atmosphere measurements,
the details of which eluded her. Kyle's understanding, of course, was
infinitely deeper than hers and growing daily. (They'd been together
long enough that she knew nothing was larger than infinite, but
she didn't care. She just wouldn't express the thought.)

The astronauts she'd met were pilots and engineers, not scientific
experts. That surely meant the payload could be operated without
a full theoretical understanding of the measurement techniques,
or the climate models in which the measured values would be

used, or the abstruse controversies that swirled around competing climate models . . . but there was no way *Kyle* would be satisfied flying without that expertise. So when he wasn't training at Johnson Space Center, he was immersed in self-study of atmospheric physics. They were once again coming at a globally vital problem from two entirely different sides.

This time, thank God, the problem wasn't eating him up. She patted his arm.

"Beautiful, isn't it?"

That could have been a reference to togetherness, the weather, the patio and its wooded setting, or the cloudless night sky aglitter with stars. Had her companion meant any of those things, he wouldn't have been *Kyle.* "The full moon? Yes, it's gorgeous."

They were silently admiring its round perfection when, as if by the throwing of a switch, the moon went dark.

"Yes, I'm serious!" insisted Kyle. "How's the weather? Look out your window."

"Sunny and warm. Basically like every day." His old college buddy, who lived in LA, sounded puzzled and not a little peeved. "Why did you really call?"

"The sun's normal?" Kyle persisted into his cell phone. He'd outwaited a call-waiting signal. Dar ran inside to answer the house phone.

"Big bright yellow ball, intends to set in the west. *Yes*, it's normal. So this is about . . . ?"

"Gotta go—I'll explain later." He hung up over annoyed protests. Overhead, stars sparkled like diamonds, as brightly as ever. How, in a cloudless night sky, could the moon be ghostly dim when in California, where it was just after six, the sun was behaving?

There was no denying the apparition overhead.

He was swinging his telescope toward the spectral moon when his cell phone rang. Dar yelled from inside, "That's Britt. I transferred the call."

"Hi, boss." As best Kyle could tell, the moon, apart from having gone ashen, was unchanged. He'd studied it enough nights to trust his impression. "Yes, I know. Yes, the moon's gone dark and no, I can't say why." He unbent from his crouch over the telescope eyepiece. "But I'm on it."

*　　　*　　　*

Too many people jammed in a consequently c
Too many speculations and too few facts. It was
the arrival day of the Galactics.

Kyle fanned himself with a folder as he digeste
ings. An obvious change from that earlier crisis
of note taking: electronic whiteboards, read/wri
Internet, had replaced walls covered in Post-it no
Ridgers could as easily have coordinated from the
hundreds of scientists worldwide whose data the
Crowding this room showed psychology trumpi

"That's one possible explanation shot to hell."
a twenty-something new hire with spiky blue ha
cell phone. "Thank God." She threaded a path th
to a terminal. On the big wall display marked "s
text appeared: SOHO READINGS NOMINAL. The S
spheric Observatory probe was permanently stat
miles sunward from Earth, at an Earth-sun gravi
point. If SOHO, with its plethora of instrumentati
ruptible view of the sun, saw no variation in the
that was definitive. The sun was normal.

There weren't many ways to dim the moon.
only reflected sunlight, so a solar problem *coul*
root cause. Nakamura was right: thank God. If t
source of the problem, they could all speedily fr
second wall was dedicated to an investigation o
phenomenon impeding the light path from sun to
to Earth. Regularly updated windows mirrored
observatories worldwide. Some big light blocker
mind where such a thing could have come fro
also darken some stars. No such dimmed stars w
That did not eliminate a filtering disk *precisely* size
obscure only and exactly the moon as viewed fro
Earth. But how could such an object be held sta
the solar-wind pressure on such a huge expanse? "
on radar sweeps for a blocker?"

"He's stepped out," answered a voice Kyle didn't
yes, there's news. Rear wall, lower left corner. Rad
between here and the moon."

"Thanks." So if there were a light-blocking obj
not only precisely positioned and placed, it's ra

CHAPTER 37

TWO YEARS SINCE The Big Dim, seven years after the arrival of the "Galactics," forty-some years since a boy fell in love with the space program ... no matter how Kyle viewed it, today had been a long time coming.

No one but he thought of today's launch as Phase Three of Project Swelk.

He was flat on his back, strapped snugly into one of two mission-specialist seats on the *Endeavor*'s flight deck. He wore the uncomfortable collection of clothing and gear that in NASA-speak was a "crew altitude protection system." Besides the spectacularly misnamed antigravity suit, the "system" consisted of a helmet, communications cap, pressure garment, gloves, and boots.

In the two front seats, as on the masersat recovery mission, were Windy McNeilly as pilot and Tricky Carlisle as mission commander. Speedy Gonzalez had the mission-specialist seat beside Kyle's. The middeck compartment was empty. A crew of four was below the norm for a shuttle flight, but this was no normal flight.

"Are we boring you, Dr. Doom?"

Kyle struggled to abort a yawn. After three weather scrubs in as many days, they'd been woken abruptly last night as the weather forecast unexpectedly broke in their favor. His limited view out the forward windshields showed merely overcast, rather than the gusty rain that had kept them grounded. "Sorry, Craig. What can

I do for you?" At this stage of the mission Kyle was simply a passenger. What *could* he do for Carlisle?

"Nothing, Doc. Ignition is not most people's preferred wake-up call."

"Don't worry. I promise I won't miss a thing." He followed the last-minute checklists and the cabin/ground-control chatter until, with a sound like the end of the world, the shuttle's main engines roared to life. Six seconds until takeoff. Then the solid rocket boosters added their thunder, and the shuttle started to rise. They began a roll, pitch, and yaw maneuver, tipping the nose for a head-down ride to orbit, in the process gaining a view through two overhead windows of the rapidly receding ground. Thrust squashed him into his seat. Amid the noise and vibration, three Gs were far harder to take than in the training centrifuge in Houston.

"Throttle-down commencing," called Windy.

Air resistance, and the attendant stresses on the shuttle, were greatest early in the launch. Throttle-down reduced those stresses until the ship reached thinner atmosphere. The shaking and din seemed to have gone on *forever*, but the pilot's calm announcement meant they were only twenty-six seconds into the flight. The jarring kept intensifying, but at a lesser rate.

"Commencing throttle-up."

Which put them at about T+60 seconds. As the shuddering reached a peak, Kyle knew how a milkshake must feel. The Earth slivers visible from his back-row seat continued to recede.

"Approaching SRB separation." McNeilly had a hand beside the backup SRB separation switch, but the computers once again performed on cue.

The solid rocket boosters burnt out in two minutes. This was farther than the *Atlantis* got, some recess of Kyle's mind reminded him. He felt the thunk of the separation. The noise began to abate, both because the SRBs were gone and from the thinning of the atmosphere. From nowhere came a maddening itch on the tip of his nose. Ignoring the tickle seemed more sensible than lifting an unnaturally heavy arm.

"Negative return," radioed ground control.

More progress. They were far enough into the launch that an abort back to the Cape was no longer possible. Milestones continued passing normally as the ship climbed and the sky turned black and starry.

"Coming up on MECO," warned Windy.

Main engine cutoff, about eight minutes into the flight. More than seventy miles up. More than seventeen thousand miles an hour. And *no* separation from the external tank—two unmanned tankers awaited to top off their nearly empty ET.

"Three . . . two . . . one . . . MECO."

Kyle's arms floated free of the armrests. His stomach lurched. His pulse raced. It was suddenly, blissfully quiet; radioed exchanges with ground control were the only sounds. As he tipped his head backward, a bony finger poked him: Speedy reaching across the gap between their seats. "Welcome to space, Doc." In the front seats, Carlisle and McNeilly tended to the details of raising and circularizing their orbit. He could not tear his eyes from the panoramic view of Earth through the overhead cabin windows. He'd dreamed of this moment for forty-some years now, had an image in his mind's eye of sparkling blue and rich brown and lacy white.

The Earth stretched out below him was a cruel caricature of that expectation. Huge, angry whirlpools of cloud dominated the Atlantic. In the black masses of cloud masking much of western Europe, lightning sparked and flashed like Thor and Zeus gone to war.

And exactly as if hostile aliens had conspired to wipe Earth clean of all life.

The Big Dim was actually quite simple.

The moon, like the Earth, receives solar energy at an average rate of 1345 watts per square meter. To darken the moon, convert incoming sunlight to electricity. To cool the moon, use that electricity to broadcast an electromagnetic signal . . . energy is removed instead of absorbed. Emit half of the incident energy that way, and—the moon being far smaller than the Earth—the transmitted energy is about 3% of the solar energy Earth receives. By way of comparison, the annual change in sunlight that causes Earth's seasons is only plus-or-minus 3.4%.

And if the goal is at the same time to sterilize the Earth? Merely broadcast in a suitable microwave frequency. Pick a frequency to which the Earth's atmosphere is transparent, a frequency strongly absorbed by liquid water—then focus all of that energy on the Earth. A frequency of 2.45 GHz works well . . . the frequency used inside every microwave oven.

Solar energy to electricity? That's easy: solar cells. Electricity to microwave beams? That's also straightforward: masers. Solar cells and masers are readily fabricated from semiconductors, with well understood human technology. The most common semiconductor is silicon. By weight, a fifth of the lunar surface is silicon.

But what could cover the whole surface of the moon with solar cells and masers?

Krulchukor laser cannons had already been grown on the moon, enclaves of solar cells and semiconductor lasers reprogrammed to project the mirage of the mother ship. That which has been reprogrammed can be reprogrammed again.

What humans call light and microwaves are only different regions in the electromagnetic spectrum, so resize and recalibrate new semiconductor structures to emit microwaves. Move the aiming point from a tiny, fast-moving radar buoy to the impossible-to-miss globe of Earth. Delete the code that limited the growth to small regions. Wait until the nanotech-produced texture—no dimension of its surface manifestation larger than inches, impossibly small to see from Earth—infests the entire lunar surface.

Then turn out the lights and crank up the heat.

"Like a freaking ballet outside, only interesting." Speedy was admiring an ET/unmanned-tanker rendezvous through a flight-deck window. "Doc. You gotta see this."

Kyle was out of her sight, on the middeck. "I caught the first act." The ET had already drained one remote-controlled tanker. The load from the second tanker would bring the ET to about half filled. That would more than get *Endeavor* where it needed to go. The hard part of space travel was reaching low Earth orbit.

"You staring dirtside again, Doc?" she persisted.

"Uh-huh." Doctor Doom was too many syllables for regular use. He'd lucked out—Doom would have gotten old. "It keeps me focused on why we're up here."

They were over the eastern Pacific, approaching the Panamanian coast. Two enormous tropical depressions were converging on the area. By historical standards, it was early in hurricane season, but the National Hurricane Center was already up to Norman on this year's second pass through the alphabet. Central America was going to get clobbered again. He couldn't help but remember that kid who washed out to sea. It had been one death among thousands in a single storm, and there had been hundreds of hurricanes, typhoons, and cyclones since—and it was *the* tragedy that still gave Darlene nightmares.

His eyes were glued to the ten-inch window in the side hatch. Logically, the view was no different than what he'd seen often in satellite imagery. Maybe so, but it was more real with only a pane of glass and vacuum between him and the unfolding catastrophe. As he watched, lightning erupted like popcorn over the cloud-cloaked mountainous spine of the isthmus. More mudslides in the making? *Damn* Grelben.

"Doc. Since you're downstairs, check on the MDS, willya?"

"Sure, Craig." The microwave dump system was one of the postapocalypse retrofits to the orbiter. *Endeavor* had launched during a waning crescent moon; there was comparatively little Earth-bound microwave energy. Even if the moon had been full, its microwaves were a different sort of hazard than the defeated masersats. Those had focused weapons-grade bursts on small targets. The endless lunar emissions blanketed all of Earth facing the moon. The MDS reradiated the incoming, comparatively diffuse microwaves. "The panel shows all green."

"Thanks, Doc."

"Coming through." Speedy dove through an interdeck opening, with a grace in micro-G he could only envy. She retrieved a camera from her locker on the middeck. The storm caught her attention on her return soar. With a tuck, roll, and light kick off a bulkhead, she stopped gracefully in midair. "Je-sus!"

"I wouldn't want to be wherever that monster comes ashore."

Another well-placed kick propelled her closer. She stared out the hatch's inset window. "You understand this stuff? Really?"

The implicit admission surprised him, since there was so much *he* had yet to learn. Maybe he'd feel more at home when the puking stopped. That half of astronauts had a few days of space adaptation sickness was little comfort. The old hands recommended keeping busy. " 'This stuff'? You mean how The Big Dim hoses the climate?"

"Right, Doc." She took a snack bar from a jumpsuit pocket. "You want half?"

His stomach gurgled. "No thanks. All right, the weather. The moon used to reflect about ten percent of sunlight hitting it, and that was scattered. Now, about *half* the incident light is reemitted, and it all comes Earth's way. As microwaves. If the microwaves hit water—and Earth's surface is seventy-percent water—they increase evaporation. Vast regions of moist, warm air rise, spun up by Coriolis forces." He pointed at the huge storms forming below. "Okay?"

"So far, so good."

"But more energy and more storms are just the start. Greenhouse effect is the kicker."

She nabbed a crumb that had floated off. "I don't get it."

Not her field, not her fault. "During the day, solar energy soaks into the ground. The heat reradiates to space at night, as infrared. But some gases block IR, trapping heat in the atmosphere. The effect is like glass in a greenhouse."

"Like carbon dioxide."

At five miles per second, crossing Central America didn't take long; the *Endeavor* made the traverse while Kyle was in what Dar called pedantic mode. A hurricane was brewing in the Caribbean. "Right. But not only carbon dioxide. Water vapor is another greenhouse gas."

"Aha. The microwaves increase evaporation, producing water vapor, which traps heat, which further increases evaporation. A vicious cycle." She finished the snack bar and carefully zipped the wrapper into a pocket. "The evaporation leads to more clouds, and so to more rain."

"Yes, but not indefinitely. Hot air rises. The water vapor-laden air rises. Rain, of course, begins as airborne droplets forming in the cool upper atmosphere, condensing around airborne dust. Condense enough water, and the drop gets heavy and falls. But these microwaves evaporate water from would-be raindrops. So the new vapor rises still higher, into colder and colder parts of the atmosphere. Drive the vapor high enough, and you get permanent upper-atmospheric ice crystals instead of rain."

"I'm a simple mechanic, but haven't we had *more* rain since The Big Dim, not less?"

Simple mechanic? Speedy had a PhD in aeronautical engineering. He made the mistake of looking at her. She was suspended in midair, her body at almost a right angle to what his confused senses considered the vertical. The little food he'd kept down that day made a fresh attempt to escape. *Keep busy.* "True observation, but not a rebuttal. It means that for now the increased oceanic evaporation is a bigger effect than vapor trapping in the upper atmosphere. Both effects are bad. Both are incontrovertibly ongoing."

Grabbing his arm, she pulled herself toward the deck. The enormity of the situation had just registered—there was horror in her eyes. "So left to itself, this process cranks along until greenhouse effect makes Earth too hot for us, or until all water is locked up in the atmosphere."

He favored her with the optimistic smile he'd been practicing on Dar. "That, my friend, is the reason for our jaunt to the moon. We're going to find a way to stop the process."

CHAPTER 38

THE UNGAINLY VESSEL sparkled in *Endeavor*'s floodlights. The fifty-foot-long spacecraft cautiously receded from the orbiter, puffs of gas gradually increasing the separation. Bulbous tanks, exposed struts, and an aggressively unstreamlined configuration made plain that the newly disgorged ship was never meant to touch an atmosphere.

The nearby moon, around which both vessels now orbited, cast only a pale, ghostly glow—as far as the human eye was concerned. The torrents of microwaves continued unabated.

"Everyone comfy?" Windy's light tone fooled no one—she wanted, as much as anyone, to walk on the moon. But someone had to stay on the orbiter—it landed on Earth as a glider, hardly a practical approach for alighting on an airless body—and the person best able to bring the *Endeavor* home, if for whatever reason the lander failed to return, was the logical choice.

"Roger that, Windy," The mission commander answered for the three strapped in on the lander. "Ready to go . . . except for one final detail. Doc?"

It was a moment of high historical drama and great personal honor. The President herself—Harold Robeson's second term had expired before the lander was completed—had asked Kyle to christen the lander. She must have ordered NASA and his USAF crewmates to keep to themselves any opinions on the subject. What could possibly compare with "The *Eagle* has landed"? Beyond memorability, he wanted a name that conveyed hope and confidence and, despite the ship's wholly American provenance and crew, an entire world's aspirations.

The timer decrementing before him insisted that, named or not, this vessel would begin its deorbiting burn inside five minutes. "Ladies and gentlemen, I give you the good ship *Resolute*."

The moon-spanning circuitry very precisely, in some way yet unknown, tracked the Earth and focused a myriad of maser beams upon it. No one wanted to learn the hard way whether proximity detection could instigate a close-in defensive retargeting. So, although the tangential approach of the *Endeavor* had evoked no discernible response, *Resolute* deorbited above the night side, where the solar-powered masers were inactive. But they couldn't accomplish their mission by hiding in the dark. Speedy set them down inside a small crater, entirely unremarkable but for its position about an Earth day to the predawn side of the onrushing day/night terminator.

"Houston," reported Tricky Carlisle, "the *Resolute* has landed." He covered the mike with his hand. "Resolutely, I may add."

Applause from Mission Control, after the unavoidable but annoying two-and-a-half second round-trip delay, almost drowned out CAPCOM's equally businesslike "Copy, and congrats." There was a short silence, into which Windy McNeilly from lunar orbit injected her own "Well done," before Houston continued. "*Resolute*, you're cleared for a stroll."

The few minutes it took to seal the space suits worn for the landing were interminable. Kyle was second through the single-person airlock. He found Carlisle standing on a large mat; more pads, with adhesive backs and Velcro tops, remained in the airlock. Peeling paper sheets from the adhesive, Kyle handed down several pads before climbing gingerly down the landing leg that doubled as a ladder. The crescent Earth floating above the crater wall nearly took his breath away. Carlisle gave him a friendly nudge, reminding him to clear the area. The crater floor glittered and shimmered in the earthlight. Faint crunching sounds accompanied his footsteps, transmitted through mat and boots into his suit—brittle circuits crushed by his weight. Moments later, Speedy reached the foot of the ladder.

Carlisle's voice came over a private radio channel. "One more presidential curse, Doc. Say something catchy."

Kyle, having suspected this was coming, was prepared. He switched to the mission's unencrypted main frequency. "On behalf of all humanity, we reclaim our moon." Faint green digits floating on his head's up display counted down to local sunrise. He returned to a secured band. "Now what do you say we reclaim our first acre?"

They had an aluminized plastic tarp spread across the crater with hours to spare.

Kyle stood on the lip of the crater they now called home. From a thin crescent when *Resolute* had landed, the Earth had waxed near to half full. An enormous cyclone threatened Japan, and a second, the Philippines. Would those storms have formed absent the alien attack? There was no way to know.

He shivered, and it had nothing to do with the menace they battled. His suit thermostat was cranked low to minimize the drain on the batteries. In the tarp's shadow it was cold enough to liquefy nitrogen. "Speedy, I'm ready to walk the back forty."

"You're on camera," she assured him.

Kyle stepped out from under the awning, the direct sunlight all the more blinding for the contrast with the light-stealing surface. A metallic mesh was embedded in the glass of his helmet's visor, like the window in a microwave-oven door. Exactly like a microwave oven . . . the openings through which he gazed were too small to admit microwaves. Downhill, like a rock garden arranged by drunks, stretched their experimental plots: dozens of regions of varying sizes, shapes, and textures. Pole-mounted videocams swept back and forth, monitoring each plot. It was ironic, Kyle thought, that they'd had to bring solar cells from Earth to power the cameras.

He made his way carefully down an intersector boundary, along what Carlisle had dubbed a carpet runner. Nails driven by rivet gun into the rocky surface held the walkway in place; an adhesived patch had been set carefully over each nail head to seal the hole. The Velcro'ed surface gripped Kyle's boots, holding him to the supposed nanomachine-free safety of the from-Earth path. It wasn't as though on a microscopic scale the adhesive didn't have gaps—they had no choice but to trust the shadows from the patches to keep the nannies underneath inert.

As on every sticky-footed excursion from the *Resolute*, Kyle felt cheated. He longed to move about in the kangaroo hop made famous on the Apollo missions. Status lights in his helmet reported all three microwave reradiators in his suit were operational.

"Are you done yet?" Carlisle's words, accompanied by a chuckle, were more an old joke than a status inquiry.

"Just medium rare." Humor was the only way to cope with the ever-present danger. Untreated, each square meter of the sunlit surface generated close to seven hundred watts—like the interior of a standard microwave oven at its full-power setting. He was in line of sight of *many* square meters. Line of sight . . . or line of fire. It was a disconcerting thought. The gauge on Kyle's wrist detected none of the microwaves that, had they been directed at him, should be immediately dispersed by any of the three reradiating systems he carried. Despite the redundancy, he yearned for a physical, foolproof, grounding cable. Alas, a trailing tether would almost certainly slide off the protective runways and onto the nanny-covered lunar surface.

Their crater was a dimple within a great flat plain, one of the lunar maria. Standing on that "sea-level" surface, he could see barely a mile in any direction, the horizon foreshortened by the moon's diminutive size. Small relative only to Earth, of course: the surface area was close to fifteen million square miles. As many stars shone overhead, diamond-brilliant and unwavering.

"Quit your sightseeing," called Carlisle.

"You caught me. Again. Starting with plot one." Bending and crouching, pacing back and forth along a runner, he examined the first plot from several angles.

Soon after landing, in the shadow of plastic sheeting temporarily stretched between poles, this slice of territory had been bulldozed clean of visible infestation by radio-controlled robots. The little RC vehicles would stay behind and be teleoperated from Earth; Las Vegas bookmakers were taking bets on how long the devices would last. Alien circuits began refilling the area as soon as the sun-blocking sheeting came down. The masers and the solar cells powering them were completely restored within minutes.

They'd "fenced" the area with shadows before the robots scraped it clean again. The field regenerated almost as quickly the second time, this time entirely from random spots within the torn-up field. It was, apparently, hard to remove every trace of nanotech "seeds" too small to see. That result reinforced the mission directive against touching the surface. They'd mechanically cleansed plot one repeatedly, and the results never changed: rapid regrowth. Repeating the experiment at scattered test spots gave comparable results. The propagation rate was always in the neighborhood of seven miles per day. "No surprises, Craig. Plot one is entirely regrown since your last inspection. No holes or gaps. I'm moving on."

The next few plots had, like plot one, been wiped clean and allowed to regrow to calibrate growth rates. There was some variation, correlated to robot-measured differences in trace-element concentrations. Plots two through ten had been treated with acids, bases, and other pollutants. No chemical made a significant difference to the regeneration rate. No coating disabled unplowed masers or solar cells for any useful length of time. For completeness—Kyle privately considered it more a matter of desperation—they were trying combinations. "We're not accomplishing a damn thing here."

"Any thoughts why?" asked Speedy.

"Sure. Nanomachines manipulate individual atoms. With such abundant solar energy, the nannies have no problem repairing themselves or cloning themselves or disassembling any inconvenient molecules created by our chemical spills. We must concurrently destroy *every* smaller-than-microscopic nanomachine, and keep new ones from migrating in from neighboring areas, to make any difference. The little critters are too hardy."

"That sounds a lot like admiration, Doc," said Carlisle. "By the way, no progress here, either." The commander was inspecting another stretch of plots, these heat-treated. They'd tried, among other methods, a rocket-fuel flame thrower, an electric-arc furnace, and a large, sunlight-concentrating, paraboloid mirror. It took three thousand degrees to purge a shadow-fenced area. No one could imagine a way to apply the technique on a moonwide scale.

"It is admiration, but don't worry." Kyle straightened from the crouch in which he'd been eyeing yet another plot. "Respect for their ruggedness doesn't detract from the scariness." If only there were some way to tame these beasts.

It didn't help Kyle's mood that by the time he headed back to the ship a new typhoon was forming in the Indian Ocean.

✳   ✳   ✳

Kyle resisted the inane urge to wave at the fast-moving glimmer that was *Endeavor*. "How's the R&R, Windy?"

The pilot mocked retching. "It's no holiday when all the food is reconstituted."

The meals down here were squeezed from tubes. There hadn't been weight margin or physical space in the lander for a fancy, shuttle-style galley. Of course, Windy would trade places with him in an instant. "How's our farm looking from up there?"

"Huh. I thought the idea was to *not* grow stuff."

"Ahem?"

"Lessee." There was the unmistakable flipping of paper in a clipboard. "Okay, these are my notes. I'll downlink the details in a minute. For fields one through eighteen and twenty through thirty-six, the emissions as always correlate nicely with the size of the plot and the regrowth rate you're reporting from the ground."

"And nineteen?" Kyle didn't let himself get excited. Most anomalies were data-collection glitches.

"This is interesting. Right after our noble commander last flame-broiled nineteen, not only did nineteen turn off, but I noticed that a whole region around that plot stopped emitting."

That *was* interesting. "And did that larger area come back on when plot nineteen did?"

"Roger, Doc." There was more rustling of paper. "And guess what: plot nineteen is smack in the middle of the larger blanked-out region. What do you suppose it means?"

"I am without clue." With a fat gloved finger, Kyle poked at the keypad on his suit's left sleeve. His head's up display showed that three of their little robotic tractors were idle. "Windy, how much longer are you in range?"

"Directly? Three minutes plus. But one or more of the satellites we deployed always has *Resolute* in line of sight."

He should have remembered that. The eighteen-hour days were taking a toll. Best to confirm his thinking. "Beside comm, they detect microwaves, too? Show if an area is on or off?"

"They have to be pretty much right above to spot beamed microwaves, but then, yes."

The planet overhead had passed full and was waning. In a few Earth days, lunar night would fall and they would pack up and rendezvous with *Endeavor* for the trip home. There could be no more unique clock, nor a better reminder of why they were here.

How much longer did they have to save the Earth? Climatologists, when pressed, threw up their hands. Before The Big Dim, they had invested years, even decades, on competing models of global warming—simulations envisioning nothing *remotely* like recent conditions. The not-for-attribution best guesses were that temperatures would creep up and up until upper-atmosphere vapor levels crossed a much debated threshold . . . followed by runaway greenhouse effect. After that, planetary temperature would skyrocket.

Can you say Venus?

His exhausted mind had wandered again. "Trickster? Speedy? Were you listening?" Both responded in the affirmative. "I'd like the untasked robots to go over plot nineteen with a fine-toothed comb."

"Agreed," said the commander. "Windy, you and your flock of birds keep an eye on us."

Neither the patiently surveying robots nor their human controllers had noticed anything different about plot nineteen when, once more, it and the surrounding region went inert.

"Good morning, *Resolute*," called the familiar voice. "This is Carlene Milford."

"Good morning, Madam President," answered the three crew. It was morning in Washington, but here lunar nightfall was fast approaching. They were nearly packed and entirely eager to go home, even though they had left not a single bootprint on the moon's surface. The *Resolute*'s landing stage, like the mats and runners on which they had trod, would stay behind with its certain contamination of dangerous nanotech.

"My compliments, and the world's appreciation, for your bravery and discoveries. We wish you a safe journey home."

At least, thought Kyle, *the rest of the world has finally accepted reality: that the aliens had been a threat.* "Madam President, are you linked into our video system?"

"Yes, Dr. Gustafson. Those are cramped quarters you've been living in."

While true, the Apollo astronauts had managed in a fraction the space. "If you can, ma'am, I suggest you switch to our camera six." Presidential calls are scheduled well ahead of time, giving

Kyle ample opportunity to pre-position the videocam. One of the lander's monitors showed the recommended fisheye-lens view of the pallid surface, across which, if one looked closely, several black rectangular mats were distributed.

"You've worked with presidents, Doctor. You know how busy are our schedules. I've been briefed, of course, but I'd like to hear from you directly a short summary your findings."

The operative word, Kyle knew, being *short*. What on her docket was more urgent than preventing life's extinction on Earth? "Yes, ma'am. You're aware the aliens covered the moon with self-growing, self-regenerating masers, and solar cells to power the masers. These structures are tiny, on the scale of inches. We also knew there had to be, but did not at first find, components for control. There had to be sensors for locating the Earth in the lunar sky."

Viewed from the moon's surface, Earth spanned a mere two degrees of arc. Due to the tilt of the moon's axis and the ellipticity of the moon's orbit, Earth from the same lunar vantage point migrated around a celestial box of about fifteen degrees by thirteen—movement the astronomers called libration. These weren't details any politician wanted or needed. "As there has to be computing power somewhere giving very precise directions to the masers." Any single maser was a physically rigid structure, the direction of whose output was fixed. By precisely controlling the emissions of *sets* of masers, however, those outputs could be aggregated into vast steerable beams. It worked just like a military phased-array radar.

"Not my specialty, Doctor, but it seems logical."

Kyle fancied he heard the sound of eyes glazing. *Simplify!* "Our work involved altering test plots on the lunar surface. As expected, a cleared region did not radiate until the masers regrew. To our surprise, however, one experiment rendered inert an area much larger than had been temporarily cleansed. We had happened upon a sensor that gave steering guidance. When that sensor could no longer spot Earth, the masers that it controlled stopped firing." Emissions from a blinded region would likely interfere with an adjacent well-aimed beam; suppressing an area whose sensor was for any reason targetless made sense.

"It sounds like we finally got lucky," said the President.

Now that the explorers could recognize the sensors, they knew how widely those sensors were dispersed. They had actually been *un*lucky, considering how much landscape had been tested, to go as long as they had before randomly encountering a sensor. "We've been using our utility robots to blind sensors with opaque scraps." While nanotech quickly regrew a *destroyed* sensor, an intact sensor could be covered. The nannies didn't distinguish shadow from nightfall.

"And the robots can spot sensors?"

If only it were that easy. "You might have heard of archeologists hunting for lost cities with space-based, ground-penetrating radar. Major McNeilly"—he caught himself before calling her Windy—"used *Endeavor*'s radar to map beneath her orbit. A subsurface view, and only using a narrow range of frequencies, reveals a nonobvious large-scale structure. The alien infestation repeats on the scale of a square kilometer. There's a sensor at the center of each region.

"This is what we do. Using the radar survey, we guide a robot to the center of a region. As the robot trolls back and forth, we use its videocam to hunt for a small and subtle discontinuity in the artificial surface: the sensor. The robot then parks atop a suspected sensor until a satellite passing overhead can confirm that the surrounding area has stopped emitting. The robot sets a scrap of asbestos over the confirmed sensor, then heads off to the next region." At a snail's pace.

"It sounds ingenious, Doctor. Is it too soon to say our problem is solved?"

He suppressed an oath. The moon was *big*. "I'm afraid, ma'am, that it *is* too soon. Disabling all the masers this way will take an armada of moon-orbiting satellites and myriads of moon-crawling robots. There are millions of sensors to be blinded, one by one." And, perhaps, again and again. Kyle expected the nanotech to eventually, atom by atom, carry away the obscuring mats—as they had, on the day of The Big Dim, removed the last thin skin of lunar dust that had disguised the spreading infestation.

"It sounds like an epic undertaking, Dr. Gustafson, but nonetheless something we *can* undertake. We have far greater cause for hope than before this expedition. I look forward to discussing it with you, and to meeting with the whole crew, very soon."

The President did not articulate the thought in everyone's mind. The four astronauts were returning to a remote quarantine, their exit from which was far from certain.

CHAPTER 39

"READY FOR ANOTHER first, guys?"

McNeilly sounded altogether too chirpy, but it was probably just pilot bravado. The alternative explanation, pilot exhaustion, didn't bear thinking about—nor could Kyle do anything about it. "I say we get out and walk."

The first to which Windy referred was a manned aerobrake maneuver. The heat tiles that insulated *Endeavor* during its fiery reentry had been designed for near-Earth missions. Symmetry was a cruel mistress: just as the orbiter had had to add speed to reach the moon, it now had more speed to shed than any previous returning shuttle. That faster-than-spec reentry turned directly into unacceptable thermal stress on the tiles. Instead of reengineering yet another critical system, the mission had turned to a technique previously tried only with robotic interplanetary probes.

"Hold on to your helmets, folks." The orbiter shuddered as it bludgeoned its way through the Earth's upper atmosphere. The angle of attack was by intent shallower than any previous reentry. "Getting toasty up here." The "up here" was because Windy, for her own protection, was alone on the flight deck. Those who had been to the lunar surface remained sealed in *Resolute*'s claustro-phobic ascent stage, inside *Endeavor*'s cargo bay. Darkroom-style red bulbs provided their only, and decidedly dim, lighting.

"Nearing fourteen hundred degrees C." Carlisle meant the tiles, not the flight deck. He was studying telemetry from the cockpit. His remoted instruments reproduced everything he would have seen in his now-empty command seat beside the pilot. "I'd say that qualifies as warm."

"And back out we go."

Kyle clutched the arms of his acceleration seat as the cabin vibrated like mad. Aerobraking was such an antiseptic term. In reality, the *Endeavor* had hit the atmosphere at almost seven miles a second. The Earth's skin of air was softer than, say, a brick wall . . . but at these speeds, not by much. The trick was to strike a glancing blow. Each dip into the atmosphere removed a bit of velocity, followed by a return to space to shed the friction-induced heat. If they entered at the wrong angle, the *Endeavor* would bounce like a stone skipping off a lake, or heat up past the thermal tiles' capacity to protect them.

"Whee!" Gonzalez was either having a great time or had forgotten their thin margin of safety. Maybe both. "Once more, Windy."

"Anything for you, Speedy."

A few tooth-rattling repetitions slowed them enough for a sedate, five-mile-per-second low Earth orbit, circularized at an altitude of two hundred miles. Landing from LEO should be a piece of cake—if all the aerobraking shocks hadn't dislodged too many tiles.

"Great job, *Endeavor.*"

"Copy that, Houston. Quite a ride, actually."

"Sorry to be the bearer of bad tidings, but you'll have to wait a bit longer. Storm in the Marshalls." That put off until the weather cleared another item for the record books: the first shuttle landing at a remote Pacific atoll.

Quarantine Central.

Endeavor smacked the isolated runway, bounced, and settled into a fast roll. The landing strip had been lengthened for them, but the curve of the atoll limited what could be done. They shook with relief when the orbiter coasted to rest with only a few hundred feet to spare.

"You make it look easy, Windy. Whenever you're ready."

"Thanks, Houston." Over the in-ship radio Kyle heard flung metal buckles striking whatever—and a meaty thud. "Head rush."

It was a wonder, thought Kyle, the shuttle pilot could stand at all. Except for a few minutes acceleration and deceleration, she had been weightless for almost a month. By rights, someone should have helped her from her seat. That was a risk no sane person would take.

"Tricky, Speedy . . . Doc." The pilot was breathless merely from struggling back to her feet. "It's been . . . fun. See you . . . in a few weeks."

They watched by close-circuit TV as their shipmate stumbled to the middeck. Braced against a bulkhead, Windy waved at the videocam. "Stay out of trouble, guys." She struggled briefly with the hatch's release. As the door slid aside, TV showed the three (still sealed in the *Resolute*'s ascent stage) an approaching, teleoperated motorized staircase. Windy would be taken, entirely by remote-controlled vehicle, to the farthest part of the atoll. They, once she was safely away, would go to their own, separate quarantine.

They had one final task to perform first.

Kyle and Craig Carlisle struggled with the suddenly heavy cooler-sized chest, in which nested smaller vacuum-sealed vessels. Each inner container held lunar-dust samples, harvested by abandoned robots. Gonzalez, meanwhile, opened the hatch into the *Endeavor*'s payload bay. Two weeks in one-sixth G, Kyle decided, were little better than free-fall the entire time as McNeilly had experienced. All three were panting before they'd wrestled the chest from the ascent vehicle, through the orbiter, and down mobile stairs to the concrete runway. It was the middle of the night, as per plan, and the electric lighting on the stairs was decidedly dim.

Out of breath, Kyle awaited another remote-controlled vehicle. Out to sea, warships were discernible only by their running lights. They were here to enforce the quarantine.

A driverless truck rolled up. "Excuse the informal welcome," announced an unseen speaker. Grunting, the astronauts hoisted the chest onto the flatbed and slammed shut the tailgate. The truck looped around them and drove to a pier jutting into the lagoon. Darkness and distance kept Kyle from seeing exactly how the chest was transferred to the awaiting submarine. No one knew how best to isolate the nanotech samples, or how rapidly the contagion might reproduce in terrestrial conditions. For lack of an alternative, the safety protocols in the onboard labs, converted torpedo rooms, were based on biohazard containment.

The submarine sailed off into the midnight darkness, headed, Kyle knew, for the deepest point in the island's lagoon. Nuclear powered, the sub extracted oxygen by electrolysis and desalinated its drinking water. The Navy boasted that its subs could remain submerged as long as the food lasted.

In the worst-case scenario, *this* sub would never surface.

The driverless truck returned. "Hop in, folks," crackled the speaker. "Time for your all-expenses-paid tropical vacation, courtesy of Uncle Sam." They climbed in for the ride to a nearby cluster of huts. It went unspoken that their stay could be permanent if the coming dawn revealed an outbreak of alien nanotech.

No one slept until an entirely ordinary sunrise became a gloriously ordinary day.

EPILOGUE

KYLE AND DARLENE STROLLED hand in hand along a serpentine strip of sand. Combers rolled lazily into the lagoon of the lonely atoll. Wind sighed through the fronds of palm trees. Stars sparkled overhead, all the brighter for the pallor of the altered moon. Both were barefoot, wearing only thin shirts over swim suits. Humidity had frizzed her hair.

"You shouldn't be here, you know." The gentle squeeze he gave her hand belied his words. "It's dangerous."

She snorted. "Yeah, I can see what hardship duty this is."

"It didn't tell you something that the only way you could come was to be lowered in a harness from a helicopter?" And that the chopper pilot then jettisoned the cable, a very *long* cable, instead of rewinding it?

"I missed you, too."

They'd talked for hours. Cat anecdotes. Weather disasters possibly caused by the microwave onslaught. The paperwork minutiae of modern life. Cat anecdotes. Radioed progress reports from the submerged lab. There was, at last, some unmitigatedly upbeat news: discovery that the nanotech was optimized for unfiltered-by-atmosphere sunlight. The nannies, should any escape, would spread *much* slower on Earth than on the moon.

With miles of tropical beach to themselves and, for the moment, perfect weather, apocalyptic scenarios and civilization's routines seemed equally improbable. Kyle whistled softly to himself, at peace with the world.

Darlene stopped short. "I know that look."

"What look?"

"That cat-that-ate-the-cardinal expression." Stripes was quite the huntress; and there were no wild canaries in Virginia. "Like someone who thought his hidden agenda for refueling shuttles in space was, well, hidden."

"You *knew?*"

"Honey, we all suspected." She pecked his cheek. "Retrieving the masersat was the right thing to do. It didn't matter that the capability to do so might also make other things possible."

"And you never said anything." He said it wonderingly—one who conspired had no standing to complain about others holding their tongues.

"So . . . about that *look* of yours."

"We, mankind, have no choice but to develop a major lunar presence. People manufacturing robots and dispersing them across the moon's surface." He rotated slowly, drinking in the beautiful night sky. This near the equator, many of the constellations were unfamiliar. It still took him a moment to get his celestial bearings. "Maintaining that human presence will mean mining the ice in the eternal shadows, the forever nanotech-safe shadows, of the moon's polar craters. If permanent defeat of the alien nanotech does not come quickly—and nothing about this battle has gone smoothly—supporting lunar outposts will mean more space travel, to harvest icy asteroids. But that's okay, because just as reaching low Earth orbit is most of the work of getting to the moon, a lunar base is the hard part of reaching the planets."

His thoughts churned faster than he could find words. His mind's eye pictured mechanisms for *aiming* banks of masers, rather than simply blinding their sensors. Steer the microwaves to antenna farms in the deep desert, where water vapor won't be increased, and the moon became Earth's solar-energy power plant. And if research could recover the original programming of the Krulchukor laser cannons? It would mean human sail-equipped spacecraft.

"Swelk never meant Earth any harm, so the outcome is fitting. The result of her visit will be, not disaster, but a rebirth of human exploration. I sincerely believe that her legacy will be mankind's dominion over the solar system."

"Keep going."

"Huh?" Gentle amusement wasn't the reaction he'd expected to his impassioned speech.

"Don't even try to bluff a diplomat. It's never going to work." She peered at the ghostly crescent overhead. "Since long before we met, the moon has been your obsession . . . yet you've scarcely glanced at it since I arrived. So I want to know, what has taken its place in your always scheming mind?"

He indicated a brilliant red spark near the horizon. A telescope for the object's proper study topped his wish list for the next airdrop. "I don't expect it to be me personally"—not that I expected to go to the moon, either—"but *that* is what. *That* is mankind's next big step.

"Mars."